THE SIMPLE DELIVERY

CHRONICLES OF THE DAWNBLADE

ANDREW CLAYDON

The Simple Delivery

By Andrew Claydon

Published by Andrew Claydon

Edited by Danielle Fine

Cover Design by MiblArt

Written in UK English

Just because you're chosen, doesn't mean you want to be

    Nicolas loves his village life just the way it is, everything as it's supposed to be.

    When he is chosen for a task, he finds himself going out into a world he knows little about and feels completely unprepared for. His only comfort is that all he has to do is deliver a message. That should be pretty simple, right?

    One near death experience later, Nicolas finds himself in a world of heroes', villains', magic and far too many undead creatures for his liking.

    Caught up in events he can't control, he must, with the strange companions he meets along the way, foil a plot that may destroy his Kingdom as he knows it, maybe even the world. Thousands of lives are in the hands of someone who has never even picked up a sword, but at least he knows not to hold it by the pointy end.

Dedicated my Mum, Christine, who was my first fan, and to everyone who loves a good adventure.

'Yarringsburg is one of the wealthier of the Nine Kingdoms of Man. Much of that wealth is derived from the silver veins of Mount Yarrin, from the side of which the capital extends. The city itself boasts many beautiful mansions for travellers with a keen eye for good architecture, provided you can turn a blind eye to the snobbery of the owners of said buildings. For an excellent meal I highly recommend Tal's Bistro in the commercial district. Reasonably priced and delicious.'

Etherius, A Travellers Guide – Dieter Von Ostric

Yarringsburg

Hablock

CHAPTER 1

Nicolas grimaced as the wagon hit yet another dip in the 'road,' his top and bottom teeth clacking together in time with the jolt. He rubbed his cheek gently, as if it would magically make the pain of the fresh bite in his mouth disappear.

What else can happen to me today?

With a sigh, he looked longingly back in the direction from which they'd come.

Since leaving the main road, the track had become progressively less suitable for actual travel. Were people even supposed to come this way anymore? Unfortunately, that question did not perturb the driver, who carried on with a relentless determination to get to their destination in as straight a line as possible, which included not doing anything as complex as avoiding the frequent potholes.

No, he was being unfair. The track was hardly wide enough for any kind of manoeuvre, potholes or no. The impenetrable tree cover to either side of them made sure of that, constantly asserting its presence with hanging branches that scraped skin off the wagon's passengers. It wasn't the driver's fault that Nicolas was here; he was just a symptom of the problem.

This wasn't where he was supposed to be nor what he was supposed to be doing. He had chores and responsibilities at home, a life to attend to. Yes, fine, the air was cool and fresh with the smell of nature and its rich tapestry of greens and browns. And sure, the birds sang sweetly. But all that paled beneath the incessant plodding of the horse and the creaking of the wagon that had entrapped him.

'You look like you don't want to be here, friend,' the man opposite Nicolas grinned from behind a bushy beard which, other than his eyebrows, was the only hair on his head. 'If you don't mind me saying.'

Since boarding the wagon, he'd made no attempt to speak to any of his travelling companions, instead defaulting into a mopey silence. In contrast, the other seven people in the wagon had been engaged in cheerful, expectant banter for the whole journey thus far. Their happiness about something he wanted no part of only served to make him resent being on the trip even more, but at least up until now, his fellow travellers had chosen to respect his mood.

For a moment, Nicolas considered not replying and hoping the man's attention would drift elsewhere. Yet he hadn't been brought up to be rude, and the man seemed genuine enough. Being friendly to a fellow passenger was no bad thing.

'I don't, truth be told,' he replied awkwardly, before adding for clarity, 'Want to be here.'

Even before the words left his mouth, he'd known the reaction his answer would provoke, and the man didn't disappoint. The well-meaning smile dipped slightly as his eyebrows rose in surprise. He even went as far as to sit back in his seat and let out a whistle as he contemplated what he'd just been told and attempted to understand it. This process involved a lot of head nodding and humming noises. In his peripheral vision, several of the travellers nearest them had stopped talking and homed in on their conversation.

'Oh,' the bearded man said finally, if hesitantly. 'Sorry to pry. I just thought...isn't this an honour?'

In Nicolas's experience *'sorry to pry'* was what someone in the process of blatantly prying was likely to say, usually followed by more prying. Which meant...this conversation was not about to just go away. Deities damn him for answering honestly.

In truth, being of age when The Choosing was called *was* considered a great honour, even if you didn't get chosen. Though that honour only extended as far as the boundaries of the village of Hablock. Letting outsiders know that people from your village could be chosen to carry messages from the Deities themselves was not at all wise. The outside world was a dangerous place. It had to be or surely you wouldn't need champions like the ones from that Hall of Guardians people liked to gossip about in such an awestruck manner? And if the dangers weren't serious, why would the Deities feel the need to send divine messages to put those heroes on the right path to slay this and rescue that?

Though presumably they only got involved in the really important stuff. He couldn't see Deities bothering with day-to-day bandits or angry trolls or anything like that. That had to be why the Choosings were so far apart. Again, he cursed his luck; he'd only been twenty-one for a few days and this happened.

Even the idea of being entitled a *'Word Bearer'* was unappealing, as was the prospect of all the unwelcome adulation if you returned triumphant. Never having to buy yourself a drink in the tavern again meant little to him. He found it a little peculiar, not to mention a lot of wasted energy, to spend a year waiting for a calamity to nearly occur so you could get some second-hand glory from it. Yet the people of Hablock had done it for generations. But he knew his place, and this wagon was not it. This, right here, was the furthest he'd ever been from the village, and he didn't care for it. Breathing exercises and calming thoughts were having no effect on his frustration.

Today was meant to be just like all the others preceding it: the usual daily routine and the reasonable expectation of not being thrust into potential danger. Instead, his mother had smiled with pride when the news came that a Choosing had been called—which was the only reason he'd kept his composure long enough to find a pillow to scream into, once the many, many hugs and congratulations had died down.

'Don't get me wrong. It is a great honour,' he told the man diplomatically, aware he was flying in the face of popular opinion. 'But it just isn't for me.'

Though nodding sagely, the man clearly didn't understand his response, but he seemed to accept it, nonetheless. That endeared him to Nicolas.

'To each their own,' the man said with a roguish grin and a shrug.

That seemed like an excellent point at which to end the conversation. There'd been an exchange of ideas and a nice closing point. So he was quite shocked when a hand thrust towards him.

'Garus Potter,' the bearded man introduced himself. 'I just go by Potter, though.'

'Nicolas Percival Carnegie,' he replied, taking the offered hand and shaking it reluctantly.

The shake was returned with firm enthusiasm, his hand compressed like kneaded dough.

'Carnage?' Potter asked as he withdrew the hand and sat back again.

'No, *Carnegie.*' Nicolas replied as he discreetly rubbed his hand.

'Shame,' Potter chuckled. *'Nick Carnage,* that sounds like a real adventurer name. Much more impressive.'

Smiling thinly, he kept what he thought of having an adventurer name to himself. Potter would surely not understand, and he seemed like a nice fellow.

His companion took the smile at face value. Leaning forwards, Potter motioned to him to do the same. 'Perhaps, if you don't want any part of this, you could do me a favour?' he whispered. 'Maybe you can tell The Oracle that you don't want to be Chosen. Thin out the competition a little and make my odds a bit better, eh?' Potter finished the request with a cheeky wink.

'You want it that badly?'

Why would anyone want that? Was he the only sane person on the wagon? He couldn't truly get his head around it. But maybe he didn't need to, maybe he just need to accept that some people would want it. To each their own, after all.

'Yeah,' Potter said with enthusiasm. 'This is my time. I can feel it.'

Suddenly Nicolas found himself fixed with an uncomfortably intense gaze.

'You never felt like you have something more destined for you Nick?'

He did not, nor did he care for being called *Nick* repeatedly. He shook his head.

'Well, I do. I'm ready to go and make my mark on the world. I've got something to give beyond this village, and it's my time to prove it.'

Potter sat back, seemingly lost to daydreaming. Presumably picturing whatever glory he thought destiny had in store for him.

'Good luck to you,' he replied, determined to finally end the conversation.

* * * *

The closer the wagon got to its destination, the more the conversation in it slowed, until it petered out altogether. Instead, they seemed to travel in a respectful silence to honour the gravity of the occasion—except Nicolas, of course, who was silent for his own reasons. The driver was also silent, but he was a miserable wretch who seemed content to communicate with his passengers via a series of grunts and head motions.

Nicolas thought back to when he had first boarded the wagon, the driver looking at him more like a piece of cargo than a person, the man's sullenness matching his own at being part of this *'trip'* at all. Things were now changing, not for the driver, but for him. Potter had given him the perfect idea and a fine dose of optimism to go with it. It was so simple and obvious he couldn't believe he hadn't thought of it sooner. He would simply tell The Oracle he didn't want to be chosen. Surely the man would have no interest in choosing someone who had no interest in being chosen? Where was the sense in that? Nicolas just had to explain his position, and The Oracle, being as old and wise and reasonable as legend suggested, would agree. Then it would be back home to the day-to-day stuff, forgetting about this little hiccup in his otherwise straightforward life. His family would be disappointed, of course, but he could spend the ride home practising his humbly disappointed expression until he had it perfected. Best of all, The Oracle was a recluse, so no one back at the village would hear about his little deal. As far as he could tell, there were no negatives here.

6

Fixed on his plan and its inevitable success, he mentally rehearsed exactly what he would say and how best to deliver it. He played the whole scene out his mind repeatedly, working out potential threads of replies from The Oracle and how he would respond to them. Nicolas became so certain of his success that when the forest canopy thinned and rays of sunlight broke through the green, he took it as a sign that he was right and this would all work just as he intended.

The wagon finally emerged from the forest with a happy Nicolas aboard it. The treeline stopped advancing and instead circled outwards, forming a round clearing in which the fabled Tower of the Oracle was located. The name of The Oracle's home was always whispered in awestruck voices. Maybe because of the mystery and superstition surrounding the tower and what was inside it? The building allegedly predated Hablock. For a place shrouded in secrecy, everyone was keen to speculate about it, leading to plenty of embellished descriptions of it, making it an intimidating place to travel to, even before you entered the whole *Choosing* thing into the equation.

Passing through the edge of the forest, his skin began to tingle as they entered an area with an unmistakeable mystic quality to it. It was in the very air itself and the glow of the nature around them. As if the air were fresher here, the grass greener. The travellers gasped in what he assumed was awe as they took in the majesty of the clearing. Nicolas gasped at the blatant misuse of the word *'tower'*. From the many and varied descriptions, the last thing he'd expected was the shabby cottage that drew his eye, its worn and dilapidated look in complete contrast to the ground around it, which seemed to be teeming with life.

The cottage could most politely be described as 'ramshackle'. Thick moss and webs decorated dry, cracked walls, and the thatched roof seemed to be thinning like an old man's hair. Debris sprawled around the cottage as if the place were attempting to spread its unkemptness to the rest of the clearing via the use of rusty buckets and old gardening tools. If someone had told him the place was abandoned, he would've had no legitimate reason to argue with them. Indeed, he may have argued with anyone who suggested otherwise. Maybe this was some kind of elaborate jest? As much as he hoped that true, he felt this was real.

As they got closer and the extent of the mess became clearer it was all he could do to not leap from the wagon and begin to tidy the area, though it was tempered by his wish to touch nothing here. He wouldn't have called himself obsessively tidy, but everything had its place at home and frankly, what he saw here made him itch.

'It looks like a ruin,' one of the travellers muttered in a disheartened tone.

'This can't be it,' suggested another.

Obviously, whoever had first called this place 'The Tower of the Oracle' was guilty of romanticising of the worst kind, bordering on outright bullshitting. How could no one know the truth? Clearly, none of the previous participants in the Choosing had wanted to admit they'd visited the 'Crappy Cottage of the Oracle'. It just didn't have the same gravitas.

'I am sorry my humble abode does not meet your lofty standards, lords and ladies,' barked a voice from just inside the cottage's limp-looking door.

All the travellers flinched. How had this person heard what they were saying at this distance and over the background sounds of the wagon? Uncomfortable glances were exchanged as high expectations began to lower considerably.

Coming up to the front of the cottage, the driver pulled on his reins, slowing the horse and turning the wagon parallel to the building before coming to a stop, dispersing a group of chickens, who made their displeasure known. Half-turning to his passengers, the driver gave them a sharp nod, which seemed to translate to *'get out.'*

After dismounting the wagon, which bounced with every shift in weight, Nicolas and the other travellers formed a line before the cottage, shuffling uncomfortably, and waited.

Nicolas winced at the sharp creak that heralded the door of the cottage opening then found himself wincing again at the smell released from within. From the dark interior of the building shuffled a figure in a long, tattered robe, leaning on a knotted stick.

Much like his home, The Oracle was wrapped in a veil of mysticism and legend, only ever seen by those brought to him for the Choosings. Those people told of a venerable wizard, powerful and dashing. Clearly, *'venerable'* was a very polite way of saying *'ancient'*. Any skin visible beneath the tattered robe was so wrinkled it resembled the bark of a tree. Long, straggly hair and matching beard moved in time with his laboured steps.

'My balls are less wrinkled than this guy,' whispered the man to Nicolas's left, drawing a slight chuckle from Potter.

The old man's head snapped round a lot faster than it seemed capable of. Cold blue eyes fixed the joker with a stare like a hunter lining up an arrow on a rabbit. Even though he'd said nothing, Nicolas tensed, guilty by association. The Oracle approached the man and fixed him with a jagged, yellow-toothed snarl.

'I am more useful than your balls will ever be, you mouthy little piece of troll dung.'

The man he'd addressed looked like he might weep as he directed his gaze firmly at his feet instead of meeting those hard eyes head on. Satisfied the joker had been put in his place, The Oracle paced the line, looking at each of them in the way a wolf may look at a lamb at suppertime.

'I am The Oracle. You are here for the Choosing. Go inside so we can get this over with, and you sorry lot can get the hell off my property.' To emphasise his point, The Oracle pointed a bony finger towards the door of the cottage.

From the awkward silence, it seemed his fellow travellers were now not as sure that they wanted to be here as they had been. Still, they began to shuffle towards the door while Nicolas waited for his moment. From the look on his face, The Oracle wasn't happy someone was still waiting in his—for want of a better word—garden. As the eyes fixed on him, he found he didn't care to meet them any more than the joker had. But he would achieve nothing by staying silent, so he resolved to say his piece and be done with this nonsense, looking at a point between the old brows on The Oracles forehead to avoid the cold pupils beneath them.

'Yes?' The Oracle said coldly.

'Ahem.' He wasn't sure he could find the courage to speak, but somehow sputtered the words out anyway, 'Oracle, I was wondering if I could have a moment of your time.'

The Oracle's eyebrow rose as he made an open-handed gesture for Nicolas to continue.

'Okay, thanks.' He gathered what little intestinal fortitude he had. 'About the Choosing. I just wanted to save you a bit of time and effort and say that I'm not really interested...in being Chosen. Sorry, but it just isn't for me.'

The old man stared at Nicolas with an expression somewhere between surprised, incredulous, and flat-out raging. After a few moments of silence, The Oracle shuffled forward—more quickly than he ought to be able—until he was in Nicolas's face, save the height difference. Nicolas found himself engulfed in the unpleasant mouldy stench that seemed to surround The Oracle like a protective aura. He wasn't sure if it was fear of the man or the smell making his stomach turn.

'You are not interested?' the old man asked slowly with the full force of close-quarter halitosis to back him up.

From the tone and the look on The Oracle's face, he was on dangerous ground. Maybe he had made a mistake? This was definitely not playing out the way he'd rehearsed it. Unfortunately, he was now committed to this path and offered a sheepish nod in reply.

'Let me see if I understand this properly,' The Oracle said in a faux-sweet voice. 'You are here because the Deities themselves require a message to be delivered to a hero so that people may be saved, but you have decided this isn't for you? The World of Etherius and the Nine Kingdoms of Man can all go hang because you aren't interested? Well, guess what...I'm not interested that you aren't interested.' Each use of the word *you* was punctuated by a painful jab from The Oracle's long-nailed finger.

Nicolas opened and closed his mouth like a flapping fish. He had no words, which seemed a boon as The Oracle held up a silencing finger anyway.

'Get in the cottage,' the old man said, enunciating every word.

Nicolas did as bid, at a quick pace, lest he annoy The Oracle further. As he entered the abode, he cursed himself for trying to worm his way out of this and cursed the whole sorry situation. This day was not turning out as it should at all.

CHAPTER 2

Somehow, the interior of the cottage seemed far worse than the shabby outside had suggested. *'Squalor'* was the word that came to mind as his eyes adjusted to the dimly lit room, every visible surface covered in grime and clutter. The size of the cobwebs spoke of spiders so large that he squirmed at the thought of them, though they must be well-fed, considering the abundant flies buzzing around. The cherry on the mouldy cake was the smell, which made it necessary to fight the urge to gag as he lined up with the rest of the travellers.

Architecturally speaking, the inside of the dwelling was sparse, with everything confined to a single room. A brief glance showed him what passed for a kitchen, and a bedroom, and toilet. The lack of separation of rooms bothered him almost as much as the condition of the place.

As The Oracle fussed with various piles of clutter, it became apparent that he was having difficulty finding something. Not surprising, as the mantra of this place seemed to be *'dump it wherever'* and he had plentiful crap to root through. The Oracle finally shoved something into his robe with a triumphant grunt.

Hobbling back to his guests, The Oracle pushed a stack of books off something that turned out to be a stool. The books hit the floor and threw up a cloud of dust, in amongst which he thought he caught sight of something scuttling away. He shivered in revulsion as The Oracle lowered himself onto the stool carefully, his legs giving out at the last second and his rear hitting the seat with an audible thud. Resting forwards on his stick, The Oracle contemptuously regarded those before him.

'I take it you are all clear on why you are here?'

Nicolas shied from The Oracle's scowl, instead directing his gaze at the man's thick nostril hair.

A woman in the group opened her mouth to speak. The silencing finger was raised before she'd even completed the motion. The finger was then brought to The Oracle's lips to emphasise the unsubtle point.

'You are here for The Choosing,' The Oracle began. 'Where one of you rabble will be chosen to deliver a message from the Deities themselves.

You think that this makes you special, and you puff your chests out in pride at the great honour being bestowed upon you. Dragon crap. You are here because you happen to be at the right age at the right time, and I am too old to do it myself.'

It was becoming clear why the previous candidates of the Choosing told so many tall tales about The Oracle. No one would want to admit what this undeservedly venerated figure was really like. He was supposed to be the Deities own prophet, after all. Those poor expectant souls he'd travelled here with; *he* was disappointed, and he didn't even want to be here. They must be completely crestfallen.

Looking down the line, he expected glum, disenchanted faces, but this was not the case at all. All of them stood proudly to attention, ready to be chosen for an honourable and sacred duty. Were they not seeing what he was seeing? The Oracle seemed to notice this too and rolled his eyes.

'The chosen Word Bearer will receive the message from me, as well as a time and place to deliver it,' the old man continued, as if repeating a speech that bored him. 'You go there at the time, deliver the message, and come home. Simple. I expect when you return there will be lots of praise, pats on the back, drinks bought for you, and plenty of amorous attention from whichever gender is your preference. Bully for you,' he finished sourly. 'Any questions?'

He would undoubtedly make the asker regret even trying to speak, and his fellow travellers seemed to have gotten the message, judging by their silence. Seemingly satisfied that no one was going to interrupt, The Oracle jumped down from his seat. There was a loud creak that may have been the stool, or possibly his bones.

All his muscles clenched as the old man approached them. This was it: the moment that could change someone's life. The moment someone from a quiet village would get to go out into the world and make their mark on it. He wanted to run, or cry, or both. What he didn't want was the job.

The Oracle rummaged in his robe, finally pulling out a small stick. The only thing even slightly noteworthy about this stick was that its end had been fashioned into a small arrow and the single dead leaf hadn't been removed when it was yanked from whatever tree or bush it came from. With a few impatient gestures, The Oracle directed them into a vague semicircle then threw the stick in the air with a huff.

What was going on? Nicolas's eyes followed the trajectory of the stick as it climbed upwards before rolling back down to the ground. Landing in the centre of the semicircle, the stick's arrow pointed towards a nearby chair leg. Tutting loudly, The Oracle bent down carefully, picked up the stick, and repeated the process. This time when it landed, the arrow pointed towards the door.

The old man did this three more times, cussing more profoundly with each failed landing. The other travellers looked as confused as he was. *Was* this some kind of joke, after all? On the sixth throw, the stick hit the floor and the arrow pointed at him. Nicolas's world closed in around him as he stared wide-eyed at the stick and its proclamation.

'You are Chosen. Congratulations to both you and irony.' The old man kicked the stick aside thoughtlessly.

He could feel his jaw work up and down as he attempted to understand what had just happened. He failed completely.

'But...but...' he stammered.

"*But...but...*what?' The Oracle snapped impatiently.

'That can't be it,' someone beside him said, giving voice to his own opinion. It may have been Potter, but he was too fixated on the stick to bother checking.

'If you want some chanting, or incense, or a fancy light show...tough.' The Oracle snorted. 'You came here for the Choosing, the Choosing is done, and he has been chosen.' He gave a half-hearted wave in Nicolas's direction.

'There's been a mistake. All you did was throw a stick in the air,' the person, who Nicolas was now sure was Potter, protested.

The Oracle held up a silencing hand. 'There are no mistakes and no accidents. You came here for the Choosing and someone has been chosen. I really do not want to have to repeat that a third time.'

'But I don't want to be chosen,' he protested, finally finding his voice.

'Did we not have this conversation outside?' The Oracle hissed. 'Are you deaf? Guess what, precious, you're it, and you need to get your head around that fact quickly because we have things to do.' Not taking his eyes off Nicolas, he continued, 'The rest of you, this isn't for you, so get out of my house.'

There were angry mutterings as the group filed out of the cottage. As Potter passed Nicolas, he gave him a resentful look. That was hardly fair, he hadn't asked for this, quite the opposite in fact. The last to leave, Potter shut the door behind him, with force, and he found himself alone with The Oracle.

Once they were alone, The Oracle's disposition seemed to soften, a little. He almost seemed...sympathetic.

'I understand more than you might think, kid,' he said as he shuffled around the cottage looking at various jars. 'I didn't have a say in this either. Born to it, you see. Came from a line of sages. No choice, just a burden I can't shake. I just get told one day, *'Hey, exciting news, you'll get visions from the Deities.'* That's it, lucky me.'

Nicolas thought hard about keeping silent. He didn't want to raise the old man's ire again, but curiosity got the best of him. 'I thought that being The Oracle was an honour. I thought—'

'You thought what? That I would have a nicer home? That this place would at least be tidy? That I would have servants at my command and virgins at my whim? That I was some sort of mystical entity? Please enlighten me as to what you *'thought."*

'I'm sorry, I—'

'I am exactly what I appear to be.' The Oracle chuckled. 'Just a crazy old man living in the woods who no one visits because whilst they revere someone touched by the Deities, they fear being around me, and those who have met me do not want to do so again. The only person I see is the wagon driver, and he has no personality to speak of. And I cannot leave this place in case I get a vision—you'll see why in a moment. And I certainly get none of the glory that any of you lot I send out get.'

'So, they don't speak to you all the time?' he asked, knowing he may be pushing his luck.

'Only when they want something,' The Oracle grumbled as he unstopped a jar and began to pour the powder it contained into a small pile on the floor in front of him. He then lit a single candle and placed it next to the pile. This seemed very important, but Nicolas couldn't fathom why.

'I get a sign that they have something to say then when I've chosen someone to deliver it, they give me the message. There isn't any small talk, not even a *'thank you, Oracle.'* Just business.' The Oracle stopped fussing with his jars and turned to Nicolas. 'Let me ask you, kid. Do you consider being chosen an honour?' The Oracle didn't wait for a reply so clearly the answer was written all over his face. 'I rest my case.'

The old man kicked away a few items on the floor to make a space. He raised the bottom of his robe, showing thin, gnarled legs, and lowered himself to the ground. When he was halfway down, he obviously required assistance, so as much as he didn't want to touch the old man, Nicolas stepped forward and offered him an arm to use. The Oracle took it without a word of thanks but did give Nicolas a tight smile of acknowledgment.

Once he was on the floor, The Oracle laboriously crossed his legs. He closed his eyes and began to chant under his breath. What was he saying? That was no language Nicolas had heard before. For a moment, his anxiety about being chosen and everything it would entail was overrun by his curiosity about the strange ritual before him.

For a moment, everything was still.

He jumped back with a cry as The Oracle's head suddenly and violently snapped backwards. When it came forward again, the man's blue eyes had been replaced by white orbs. As foam appeared in the old man's mouth, he found himself backing away until he knocked over a stack of books. The dust cloud it produced caused him to cough hard.

The body before him became wracked with spasms, starting with a twitch or two and rising to a crescendo of random, violent movements. He had no idea what to do. Was this normal? Should he try to help somehow? How did the man remain seated while losing control of his body?

In lieu of doing nothing, he found himself tentatively approaching the convulsing body, his hands held before him, ready to catch The Oracle if he fell. What was that terrible smell? Initially he stepped back, hand to his mouth as he fought his gag reflex.

Nicolas retreated another step at the realisation that the old man had soiled himself.

How can I step back when this man needs my help?

Though his self-chiding was moot as The Oracle's body suddenly became still, the colour returning to his eyes just in time for him to pitch forwards and vomit. Concerned he may copy the Oracle's action, he turned away, just the sound of it being enough to stoke his nausea.

When he finally turned back, The Oracle had risen to a seated position. He appeared drained, his skin a deathly grey and his breathing laboured. How was he even alive after all that, never mind moving? The old man's mouth worked hard to control his lungs. Maybe the air in this room wasn't the best to aid recovery?

Though he wanted to step forward and help, he could only watch as a shaking hand took hold of the candle beside him and plunged its flame into the pile of powder. With a small *whoomph*, the powder ignited, billowing red smoke into the air. The Oracle bent forward and inhaled the smoke greedily, his tremors easing and the colour returning to his skin with each lungful.

'And that,' The Oracle groaned weakly as he leaned back and let the nearby table support him, 'is what happens when higher powers speak to a mortal.'

The worst of the ordeal over, Nicolas finally found himself able to act, grabbing a passably clean rag and soaking it in water from a bowl from the kitchen. The Oracle took it with an appreciative nod, using it to dab his weathered face before discarding it and motioning for Nicolas to help him up.

Gently, he took The Oracle's arm and helped him rise. The combined smell of diarrhoea and vomit made that difficult, but he forced himself to ignore it lest he become light-headed and drop the man. He'd been through enough already. Keeping his composure, he settled the old man back on his stool before backing away as quickly, but respectfully, as he could.

'Is it always like that?' he asked, stunned by what he'd just witnessed.

'Every time,' The Oracle whispered hoarsely in reply. 'And I am attuned to it. Imagine what it would do to you. Blow your head clean off, most likely.' He reached out and grabbed a nearby glass of old looking water, taking a long drink from it. 'The red powder helps me recover, otherwise I would spend at least a day lying on the floor in my own mess before I could even crawl again,' he continued. 'Now you see why I don't go out. Imagine getting a message in the middle of the local tavern and crapping all over the place. I doubt I would be welcome back. It would definitely ruin my reputation as a revered figure.'

'I'm so sorry,' he said sincerely.

'You can cram your *'sorry'* in the hole between your ass cheeks,' The Oracle snapped. 'I don't need your pity. I had a job to do, and I did it. Now you have to do yours.' He pointed to a rolled-up piece of parchment on the far side of the room.

Nicolas fetched it for The Oracle, who unfurled it after sweeping a stack of bowls from the surface. It showed a map of Yarringsburg. The mountain at the centre of the kingdom made identifying it easy—that same mountain's rich silver veins had turned a small mining community into a thriving kingdom. On the far side of the mountain he saw a familiar mark: Hablock.

'Do you know Caring's Crossing?' The Oracle asked, pointing to a specific point on the map.

Nicolas nodded.

The crossing was a bridge over the river that separated their part of the kingdom from the more populated areas. Finally, some good fortune. The crossing was only a few hours' walk from the village. Some Word Bearers had travelled half the world to deliver their messages. He was getting off lightly by comparison.

'Well, bully for you.' The Oracle snorted. 'Be on the bridge tomorrow afternoon. When the hero comes along, the message you need to give him is: *'I've heard bad omens from Stranom Crag. No one goes there after dark.'* The message is for its intended recipient only. You do not repeat it to anyone else. Am I clear?'

'What?' he asked. 'I have to say that? It makes no sense.'

'Did I stutter?' The Oracle asked. 'Just repeat it exactly as I said.'

'To whom?'

The Oracle cried out in exasperation. 'A bloody hero, kid,' The Oracle said. 'And before you open your mouth and utter your next stupid question, just keep an eye out for someone who seems heroic who passes the bridge tomorrow afternoon. I'm sure you can figure out what *heroic* looks like for yourself.'

Be at a random bridge and look for someone who looks heroic. That can't be it?

'But...' Nicolas stammered.

'Get out.'

He obeyed dutifully, walking to the door as he desperately tried to commit the message to memory. So much had just happened, and now he was expected to remember that obtuse message? He prayed the words stuck in his mind.

Reaching the door, he found himself turning back. He couldn't leave the old man in his still-weakened state. He appeared to be recuperating, but it didn't seem right to just walk out.

'Is there anything I can do?' he asked.

The Oracle raised his head and turned to look at Nicolas like it was the most painful thing he'd ever done. Despite this, he still fixed him with a steely glare.

'Yes,' he snarled. 'You can listen when I tell you to get out, moron.'

CHAPTER 3

Though his world was now expanding rapidly, everything also seemed to be closing in on him; the weight of his new responsibility and the danger it entailed pressed down on him. Time was a lost concept as the wagon made its return journey to the village, and he struggled to grasp the events he'd just witnessed. How had this happened? How was he supposed to do this? What if he forgot the message? All it would take was a single distraction and it would be lost in his mind for all eternity.

Maybe eternity wouldn't be that long anyway. There were so many ways he could die out there. He could fall and trip on a rock; he could be trod on by a giant who simply didn't see him... Soon, his mind became a single track on which passed images of various terrible fates that may befall him on his trip. From the tight feeling in his chest, a panic attack could strike at any time.

In the eye of a storm of fear and self-doubt, he still managed to be keenly aware of his fellow travellers. It seemed it was their turn to endure the wagon journey in sullen silence. Who could blame them? The 'Tower of the Oracle' and the man himself were frauds and the ceremony a joke. What chatter he could hear around him reflected the general dissatisfaction of the whole trip. Judging by the glares flashed at him, this was manifesting as resentment towards the one who'd not only been chosen but hadn't wanted to be.

'We're nearly home,' Potter said with no warmth in his voice as he nudged Nicolas.

Shaking himself from his self-absorption, he saw that they were no longer in the forest, but instead in the open fields that surrounded Hablock and its widespread farming community. The road was actually fit for travel, sided by bushes and old stone walls. On the horizon were silhouettes of the smattering of buildings that made up the village square of Hablock.

'You're about to become very popular, Nick,' Potter said, poorly hiding the jealous edge to his voice.

'Am I?' he asked, certainly not feeling popular.

'Of course.' Potter smiled. 'You are the Word Bearer now, friend. You leave on your quest a boy and come back a legend...in these parts, anyway.'

'I suppose.'

'He supposes.' Potter laughed.

Several angry mutterings suggested what his fellow travellers thought of that. Why were they mad at him? If he could find a way to undo it and let any of them have their moment, he would.

'I know I'm not supposed to ask,' Potter began quietly as he leant in. 'But what did the old crank say to you after we left?'

'I can't tell you that,' he replied, taken aback by the audacity of the question. 'The message is meant only for the hero.'

'What if it wasn't.'

This seemed to be heading somewhere and he wasn't sure he liked where. 'What do you mean?'

Potter ran a hand through his beard before he spoke. 'What if you give me the message and I deliver it?'

'Just give it to you?' he whispered incredulously.

'Sure.' Potter half-smiled. 'You don't want to do it. We all heard. So don't do it. Give the message to someone willing to deliver it.' He pointed to himself as if it needed emphasising.

Looking at Potter, he tried to fully absorb his proposition. He could avoid a job he didn't want and all the danger that went with it. Surely someone who actually wanted the task would do a better job? Was the result of a ceremony in which a stick was thrown into the air something to strictly adhere to?

Though it seemed ideal, the message was from the Deities, after all, and he'd been specifically told not to repeat it. Shirking a duty given by all-powerful higher beings seemed a recipe for disaster, no matter how they chose their messengers. Plus, there was something just plain wrong about handing the task off because he didn't want to do it. Chosen was chosen.

'I'm sorry but I can't,' he replied finally, surprising himself. 'I was told to share the message with no one else. The Oracle was very specific about that. It would be wrong.' Mentally, he uttered an apology to any of the Deities who knew how close he'd come to agreeing.

Potter held Nicolas's gaze, his face unreadable.

'I'm sorry you didn't get chosen. I wish you had been,' he offered, hoping to soothe any ill feeling. It seemed weak even as he said it.

'Not your fault, fella,' Potter replied finally with a nonchalant shrug, 'Sorry, but I had to try. Looks like I'll have to take the scenic route to my destiny, eh?' Potter sat back lazily and took in the world around them.

Nicolas tried to do the same but could only focus on the dangers that world contained.

Soon he found himself looking up as the wagon passed slowly under the arch marking the boundary to Hablock's village square. Fields were replaced by rows of blocky wooden buildings, designed and placed with pure practicality in mind. The founders' of the village were evidently not a artistic lot. As he passed the tavern, the single road through the town opened in the centre, where the statue of town founder Cyrus Hablock stood gazing off into the horizon. The local birds were doing their best to undermine his dignity with their droppings.

A large crowd was gathered around the statue. It was expected, of course, but that crowd would soon turn all its attention to him, a prospect that made his heart thunder in his chest and his palms sweat. This was his worst nightmare come true—a nightmare made worse by the silence, the expectant hush of a mass of people waiting for an answer.

Easing the wagon to a stop, the driver used one of his eloquent head nods to tell them to leave his conveyance. No one seemed inclined to thank him for his service. Nicolas nearly did, but the man had a less open personality than The Oracle.

For a moment, he stalled on the dirt road, but there was nowhere to go but forwards, towards those curious faces and hopeful eyes. There were some deflated expressions as families caught the eyes of their kin and realised this hadn't been their time. The silence of the crowd was deafening, but it was shortly broken by thunderous applause.

One of the others must've indicated him as the Word Bearer. Hablock was a quiet village, but when they had reason to celebrate, they did so with gusto. As all eyes fell on him his step wavered, his cheeks flushing as he avoided their gazes. His parents broke from the crowd, his mother bearing down on him with a speed that would've impressed a charging bull. Before he had chance to react, her arms were locked round him, his face full of her bushy, curled hair. None of it made him feel any better.

Knowing his mother wouldn't let go until she was good and ready, he scanned the rest of the crowd, careful to avoid actual eye contact with anyone. Many looked at him with simple joy, though he couldn't help but notice thinly veiled glares from the relatives of the unsuccessful. Yes, the choosing was taken seriously, but such bad sportsmanship was a bit much. It made him feel more like a victim than he already did.

'I am so proud of you,' his mother said with a beaming smile. 'First Word Bearer in three years, and it's my boy. I can't believe it.'

He still couldn't.

It was only when her grip slackened that the rest of the crowd approached, giving him congratulations and adulation as unwelcome as his Choosing.

'I didn't do anything,' he mumbled. 'He just threw a stick.'

It sounded sillier every time he thought of it, but his words were drowned out by the voices of well-wishers and applause. He realised that all he could do now was put on a happy face, as was expected.

Feeling a familiar hand on his shoulder, he looked up into his father's rugged face. Was that a hint of sadness in his father's smile?

'Well done, son,' he mouthed.

Any dwindling hopes of trying to palm off his burden dissolved like sugar in hot water. He couldn't let his parents down, let his village down. It looked like he was going to do this, despite his better judgement.

'All right, you lot,' his mother shouted over the noise of the crowd. 'Step aside so I can take my son home.'

Nicolas knew that she'd wanted to add *The Word Bearer*' after *'son'* but was restraining herself. Pride was one thing, showing off was another, and his mother took her dignity and standing in the community very seriously. There would be no showboating for her.

Obliging without question, the people parted like the grand double doors of a castle, though the chattering and congratulating continued as they passed through. Why were people so keen on touching him? Was he now some kind of lucky charm? More fool them, there was no good luck here, he just hoped his bad luck didn't rub off on them

Taking in the sea of faces surrounding him, Nicolas only had two desires right now: to sit on something that didn't bounce under his butt and to be alone.

As it turned out, a decent seat was an achievable goal. Being alone, not so much. Somehow, his mother had managed to have a celebration ready for Nicolas's triumphant return, to congratulate him on the great honour bestowed upon him. Nicolas knew this because the word *honour* was thrown around quite shamelessly. Apparently, showboating in the right circumstances was okay. When his father produced the cake he'd already prepared, Nicolas began to wonder whether his parents had conspired with fate to get him picked. If not, they were lucky he had been, or a lot of food would've gone to waste.

Nicolas had to give credit to his parents: they put on an amazing spread of potatoes, various meats and vegetables. Though he was famished from the long day, the events of it still had his stomach in knots, so he found it difficult to eat much. He found it even more difficult to make merry, displaying half-hearted smiles when the pats on the back came. The questions were worse, people wanting to know everything about The

Oracle and The Tower. He was sure they didn't want to know *everything* so he towed the line with the popular tales, and his audience lapped it up despite his awkward delivery. If he had decided to tell them the truth, he doubted he could've accurately portrayed the ridiculousness of the whole thing anyway.

Soon enough his voice was hoarse from talking. Was it bad for wishing a party in his honour to end as quickly as possible? For someone keen on avoiding being the centre of attention this was a nightmare, as was the reason why. Yet somehow he endured it, keeping his anguish inside as he conversed with people he barely recognised.

When time came for his mother to call an end to the celebration, he could've hugged her as tightly as she'd held him in the square. Politely, she began to shoo the guests away. The Word Bearer needed his sleep, didn't you know? Truer words, he thought, exhausted under the weight of people telling him how lucky he was.

Naturally, he offered to help clear up—despite his own needs, he couldn't just walk away and leave the mess for his parents—but his mother wouldn't hear of it. He would've hugged her again for that had the threat of breaking down in tears not hung over him. Using his last embers of energy, he climbed the stairs to his room.

Once the door was shut, he half fell onto his bed, mind racing. Trying to avoid the thoughts plaguing him, he looked to the ceiling of his room, trying discern images from the knots in the wood, but they kept struggling back to the surface. His mind soon became consumed by the deadly fates that may await him on his journey, both the possible and the ridiculous. There was not one of them that he felt capable of handling, reaffirming his belief that they had picked the wrong person for this job.

As he lay there, tired as he was, he knew sleep would elude him. Maybe planning the journey would ease his fears? Rooting through his bookshelf, he soon found what he sought, a book containing charts of the area. Placing it on his lap, the old book opened with a creak as he leafed to the page he needed. Finding the local area, he marked Hablock with his finger, tracing a line between it and Caring's Cross. It was close; that was good. Though to make it to there in time meant going through the nearby forest, the road winding around it too far out of his way. What hid amongst the trees waiting for unwary travellers? This area wasn't known for natural predators or bandits, but he felt luck had forsaken him, so that meant nothing. With a derisive chuckle he realised not once had he considered the possibility of his journey being successful. Was it a lack of faith in himself, or in the world around him?

He hadn't known exactly how on edge he was until a knock at the door made him start. Maybe a distraction would be good?

'Come in,' he said hesitantly.

When the door pushed aside, his father came in with his usual genial smile. The years of carrying sacks of flour, and eating his own cakes, had made him an imposing figure. Nicolas looked at his own gangly arms. Were they even really related? If only he was even half his father's size.

'Big day,' father said simply as he sat next to him, the bed creaking slightly under his weight.

That was a massive understatement in Nicolas's opinion, but he kept it to himself.

'Planning your journey?' he asked, noting the map.

For some reason, he found saying his destination aloud difficult, as if it would make it all the more real. Instead he tapped the map with his finger.

Studying the map, his father smiled warmly, looking almost as if a weight had been lifted from him.

'Caring's Cross, that's good. That's close.'

He gave a tight smile in reply, hoping his father's positivity might rub off on him but doubting it.

'Nicolas,' he began after a moment of silence and in the tone of a man trying to be as diplomatic as possible. 'I know you aren't very savvy about the world beyond the village. But it's only a short trip. You just need to keep your head down, get there and back again, and it'll be all good.'

Though the advice was sound, what was behind it scared him. Even his father knew he wasn't cut out for this. His worst fears were confirmed.

From his belt, Father suddenly produced a small knife. It wasn't an elegant weapon, just a simple blade, but very recently sharpened by the look of it. As the knife was handed to him, he took it hesitantly. Deities he hoped he would never be in a situation where he needed it.

'If there's trouble,' Father said, 'the pointy end goes into the troublemaker. And if that doesn't work, there are two simple rules to go by. No matter what species it is, orc, dwarf, or whatever, a punch to the throat or kick in the balls will do.'

Again, sound advice, had he any experience in punching and kicking. Hopefully, the explanation on how to use a knife was to lighten the mood, but who knew? The man was trying, though, and that meant something.

'Thanks, Dad.'

An arm like a tree trunk wrapped around Nicolas and gave him a single tight squeeze. He couldn't shake the feeling it was a hug of sympathy more than anything else. Caught off guard by the gesture, the pressure of his role weighing heavy on him a single tear rolled down his cheek.

'You'll do just fine,' Father said as he rose and patted Nicolas on the shoulder. 'You can do this. But you need to rest. It's a big day tomorrow.'

That was the best advice so far. The door closed and he lay back, closing his eyes and wishing for a peaceful sleep.

CHAPTER 4

Sleep had eluded Nicolas. Like playing tag against the fastest child in school, it kept jinking and dodging him, yet always stayed frustratingly within reach. His nightmares had been kind enough not to wait for sleep to come to him, providing him with images of failure and danger and death. Not matter how many times he reminded himself of the safety of the area or the simplicity of the task, they wouldn't abate.

As he finally trudged downstairs, unwilling to start a day he already knew would spiral out of his control, he walked into a hive of activity. Both his parents fussed to and fro as they prepared his travel bag, and the table was loaded with a hearty breakfast to ready him for his journey. These home comforts made him want to leave even less, despite the promise of being home again that same day.

Feeling as if he were really asleep and in a dream, he sat at the table. It was as if he was slightly out of sync with reality, which almost suited him as it was a reality he didn't want to face. Without any hunger, but knowing he'd need his strength, he began to eat. The food was hot and delicious and he took a second to enjoy the simple pleasure of being at home with his parents. Who knew when he would see it or them again? The only thing sullying the moment were the worried glances his parents were barely concealing.

He seemed to be back at the statue in the village square in the blink of the eye. Unsurprisingly, a Word Bearer leaving on his journey was a point of pride for the people of Hablock, and therefore an occasion to be marked. Had the crowd even left last night? Maybe they'd just camped here? Did they not have homes to go to and chores to do?

More well-wishing was lavished upon him, laden with nuggets of advice he couldn't hear over the band playing a fast-paced jig on the stage that had been erected nearby. Being the centre of attention almost made him yearn to get on with his quest. Sighing, he realised they would be just as bad on his return. Maybe he should take the scenic route, stretch it out at least another day? Finally considering a return journey made him smile despite his mood.

Then the mayor took the stage, shushing the crowd in the no-nonsense style for which he was famed before summoning Nicolas to join him. He wanted to run, but there was no escaping this. He wanted to scream at all of them, to tell them what a fraud he was, how unsuitable he was, how stupid this all was. He knew these things. Why didn't they?

Fighting down the emotions broiling inside him, he managed to say a few words when the mayor called on him. He had no idea what he said, and never would, but whatever it was, the crowd seemed to lap it up. Maybe they were simply so set on cheering today, that they'd cheer anything he said? Maybe he could've discussed the pros and cons of using horse manure to clean yourself and they would've enjoyed it just as much?

Once the speeches were done, the local priest joined him on stage, calling on the Deities to bless and aid him on his journey. He alternated between feeling that he needed them and wanting them to shove their blessings right up their backsides for putting him in this position.

All that was left then was to depart. The crowd applauded as it parted, marking his route out of town and making him feel naked under their gaze. The urge to throw up or run home were incessant, but he put one foot in front of the other and continued to do so as the adulation carried him forwards, while drowning out every calming mantra he attempted to recite. He could hardly blame them. It wasn't just a message he was carrying, it was also the village's pride and hope and the hope of everyone whose fate would be determined by the hero receiving his message. He felt every gram of its weight on his shoulders.

Half-heartedly, he returned the beaming smiles and waves of those he passed—one of whom was Potter, the bearded man giving him a small salute. At least there were no hard feelings there; he kind of liked the guy. Or maybe Potter just knew that his life had been saved by not being chosen and was saluting a man walking to his impending doom?

At the end of the crowd, his mother and father awaited him, hugging him tight without a word. Everything had been said. It was time to begin his journey.

****

'Beseeching the Deities for blessings.' Nicolas laughed. 'They should've already blessed my trip. I'm running an errand for them, after all.'

Travelling through the numerous fields around Hablock had given him ample opportunity to go from fearing his task to resenting it. You see one field of crops, you've seen them all, and the crops didn't care how much he grumbled—they were content to dance lazily in the gentle breeze. All around him was tranquil; Nicolas was not. Having only his own mind to keep him company save for the thousands of chirruping crickets surrounding him, he'd decided that besides being a frightening prospect, this whole quest was unfair and he was well within his rights to be pretty damned upset about it. Upset about the way he was chosen, upset about being chosen, and upset about all the bull crap stories that surrounded The Oracle and his Tower.

Nicolas was also upset about the message itself. *'I've heard bad omens from Stranom Crag. Nobody goes there after dark.'* What did that even mean? That wasn't the kind of thing someone just walked up to another person and said. What if there were follow-up questions? He didn't even know where the bloody Crag was. So not only was he risking serious injury on this journey, he was also about to walk up to some noble hero and make a complete idiot of himself.

Then another issue struck Nicolas. How would he even recognise this hero when he came along? What if he gave the message to some random traveller? Lives were at stake, or the Deities wouldn't have gotten involved. He barely felt in control of his own life right now; how was he supposed to be responsible for others?

A change in scenery pulled him out of his own head. It had taken a couple of hours, but the end of the fields was finally visible in the distance, the forest beyond marking out its edge with bark and leaf. This would mark the second leg of his journey, and the most uncertain part. It was easy to see anything around you in a field, but in a forest, there were numerous spots for dark things to hide.

Rising above the forest in the distance was Mount Yarrin, the mountain for which the kingdom had been named and the reason for its prosperity. On its far side would be the city itself. What would a city even look like? He'd heard tell of its size, but he couldn't grasp the scale.

All around the mountain, large rock formations stood tall and proud, but Yarrin was king of them all, rising so high that cloud obscured its topmost peaks. He was glad he wouldn't set foot on it, for if the wood made him unsure, the thought of anything lurking in those foothills and mountains terrified him. And yet he couldn't help but be awestruck by the wonderous creation of nature.

Reaching the border between the fields of crops and the unrestrained forest, Nicolas readied himself for the second leg of his quest. What was between him and his destination?

'I won't find out if I just stand here,' he said to himself, taking a long swig from his canteen.

The bushes formed a thick wall between him and the forest, and naturally there was no visible gate. It didn't take long for him to figure out what he had to do; he just didn't like the idea. Over it was the only way. He knew he shouldn't have given in so easily when mother insisted he wore his best jacket.

His pack went first, requiring a bit more effort to launch over the bush than he'd hoped. He was satisfied when he heard the clump that signalled it landing on the other side. Now for him. Taking a few paces back, he readied himself, eyeing his obstacle, which wasn't that high. Really. With a deep breath, he ran at the bush.

By his third false start, he was becoming quite aggravated.

'It's just a stupid bush!' So then why was he treating it like a ten-foot spiked wall?

Channelling that annoyance, as well as his upset at The Oracle and the task, he let out a cry as he charged the bush a fourth time, working his legs hard before launching himself into the air. At the moment his feet left the ground, it occurred to him he had no idea how to land properly on the other side.

As it turned out, it was a moot point. He ended up directly atop the bush, the leaves rustling in annoyance at having their restful photosynthesis violently disturbed. Twigs poked Nicolas from every angle, and the bush boasted some truly painful thorns as well. He cursed the bush aloud. The bush didn't care. With agitated rustling, he squirmed over the foliage like a sea creature washed ashore. The bush fought him every step, but he eventually half-landed, half-rolled onto the forest floor beyond.

'Brilliant start.' Nicolas sighed as he inspected the toll the bush had taken.

Ripped clothes and a few small cuts seemed to be the sum total of the damage, so he picked himself up and dusted himself off.

Looking around the forest, he tried to acclimate to his new surroundings. Compared to the open fields, this place felt dark and enclosed, with the noises of nature all around him but no idea where or what they emanated from. He knew he was in a paranoid person's worst nightmare, because he was that person. Eyeing the trees suspiciously, he leant down and grabbed his pack, which seemed to have fared better in its trip over the bush than he had. Hefting the pack onto his back, he tried to ignore his mind telling him that the rustling of the leaves was the forest laughing at him, the trees saying to each other, *'Look at this scrawny guy who's come here to die.'*

Paranoia or not, he had to get through this forest to the crossing. If he travelled in a straight line, he would be there soon enough. Hopefully, this hero would also arrive in a timely fashion so he could make the journey home in the light. He doubted the Deities would send him to meet someone who wasn't going to show.

And so he advanced into the forest, wincing with the crunch of every leaf and snap of every twig that announced his presence to any listeners. Despite that, the forest was relatively easy to travel through. It seemed the only problems were in his mind, after all.

After about a half-hour's walk, he came to a halt. He'd become accustomed to his new surroundings and almost nonchalant about it when something made him freeze on the spot. It took a second to register the reason: he'd heard something—something out of place in the ambient noise of the forest. Something that caused an alarm bell to ring. He listened intently to see if the sound repeated itself.

After standing still for several long moments, he began to believe he'd imagined the sound, that his mind had played a trick to warn him to take more care. Then the sound came again: a wet, mucous laden snort from somewhere off to his right.

Calm down Nicolas.

Animals were to be expected in a forest, he *knew* that, yet still he didn't move, his feet seeming to have planted roots deeper than the ancient trees around him. Should he be staying still when danger maybe close by?

Moving his head slowly, lest some errant crick of the neck summon danger, Nicolas scanned the tree line as far as he could see. There appeared to be nothing, until a flicker of movement told him he should be looking much closer.

His legs weakened as a large shadow emerged from behind a nearby tree. Out of focus, disproportionate limbs soon resolved into leathery appendages covered with matted fur. The muscular torso was topped by a squat, tusked head that appeared displeased with everything around it. He had no basis for comparison, but he was sure that was a troll. He was also sure he could soil himself imminently.

Trembling, he watched the creature amble forward and pick up a nearby log with ridiculous ease, as simply as one may pick up their plate after supper. After a brief examination, during which the troll seemed to find nothing of interest, it tossed the log aside with a guttural bark. If it could throw a log so easily, what could it do to him?

The log hit the forest floor with a loud crack, and Nicolas let slip a small cry. *Dammit.* Any hope the crashing log may have drowned out his cry was dashed as the troll abruptly turned in his direction and barked a challenge. Apparently, its large ears were not just for show.

The troll rose to full height and beat its chest several times before thumping its fists on the forest floor. If this was a display of dominance, it was unnecessary. He knew who was in charge here. Confident the predator-prey relationship had been established, the troll loped towards him. He highly doubted he could outrun the creature, even if he could've moved his legs. *So what now?* The only thing he could really do was try not to provoke it.

What had he learned about trolls? One thing: they dwelt in mountain caves and underground. As this was—clearly—neither, was this a hallucination, cooked up by his overanxious brain, or were the stories wrong? The musky odour of the troll made a strong case for the latter. Being eaten by a troll had been on his list of potential deaths on this journey, just not high on it. Irony was certainly having its way with him lately. On the plus side, at least he wasn't completely paranoid.

Its shadow covering him, the troll leaned in close, Nicolas refusing to look into those fierce green eyes. It sniffed him once—a long, drawn breath—before barking a challenge at him. Somehow, he managed to stay still, though all his internal organs shook. Maybe he should play dead? No, it was far too late for that. He had the knife tucked inside his boot but attacking a seven-foot troll with a two-inch knife was insanity itself.

He finally did cry out as the troll grabbed and held up his arm, which looked like a stick in the troll's giant fist. Fixing him with a glare warning against making any other noise, the creature took another sniff, before letting his arm flop back to his side with an unimpressed snort.

Had the troll decided he was too scrawny to bother eating? Had he come across not only the sole forest-inhabiting troll in all Etherius, but the fussiest eater too? After a moment of consideration, he decided he was offended. Why was he not good enough to eat? Any creature would be lucky to dine on... *what was he thinking?*

With another large sniff, the troll ambled behind Nicolas, who decided the best thing to do was continue staying still—it was working so far and he didn't want to give the troll reason to think a light appetiser might be worth it after all.

Why won't this bloody thing just go away, though?

With another cry, he was yanked from the ground and lifted into the air, his limbs dangling feebly as he tried his best not to flail lest he accidentally strike the troll and start something he couldn't finish. Hauled around, he found himself eye-to-eye with the creature, who didn't look pleased with him. For a second, he thought he caught a glimmer of intelligence in the creature's green eyes then the world shook violently. The forest blurred in and out of focus as he was bounced up and down, the troll grunting at him in annoyance. Somehow, despite being dizzy and disorientated, he had a brain wave. The troll wasn't holding him; it was holding his pack. It wanted his pack, and he happened to be attached to it. That, he could do something about. With great difficulty, he began to wriggle one of his arms free of the strap. It seemed to take an eternity, but finally his hand slipped out of the pack, and the forest floor came to meet him at speed. There was a thud.

Through the pain of the fall, he crawled as far from the troll as he could while the creature roared in triumph behind him, the sound bouncing from tree to tree. After slipping behind the nearest tree, he peered out to see what the troll was doing, despite his brain frantically listing the reasons he shouldn't. The creature had dropped to the floor, and it tore the pack apart as if it were nothing, before sorting through the debris until it came across the provisions Mother had packed for him.

Within seconds, jagged teeth were tearing through meat—the troll seemed determined to consume its prize as quickly and messily as possible. Not wanting to waste the opportunity, Nicolas turned and ran like the wind in the opposite direction, thanking any Deity that would listen that he was still alive and his britches unsoiled.

CHAPTER 5

On the positive side, coming across the only troll in Etherius who liked a nice stroll in the forest had allowed him to reach his destination in record time. Lying on the bank of the river gasping for breath, he could see the hole in the bushes from which he'd burst, leaving scattered leaves and broken branches in his wake. Fear had driven his limbs far beyond his anything his own fitness would allow, but as that fear dissipated he began to feel the price his body would pay for it. His whole body burned, and his heart hammered in his chest from the unaccustomed exertion.

Fighting to regain his breath, he closed his eyes and tried to concentrate on the trickle as water made its way down the river, calm and relaxed in contrast to the man lying on its bank. The pounding behind his eyes made this difficult, but he persevered until he felt a semblance of self again.

'I'm alive,' he half-laughed, half-cried in surprise.

He'd survived an encounter with a troll, of all things. But had he come away unscathed? He patted himself to see if the creature had taken a chunk from him and he hadn't noticed, and was relieved to find himself whole. But what was next? He was only halfway through his short quest and already one of his worst fears had befallen him. Wasn't this supposed to be simple? What else was waiting for him? Maybe a dragon had claimed the bridge?

Raising himself to his knees, he took in his surroundings properly. How could the river be so calm? Did it not know there were trolls on the loose? One troll in the forest did not a rampaging troll horde make, but there shouldn't have been one to begin with. What did reassure him was the bridge just down the river from him. Caring's Cross. At least he was where he was supposed to be, and alone.

Crawling to the water's edge, he looked out over the bank, gasping at the pale and haggard reflection that looked back at him. Cupping his hands, he took a scoop of the cool liquid, splashing it on his face. Instantly he felt reinvigorated, though maybe the euphoria of surviving had a hand in that. One thing was for sure, though, on the journey back, he was taking the long way home.

Rising slowly, unsure his legs would take his weight, he looked towards his destination. He was famished, his energy burned off, and his provisions in a troll's belly, but he still had a task to complete. It was getting on for afternoon, so this hero should appear soon, then he could worry about scavenging some food. Maybe the hero would be grateful for the assistance and share some provisions? Either way, he needed to be on that bridge.

As he approached, he saw a worn sign pointing off in two directions, the writing on either arrow old to the point it was no longer legible. He hoped travellers who passed here already knew where they were going. He certainly had no interest in what lay in either direction. He strolled to the centre of the bridge and looked around. There was no sign of anyone. A distinct lack of heroes. The only thing here was a simple stone bridge, but what else had he expected? Maybe that dragon lurking around?

'I'm here,' he said to no one in particular as he leant against the stone wall along the bridge's edge.

All that was left now was waiting. After that, he could deliver the message and get on his way back home. Hopefully this hero was the punctual sort.

* * * *

It had been hours. The sun was starting to get low in the sky as he paced impatiently. He *had* been quite calm, ready to do his job so he could return to Hablock. He'd even managed to find some berries nearby which, while not slaying his hunger, did appease it slightly. In a wild fantasy, he'd hoped to find a lost pack containing provisions of the meat variety, but reality had dashed that hope. Then time had begun to drag.

Does this person not know I survived a troll attack to be here? The least they can do is turn up on bloody time.

Of course, The Oracle hadn't specified a particular time, just giving him *afternoon* to go on. Maybe the crazy old coot had given him the wrong day? He doubted translating messages from Deities was an exact science, and he hardly seemed reliable to start with.

Hang on, what if this guy doesn't turn up at all?

He had a message that could potentially save lives; what was he supposed to do with it if the hero didn't show up? Find some soldiers maybe? There was no way he could do anything about it himself; the encounter with the troll had proven the level of his courage. He certainly didn't want to be out here by himself, at night, with no provisions.

Maybe he should just go home. He'd done his bit. If the other party was lackadaisical then that was on them. No one at home would know the difference. On the other hand, he'd been given a sacred duty...not that the object of that duty had bothered turning up. But it was still a duty, and he had to fulfil it as best he could, especially when he risked upsetting the Deities if he didn't. Which left him stuck on a bridge until something happened.

Then something happened.

There was the unmistakable neigh of a horse and the distant clopping of hooves that went with it. Standing up straight and brushing off his jacket, preparing to finally get this done, he rehearsed the message and how he would deliver it in his head. This time tomorrow, all of this would be a silly memory, hopefully one that included an apology from a certain hero for being so damned tardy.

Up ahead, where the road disappeared around the trees, a pair of horses emerged. He was about to call out, but something stopped him, that same danger sense that had stopped him in the forest when he heard a noise that turned out to be a troll. That instinct told him not to draw attention to himself, and he found himself shrinking back towards the wall again.

As it turned out, the pair of horses was not alone. Eight riders appeared on the road ahead, escorting two wagons. If asked to describe a bandit, he would've described these men. They had hard eyes and worn armour and rode with the easy posture of men who were worse than any trouble they might encounter. And here he stood in the middle of a bridge, plain as day. He pressed himself to the wall harder, nearly tipping over into the water below.

He needed to do something, but what? If he ran, they might give chase. If he tried to fight, they might laugh at him before they beat him to death. He could jump into the river, but what if he cracked his head on a rock? In the end, he decided to do what he'd done with the troll, stay still and hope they passed. It had worked with the creature, so why not now? Okay, so there were many reasons, but he didn't think he could move if he tried.

As the convoy began to pass him, he allowed himself some hope. They had to see him. He was right there. Yet they paid him no heed. Maybe they didn't care about him, just like the troll? He could definitely live with that. He was already learning to live with heart-wrenching fear, and he hadn't been at this a day yet.

Keeping his eyes low, guessing that making eye contact with any of the riders would be a deadly error, he ended up instead looking at the wagons. Why did they have cages attached to them? The metal bars looked thick and durable. Despite his better judgement about prying into the business of dangerous men, his curiosity got the best of him, and he looked in the wagons.

As the first passed, he saw a group of robed individuals who sat dejectedly, shaking with the motion of the wagon. In amongst them was a large shape covered by a red cloak. It was bigger than any of the other people, but he couldn't make out what it was as the tattered cloak covered it completely. What were the collars around each of their necks?

The second wagon also contained people, though more densely packed, with no room to sit. From what they wore, he guessed they were all village folk. These people had chains around their wrists, but no collars. Odd. The villagers all stared off into the distance, possibly contemplating their fate when they got where they were going. It didn't seem like it would be a happy one. None of them looked at Nicolas.

Except one.

His gazed locked with a pair of pleading green eyes. The owner of them was likely about his age and the most beautiful woman he'd ever seen with pale skin contrasted by short auburn hair. She looked to him for salvation. He could only gawk back at her.

What he needed to do was help her, and by extension all of them. He just had no clue how to do it. Grand intentions were no match for ten hardened fighters. He was barely a match for a slight breeze. But he had to do something. As the final wagon passed him, he wracked his brains. The only productive idea he could come up with was to wait for the hero and set him on the evildoers. Hopefully, he would be here any second now.

'Enjoying your sightseeing?'

Nicolas wheeled around. Behind him were two other riders, very different from the ones who preceded them, more intimidating and malicious.

The one who'd spoken could be summed up in a single word: muscle. He knew this because the man had as much of it on show as possible. What drew the eye, though, was the bearskin cloak he wore, the dead creature's head draped over the warrior's as if it would bite it off whole any moment now. The man's gaze was contemptuous to say the least, but he wouldn't challenge it.

'I do believe we have an innocent bystander of some sort,' his companion commented.

The voice was feminine, but that was the only way he could tell the figure was a woman. She was covered head to toe in sturdy armour, obscuring her form and features, yet even from behind the visor he could feel the fierce eyes watching him. Across her lap was a sword with what seemed to be a rising sun carved on its hilt that drew his eye. To her sides, secured to her saddle, were a crossbow and a long lance.

He knew he was in more danger now than when coming upon the troll in the forest.

'Another for the cage?' the big man asked as he stroked his beard.

'We're on a schedule,' the woman replied in a cold voice.

'We stopped for the girl.'

'She was worth stopping the convoy for. I don't think this scrawny boy warrants the same effort,' the woman retorted as she gestured with her gauntlet towards him. 'Hardly a fitting tribute.'

The big man looked back at Nicolas and nodded with a chuckle.

It seemed Nicolas was inadequate for a lot of things today.

'Maybe you would care for a bit of sport, Grimmark?' the woman suggested.

'I would hardly call it sport,' the big man, Grimmark, sniffed. 'But I will kill him anyway. Unless the lady wishes to?'

'I've had my sport for today.'

Both riders laughed at some sort of private joke as the woman caressed the sword on her lap. It was then that Nicolas registered that one of them had used the word *'kill'* in relation to him.

'Besides,' the woman continued, 'it's a lot of effort getting on and off the horse, and I don't wish to expend it on some boy on a bridge.'

'I've told you time and again that you wear too much armour.' Grimmark chuckled heartily. 'It will get you in trouble one day. Warrior women should wear as little armour as possible and be proud to bare their flesh in battle.'

The helmet on the woman's head turned until the visor was pointed directly at Grimmark. Even from where he was, Nicolas could feel the contempt directed at the big man, who seemed completely indifferent to it. 'More than the boy will die on this bridge if you make such suggestions to me again.'

'Don't I get a say in this?' he heard himself say. Why had he spoken?

Both riders looked back at Nicolas and laughed again.

'I promise I won't say anything to anyone' or trying to beg for mercy. You've seen something you shouldn't, and now you have to die. If it makes you feel any better, it isn't personal, just bad timing on your part.'

That didn't make him feel any better at all.

The world seemed to slow in a haze of thumping heartbeats and shallow breaths as fear took him. The warrior, Grimmark, dismounted his steed with more grace than he would've expect from someone his size. After rolling his shoulders a couple of times, the warrior reached behind him and pulled a long-handled warhammer from the harness on his back. Nicolas gulped. The hammer's head was carved into the visage of a snarling bear. Grimmark swung the hammer lazily a couple of times, obviously in no hurry to commit murder.

'No whimpering now, boy,' Grimmark said as he finished his little warm-up and approached Nicolas. 'I will get little enough satisfaction from killing you, and I don't want that marred by you wailing like a baby.'

For the second time, his traitorous legs betrayed him. As the warrior bore down on him, Nicolas found himself stuck to the spot as if he were part of the bridge itself. At least he'd proven himself right that he was the wrong person for this task. Not that it was much comfort now.

The warrior came nearer. This was it, how he died. He'd always thought himself dying an old man, surrounded by family, on the odd occasion he thought of such things. But no, instead he was to be beaten to death on a bridge because of a stick. Feeling a sense of the inevitable, he thought of his mother and father, may the Deities watch over them. He loved them both dearly and wished he'd said so more often. Would they ever know what became of him?

All he could do was watch as Grimmark closed the distance, hefted the heavy hammer high, and swung it down towards him. Around him the time slowed to a crawl, cruelly ensuring he missed no tiny detail of his last moments alive; the murderous glint in the warriors eyes, the tension in his muscles as he swung, he saw it all. Then his whole world narrowed to the leering metal bear head arcing down upon him. Not wishing to watch his oncoming death he closed his eyes. He'd failed in his task, but that shame would only last another second or two.

Muttering a final prayer, he heard a sharp cracking sound somewhere near his feet, coupled with a grunt of surprise. Quickly realising his head hadn't been caved in, he slowly opened his eyes. Then opened them wider in surprise as he realised he was actually still alive. Grimmark stood before him with an equal look of surprise, still holding the hammer, whose deadly head had smashed a stone tile where Nicolas had been standing a moment before, sending pieces of stone scattering in all directions. Somehow, as far as Nicolas could tell, once he'd taken his brain out of the equation by closing his eyes, his body had actually done something useful and sidestepped the blow at the last second.

Fighting the urge to whoop for joy at still being alive, he knew he was still in great peril. The angry look on the big warrior's face suggested life span was now measured in seconds..

With a roar, Grimmark swung the hammer at Nicolas's midsection. Letting his natural reactions guide him, Nicolas jumped back a step and the hammer swung harmlessly by him, though close enough that he felt the breeze from the hammer's motion as it passed.

'Is there some kind of problem?' the armoured woman asked mockingly from her horse.

'No problem,' Grimmark snarled through bared teeth. 'Just taking my time with the runt.'

The woman gave a single sharp laugh, and the warrior's face reddened with rage. Uttering a more passionate roar, Grimmark charged directly at Nicolas, swinging wildly. The warrior was big and strong but had obviously traded muscles for speed as Nicolas found himself able to dodge the frantic blows, even if they did come close too often. He ducked and weaved as the hammer swung from all directions, taking many more chunks out of the poor bridge. It was like they were dancing, though in most dances one participant doesn't usually end up dead.

Roaring in frustration with every miss, Grimmark seemed more bear than man, a monstrous creature with no feeling. Though Nicolas was pleased he hadn't been beaten to death with a hammer yet, the end of this dance was inevitable. With each dodge, he could feel himself getting more tired and a little slower, and with each swing, Grimmark's anger made him faster. Nicolas needed to find a way out of this situation, but he was so busy dodging he had no time to think.

Even as his feet began to move to step away from the next blow, Nicolas knew he was a fraction of a second too late. The impact was jarring as the hammer struck, whipping his head to the side. There was a moment of flashing blackness, replaced by a reality that was fuzzy and distorted. He couldn't control his limbs, though they were moving, his hands reaching out slowly as if underwater, ghostly ripples of motion showing the path of their movement. What was he reaching out for? He expected pain, why could he feel nothing?

Everything around him swayed, except for Grimmark, resting on the shaft of his hammer, the only fixed point in his vision. He was vaguely aware of the satisfied smile on the warrior's face. That was it then, Grimmark's work was done, he was dead. How could he still perceive the world around him? Maybe he was dead and death just hadn't caught up with him yet? Nothing made sense.

There was some pressure behind his legs then he turned upside down. Or maybe the world had turned upside down and not him? An impact jarred his neck and shoulders, and ice cold travelled through his body in an instant. He felt a crushing weight around him, constricting his motion. Everything was now shaded blue and green. Why could he see bubbles in front of him? Was that a fish?

CHAPTER 6

He gasped for breath, his body spasming as his mouth filled with water instead of air. His diaphragm constricted as he tried to force out the unwelcome liquid, but there was nowhere for it to go. He cried in panic, but there was no scream, only bubbles. Where was he? Why was everything dark? His lungs heaved again. He flailed, trying to stand upright, but there was no ground beneath his feet. What was happening? What had happened? Images of a bear on a bridge flashed before him… No, not a bear, a warrior. The bridge. He'd been on the bridge and now…now he was in the water. With that realisation, his flailing became purposeful as he pushed himself up through the water, his lungs desperate for air. Was that light? It was, though distorted by the water it passed through. He headed toward it.

Bursting from the water as if he'd been born again, he heaved and coughed. Vaguely aware of land nearby, his pushed his body toward it until he finally felt something beneath his feet. Desperately he crawled and clawed his way onto the bank. His little energy spent, he collapsed in the mud and blacked out.

Opening his eyes with a pained cry, he began to hack and cough out the river water he'd swallowed. Once it had been expelled his burning lungs fought to breath normally again. Slowly they settled back into a normal rhythm, though the pain was still great. Weakly, he turned his head back to the river, the water continuing on its path, dispassionate to his near death. Half his body still lay in the water. Slowly he fought to get himself out of the river, his wet clothes dragging him back and the mud of the bank refusing to give him decent purchase. Despite this, he managed to shuffle on his belly until he was fully onto the soft grass, turning onto his back and crushing bright blue flowers that, until now, had bloomed unmolested. Taking some time to just breathe, he waited for feeling to return to his body.

With the return of feeling came pain. His temple throbbed angrily. Tentatively touching his head, he cried out, nearly passing out again. When he withdrew his fingers, they were red with blood. The pieces of his memory fell back into place. The bridge. The warrior Grimmark had caught him with his hammer, but it must've been a glancing blow or his head would no longer be attached to his neck. He must've fallen into the river and been carried away after stumbling back from the strike. At least he was alive.

'Two near death experiences in one day,' he moaned weakly.

He hoped the two warriors thought their work done and didn't feel the need to come looking for him—though they hadn't seen fit to waste much effort on him in the first place. Hopefully, that was still the case. He was in no state to defend himself. Nor help the people in the wagons. What would become of them? The girl had needed his help so badly, and now he could barely raise his arm.

Something needed to be done. However injured he was right now, he couldn't, in good conscience, leave those people to their fate without at least trying to help them. What could he do in his current state? His only option seemed to be finding someone to help them. You couldn't just go around kidnapping people without someone noticing, so there had to be soldiers looking for the captors. All he needed to do was find them and point them in the right direction. If he found the road, hopefully he would be lucky enough to stumble on these imagined soldiers—though he and luck had been at odds so far that day.

Unfortunately, finding people required him to move, and he wasn't sure he could. His body numb from cold, shock and pain, he concentrated on moving his arms and legs. Finally, they twitched. Not a lot, but enough to think he had some kind of control over himself again. As long as he was careful, he should be able to get up and eventually get going, but he wouldn't know for sure until he tried.

He began to crawl towards the nearest tree so he could work on standing. His vision was hazy, and the single tree became three, but he headed for the middle one. As he reached it, his vision cleared, focusing with startling clarity on the person lying against the base of the tree. He screamed, and then passed out.

Several minutes later, consciousness returned, bringing a horde of painful sensations with it. He tried to think, but everything was fuzzy. Why had he passed out? Coming up with nothing, he opened his eyes, saw the body, and screamed again.

Scrabbling back to the water's edge like some sort of crazed insect, he couldn't take his eyes off the body, much as he wanted to. He only managed to make himself stop when he reached the natural barrier of the river and it still hadn't gotten up and come at him. Was the person dead? He crawled slowly back towards it.

Yup, definitely dead. He didn't need to be a healer to identify the large arrow sticking out of the man's chest as the cause. The corpse's eyes were open and wide with surprise, but also terribly empty, devoid of any spark of life. His jaw was slack and skin pale as flies buzzed around, drawn by what promised to become an unbearable stench.

Alive, the man must've been ruggedly handsome, if that was your thing. His jawline was solid, and stubble had been expertly cultivated. His short brown hair was braided on one side and ran down his shoulder. He must've been a warrior of some kind, judging by his stylish blue leather armour with a rising sun motif, which was now covered in a large blood stain. The only other thing ruining the warrior's aesthetic was that he had his trousers around his ankles and was showing things Nicolas was trying very hard not to look at.

He should probably do something about that, but...yeah, not happening. Instead, carefully, he lowered the corpse's eyelids. He didn't want to touch the body at all, but it seemed the respectful thing to do. While doing this, he whispered a brief prayer for the man's soul.

'This has been a terrible day.' He sighed as he sat back on the grass.

'How do you think I feel?'

Nicolas turned in the direction from which the voice had come, processed what he was seeing, screamed, and passed out again.

This time, Nicolas was only out for a few seconds. As he came to, he also came to a decision. *I've really had enough of today.* He was just going to stay as he was, lying on the grass with his eyes closed. If he couldn't see all the things he was seeing, they didn't exist and therefore couldn't bother him.

'Okay, kid.' A voice cut into his fake tranquillity. 'In a moment, I'm going to need you to open your eyes. When you do, we're going to break this cycle of screaming and passing out because we have a lot to go over. Do you think you can do that?'

The flaw in his plan seemed to be that not only were things *not* going away, they also wanted his attention. Which meant he had to face reality sooner or later. He nodded.

'Brilliant,' the voice replied happily. 'Well, come on then, kid. Let's get this over with.'

Light flooded in as Nicolas opened his eyes, looking directly up at the sky. Only a few dangling branches impeded his view of the oncoming twilight. Remembering what he had seen, he raised his head with more than a little trepidation. His eyes widened. It had been what he thought. With a cry, he scrambled backwards until he was stopped by the rough bark of a nearby tree that thankfully did not have a dead body leaning on it.

'At least you didn't pass out this time,' the voice noted dryly.

Blue smoke had coalesced into the figure of a human—albeit one that rippled queasily and emitted an aura of blue light. He could see the trees and bushes behind the man, distorted as if viewed through water. And he had the same features as the body by the tree.

Nicolas's mouth worked up and down without actually producing any words as the figure looked at him with a mixture of bemusement and irritation.

'You're just going to have to say it, kid,' the figure suggested a tad impatiently, his voice like an echo.

'Who...? What...?' he stammered, unsure what he wanted to say until settling on the obvious. 'You look like him.'

'Dead body,' the figure said, gesturing to the corpse without looking directly at it before gesturing to himself. 'Spirit of dead body.'

'But you're dead!' Nicolas cried.

'Hence...spirit,' he replied dryly.

'But...but...'

The smoky figure held up a silencing hand, and though his eyes were just white balls of light, frustration was clear in them. 'This really shouldn't be that hard to grasp, kid,' he began slowly. 'But we both appear to be having a terrible day, so I'll make this as clear as I possibly can. I was killed. That's my dead body under the tree, and what stands before you is my spirit, which for some reason is not relaxing in the afterlife as I'd hoped.'

Nicolas nodded all the way through this, only half listening due to the shock at what he was seeing. But he got the gist.

'Now to a more important issue,' the spirit said after a pause. 'How can you see me?'

'How can I see you?' Nicolas echoed.

The spirit clenched his jaw and shook his head slowly. 'Some kind of village idiot,' he muttered to himself.

'Hey!'

'Oh, you don't like that?' the spirit asked. 'Then prove me wrong.'

That seemed like a lot to ask at this point.

'Let's try some introductions,' the spirit suggested. 'Though I think it's just a formality in my case. Auron of Tellmark, The Dawnblade. At your service.' The blue form gave an elaborate bow and looked expectantly at Nicolas.

'Should I know you?' Nicolas asked, feeling like he was missing a great many things right now.

Auron's ethereal blue face was unnervingly expressive for something...so unreal. Right now, it looked a mixture of shocked and annoyed. Blue lips pursed, Auron seemed to struggle to understand what he was being told. After taking a moment to compose himself, the spirit spoke again.

'Known as *The Dawnblade*? Slayer of Golgruk? Saviour of Danith? Bane of the Black Marsh? There's quite a list of accolades to go through. Does any of this ring any bells?'

He shook his head awkwardly.

'Brilliant,' Auron cried, flinging smoky arms into the air in frustration. 'I die, and my spirit ends up being seen by the only person in the Nine Kingdoms and beyond who's never bloody heard of me. Isn't that the icing on the mouldy bloody cake?'

As the spirit ranted, Nicolas raised his hand slowly.

When he finally noticed it, Auron looked incredulously at the raised appendage. 'What?' he snapped.

'Um...why are your pants around your ankles?'

It was probably a strange thing to focus on, considering everything else that had happened to him that day, but it had suddenly become very important to have closure on at least one thing, and for reasons he couldn't fathom, he'd chosen this.

Auron didn't seem happy about the question, and for a while, Nicolas thought he wasn't going to answer. 'Because the world is a cruel and ironic place,' Auron finally snarled. 'Because a legendary hero doesn't get to die in mortal combat, fighting for all that's good against insurmountable odds. No, sometimes a legendary hero gets bushwhacked when he's answering the call of nature. No grand ending for Auron of Tellmark, just an arrow in the chest while I'm taking a dump.'

Nicolas was kind of sorry he'd asked, but at least he had a decent explanation for *something*. That was terrible, poor guy. Having nearly been killed twice in one day, he couldn't imagine what it would be like to actually die, let alone in such a stupid way. And then to have to stick around to see the aftermath and be asked daft questions by some boy from a village?

'Do you know who...did it?' he asked, unable to say *'killed you'* aloud.

'No idea,' he said. 'I was summoned by the king of Yarringsburg on urgent business. On my way, I made a pit stop, saved someone, went to answer the call of nature, and next thing I know I'm stood over my body, my mare's been killed, and the scumbag who did it stole my sword to boot.'

Looking again at Auron's dead body, he recalled something he'd seen earlier. 'Does your sword have a rising sun on the hilt like the one on your armour?'

Auron fixed Nicolas with a stare that seemed to look right into his soul. 'You've seen it?' he asked slowly. 'You've seen the Dawn Blade?'

'Yes,' he said enthusiastically, happy to be of some actual use. 'There was a woman in armour. She had it.'

'Woman in armour?' the spirit repeated.

'Yeah, like a lot of armour. She had a big guy with her.'

Auron's eyes widened, and his aura took on a red tinge. 'That bitch!' he cried in a terrible, echoing voice.

'You know her?'

'Silva Destrone, *The Rose of the Southlands*. The big guy is Grimmark Bear-Slayer. We used to work together, after a fashion.'

'You did?' Nicolas asked warily. Was this Auron really a hero when he'd worked with such villains before?

'Long ago,' Auron said, picking up on Nicolas's reaction. 'Like me, they used to belong to the Hall of Guardians. However, unlike me, they found gold preferable to peace and justice and started selling their skills to the highest bidders. Generally, people who wanted skilled hands for dirty jobs, which they showed a real aptitude for.' The spirit glanced at Nicolas's head. 'I take it they're the reason you washed up here with a bloody headwound?'

'Yes!' he cried. 'I was on a bridge, there were these carriages with prisoners, and next thing I know that maniac with a hammer is trying to kill me. He hit me, and I fell into the river and ended up here...with you.'

'Consider yourself lucky, kid. The sum total of people who've survived either of those two trying to kill them is...you.' Auron went on bitterly, 'I'm now amongst the number who didn't.'

'Sorry.' The word was empty but worth saying, nonetheless.

Auron looked thoughtfully towards the river before turning back to Nicolas. 'So, who are you then, random kid who washed up nearly dead and can see me?'

Nicolas stood up and brushed himself off, thankful his legs supported his weight. For a moment, he almost offered Auron his hand to shake. Hopefully, the spirit hadn't noticed.

'Nicolas Percival Carnegie,' he said finally with an awkward wave.

'Very formal introduction.' Auron chuckled. 'Nick Carnage, is it?'

'No, it is not.' The stupid name was following him.

'Fair enough. Sounds more heroic the other way, but it's your name.' Auron shrugged. 'Pleasure to meet you, kid.' Auron held his gaze for a moment. 'Now that we know each other, I need a favour. I know it's been a strange day and all, but I can't do this myself, and it needs doing...once you've tended to nasty head wound, of course.'

'What is it?' he asked cautiously.

'I need you to take care of that.' Auron pointed at his dead body. 'Please?'

He sighed. If only that damned hero he'd been waiting for had turned up on time, maybe all of this could've been avoided? Nicolas hoped wherever the hero was he was having fun whilst he was here living his worst nightmare.

CHAPTER 7

Burning brightly in defiance of the inky night sky that had set in around it, the fire cast a glow which lit the immediate area until it could go no further, and the blackness reasserted itself. Nicolas watched the flames dance with his head bowed, partly out of respect and partly so he didn't have to look directly at the body burning atop the funeral pyre.

Auron stood closer to the flames, seemingly unaffected by the heat, staring silently as his body was reduced to ash. Maybe he'd disappear once his body did? Nicolas waited to see if he would just fade away.

It hadn't been easy work. Summoning the courage to touch a dead body was one thing, and having to redress the lower half of that body was another. Then there'd been the matter of getting it onto the pyre. He'd hoped to bury the body, but Auron had insisted, some kind of warrior honour thing, and Nicolas couldn't refuse the man his dying wish. Dead wish?

The trade-off for Auron had been having to put up with him trying to heave his dead weight into place. Nicolas was learning his limits today, and one of those was upper body strength. Several times he'd tried, and failed to get the corpse atop the pyre, but Auron had said nothing—his stare of silent judgement saying everything for him.

Then Auron had needed to assure him that setting what amounted to a huge beacon fire wasn't actually suicidal or insane. The bandits would be long gone, he'd said, and no sane animal would approach such a large fire. It wasn't the sane animals Nicolas worried about. Grimmark wouldn't be too happy to discover he was still alive, and he'd undoubtedly try to correct that as soon as he could.

'Where are you from, kid?' Auron spoke for the first time in a while, back still to Nicolas.

'Uh...' Nicolas replied, surprised by the sudden question. 'I'm from a village southwest of here.' He wasn't keen on giving out his address to just anyone, let alone a ghost.

Ghost was the wrong word. He'd used it earlier and Auron had explained, at great length, that he was a spirit, not a ghost. Nicolas couldn't remember the specifics of the lecture, but got the idea Auron thought the term *'ghost'* a bit common for him.

'Must be pretty out of the way if you've never heard of me,' the spirit replied. 'I take it you've heard of the Hall of Guardians.'

'In passing, yeah.'

Auron turned his head and looked at him from the side with a chuckle. *'In passing,* he says.' Turning away from the fire completely, the spirit approached Nicolas, looking at his temple. 'How is it?'

Nicolas flexed his eyebrow. The skin still felt tight where he'd bandaged the wound after treating it with medicinal herbs from Auron's belongings. Beneath the bandage, it was still sore, but it was more of a background throbbing than outright pain. 'It's mending, I think.'

'You cheated death today, kid,' the spirit replied casually. 'You were lucky. Very lucky.'

That was pushing it, he thought, but after being smacked with a hammer, nearly drowned, and passing out several times, he *was* quite surprised at how well he was functioning, all things considered.

'So you said there were people in those wagons on the bridge?' Auron asked so casually that it made a little alarm bell ring in Nicolas's mind.

'Yes,' he replied carefully. 'Two wagons full of people.'

Auron nodded thoughtfully. 'You know we're going to have to save them, right?'

And there it was. Nicolas had a sinking feeling he was getting chosen again. 'Did you say *we*?'

The spirit nodded.

'Nope,' Nicolas said, holding up his hands in an apologetic way. 'Sorry, but no. Not happening. I'm not going after those wagons, ghost or no ghost.'

'Spirit,' Auron corrected sourly.

'I don't care, it's still no.'

'So you're just going to leave those people to their fate?' Auron asked simply.

'I didn't say that,' he retorted. 'I said that I'm not going after the wagons. I have a plan.'

'Oh, well, in that case...please, enlighten me?' Auron gave a sarcastic wave of his hand.

'Go to the nearest town, find some soldiers, and tell them about it. The soldiers find the wagons and save the people. Easy.'

There'd been a moment on the bridge when Nicolas had wanted to follow the convoy himself, but nearly getting his head caved in had reinforced how unprepared he was for anything even remotely like saving people. But he had a solid plan to help them without endangering himself again. He wasn't dodging the responsibility...just sidestepping it slightly.

'And how long do you think those people have?'

He didn't reply.

'Listen, kid,' Auron began slowly, 'when people are carted off in cages by bad guys, they have a very finite life expectancy once they reach their destination, whether they're worked to death, starved to death, or just flat-out killed to death. One thing is for sure: the longer they're alive, the less they'll want to be. So time is of the essence, and we can't waste it running around the forest looking for a random army. It's already been too long. It's up to us.'

He wasn't naïve. He knew that bad things were going to happen to those people. But today had shown him his limitations clearly. He had to be realistic. Though after hearing the list of potential fates, he found it harder to just walk in the other direction on something that could easily be a fool's errand.

'It can't be me. I can't do it,' he pleaded.

'Believe me, kid, I know you're not the type for this.' Auron looked him over. 'But you've been thrust into one of those *you're my only hope* situations. There's no choice.'

'You're a hero...why can't you do it?'

The spirit walked to the nearest tree and put his arm through it. 'That doesn't mean I'm useless,' he said, looking at his half-immersed arm. 'I can guide you and give you the benefit of my considerable experience.'

The blood drained from his face as he thought about what going after the wagons would entail. Picturing Grimmark and his hammer. No matter how many scenarios he played out in his mind, they all ended the same: him in a puddle of blood on the floor.

'Can you really stand by and let those people suffer?' Auron asked. 'People just like the ones who live in your village. Can you let what happened to me and nearly happened to you happen to them?'

Somehow, and he had no idea how, that was the clincher. He thought about the girl again, her soft skin covered in blood with her face contorted in terror. Truly, he knew there was no time to find soldiers, which left it down to him and his odd new companion. Anyone whose fate was in his hands didn't have much hope, hero spirit or no. But people were in danger, and there was no better alternative. His parents wouldn't want him to shirk such a responsibility. Thinking of his parents reminded him how overdue he was in returning home. They'd be worried, but this was more important.

'I'll do it,' he said quietly. 'I'll do my best.'

Auron beamed at him. 'That's all I'm asking, kid.'

He was asking a lot more than that, but it was probably impolite—and unnecessary—to point out that he was putting his life on the line.

'We can save the prisoners and you can avenge me while we do it.'

Distracted, it took him a moment to realise what Auron had said. 'Wait, what?'

'You can avenge me.'

'Oh, you're just casually dropping that in too?' he asked incredulously. 'And how exactly do you expect me to face Grimmark and Silva again? I barely survived last time.' Nicolas pointed to his head for emphasis.

'But you did survive.'

"*Barely*!' Nicolas shouted, his blood boiling. The gall of this guy. 'I can't hurt people. I can't even fight. What do you want me to do, hurt their feelings? Bruise their knuckles with my face? That's about the level I'm at.'

'Details,' Auron said confidently. 'I can teach you that stuff on the way.'

'Oh, as easy as that?' He very much doubted it.

'Look, kid,' the spirit began. 'I should be living it up in the afterlife right now, swapping tales with heroes of old, drinking all the mead I can find, surrounded by doting virgin girls. But instead, I'm stuck here, between life and death. I must have unfinished business, which has to be avenging my murder by kicking the arses of the scum that killed me. I can't do it, and you can see me, so we're in this together.'

He glared at the spirit.

'I wish it wasn't you either,' Auron continued. 'Neither of us chose to be here, but here we are. So are you going to step up to the responsibility? There has to be a reason you can see me.'

He couldn't believe someone could be so annoying yet so right. As much as he didn't like the path he currently seemed stuck on, the idea of Silva and Grimmark simply getting away with what they'd done and condemning Auron to forever walk the land was terrible, as was thinking of the fate of their captives.

'Great stuff.' Auron beamed from his hesitant nod. 'If it makes you feel better, we'll focus on the people first, vengeance later. And who knows, maybe this is where the legend of Nick Carnage begins.'

'That's not my name.'

* * * *

When he woke, there was a single moment when he believed yesterday had been a dream. It passed quickly. Then he was left with the grim possibilities of what was to come, making the new day a very unwelcome one. The dark, cloudy sky seemed a portent of what was to come.

Rising, he took several deeps breaths of cool air. Though he was in no rush to get going and put himself in danger he couldn't handle, the responsibility wasn't just going to go away, so he may as well face it. He felt like a miscast actor on the opening night of a play. The curtain was rising, and he was about to be pelted with rotten tomatoes by the audience. Except his audience today would be armed with something a little sharper.

'Morning, kid.' The spirit stood by the ash pile that had been his funeral pyre, glowing brightly in the dim surroundings.

Nicolas stretched, attempting to dispel the aches he'd earned sleeping on a thin pile of leaves. 'Morning,' he replied, still unused to talking to someone who wasn't technically there.

'You need some food and drink then we need to move.'

His new companion was all business this morning. Good for him, bad for Nicolas. Maybe finding the soldiers really was the best plan. How would his death help anyone? Yesterday had taken a heavy toll on him mentally and physically. He was in no fit state for any sort of pursuit or whatever would be required at the end of it.

'You eaten yet?' Nicolas cursed himself the minute the words left his mouth. 'Sorry,' he added sheepishly.

'It's fine,' Auron replied, seeming to take no offence. 'You still okay to do this?'

Even though the question sounded like a formality, Nicolas thought it over—the pros, the many, many cons, and the various outcomes of failure. He was one hundred percent not okay to do this. Not at all.

'Yeah.' He set about finding something to eat in Auron's discarded pack.

'Once you've eaten,' Auron said with a smile, 'it's adventure time.'

* * * *

'So, there I was, surrounded by twenty-odd stone warriors, huge things. Old Vixious the Animator stood on a ledge looking down at me, banging on about how great he was in between fits of maniacal laughter. *Soon I will be the master of all elements. Etherius will be mine to rule.* Blah, blah, blah. Pretty standard villain bragging. You could say that I was in a bit of a situation.'

'Uh-huh,' he replied absentmindedly, more concerned with the situation he was in right now.

'Well, kid, I'm not about to fight twenty stone warriors. That is a losing battle right there.' Auron continued, 'But Vixious, he was the key. He was the one making them walk around. So, one minute the crazy old goat is bleating about how amazing and powerful he is, and the next moment, *bam*, he has my favourite throwing knife sticking out of his throat. The look on his face was priceless, kid. He drops dead and the stone warriors with him. I'm not a bragger, but there was a parade.'

When they'd set off from camp, Auron had said little. That had changed dramatically the further they got from the site of his death. Now, it was a constant stream of stories. *I slayed this* and *I saved them* and *I deflowered her* and on, and on, and on. Was this some kind of therapy for him or was he always like this? Yes, he'd done many amazing deeds but listing them was getting old quickly, never mind the way he acted them out as he spoke. It was all so...repetitive. There was peril of some kind, Auron turned up, saved the day, adulation was given, and on to the next story. Nicolas really hoped these tales didn't count as the training Auron had vaguely promised him, because he'd only been half-listening since the third one.

Despite Auron talking his ear off, the world around them was serene. Leaves rustled, the river ran, and animals chattered. All was in its natural state, which made the sight of Auron all the more unsettling. His glow was still nauseating if looked at for too long, but mostly it was that he didn't really connect to anything. His feet moved and propelled him forwards, but they didn't touch the ground. The odd leaf would fall from a tree and pass straight through him. He was out of synch with the rest of the world, and Nicolas couldn't make peace with that. Yet. Would he be like this when Grimmark was done with him?

'I remember this one time I was travelling up the Nalian Coast, and I came across this temple,' Auron said, moving on to the next story without skipping a beat, 'full of priestesses who were besieged by these beast men and hadn't seen a real man in a looooong time. So I—"

The pair rounded a corner, and Caring's Cross loomed into view. By now, the earlier threat of rain had proven to be a bluff, and the sun was breaking through the clouds. One such shaft of sunlight shone directly onto the bridge, almost as if the Deities themselves were pointing to it. He'd had enough of their messages for a lifetime. Messages. Was there something he was forgetting?

Seeing the bridge again chased away that vague recollection. It was strange. He'd nearly died here. His heart quickened as he focused on the stone walkway.

'Kid,' Auron said, waving his smoky hand in front of Nicolas's eyes, 'snap out of it.'

Blinking a few times to break the connection between himself and the bridge, he turned to Auron, whose white eyes were staring at him intently.

'You're alive,' the spirit said in a stern tone. 'They tried to kill you and failed. You did not die here. That's what you need to focus on. Nearly dying isn't the same as actually dying.'

Somehow, those words resonated with him. The fear and panic didn't go away completely, but it was dampened. He *had* survived, and as Auron had said, not many people were still around after an encounter with that bear-loving barbarian.

'Scared is okay,' Auron said. 'Giving in to scared is not.'

Scared was something he had in abundance, but he closed his eyes and steeled himself. Sheer bloody mindedness forced his legs to move in the direction of Caring's Cross, Auron's eyes on him every step of the way. He only came to a halt when he reached a familiar dent in the stone. Crouching, he ran his hand over the rough edges created by the hammer blow. If that had been his head...

'Woah.' Auron whistled, looking at the dent. 'Imagine if you'd been there when the hammer hit. Strange to see it again, I bet.'

An understatement of epic proportions.

'I don't suppose they gave you any idea where they were headed?' Auron looked to the other side of the bridge.

'Grimmark wasn't very talkative when he was trying to cave my head in, and I was too busy to enquire about his travel plans,' he replied petulantly.

'Don't be a jackass, kid,' Auron chided.

'Sorry,' he replied, before gesturing to the far side of the bridge. 'They followed the road that way.'

'Then that is the way we go,' Auron said, already striding away. After a few paces, the spirit turned and looked back at Nicolas, who hadn't moved yet. 'If you've finished reminiscing, we have some work to do.'

Nicolas imagined punching Auron in his patronizing blue face. Not that it would do any good.

Just before they left the bridge Nicolas looked back longingly. Back toward home.

After half an hour of following the road as it wound around the parts of nature it couldn't cut through, they reached their first hurdle: a crossroads. One route continued around the mountainous region to the city of Yarringsburg itself, while the other rose into the foothills. As Auron considered both paths, Nicolas took a moment to sit and recover. His body was protesting vehemently against what he was making it do.

'Where to then, kid?' Auron asked.

He looked at each road in turn. There was no obvious sign the convoy had taken either route. 'How should I know?' He shrugged.

'I was hoping passing the bridge might make you remember something that would serve as a clue,' Auron replied flatly.

'I'm sorry,' he snapped. 'I told you I didn't see anything. I can't just make new information magically appear.'

Auron rolled his eyes. 'You are wound real tight, kid. You need to loosen up a bit.'

Behind Nicolas, a bush rustled heavily. In an instant, he was out of his seat and scrabbling at his boot until he finally got a decent grip on the handle of the knife, which he pulled out and waved at the offending bush.

'This is exactly what I mean,' Auron said as looked at him in bemusement. 'You can't go freaking out and drawing a knife at every squirrel that runs up a tree.'

After waiting for a few moments until he was sure, completely sure, that all was well, he slid the knife back into his boot and slumped against the nearest tree.

'Good choice. I'm not sure you'd win a knife fight with a squirrel anyway.' Auron smiled. 'Or are you worried a rabbit might nibble your ankles?'

Getting the distinct impression he was being teased, he found he didn't care for it. 'I was worried about trolls, actually.'

There was a surprised pause then Auron burst out laughing. He laughed so hard he had to put his hands on his knees to steady himself. 'Kid, you really don't know much about the world,' Auron said when the final chuckles had died away. 'Trolls live in mountain caves. They don't hang around forests.'

'Actually,' he replied testily, 'I'll have you know a troll attacked me in the forest yesterday. It took my pack and ate my supplies.'

'Trolls eat people not packed lunches.' Auron smirked.

'This one did,' he protested.

'Are you suggesting you're so scrawny that even a wild troll wouldn't eat you?' Auron asked, before laughing again. His laughter stopped when he saw Nicolas's expression. 'You're serious, aren't you?' he asked with a raised eyebrow.

He nodded once.

'We go up then,' Auron declared confidently after a moment's thought. 'The trolls in this region live in mountain caves, always have. Like any other animal, they stick to their natural habitat. That's where the food and shelter is. The only reason a mountain troll would be in the forest is if it had been driven out of its home. I don't think it's a coincidence that trolls are appearing where they shouldn't be when there are bad guys on the loose.'

He couldn't fault Auron's logic, so up it was.

As they set off on the trail of the convoy, Nicolas couldn't shake the suspicion that he'd forgotten something important. His temple throbbed again as he tried to remember and failed. Maybe it was a side effect of getting hit in the head with a hammer? What he did remember were his parents. They'd be worried sick about him by now. He should have returned yesterday. In truth, he was worried sick about himself. But if he went back now he'd let them, and himself, and the captives down. As tempting as home was, the price of it wasn't.

Chapter 8

As they followed the path from the river into the foothills, the terrain began to change remarkably. The trees that had surrounded them grew sparser, replaced by rocky outcroppings like the jagged teeth of monstrous beasts. Behind them the world stretched out as they rose, Nicolas could see the tops of the trees for miles, like a large green rug thrown over the earth, only interrupted by rising smoke from distant settlements. The view was almost as breath-taking as the chill in the air, the temperature dropping the further up the trail they went. Seeing the fog of his breath emerge from his lips, he shivered and pulled his jacket around him tightly.

Auron was quieter now as he focused on tracking the convoy. Nicolas walked in the spirit's wake, letting the hero do his work while trying not to imagine the numerous terrible fates they were closing in on, between pangs of longing for home. Used to flat farmlands, he had to stop repeatedly as the steep climbs and rough terrain took a toll on him, leaning on his knees to catch his breath. Auron wasn't subtle in his displeasure at these constant breaks, huffing audibly or rolling his eyes—an interesting trick when he had no pupils, but the spirit managed it.

At the next junction, a dirt track broke from the main road, reminding him of the trail to the poorly named *Tower of the Oracle*. On this road there were obvious signs of the convoy's passage, so obvious that even he could pick them out at a glance. Auron didn't even slow, switching to the track with conviction. Taking a moment to steel himself, he followed. It was all well and good for the one who couldn't get hurt to march on with confidence. He hoped Auron remembered that Nicolas was still mortal.

The dirt track repeatedly split away to various other routes, but this didn't deter Auron. Occasionally, he would point out a track in the mud here or a broken twig there. He was running the bandits down like a seasoned hunter. Did that make Nicolas his faithful hound?

After a while, he followed Auron without thinking, his mind working over all the possibilities of what was to come. Capture, torture, pain, injury, death; all were considered, only thoughts of success were dismissed, seeming fanciful and unlikely. He was so engrossed in his own thoughts that when Auron stopped suddenly, he didn't notice until he was almost on the spirit. Nicolas stumbled as he tried not to bump into his new companion. Auron probably wouldn't take kindly to being walked through without permission.

The road ahead of them rose steeply then disappeared in a sharp corner surrounded by rocks and so tight they could see nothing beyond it. The only view he had was the one down, which was becoming less picturesque and more nauseating the higher they went.

'What is it?' he whispered, not knowing why but really feeling like he should.

'You hear that?' Auron replied.

He listened. At first, there was just the usual background noise. Surely Auron must be alluding to something beyond the fluttering of birds? Concentrating harder and reaching out with his senses, he finally began to make out other sounds on the breeze. There were men laughing, horses neighing, the sound of wood being chopped. Now that he was paying attention, he could even smell the smoky odour of campfires in the air.

'Bad guys,' Auron said with an almost predatory tone. 'I'm going to scout ahead. Stay here, keep low, and do not make a sound.'

He didn't appreciate the stern-parent tone, but he wasn't going to argue. Finding a small break in the rock formation, he leaned into it and watched the spirit disappear around the corner, a single lingering whisp of blue smoke the only sign of his passage.

Returning moments later, Auron put a finger to his lips and gestured for him to follow. Ascending the slope, Nicolas kept himself pressed to the rocks, raising himself just enough to peer over the crest.

Just beyond him, the ground levelled into a long plateau beyond which the mountain rose in a sheer wall of rock. The fort caught his eye straight away. It looked old and worn, with great chunks missing from its stonework and moss covering a fair portion of the rest. He may have believed it deserted if not for the activity at its base.

Haphazardly placed tents stood on the far side of the bridge that led to the fort, at the base of the building itself, as men who looked like those he'd seen in the convoy moved between them. Though he was unsure, he thought he could make out part of one of the wagons between the tents. That meant they were in the right place. Focusing on the men in the camp, he knew any of them could kill him with the slightest of efforts. What was he doing here?

His stomach lurched. He was so far out of his element he may as well have been fish trying to fly. If the prisoners weren't dead already, he wished them a speedy and painless death, because there was nothing he and a spirit with high hopes could do for them now.

'We tried,' he said as he looked back at Auron. 'At least we know where they are, so when we find help, we can speed them on their way.'

Auron was studying the fort through narrowed eyes, as if assessing every detail, every chip in the stone and piece of moss clinging to the walls. 'You know we aren't done yet, kid,' he replied simply, not taking his gaze from the fort.

'I beg to differ,' Nicolas insisted. 'As much as I want to help those people, I don't think my good intentions and small knife are going to make much impact on that lot...unless they die laughing when I challenge them.'

His companion turned to him and tilted his head with a disapproving expression. 'You really think I expect *you* to fight your way in?' Auron said. 'This isn't that kind of mission. We're going in the back way.'

'The back way? What back way?'

'I don't know where it is yet,' the spirit admitted. 'But here's a hero lesson for you, kid. There's always a back way. We just need to find it.'

'Oh.' He sighed. 'For a second, I thought you meant a real door not a wishful-thinking one.'

'It has to be there,' Auron said with a big smile. 'Unless your whining has the magical property of cutting through stone?'

He didn't dignify that with a response.

'It's there,' Auron continued, ignoring his glare. 'We just need to find it.'

'Find it how?'

Auron seemed to have something specific in mind. 'I'm going to have a look,' he replied in a frustratingly casual manner.

'You're *going to have a look*?' he repeated incredulously. 'You're just going to stroll out there?'

'Well...yeah.'

'But there are guards.' Had Auron somehow not noticed?

'They won't see me,' Auron said confidently. 'I'm a spirit. You're the only one who can see me.'

'We don't know that,' he cried, still mindful enough to keep his voice low. 'I'm the only person you've met since you di...became a spirit. Everyone could be able to see you for all we know.'

'I'm standing here plain as day, and no one's raised an alarm yet,' Auron countered before adding with a reassuring wink that fell short, 'Trust me, kid.'

How could he be so damnably confident? There were too many unknowns here to put anything to chance. The logical thing to do would be—

Auron left.

His heartbeat sounding like a battle drum, he peered out and watched the neon blue figure walk across the plateau, plain as day. There was a slight hesitance in his step that just proved he wasn't thinking things through properly.

Annoyingly enough, he did turn out to be right. The guards paid him no mind as his stride became more confident, almost to the point of sauntering. Reaching the guards, the spirit even turned and waved at Nicolas, just to emphasise how right he was. Soon, Auron had disappeared between the tents, and…Nicolas was alone.

Shuffling carefully down the slope, Nicolas made his way back to the dent in the rocks, pressing himself in and waiting. What other option did he have? Running home was very tempting, but he wasn't sure he could find his way back, and…there was a small ember in him, the need to do the right thing, that kept him there despite it all. Still, that didn't stop the fear. Minutes seemed to drag for hours as he waited to be discovered, expecting some random guard to walk by and put an axe in him at any moment. Being able to hear the activity of the fort, a sign of how close the danger really was, made it all the worse. The only comfort was that it seemed no one had discovered Auron. If they had, some kind of alarm would surely have been raised by now.

'Miss me?'

When a blue head appeared around the corner of Nicolas's makeshift hideaway without warning, he jumped back, knocking the back of his head against the rock, and it was only a primal survival instinct that brought his hands to his mouth before he made a sound.

Auron seemed entertained by his own antics. 'You okay?'

He took a moment to tell Auron exactly what he thought of him popping up without any warning.

The spirit's amused expression didn't falter. 'If it makes you feel better, I've found you a way in.' The hero smiled, evidently pleased with himself.

'What's happening in there?' Nicolas asked, hoping to at least arm himself with information before delving into a ruined fort surrounded by a small army. 'Did you see the prisoners?'

'I didn't,' the spirit replied, slight concern in his tone. 'But I was looking for an entry point, not taking a scenic tour.'

* * * *

Auron's *entry point* turned out to be twenty minutes of thickly bushed, steep terrain from where they'd been. It seemed as if they were taking a broad circle around the fort, though he was too busy fighting through the near-impassable foliage to really keep track. Based on their climb, he did have a vague idea that they must be nearly level with the top of the fort.

Puffing and panting as Auron finally called them to a stop, he doubled over to catch his breath and assess the damage to his jacket, which now boasted several new tears. Every time he thought his body had reached the apex of its ability to ache, he managed to surpass himself. How much more of this could he take? The fact that his new companion stood as if he'd just awoken fresh to a new day didn't help.

'There,' Auron declared proudly.

There was a hole in the wall of the fort that looked like it had been made by some rock collapsing from above. Buckled and dented stone marked the opening, beyond which was darkness. An outcropping of rock less than a foot wide extended from where they stood to about two metres before the hole in the wall.

'You want me to shuffle across there and jump through that hole?' he asked incredulously, looking at the sheer drop between the rock and the wall.

'Yeah,' Auron replied as if it was the easiest thing in the world. 'Keep your weight against the rock, shuffle slowly, and don't look down. The edge of the ledge is close to the wall, and the floor of the fort isn't far under that hole, so it's hardly a *jump*.'

Looking at his new companion, he could feel the words ready to spill from his mouth. They were words of pleading and protest. Long, logical arguments as to why he wasn't the right person for this as well as summaries of the most likely fates he would encounter inside, all of them painful. All were ready to be unleashed in an uncontrollable wave any second now.

'These people are depending on you, kid,' Auron said calmly, as if reading his mind. 'It's absolute troll balls that it has to be you, but you are all these people have.' The spirit looked back to the fort briefly. 'One step at a time. First step, get across that ledge.'

The conviction in Auron's tone somehow steeled him just enough to do what he had to. Though calling the slightly jutting out piece of rock a *ledge* was a stretch. Staring at the hole, he tried to focus his mind on the annoying fact that his new companion was right—he really had no choice—channelling it into movement.

He stepped up to the edge of the ledge and pressed himself to the rock with a deep breath. He wanted to close his eyes so that he wouldn't accidentally look down, but yeah, that was probably suicidal. Eyes open, he inched out carefully. Far too much of his foot hung over the edge than he was comfortable with. Hugging the rock for dear life, he progressed slowly, wincing each time his foot dislodged some loose stones and they clattered from the ledge, reminding him of the length of the drop beneath him. Though dizzy, afraid, and constantly waiting for the arrow of some watchful guard to suddenly appear in his chest, he finally reached the edge.

Hopefully in another moment or two, he could unclench. There was just one jump across a precipice between him and...well, the next dangerous task, he supposed. His landing point atop the broken stone was quite narrow—not comforting when the price of failure was falling to your death.

'You can do this, kid,' Auron whispered confidently from behind him.

Readying himself, he decided not to take the time to weigh up his options or contemplate possible fates. He'd gotten this far. What was a short jump? Pushing with his legs, he hopped from the ledge towards the hole. There was a single second of propelling himself through open air, then his feet connected with the fort's wall. Quickly he grabbed the edges of the hole to brace his wavering body. Finally, he stood steady.

'I did it,' he whispered to himself in wonder.

He'd congratulated himself too soon. The stone beneath his feet slipped. Coming away from the rest of the wall under his weight, it collapsed inwards, taking him with it as he frantically tried to cling to the sides. His grip failed him no matter how painfully he clawed at the stone with his fingers. With a cry, he fell until he landed in a painful heap on the floor of the fort.

At least he hadn't fallen the other way. Holding the arm he'd landed on—thankful it wasn't broken, even though it screamed in pain—he got awkwardly to his feet.

'And who might you be, exactly?' asked a smooth voice behind him.

Wheeling around, there was a long, dark shape behind him. Who was that? Before the answers came his vision became filled with the meaty fist aimed directly at his face. He heard the slap as it connected, but by then everything was already going black. Again.

CHAPTER 9

Slowly, he felt himself coming to again. What effect was being unconscious so often going to have on his mind? He tried to remember things he should know, like his parents' names, or his birthday, to ensure no permanent damage was being done. The oncoming pain distracted his train of thought. His arm throbbed and his face felt tender.

'Nick? Nick? Nick?'

'That's not my name.' His voice was a weak groan as he tried to open his eyes.

Only one appeared to be working, but that one was stung instantly by a bright blue glow.

Auron stood directly over him, looking quite concerned, which was even more cause to worry. 'How are you, kid?'

Not good was an understatement. Tentatively, he raised his hand to his face and felt the swollen skin around his eye. 'How much head trauma can one guy suffer in a short space of time?' He moaned quietly. 'I think I'm okay.'

Auron looked away for a second before looking back at Nicolas sheepishly. 'You aren't really okay, kid,' the spirit replied grimly. 'In fact, you're in a bit of trouble.'

'What do you—?'

Two pairs of large hands wrapped around his arms tightly, hauling him roughly into the air. Coupled with the fact that everything was a bit wobbly already, the sudden movement nearly made him vomit. The hands, and the men they were attached to, dragged him a few paces before half-dropping, half-throwing him back to the ground. Taking a minute to right himself, he fought back the nausea and tried to blink away the spinning sensation behind his eyes.

'Up,' barked a harsh voice from behind Nicolas, punctuating the command with a sharp kick to his rear.

Doing his best to obey quickly, lest a second boot find him, he pushed himself from the floor and finally up to a standing position, albeit an unsteady one.

They were no longer in the corridor in which he'd landed. Instead, he now stood in a large chamber that may once have served as a great hall. He'd been deposited in front of dais, and the old chair on it. Once, it must've been quite lavish, but the years had turned it into a poor man's throne. It looked almost as old as the worn and faded tapestries on the walls, mould having spread across them over the untended years. The figure on the chair regarded him with leisurely bemusement.

Covered in a simple black robe, which didn't seem a good sign, he was lanky and oh so pale. He had rodent-like features—a long, prominent nose that seemed to twitch of its own accord and small, beady eyes full of cunning and malice.

'Apologies for the rude interruption to our earlier introduction,' the man announced in a smooth voice that ill fit the look of him. 'Unfortunately, my guards don't take kindly to intruders and like to punch first, talk later.'

Nicolas had absolutely no idea what to say, settling on a feeble, 'It's okay.'

'That looks sore,' the man said conversationally, pointing to his swollen eye. 'But I suppose that's the risk that you run when you break into forts.'

Again, all he could summon by way of reply was, 'It's okay.'

'Excellent.' The man rose from his chair and drawing himself up to his full, imposing height. 'That means we can begin.'

Interlocking his fingers and stretching his hands until his knuckles cracked, the man took a few paces towards Nicolas, close enough to use his height difference to intimidating effect. As much as he wanted to back away, he was very aware of the two men directly behind him who would undoubtedly deliver a painful rebuke.

Stooping a little so he could look Nicolas in the eye the man, surprisingly, held out a hand. 'And who might you be?' The question might've been pleasant if not for the look in his eyes.

'Nicolas Percival Carnegie.' Tentatively he took the hand and shook it.

'Never give the bad guys your real name, kid, much less a formal introduction.' Auron sighed behind him.

He felt a bit of an idiot for saying it, in all honesty, but trauma to his head coupled with fear was very seriously impairing his ability to think straight.

'Pleasure to meet you, Nicolas,' the man replied, shaking Nicolas's hand a little too enthusiastically.

'And you are?' he enquired.

The man took back his hand and smiled at Nicolas like he'd been asked something funny. 'Interesting question,' the man replied coyly, waving a finger in the air. 'Who am I? Right now, that doesn't matter. Who I'm going to become...there's something worth talking about. All you need to know is that I'm a humble necromancer. For now.' The necromancer gave him a formal bow.

To Nicolas's side, Auron made a noise of disgust. 'I hate necromancers,' he spat. 'Bunch of grave-robbing, corpse-bothering scumbags, to a man. I should've guessed by his seedy look.'

'So, who are you going to become?' he couldn't help but ask, ignoring Auron's thoughts on necromancers.

Smiling self-indulgently, the necromancer again wagged his finger at Nicolas. 'You seem like a fine young man, despite the trespassing,' the necromancer began. 'But that isn't a conversation for us. You and I have more pressing business.'

'Such as?' He didn't like where this was going.

'Such as you telling me where you came from, how you found us, and who sent you,' the black-robed man replied frankly.

'I'm just a passer-by,' he offered, scrabbling for something better but failing.

Behind him, Auron let out an audible groan.

The necromancer considered this then let out a derisive chuckle. 'And does Mr Nicolas Percival Carnegie often *just pass by* forts in the mountains and then attempt to sneak into them? I would call that a rather odd hobby, wouldn't you?'

'Well, I...'

He had no words, and he was well aware his life expectancy now was being measured in minutes. Any response he gave could lessen that considerably, but all he could do was stammer. At least someone had finally used his name correctly. An odd detail to focus on, but the brain can behave strangely in times of stress.

He could've jumped for joy when a loud creak signalled the door of the chamber opening and gave him a few extra seconds to think of something. The joy turned to despair as he saw who'd entered the room.

"*You*!' Grimmark roared as his eyes settled on Nicolas.

His jaw dropped. The warrior was as imposing as he had remembered but angrier.

'What are you doing here?' he bellowed, pointing an accusing finger at Nicolas.

Next to the bear-obsessed warrior stood Silva, her armour shaking with laughter at the sight of Nicolas. The laughter seemed to enrage Grimmark further.

With a cry of frustration, the warrior unslung his war hammer and, brandishing it, began to stomp towards him. His guards shrank back quickly as the big man bore down on him, the metal bear on the hammer's head watching Nicolas with bloodlust in its metallic eyes.

Silva walked almost lazily in her companion's wake, with Auron following Silva's every step, screaming curses and oaths at her and listing various unpleasant things he would like to do to her like he was possessed. His aura had changed from light blue to shades of red that broiled like storm clouds.

It didn't take long for his attention to return to Grimmark, as the oncoming juggernaut filled his vision. Stepping backwards, as if it would help, he soon found himself bumping against the necromancer. Even then, he couldn't take his eyes from the massive warrior. He wished he had another river to fall into. Having escaped the hammer once just to die by it again seemed like a cruel joke. The hammer rose... Grimmark sneered at Nicolas as he prayed for any kind of salvation. The salvation he received came from a very surprising direction.

Just as the warrior's muscles tensed to bring his weapon down on Nicolas's head, the necromancer stepped between the two, as casually as if he were meeting an old friend for a chat. The black robe blocked his view, so he stepped slightly to the side so he could see what was happening. He'd enough unknowns for three lifetimes already.

The warrior locked his eyes with the necromancer, who stood silently between him and his kill. Eventually, Grimmark relented, dropping the hammer to his side, though clearly displeased about it.

'You know this boy?' the necromancer asked calmly, as though no one had been about to be murdered right in front of him.

'Yes,' Silva replied for her companion, who was still seething with rage. 'We met him yesterday at Caring's Cross as we brought the wagons over. He was a witness, so I let Grimmark kill him, which he evidently failed to do.' She finished with a sneer at the big man.

The warrior took it exactly as you would expect a big angry warrior to. 'How is he here? How are you here?' Grimmark roared, first pointing at the necromancer then at Nicolas, who felt himself pale.

'Questions I would very much like the answer to.' The necromancer calmly turned to Nicolas, appraising him again. 'So, you were at the crossing, survived Grimmark's wrath, and now you are here in my fort. That is an odd coincidence, don't you think?'

He quaked under the gazes of a room full of enemies. Auron was no help as he was still engrossed in spitting furious insults at his killer. The man was no longer the *legendary hero* he claimed to be, now he was a vengeful wraith, consumed by his rage as much as Grimmark had been moments before. He seemed particularly put out by the fact Silva had his old sword slung over her shoulder. He would be no help here.

'I just happened to be at the crossing when the wagons came.' He kept his gaze on the floor. 'When I came to after I was attacked, I thought I should, um, try to rescue the prisoners.'

There was a moment of silence. Then Grimmark and Silva burst out laughing. The necromancer simply watched him curiously.

'You came here,' Silva wheezed between cackles, 'to rescue the prisoners?'

'Kid's got big balls on him.' Grimmark roared with laughter.

'Let me see if I understand this correctly.' The necromancer ignored the still-laughing warriors. 'You survive a one-on-one fight with one of the fiercest warriors in the Nine Kingdoms—barely, by the look of it—and you decide that instead of running home or going for help, you would follow him and try to break into a heavily armed fort and rescue the people he'd taken?'

Nicolas's face heated. It sounded even crazier aloud. Good job he'd left out the part where a spirit had talked him into it. 'There was a girl...' he blurted, feeling the sudden ridiculous urge to explain himself.

'You did this for a girl?' the necromancer asked in surprise before turning to the warriors. 'Silva, do you remember this girl?'

Silva's expressionless helmet turned to regard Nicolas. 'I can guess the one he meant. Some village girl we picked up after the rest,' the warrior replied coolly. 'Arguably pretty.'

It was difficult to make out what she was saying with Auron screaming directly in Silva's face, unbeknownst to anyone but him, apparently.

'Unfortunately, our horny hero here has gone to the wrong place. She went to the other site.' Silva chuckled maliciously.

Nicolas suddenly remembered that he'd only seen one of the wagons outside the fort. He hadn't expected them to have split up.

'Yeah, idiot,' Grimmark boomed. 'You're here, about to die, while she is—'

The necromancer raised a finger. 'Enough. I don't want him knowing more than he already does.' He quailed as the necromancer's beady eyes looked into his. 'That story may be just stupid enough to be true,' he said. 'But I cannot take the risk that it isn't, and I think you may be holding something back. My work here is at a critical juncture, and I will suffer no interference. So unfortunately, young Nicolas, I'm going to have you worked over until I'm sure you have no secrets left in you. Then, once we are done, Grimmark can have you.'

Behind the necromancer, the warrior smiled evilly.

'If he can handle the kid this time,' Silva added snidely.

'Silence, woman.' Grimmark grunted.

'But I *have* told you everything. I *swear*.' He felt tears welling in his eyes.

The necromancer made a faux sympathetic face then leaned in close to Nicolas. 'You left out the part about the ghost travelling with you. The one you can clearly see,' he whispered into Nicolas's ear. 'So let's see what else you left out.'

Stunned, he watched the necromancer click his fingers before two pairs of hands grabbed him and began to pull him towards the door. He looked to Auron for help, but that was pointless. He may as well ask the rat skulking around the corners of the room. There was no help for him. Even the trio had disregarded his presence already.

'I take it the delivery went well?' the necromancer asked the warriors.

'I think they're satisfied,' Silva replied. 'They seemed to receive the tribute well enough, but it's hard to tell with those disgusting leeches. So much pomp for such low creatures.'

The rest of the conversation was lost to Nicolas as he passed through the door to the chamber, which closed behind him. All he had left was contemplating what was going to happen next. Good things did not seem to be on the horizon.

CHAPTER 10

Several featureless, damp stone corridors later, he was taken through another door. He attempted to see where he was, but it's exceedingly difficult to see around you properly when you're being dragged backwards by a pair of thugs. The sum total of his effort was a sore neck and a view of some very drab ceilings.

Enlightenment soon came to him with a rusty metallic squeal just before his body was launched into the air. After a graceless flight, he hit the floor on his buttocks with a painful crack before rolling into a small pile of straw. The chuckles of the thugs in the background added insult to injury.

Trying to pick himself up, he found that being dragged all that way had made his legs numb and the thugs' tight grip had cut off the circulation in his arms. Fumbling around like a new-born deer, he soon ended back on his rump. This was, again, to the amusement of the thugs.

'Idiot,' one of them spat as he pushed the door closed with another ear-splitting screech of metal, before turning the key in the lock with a very definitive *click*.

He stared at the barred door dumbly for a moment, his head a blur of everything that had happened until now. Finally registering that he was in a cell, he yelped then ran at the door, shaking it as hard as he could. What did he expect to achieve by this? He was never in any danger of pulling it from its hinges. What he did achieve was entertaining the thugs beyond his cell no end. Following the walkway back to the main door of the jail, the pair muttered about how pathetic he was. Shutting the jail door behind them, he heard another *click*.

Looking at the bars encasing him, panic was in danger of consuming him completely. He'd believed that yesterday was horrible, yet today he was in a necromancer's dungeon, due to be tortured for information before being killed by a big, bear-loving psycho. He should've just let Potter deliver the damnable message. No, he wouldn't wish this on anyone else.

What he did wish for was a way out, but none seemed obvious. His cell was one of five, each empty save for his. The only other feature beyond the straw on the floor was the large red mound in the cell beside his. Why was the door to that cell closed?

'Hi.' The voice was casual, but the surprise of it nearly made him spring to the opposite wall of the cell as he cried out. 'That was not a macho scream, kid,' Auron chided with a raised eyebrow and a bemused look on his face.

'You…' he spluttered, fighting for his lungs to work normally, 'have got to stop doing that.'

'Stop what?' Auron asked, looking genuinely confused.

'Appearing out of nowhere and talking suddenly. Of all the things I'm going to die of soon, I'd like to take heart attack off the list.'

'Jeez, kid.' Auron rolled his eyes. 'Calm down a few notches. It's good for you. It will help you build some fortitude, prepare you for the unexpected.'

"Fortitude? Fortitude?' The nerve of this guy. 'I think I'm going through enough right now without you jump-scaring me every time you fancy. Do you not understand the amount of trouble I'm in right now? Oh, and while we're at it, thanks for all your help in the other room back there. You were really invaluable. What would I have done without you?'

'Yeah.' The spirit awkwardly rubbed his neck. 'I'm sorry about that, kid. I don't know what happened. The second I saw Silva, everything went red. I was totally out of control. I remember screaming at her, but I just couldn't stop myself. Thank the Deities she left the room or I might still be there now. The effect seemed to wear off the minute she left my sight line.'

'I suppose she did murder you. You're entitled to be upset with her.' As much as he wanted to make Auron feel guilty, he got it. He would've felt the same if Grimmark had succeeded in killing him and he was still knocking around as disembodied smoke.

Auron smiled at Nicolas, thanking him for understanding without having to say it aloud. 'Not that it did much good,' the spirit joked. 'It's not like she could hear any of it or would have felt it if I'd punched her. I was just as ineffective as the rest of them. All I wanted to do was tear her apart.'

'What do you mean *the rest of them?'*

'That room was full of ghosts,' Auron replied, like it was the most natural thing in the world. 'And they did *not* like the necromancer. They were doing pretty much the same thing I was doing. And coming up with some pretty inventive names for the guy.'

Knowing a room he'd been in had been full of ghosts made him squirm slightly. One was more than enough for him. It also made him remember something.

'He could see you,' Nicolas said thoughtfully.

'Who?'

'The necromancer. He knew you were there. He told me so.'

'He could see me?' Auron said, genuinely surprised, 'I suppose it makes sense, him being a necromancer and all. He must be able to see the rest of them too then.'

'That doesn't seem likely. I couldn't handle being in the same room while you ranted at Silva for a few minutes, never mind being followed around by a group screaming right in my face.'

'The guy did seem all kinds of crazy,' Auron conjectured. 'Maybe that's the reason.'

Maybe if they could question the other ghosts, they might have some information that could help them. He offered this theory to Auron.

'I don't think so,' Auron replied. 'The ghosts were pretty far gone. Luckily, I'm a spirit so I could tear myself away. I doubt the rest would be capable of rational conversation.'

That ray of hope was blotted out nice and quick.

'On the plus side,' Auron continued, reacting to the look on Nicolas's face, 'at least we have a bad guy now. In the hero game, knowing the bad guy is considered a big step in the right direction. Now we just need to get you out of here, find the necromancer, defeat his minions along the way, slay him, avenge me, rescue the prisoners, and you can go home. Simple.'

Nicolas told Auron exactly what he thought of his use of the word *simple*. He told him in a tidal wave of frustration that grew in speed, ferocity, and colourfulness of language. Auron looked genuinely shocked at the words coming out of Nicolas's mouth, but he couldn't stop. He thought he might *never* stop ranting when he was grabbed by the hair and yanked toward the adjoining cage, his face pressed painfully into the bars.

'Will you please calm down?' asked a deep, impatient voice.

The grip slackened slightly but still held him tight. Was the arm holding him green? He followed the arm until it disappeared under a dirty red cloak, which covered a figure around the size of Grimmark. Yellow eyes looked down on him levelly from under a hooded brow.

'Orc,' he whispered with a gulp.

The grip on his head suddenly released, and Nicolas, who'd been pulling against it, tumbled backwards onto his bottom.

The orc ran a hand through his mohawk of orange hair with a sigh. 'Very observant of you,' he remarked dryly. 'Could you and your ghost friend kindly keep it down? I'm attempting to rest while I can.'

'You can see him?' Thank the Deities it wasn't just him and the necromancer.

'You can see me?' Auron said at the exact same time, before adding, 'I'm a spirit, not a ghost.'

'I cannot,' the orc replied calmly. 'But I've had to listen to you talk quite loudly since the guards left you in the cell, having what appears to be a one-sided conversation. You are therefore either talking to a ghost, or you are absolutely crazy. I hypothesise from looking at you that you are not crazy. Distressed, beaten, and highly strung, yes. Crazy, no.'

Another ray of hope blotted out. At least the necromancer seeing him meant Nicolas hadn't gone insane, a suspicion he'd harboured since him and Auron first met.

'He's well-spoken for an orc,' Auron noted, obviously suspicious.

'You are very well spoken,' Nicolas repeated, paraphrasing his friend.

The orc rolled his eyes wearily. 'Ah, you're one of those. You meet an orc who doesn't say things like *smash yer humie skull* and *gonna get my choppa and 'ack 'im up*, and you stand there slack jawed as if you'd just seen a dragon with two anuses.'

'Um...' he began sheepishly. 'I haven't actually met an orc before.'

The orc seemed surprised by this, looking at him for a moment as if trying to detect some sarcasm. Finding none, he appeared to warm to Nicolas slightly. 'Then please allow me to introduce myself and give you a different view of orc culture to the popular stereotype,' the orc said with a flourish of his cape and polite bow. 'I am Garaz, shaman and spell weaver, at your service.'

He offered his hand tentatively, and the orc shook it carefully, has hand much larger than Nicolas's.

'I'm Nicolas Percival Carnegie,' he said after a moment, before gesturing to the spirit. Not that Garaz could not see him. 'And this is Auron of Tellmark. *The Dawnblade.*'

Auron seemed to be waiting for something. Most likely to see if the orc had heard of him.

'A pleasure to meet you, young Nicolas,' Garaz smiled warmly. 'The name of your friend is known to me. Truly these are dark days if such a legendary hero has fallen, even one whose reputation was built on a controversial foundation.'

Controversial? Nicolas looked at Auron for clarification. The spirit stood silently, glaring at the orc.

'He's helping me rescue the prisoners from the wagons,' he explained, feeling the need to fill the silence.

'A noble endeavour, but one I fear is not working out the way you intended.' Garaz smiled. 'I appreciate the effort, though. And the pains you have gone through to get here.' He looked pointedly at Nicolas's swollen eye and cut forehead.

'Well, no, it isn't exactly going the way we'd planned.' Thinking maybe things were about to improve, 'But that's okay. *Spell weaver* is like a wizard, right? So you can magic us out of here or something?'

Garaz looked at him in bemusement. 'Do you not suppose that if I were able to *'magic us out of here or something'* I would have already done so before you arrived?'

'Oh, I suppose so.' Ah, he hadn't thought of that.

Behind him, Auron *tutted* like a disappointed parent.

Garaz lowered the rim of his cloak slightly to reveal a heavy looking metal collar around his neck. It was engraved with runes and had an imposing lock at its centre. 'This is a binding collar,' he explained. 'It prevents me from conjuring or casting spells.'

'All the people in your wagon had those things on, didn't they?' he asked, thinking back to the bridge.

'That is correct. I was brought here with several other witches and wizards. Since our arrival, we've been taken from our cells one by one. None have returned. I now patiently await my own fate. Though I confess myself glad of some company...now that you are no longer hysterical. I apologise for being so rough with you just now. You were spiralling, and I did not feel that attempting civil discourse with you would be the most efficient way to calm you down.'

'No worries.' In truth, Garaz wasn't wrong.

'Those must've been the ghosts I saw around the necromancer,' Auron interjected thoughtfully. 'They did all appear to be wearing wizardly robes.'

He relayed what Auron had seen in the chamber with the necromancer.

Garaz bowed his head sombrely as Nicolas spoke. 'That they were all dead was really the only logical assumption,' he said with emotion. 'But to hear it confirmed is sad news indeed.'

'Do you know where the other wagon went?' he asked, hoping to distract the orc from his grief while finding out something useful.

'All I know is that they stayed on the main road as we broke towards the foothills and the fort.' Garaz shrugged. 'I am sorry I cannot be of more help.' The orc let out a slight chuckle. 'Though I admire your optimism, young Nicolas. I am afraid that even if I did know the information, it would do you no good. We are both prisoners now and have little time left to live, I fear.'

Nicolas feared too. Nicolas feared very much, though it was comforting to have some company other than Auron.

'Nonsense,' the spirit argued. 'We just need to figure out a way to break you two out of here, that's all.'

He repeated what Auron had said.

"*That's all?*' The orc laughed. 'I believe your friend thinks we can walk through walls as easily as he.'

How was he so calm about the idea of a ghost? Nicolas asked.

'I have seen stranger things on my travels,' the orc shrugged in response.

He may have liked to hear about that, were they not locked in a jail together. Escape was the most immediate concern. Though it felt unachievable, he wasn't about to just sit here and wait to be tortured.

'There must be something we can do?' he probed hopefully as Auron paced the length of the jail, looking for something to inspire an escape plan.

'I cannot use magic, and you, forgive me for saying, are no warrior. I do not see a way out of this other than via the afterlife.'

Openly pointing out that he was no warrior seemed a little unnecessary.

'So, you can't use magic. But aren't orcs, like, really strong? That's a thing, right?'

'Well, yes, we are naturally stronger than most, but I do not see how that can help,' Garaz answered. 'I cannot bend the bars or remove the door from its hinges. If I could, I would, again, not be here.'

He'd assumed as much, but he wanted to check every possible advantage they may have. Hopefully, talking the problem out would make a solution obvious.

Auron's noise of triumph caught his attention. 'Nicky, you little genius, you've just given me an idea,' he said with a broad, slightly unsettling grin.

CHAPTER 11

Almost an hour passed before he heard the *click* of the lock again. Eyeing the door as the two men entered, he again felt sick to his stomach. He'd always known that life was finite but being faced with it repeatedly was a different thing. On top of that, the way the men were smiling was unnerving. They didn't strike him as the type to generally enjoy dragging skinny boys around, so wherever they were taking him had to be pretty terrible. Completely ignoring Garaz, who was swathed in his cloak again, the pair stopped before his cell.

'Torture time.' One of the men sneered as he put a key into the door of his cell. 'You're off to see Old Hob. He can get anyone talking, can Old Hob. An artist, you might say.'

Brilliant.

Backing up against the wall of his cell, he intended to put every millimetre of distance he could between himself and the men. In the corner of the cell, Auron stood casually with his arms folded.

Everything seemed to slow as the door opened, right down to the flakes of rust falling from the handle like leaves caught in a breeze. Suddenly, the cell was a lot fuller as the men entered.

'Stay back!' he cried. 'I'm not going anywhere.'

Though he raised his fists in defiance of his captors, he wasn't entirely sure what he intended to achieve. As the men approached him, laughing heartily, he began to flail his arms, hoping some mysterious force would guide them to strike down his enemies. The guards didn't seem concerned. It was only moments before his feet went out from under him and he was being removed from his cell.

'No, no, no,' he pleaded. 'I don't want to go. I want to live. Please don't hurt me. I'll tell you everything. I don't want to die.' Wet tears stained his cheeks as he begged.

Just beyond his cell, the men halted with a noise of disgust. 'I think we're going to have to knock him out,' one of them said. 'There's only so much whining I can stand, and I don't think he'll shut up otherwise.'

'We can't,' replied the other. 'If we bring him to Old Hob unconscious, he might not be too happy, and the boss will be livid.'

Their conversation was cut off as Nicolas's battle to control his nausea failed. As he heaved and gagged, hot fluid rushed up his throat, burning everything it touched. His body spasmed, and the men let him go, realising what was about to happen. He fell to his knees and vomited, his stomach contracting violently just to be sure no morsel remained in his stomach. He was vaguely aware of his captors backing to the door of the next cell, evidently not wanting to get their boots ruined.

'Be a man about it,' one of the men cried, apparently having distinctly less fun now.

Stomach empty and eyes watering, he looked up at his captors. For some strange reason, he felt the need to apologise for making a mess. Who knew why. Before he could, though, two large green arms slipped through the bars of the cell the men had backed towards. Each arm wrapped around one of the men's necks, raising them from the floor and cutting off the blood supply to their brains. The men made horrible choking noises as they flailed, attempting to gain a foothold or break free from the grip. As much as he wanted to look away, he watched in fascination as the flailing decreased until both the bodies were limp, faces pale. Only then Garaz let go, and both men collapsed to the floor in a heap.

'Great work, kid.' Auron beamed as Garaz fumbled with one of the guard's key chains. 'Actually being sick was a nice touch. Great acting.'

There was no acting involved, but he wasn't about to admit that. Auron seemed so proud, and he didn't want to shatter his illusion. Plus, he wasn't sure he could speak right now anyway.

'Hey!' Another of the necromancer's men stood in the doorway, looking at his unconscious companions in disbelief.

Scrabbling to his feet, Nicolas backed away slowly as the man drew a vicious looking club from his belt and advanced. Which quickly became a charge. Again, Nicolas wanted to plead, and again, he wasn't sure he could speak.

As the guard passed Garaz's cell at speed, his leg suddenly went out from under him and he stumbled, bracing himself against the wall to keep from falling completely. There was a look of revulsion on his face as he looked down to see what he'd slipped on. Despite everything, Nicolas found himself slightly embarrassed.

'Now, kid,' Auron cried. 'There's your opening. Use it.'

Not thinking, just obeying, he launched himself towards the distracted guard, shouting a strained battle cry. Closing the distance just as the guard looked up in confusion, he threw his fist in a wide arc at the guard's head. It struck his jaw.

"Ow!" Nicolas cried, snatching his arm back and nursing his hand as pain flared through his knuckles.

With a small spot of blood on the edge of his lip the only sign he'd been struck at all, the guard rose to his full, imposing height. Putting his thumb to his mouth, he inspected the bloodied appendage. Snarling, he dropped his club to the floor, instead opting for the serrated knife on his belt.

Nicolas brought his arms up over his face just as the knife arm went back, preparing stab him. However, the stabbing never came. Garaz, now free of his cell, grabbed the man's arm, using it to spin him around before laying him out with a thunderous headbutt. The man landed in the product of Nicolas's recent regurgitation.

'I am not normally one for physical violence,' Garaz said as he looked down at the bodies. 'But some primitive part of me enjoyed that.'

Numbed by what had just occurred, all he could do was watch as the orc rummaged in the guards' pockets until he produced a small, square key with a smile. He used his fingers to probe for the lock on his collar then fitted the key and unlocked it. The heavy collar came away instantly, gravity dragging it to crack against the stone tile below. Once the collar was removed, Nicolas could almost feel the surge of energy from the orc, as if he'd been half asleep, but was now completely awake.

'Great.' He smiled. Something finally going right. 'Now you can magic us out of here.'

'You really have no idea how magic works, do you?' Garaz asked with a raised eyebrow.

'No,' he replied honestly.

'We can discuss the finer points of spell craft later,' Auron interrupted from the door of the jail, where he was keeping watch for more guards. 'We have to go.'

'We can discuss it later,' he told Garaz in all haste.

Assembling themselves by the door of the jail—Garaz with club in hand, while he'd retrieved his father's knife from one of the guards—the pair waited. He looked at the knife. Could he even bring himself to use the blade? He guessed he'd know when the moment came, though he wasn't optimistic. After a few moments, Auron's head appeared through the door, confirming the way ahead was clear. Disconcerting as it was to be talking to a disembodied head, at least it brought good news.

'Where do we even go?' he asked as they emerged into the corridor.

'We need to get out of here and find the site where they took the other prisoners,' Auron said thoughtfully. 'Our best bet for an exit has to be the way we came in, so we avoid the small army at the front gate.'

Yeah, the idea of slipping out without more confrontation was really appealing.

'Would you mind letting me in on your plan?' Garaz asked. 'May I remind you that I cannot hear your friend.'

Quickly, Nicolas reiterated Auron's idea and explained how they'd gained entry to the fort in the first place.

'That does seem the best choice.' The orc nodded in agreement.

Quickly but carefully, the trio progressed through the corridors, keeping close to the wall to minimise the risk of detection, until a stairway leading to both the upper and lower levels of the fort appeared ahead of them. Nicolas pressed himself to the nearest doorway as Auron gave them a sudden signal to hide. Following his cue, Garaz did the same on the opposite wall.

He waited, keeping his mouth as tightly closed as possible, lest a stray breath give them away. In his hand he felt his grip tighten around the handle of the knife. The blade vibrated slightly in time with the shaking in his hand.

Just seconds later, the stomping of boots indicated a large group approaching from above. Luckily, they were so busy chatting amongst themselves that none of them noticed the two escaped prisoners as they passed their floor. Why were they all carrying mining equipment?

'This will be a long journey if we have to keep stopping like that,' Garaz said thoughtfully once they were gone. 'And your absence in whatever torture chamber they had prepared for you will be noticed soon enough. They will send someone looking.'

'What can we do?' Nicolas asked.

'Keep moving,' Auron urged, as he edged towards the stairs.

About to follow his ethereal companion, Nicolas was halted by the sound of tearing behind him. Turning in alarm, he found Garaz ripping several old tapestries from the wall.

'What are you doing?' he asked in an urgent whisper. All it would take was for one guard to hear the noise he was making.

'An addition to the plan,' the orc said simply.

Garaz heaped the ragged tapestries on the floor before breaking up some rotted wooden furniture abandoned in the corridor and adding it to the pile. Using one of the torches from the wall, he set fire to the kindling. As it began to burn, Garaz held his hands towards the flames and muttered under his breath. Nicolas watched in amazement as the flames soared as if oil had been poured on them. Thick black smoke spread down the corridor quickly, the fire itself following close behind, seemingly as if it had a will and purpose of its own.

'Distraction.' Garaz smiled as he passed Nicolas and followed Auron up the stairs.

Soon there were cries of alarm throughout the fort, and the sound of men running both towards and away from the advancing flames. It seemed the distraction had the desired effect. The higher they ascended through the fort, the fewer guards they found as the ones not busy fighting the fire were evacuating. Best of all, there were no calls to look for escaped prisoners. It seemed as if they'd either been forgotten or given up for dead. Either suited him.

Though the guards were not the only hazard now. The fire may be raging several levels below them, but he could still feel the heat of it rising from the floor. At some point it would reach them. What if they were still in the fort when that happened?

Turning a corner, he finally saw the hole from which he'd entered the fort. From it, a shaft of light reached down to the floor, promising both hope and freedom.

'We made it!' he shouted in triumph, making toward the light.

'Kid, no!' Auron cried after him, but it was too late.

His reflexes kicked in just in time to stop him walking into the lethal spear tip as it advanced from beyond the light. Maybe it hadn't been his reflexes at all? He got the impression if the wielder of the spear had wanted him dead, he would be. As the backed away slowly, Silva emerged from the light. Beside her came Grimmark, smiling with satisfaction as he cradled the head of his beloved hammer in one hand.

'I thought so,' Silva said in a self-congratulatory manner. 'The minute I heard about the fire, I suspected there was a rat was on the loose.'

'The orc too,' Grimmark snarled, noticing Garaz. 'Probably set the fire. This scrawny boy would think of nothing so cunning.'

He may not have thought of it, but he was still offended.

'So, is it true?' Silva asked as she withdrew the blade of her spear and stood the weapon on the ground next to her. 'That you aren't here alone?'

'The necromancer told us you have a ghost travelling with you,' Grimmark added as he looked around with a half-smile.

He didn't answer, but from the look the warrior gave him, his face must've given it away.

'It is true,' Silva cried in glee, before talking to the air around them, 'Is that right Auron? Is your ghost here? Tell me, hero, have you had any good bowel movements of late?' Silva cackled coldly.

Grimmark chuckled in his deep bass voice. 'He cannot even die properly,' the big man added. 'Has to hang around and pester the living some more.'

Auron, who until this moment had been content to glare coldly at the pair, took the bait. 'Damn you, you murdering wench,' he screamed, pointing an accusing finger at Silva as the redness began to overtake his aura again. 'I'll kill you and that big, shaved ape you hang around with too.'

'Creates a reputation based on blind luck and dies on a riverbank with his pants around his ankles. Hardly the poetic end of a great warrior. Funny, though,' Silva continued. 'Thanks for the lovely sword, by the way. Nice to have a memento of your passing.' She touched the hilt of the sword that still sat on her shoulder.

'If you had dared fight me like a warrior, it would've turned out differently, you dirty assassin-whore. I would've cut each piece of that stupid armour from you before doing the world a favour and running you through,' Auron roared in reply, ignoring the fact that neither of them could hear him.

'Do not worry, boy,' Grimmark said to Nicolas. 'Your death will be more epic than the *Dawnblade*'s.'

Auron's aura was now fully red again, and he was lost to his rage. Nicolas didn't have the time to try to snap him out of it. He had more pressing concerns, like trying not to die himself.

'But you aren't supposed to kill me yet. Your master will get mad.'

The pair of mercenaries looked at each other and laughed.

'He isn't our master, as much as he may believe he is,' Grimmark said between laughs.

'We indulge him, but he has no real power over us.' Silva snorted.

'Oh,' he said quietly as the events of the next few minutes played out in his mind. The end of those minutes promised to be bloody.

During this exchange, no one had been paying much attention to Garaz. The orc had closed his eyes and began chanting under his breath, quiet enough to be drowned out by the mercenaries' insults. Now, his labours were paying off.

Smoke formed around their ankles—summoned from the fire, no doubt. The mercenaries only noticed the black cloud when it reached their hips, by which time it was growing faster and faster. The pair swiped urgently at the smoke, but each time, it scattered only to reform in the same place again moments later.

Oddly, as the corridor was enveloped, he could see through the smoke clearly, when Silva and Grimmark's flailing and cursing suggested they couldn't. He looked over at Garaz, who winked at him.

'Let us go,' Garaz whispered to him. 'This will not take long to clear.'

The fact that neither of the warriors could see wasn't making them any less deadly as they blindly lashed out with their weapons in all directions, making up their lack of vision with the sheer quantity of strikes. Garaz moved to the far side of the hallway to circle around Grimmark. Nicolas went the other way, around Silva.

Her spear gave her a long reach that she was using to great effect. Several times, he took a step closer only to be driven back by a wild swipe from the weapon. Across from him, Garaz was making no better progress as Grimmark took chunks out of every surface with his hammer. However, the big man was slowing with each strike and, seeing the opportune moment, Garaz slipped past the warrior to await him under the hole. His turn now.

With a deep breath and firmly clenched buttocks, he let a high swing of the spear pass him by and made his move. His plan was to keep close to Silva to stay out of range of the sharp tip of her spear. In reality, what happened was that he barrelled straight into the armoured warrior. His attempt to duck low ended with him colliding with the side of Silva's knee. With a cry of outrage, Silva buckled, the spear clattering to the floor beside her as it slipped from her grip.

Silva, her reflexes evidently honed, recovered quickly, managing to half turn and grab at Nicolas, clutching a handful of his jacket. Frantically, he slipped his arms from the piece of clothing, ducking behind Silva. Seeing something he could use for leverage, he grabbed an item on Silva's back, using it to pull her down until the weight of her armour did the hard work and she crashed to the floor. As the warrior toppled, a strap gave way and the item fell into Nicolas's hands. He quickly secured it around his own shoulder and made for Garaz.

'Grimmark!' Silva screeched from the floor. 'Help me up, now!'

He ran to Garaz, and the orc lowered himself and cupped his hands below his hips. Understanding what he wanted, Nicolas put his boot into Garaz's hands and let the orc propel him upwards through the hole in the fort's wall. Scrabbling ferociously, he finally found a decent handhold with which to pull himself up, ensuring this time that the stone beneath his feet was steady and could take his weight.

Turning, he crouched and offered his hand to Garaz. Taking it, the orc began to pull himself up while Nicolas began to worry his arm would tear from his shoulder or he'd burst a blood vessel and pass out again. Surprising even himself with his efforts, he managed to lift the orc just enough for Garaz to grab the side of the stone and haul himself up. He couldn't feel his arms anymore, though they were surely a few inches longer now.

Below, the smoke was starting to clear.

'There!' Silva shrieked.

Whereas moments before, the two warriors had been confused and blinded by the smoke, now they both bounded towards the pair, weapons in hand. He stepped back just in time as Silva launched her spear. He felt the breeze as the weapon passed his ear, before it clattered down the rocky face of the mountain.

'Where now?' Garaz asked, looking around in confusion.

The orc didn't appear happy when he pointed to the thin ledge he'd used to get to the broken wall, but with enemies on their heels, they didn't have the luxury of options.

They made the jump in turn, and this time, he didn't hesitate, his fear of what was behind him greater than his fear of the jump. Garaz looked as if he were barely on the ledge, more of him overhanging it than on it, but he managed to shuffle its length without falling to his doom.

Before leaving the ledge for the ground proper, he looked back. Billowing black clouds were rising into the sky and he could see licks of flame emerging from any break in the fort's wall as the blaze consumed the building. Beyond the crackling of fire he heard the urgent calls of the men battling the blaze. At the hole from which he exited the fort, he saw Silva and Grimmark.

'You are dead! Do you hear me, boy? Dead!' Silva screamed and cursed.

Grimmark simply glowered at him with evil intent. Apparently, neither of them fancied their chances on the ledge. Considering the size of Grimmark and the amount of armour Silva was wearing, he couldn't blame them.

'I will carve every inch of skin from your body,' Silva roared, making him believe it.

He would've loved a moment of smugness to revel in slipping away from the pair, again, but poking the beast would be unwise. The warriors disappeared back into the hole, which meant they were probably now running for the fort's entrance. Which meant Nicolas needed to be running get as far from it as he could.

Following Garaz, he made for the treeline. Next to him was a sullen Auron, who'd appeared from who knew where. His aura was still tinged red, but he seemed a little more in control. The undergrowth was as thick as before, but with murderous mercenaries on his heels he ploughed through it regardless, leaving the smoke-vomiting fort behind them. Their only advantage was their head start, and he wasn't about to waste a second of it.

CHAPTER 12

The now-setting sun threatened to cut the trio's flight short as the sky changed to a multitude of red hues before darkness began to set in. With the light went decent visibility, making fleeing down a mountain at speed practically suicidal. His one advantage was Auron, whose bright aura gave enough light to guide them away from the main trail without tripping over one of the many obstacles or walking right off the edge of the mountain itself. Though guiding Garaz, who was oblivious to the aura, did slow them marginally.

'Over here,' Auron called from beyond a set of bushes.

After struggling through, branches snapping back into place after he'd passed them, Nicolas found himself facing a rocky outcropping. With thick foliage all around and no direct line of sight to the main trail, this seemed a decent enough place to hunker down for the night. He needed to rest so desperately he wasn't sure he could make the last few steps to the shelter. Between both the physical exhaustion and the sheer emotional and mental trauma of it all, he was nearly spent. How was he not just curled in a ball, sobbing?

Even settled under the rocks, he jumped at every rustle around him. There had to be people out looking for them, and any bush could conceal a potential attacker. His paranoia only subsided slightly when he realised that the elements were the more immediate threat. The temperature had dropped rapidly until he was unsure whether he shook from fear or cold.

'Come here,' Garaz whispered to him, opening his cloak.

Though he would've felt awkward about sharing a cloak with anyone, let alone an orc he'd just met, survival trumped awkwardness. He shuffled across and allowed Garaz to wrap his arm around him. Already, he felt slightly warmer as he tried to compress his body into as small a ball as possible to keep warm.

'I'm going to check the trail,' Auron said, turning to go.

'No wait,' he cried. 'What if the necromancer sees you and finds us?'

Auron looked at him then let out a single laugh. 'Chasing escaping prisoners is henchman work, kid. No way he comes running down this mountain after us. Don't worry.'

Right. He may as well have told the tide not to come in. But the spirit did seem confident, so he didn't press the issue.

Twenty minutes later, their pursuers caught up to them. It started with men calling to each other in the dark. Then bobbing torchlights in the distance. Then came the audible stomping of boots on the track. He held his breath, fearing an errant cough or sneeze may give them away. Praying, he saw the light from the torches grow brighter. They were so close.

When they began to dim again he allowed himself to hope, only letting himself relax completely when the light had vanished altogether. It appeared their pursuers assumed they would make for the forest despite the dangerous terrain. Thank the Deities they didn't think to look for side trails.

All that was left now was to try not to freeze to death. He wasn't optimistic. Already his fingers and toes were numb, despite the shared cloak and body warmth, and he couldn't physically stop himself shivering. This only got worse when Garaz moved, taking the cloak with him and allowing the cold to renew its assault.

He wanted to ask what the orc was doing but thought better of it. Whatever it was, Garaz seemed to have a purpose. The orc made a small pile of stones in front of them before drawing some symbols in the ground. Putting his hands over the stones, the orc chanted under his breath, and the hairs on Nicolas's arms raised with the energy he was giving off.

'Just a simple technique to channel the warmth of the earth through the rocks,' Garaz said as he returned to his side, sharing his cloak with him again. 'It will not be much, but it will prevent us from freezing and will not draw attention.'

Almost instantly, there was warmth in the air around him. It was just enough to take the edge off, and with Garaz's cloak, he felt almost comfortable.

'They're gone,' Auron said as he reappeared through a bush. 'I don't know how they expect to find you the way they're charging about hollering.'

'We're hoping they don't,' he replied sourly.

The spirit didn't reply. Instead, he studied Garaz's stone pile. 'How long have you been a wizard?' Auron asked.

When the orc didn't reply, the hero looked annoyed then realisation crossed his face. It seemed even Auron hadn't gotten used to being a spirit yet. Was that something you could ever get used to? From the look on his companion's face, Nicolas hoped he could find it in him to help Auron with his unfinished business so he could move on. He relayed the spirit's question to Garaz.

'Since I was young,' the orc replied. 'I was found to have the gift for magic as a child. For many years, I studied under the tribal shaman. I learned much, but always felt I was only skirting the edge of my potential. When I was probably slightly younger than you, I left my tribe and made my way to the Academy of Magic.'

'The actual academy itself?' Auron let out an impressed whistle. 'Can't have been easy getting in there. They tend to be a bit of a 'human only' club.'

He repeated what Auron had said.

'It was not so bad,' Garaz said thoughtfully. 'They could not deny my talent, and I was lucky to find someone willing to be my patron. Once my foot was in the door, so to speak, them wanting little to do with me gave me ample time to concentrate on my studies.' He finished with a half-smile.

'So now you're a wizard?' he asked, curious as he knew little about magic.

'You need to understand, young Nicolas, that *wizard* is not an all-encompassing term,' Garaz replied patiently. 'Just because I am a wizard does not mean I can therefore do all magic. The body—human, orc, or otherwise—can only produce a certain amount of energy at a certain time. Spells are a way of channelling that energy to produce changes in our environment, expending the energy as we cast them. The bigger the spell, the more energy is required to cast it. Afterwards, the wizard needs time to recharge and restore the energy. You can increase your energy through training, just like with any activity, but there is always a limit to how much magical energy any single body can contain and produce. That is why no wizard knows 'all magic,' and we work on focusing and channelling our magical energy through a preferred discipline.'

'Discipline?'

'There are many different magical disciplines, ranging from battle magics to things such as conjuring and illusion. Generally, a wizard will have a main discipline that he is highly skilled in and maybe one or two others that they have enough knowledge of for the odd spell. Even the greatest wizards only know three or four disciplines. I suppose it is nature's way of keeping balance, ensuring that no one wizard can become too powerful.'

'Necromancy is a magical discipline, right?' he asked.

Garaz winced. 'Unfortunately, yes,' he replied with distaste. 'Though a forbidden discipline, because it is wrong and unnatural, and because it tends to draw individuals who are not mentally stable. No good ever came from messing around with the dead, and anyone who decides that they would like to spend their time raising zombies and such has serious issues. I find it particularly abhorrent because my chosen discipline is that of healing and restoration. I have dedicated myself to preserving life. Those who prey on death disgust me.'

'The necromancer did seem pretty odd.' A chill ran down his spine at the memory of the man in the black robe and his rodent eyes.

'He seemed pretty standard for his breed,' Garaz answered with a small snarl. 'A sad, mad little man with a need to prove himself. Necromancers generally have a large inferiority complex because they are forced to practise their arts in back alleys and crypts. When we were delivered to the fort, he made a big show of having us all bow before him whilst he slated our disciplines at great length. He took particular exception to me, the disciplines of life and death having always been at loggerheads. I presume that is why I was left until last, to draw out my suffering.'

'What about you, Auron?' Nicolas asked, having to squint slightly to look at him because of the light of his aura in the dark. 'Have you had experience with necromancers before?'

'Yeah, once or twice,' Auron said. 'Garaz isn't wrong. But like anything else, stabbing them in the vital places tends to do the trick.'

He repeated the remark for Garaz's benefit.

'He was powerful, though,' the orc mused, more to himself than anyone else. 'I could sense it radiating off him. It felt…unnatural. He claims that whatever he is doing will be on a grand scale. He spoke of changing the world.'

'How?

'He would not go into specifics,' the orc replied. 'He said we were too rigid and small to understand his vision. Part of him was clearly dying to tell us and rub our noses in it, and I am sure I could have goaded him into saying more, but by that time, I had been abducted and beaten, and there was only so much listening to a raving maniac I could stand.'

'Maybe it's something to do with those men with the mining tools?' Nicolas suggested.

'Pfft.' Auron grunted. 'I would bet good money that those guys were just digging up a load of dead bodies. Classic necromancer stuff. Dig up some bodies, make them move around then pretend you've done something amazing and out of the box while trying not to breath in and gag on the death stench.'

Despite himself, he chuckled slightly before passing the comment to Garaz, who also smiled at the remark.

'I cannot help but wonder why this necromancer wanted wizards especially.' The death of Garaz's peers seemed to weigh heavily on him. 'Beyond him simply being insane and having an axe to grind with other magic users. I got the impression we were there for a specific purpose.'

'The people in the other wagon didn't have collars on like you,' Nicolas noted, thinking mainly of the girl with the green eyes.

'They must have been non-magic folk then,' the orc replied. 'Unfortunately, I did not see the other wagon as I was rendered unconscious before I was taken.'

'That makes sense. I'd think carefully about tussling with him even before you take the magic into account,' Auron said as he appraised their new companion.

He also looked at Garaz. The orc had a gentle manner, but there was no mistaking his imposing size and physique, and he couldn't forget what he'd seen Garaz do to the guards in the fort with seemingly little effort. How had they managed to capture him? Once the question was in his mind, it wouldn't go away, conjuring up paranoid ideas that maybe their new companion wasn't what he appeared to be.

'How *did* they grab you?' he asked, trying to make the question sound casual.

'Once I completed my studies at the Academy of Magic, I decided to travel. I wanted to see the world,' Garaz replied. 'If I find somewhere I am welcome, I tend to stay for a week or two ministering to the sick.'

'Somewhere you're welcome?'

The orc smiled to himself before he answered. 'Generally, humans are suspicious of orcs, for good reason. My people have a long and violent history with yours. It is...difficult...to find places where I am accepted. I found one such place in a logging hamlet by the river. I had been there a few days when a woman approached me. She blew some kind of powder into my face, and everything went black. When I awoke, I was being dragged from the wagon. Apparently, one of the guards had lost a brother to an orc incursion, so he and his companions worked me over before presenting me to their master.'

The story seemed genuine enough, but what did he know? He looked at Auron, who seemed to be taking the tale at face value. That reassured him slightly.

'So, what's our next step? Go and find some soldiers?' he asked hopefully.

He had rescued one person. Or had Garaz actually rescued him? Either way, he'd done something and nearly died for it. Repeatedly. Now must be the time to allow the professionals to do their work.

'I doubt we have the time,' Garaz replied after some thought. 'Whilst this necromancer seems quite mad, I did pick up a sense of finality from his ranting, like we were coming close to his end game. We need answers as to what that is. The fort will be too heavily guarded now to allow a return, but this second site might have information. Plus, there are people there in dire need of our help. What we need to do now is find this other site and the other captives.'

"*We?*' he repeated, slightly shrilly. 'We who?'

Garaz pointed his large-clawed finger firstly to himself then to Nicolas then to where he assumed Auron was. He was close but was actually just pointing at a bush.

'Look,' he protested, 'I saved you…'

'Kind of,' Auron added unhelpfully.

'…but now you're free, you can go and save the others. I think a wizard and a hero ghost…sorry, spirit would do a great job rescuing those people. You don't need me hanging around, slowing you down when I can be more useful finding people who can actually help, like soldiers.'

'Your logic is intriguing, but the big hole in it is that I cannot see Auron,' Garaz replied flatly. 'His soul is bonded to you, for some reason, so I need you to come with me. I know you are no warrior, young Nicolas—the punch you threw at the fort proved that—but you have come this far. That tells me you have a reserve of courage in you, and that you can be more useful than you think. Neither Auron nor I can complete this task without you.'

Nicolas's mouth opened and closed a few times as he searched for the perfect combination of words to get him out of this. There was none. That ember of courage of his was becoming more of a burden than the bloody choosing stick. But he'd come this far to help save people, and there were still people to save, so it would appear that was that.

'Dammit,' he muttered to himself.

'The orc is right,' Auron added. 'We can't do this without you. Do you really want to let the others face a similar fate, or worse? Plus, there is that pretty girl.'

'No,' he replied. 'And shut up.'

'So, you will not join me?' Garaz asked in surprise.

'I was talking to him.' He jerked his thumb towards Auron. 'I'll go. But how do we even know that they're still alive?'

'We cannot give up on trying to rescue them simply because they *may* be dead already,' Garaz counselled.

It was a fair point.

'Brilliant,' Auron grinned. 'Just imagine the reward that girl will give you when you save her from the jaws of certain death.'

To make his point clearer, Auron punctuated his sentence with kissing noises. Despite his outrage, a small smile crept out. Even though he wasn't doing this for a kiss, of course.

'It's going to be dangerous.' Nicolas knew the reality of their situation. His smile dropped. 'More dangerous. They're looking for us now.'

'At least you are armed now, young Nicolas.'

For a few seconds, he had no idea what the orc was talking about. Then it dawned on him that he had something strapped around his shoulder, something he'd taken from Silva on their escape from the fort. In all the running and numbing terror, he'd completely forgotten. Mortal danger was hard on the memory. He kept forgetting things, sure there was something else he needed to recall.

Reaching behind him, he took the leather scabbard from his shoulder and held it in his hands. The carved sun on the hilt of the sword was swathed in Auron's blue light.

'No way,' Auron gasped.

Nicolas drew the blade from its scabbard. Even in the darkness he could tell that the blade was perfectly reflective, like no metal he'd ever seen, and razor sharp. He held it in his hands in exactly the way someone who'd never held a sword might.

'The Dawn Blade,' Garaz said in awe as his eyes traced the length of the blade.

Auron stepped towards the sword with his hand outstretched. He looked almost hypnotised, like someone who's seen a loved one they thought lost to them. The neon blue hand wavered inches from the sword then closed into a fist and withdrew, though he continued to look longingly at the blade. Was he happy or sad? Nicolas couldn't tell.

'I grabbed it from Silva in the smoke,' he said, 'Well, more like I bumped into her, and it ended up on me.'

'Thank you, kid.' Auron's voice was full of emotion.

'I never thought to see the Dawn Blade in person,' Garaz muttered. 'A sword so legendary and so controversial.'

'Hey,' Auron shouted, making Nicolas jump. 'Nobody disparages my sword.'

'Um,' he began, curiosity getting the better of him, 'what's with the whole *controversial* thing anyway?'

He looked at his orc companion, who gestured to where he believed Auron stood, though he was wrong again. Auron stood over Nicolas, looking annoyed at the question, but finally relented and sat in front of him—as much as he could, anyway.

'My moniker comes from my very first heroic deed, slaying an orc warlord called Magrax the Defiler,' Auron began. 'He was a big deal at the time and on the rise, trying to unite various tribes into a coherent army to start a war as they like to do. There were a few tribes still holding out, so he decided to put on a big show of bravery to get them in line.'

Nicolas listened intently, while Garaz, who couldn't hear a thing, got himself comfortable and watched the stars.

'To do that, he decided to ride through the human lands by himself. I think he planned to rough up a couple of villages. Show that he didn't fear humans and that he was a mighty warrior. Then every orc tribe within fifty leagues would flock to his banner. Me, I was a courier at the time. I'd hoped to make my name as a hero but had only got as far as delivering messages and having a fancy sword. I was returning to my village from a job at night when suddenly there was this huge orc in the road, red eyes staring straight into me.'

'What happened next?' he asked, actually engrossed in one of Auron's stories.

'I had two options: stand and fight or make my escape and alert the nearest village. Being just about your age and having a sword I'd never blooded before, I chose to go find help. Naturally, the orc chased me, not wanting the alarm raised until after he'd caused some chaos. In the dark, I ended up lost and cornered on a cliff. The only choice I had then was to fight.'

'Did you win?'

'Will you just let me tell it?' Auron snapped before continuing. 'So, I drew my sword and stood my ground. Turned out, I wasn't a bad fighter and actually held my own for a while. Between the chase and the fight, enough time had passed for the sun to start rising. As it did, it reflected right off my blade into Magrax's eyes. Knowing he was blinded, I took the opportune moment to lop his head off. And thus, a legend was born.'

'So why the controversy?' he asked, confused.

Auron glowered for a moment before answering. 'Apparently there are two schools of thought about my victory. The first, and mine, was that I heroically attempted to warn others then used strategy to defeat a much larger opponent and win the day. As far as my *'detractors'* are concerned, I ran like a coward then got lucky. Either way, though, the Dawnblade was born that day.'

Either explanation was equally plausible, but he wasn't about to say that to Auron. And he certainly wasn't about to belittle someone for fleeing when that was all he wanted to do himself. The only difference being he doubted he would stand and fight after all was said and done.

The spirit seemed to sense Nicolas's hesitance and became indignant that he wasn't immediately on his side. 'I'm going to scout the area,' he huffed, rising. 'You need to get some sleep. Big day tomorrow.'

Before he could say anything, Auron had disappeared back through the foliage concealing their hiding place, the slight blue glow in the air showing which way he was going.

Awkwardly, Nicolas sheathed the sword and tried to find some way of getting comfortable on the cold, hard ground. Would he fall asleep or simply pass out? Either way, the world around him vanished.

CHAPTER 13

The elation of simply being alive greeted him as he woke, the air around him cool, but fresh and invigorating. The night hadn't been a restful one, the constant threat of discovery causing him to wake with a start multiple times. And then there was the pain, his body feeling every nick and scratch it had suffered recently. Added to that was the fear. His days going from his usual predictable, comfortable routine, to being filled with danger and the unknown. Despite all of that, he was alive, and for a moment he intended to enjoy it. Rising, he opened his one good eye and took in the wonder of the new day.

'I'm ok,' he whispered to the morning air, as if it would carry his words across the landscape to his parents ears.

Even from their concealed hiding spot, he could see the world laid out beyond the mountain. This early, a mist had descended on the forest below, weaving around the green islands of trees like a white sea. Something about the natural beauty gave him his first moment of peace since some idiot had knocked on his parents' door to tell them a choosing had been called.

Hushed crackling and the smell of cooking meat broke him from his trance. His stomach growled ferally at the promise of food. Now it was light, it seemed Garaz had risked a small campfire and found some kind of animal to cook on it. He wasn't about to ask what it was, because he didn't want to know. It smelled delicious, and that was all he needed to know. Though he was surprised the orc had done all this without him noticing. He'd thought he would've been more alert, considering.

Garaz smiled when he noticed Nicolas was awake. 'For you.' In one hand, he had a cooked creature on a skewer, which renewed the growling in his stomach. In his other hand was a cup fashioned from some folded bark.

'It is a herbal tea,' Garaz informed him. 'It will help. And once you have eaten, we will see to those wounds.'

After taking both the skewer and cup from the orc, he gobbled down the meat greedily. Though the animal was small and chewy, after the last two days, it felt like a feast. Not giving himself time to swallow properly, he drank the tea in one gulp, coughing and spluttering as the food he was still chewing was suddenly washed down his throat.

'And they call us savages,' Garaz remarked as he looked at him with amusement.

Once he'd finally recovered, the orc bade Nicolas sit by him so he could inspect his injuries. Despite the way in which he'd drunk it, he could already feel the tea working. His muscles relaxed and aches dulled as it warmed him from the inside out.

'Keep your eyes shut. Sorry, eye,' Garaz said as he laid one hand on Nicolas's swollen eye and the other on his wounded head.

'Very funny,' he replied.

The orc smiled then began to chant. He was aware of light emanating from the orc's hands, its energy passing into him, revitalising him. After a few moments, Garaz drew back, and Nicolas could open his eye. Also, the wound on his temple was mostly healed. He still felt the lingering echoes of pain and swelling, but it was a massive improvement.

'I cannot magically make your wounds disappear,' Garaz explained, 'but I can speed up the healing process.'

'Thank you,' he said.

He needed to blink a few times until his eye adjusted to being able to see again. Things were blurred slightly, but it was a vast improvement.

'You're back,' Nicolas said suddenly, looking over the orcs shoulder.

Through the bushes, Auron approached. The spirit looked longingly at the remains of the food on their skewers. It must be difficult to know you could never enjoy food again.

'Did the hunting party come back?' he asked, hoping to take the spirit's mind from his woes.

'Yeah, early this morning,' Auron confirmed with a chuckle. 'Idiots didn't even know they walked by you twice.'

Nicolas told Garaz what he'd said.

'I, for one, am glad of their failure.' The orc chuckled. 'The problem we have now is finding the other site. The other wagon could not have travelled that far from the fort as there are garrisons nearby, and they would be spotted. However, we could also spend days searching this area and still find nothing.'

'Trouble with this area is,' Auron began, as Nicolas repeated his words for Garaz's benefit, 'there are so many caves and nooks. We can't afford to search each one, especially as there will most likely be parties hunting us again in the day.'

'So what do we do?' he asked.

'If only we had some way to narrow our search,' Garaz mused. 'I wish I had been conscious enough to see where the wagons parted.'

The party was silent for a moment, each retreating to their own head to think about how to proceed. He couldn't shake the feeling he was forgetting something; it was right in front of him, but he couldn't touch it, almost like Auron.

'Without divine intervention, we're just going to have to search and hope that luck favours us,' Garaz said, seemingly coming up with nothing more useful to contribute.

Divine intervention? That struck a chord, but for a moment, he couldn't think why. Then a name popped into Nicolas's head.

'Is Stranom Crag around here?' he asked, almost absentmindedly.

'Yeah, near enough.' Auron looked out at the horizon, still lost in his own thoughts.

Something clicked in Nicolas's brain.

"I've heard bad omens from Stranom Crag. No one goes there after dark.'

Both Garaz and Auron were looking at him very strangely.

'You what?' Auron asked, and Nicolas repeated it.

'I appear to be lost,' Garaz interjected. 'Are you quoting someone?'

He felt really foolish all of a sudden. This was the whole reason he'd been out here, and especially on that cursed bridge, in the first place. There was no chance at all that his message and what was happening were not connected; he kicked himself that it had slipped from his mind for so long. His head had taken a lot of abuse of late, in his defence.

'Umm, yeah.' He coughed sheepishly. 'It was a message I was supposed to deliver.'

'That is a strange form of message,' Garaz commented with a raised eyebrow.

'It's something the people of my village do,' he replied vaguely. 'I was on a bridge waiting for a hero to give the message to. The hero never turned up, though, and I ended up knocked into the river.'

Auron was suddenly looking at him as one may do a capering fool.

'Oh, do you—'

'Think that message was meant for me?' Auron finished in a voice thick with sarcasm. 'Yeah, I do. Idiot.'

'Oh.'

'All this time you knew exactly where we should go,' Auron said, perfectly imitating the look of his father when annoyed. 'Why didn't you tell me you were from Hablock?'

Nicolas began to feel a brilliant combination of awkward and embarrassed. 'I'd just met you, and you were dead....'

'And not once did it occur to you that I may've been the hero you were supposed to give the message to?'

'I've been hit in the head, twice. And in plenty of mortal danger. So...no,' he protested weakly.

Auron gave his view on that in a very rude fashion.

'Hey,' Nicolas shouted, standing up. 'There's no need to talk to me like that. I nearly died on that bridge.'

'I *did* die, moron.'

'I...um...yeah.'

That fact blunted Nicolas's building anger. 'Sorry,' he said quietly, as Auron glared at him. 'Wait...you know Hablock?' he asked. 'I thought that what we did was pretty much a secret beyond our village.'

'It is, for the most part,' the spirit replied, not breaking that glare. 'But when you've been a hero at my level for as long as I have, a secret or two happens your way.'

'As amusing as it is watching one side of an argument,' Garaz interjected, 'can you please give me the full picture so I might understand the nature of your disagreement?'

Nicolas took a moment to fill Garaz in on Hablock, the notion of a Word Bearer, and the full events of the last few days. The orc listened thoughtfully while Auron paced, shaking his head and muttering.

'I see,' Garaz said as he finished his tale. 'Well, as far as oversights go, I cannot say I am too upset with this one. If not for your forgetfulness, I would be dead right now.'

Both Nicolas and Auron conceded that point. He was thankful for any point that made him look less of an idiot.

'And what were you doing travelling on that road, Auron?' the orc asked, not quite looking at him.

'I was urgently summoned to Yarringsburg by the king,' Auron said. 'The message didn't state why, just that it was urgent. Generally, if a king summons you personally, it's more than your day-to-day troll slaying. On the road, I came across a hamlet where the people had been taken. After that, this necromancer had six less men than he started with. I just wish I'd taken a moment to go to the toilet before I left the tavern that morning.' He finished with a grim look.

Nicolas relayed the response.

'Interesting,' Garaz replied. 'This has to be connected, but I do not see how.'

'I'm sure it'll become obvious once we get to the Crag,' Auron replied, through Nicolas.

He winced slightly at the use of the word *we*. Some part of him had hoped that finally delivering the message would end his part in this affair, but that was wishful thinking of the worst kind. For better or worse, he was now part of this until whatever end played out. At some point, he would have to make peace with that, but the internal struggle between what he knew he had to do and every sense telling him not to do it wouldn't cease. Neither would his longing thoughts of home and his parents.

* * * *

With no camp to have to pack up, it was quite easy for the group to be on their way after their less than hearty, but satisfying, breakfast. He was pleased to learn that Auron had been to the Crag, and that it was back down the mountain trail from where they were, so there was to be no tedious uphill climb. Though didn't that just get them to their doom faster?

As they travelled, it seemed Auron's irritation with Nicolas dissipated. He could tell, because Auron decided their trip wouldn't be complete without more tales of his adventures, complete with dramatic hand gestures and sound effects. Or perhaps he was still annoyed, and this was a form of punishment? Either way, he found himself envying Garaz, who could neither see nor hear any of it and was happy to travel with them in quiet contemplation.

The trip down the mountain was decent as the day came into its own. The sun broke through the early morning clouds and cast light over a beautiful landscape as far as the eye could see. Even the animals around them seemed delighted by the new day, chirping or tweeting to each other gleefully. The best thing so far for him was getting further from the fort, despite the unknowns of their destination.

It wasn't too long before the mountain trail became a proper road, thankfully. Though there was no sign of others around, they still proceeded warily, save Auron, who still had plenty of stories.

'Does Auron know what we should expect at the Crag?' Garaz asked as they continued.

'I told you just now, kid,' Auron said testily when Nicolas asked him.

'Well, yeah.' He didn't want to admit his mind had been wandering. 'He just means what to expect...specifically.'

Auron, who was leading the group, took a moment to look back over his shoulder at Nicolas. The look on his face suggested he wasn't fooled at all. *'As I said before*, I don't know specifically,' the spirit replied. 'There's a network of old caves there. Some bandits were using the place as a base to rob travellers on the road, way back. When I turned up at their doorstep, they surrendered on the spot, my formidable reputation preceding me, of course. I didn't actually go into the Crag itself. I let the local guards clear out the loot and tidy up and gave myself the rest of the day off.'

'I see,' Garaz replied simply as Nicolas told him what his companion had said.

'Off the road.' Auron's voice was urgent as something behind them caught his attention.

Grabbing Garaz—or in truth tugging on his cloak gently until the large orc got the message and followed—they moved to a nearby clump of bushes, concealing themselves behind them awkwardly, waiting. Even Auron hid with them, just in case. Though the leaves of the bushes bent and stretched around Nicolas and Garaz as they pressed themselves close to it, they passed straight through Auron, so he looked as if parts the bush grew from his form itself.

Several moments later, distant sounds resolved into the neighing of horses and clopping of hooves on the stone road. Maybe it was a hunting party from the fort set to ride them down? Maybe a search party from home? Though he had no idea how to use it with any degree of skill, he closed his hand around the hilt of the Dawn Blade. If the worst came, he would just swing and hope for the best.

Twenty men on horseback were moving in their direction, seemingly escorting a group of villagers. The riders looked kind of splendid in their silver helms, purple plumes bouncing in time with the stepping of their mounts. They carried oval shields and long lances, and their armour displayed the heraldry of Yarringsburg. They looked proud and at attention, in contrast to the villagers, who looked tired and resentful, each carrying packs on their back or wheeling little carts behind them filled with personal possessions.

'Soldiers,' he whispered with glee.

Finally. After all his hoping, there were finally soldiers, professional fighters who could take his burden—sorry, quest—and do a damn sight better job of it. Rising, he stepped into the road, vaguely aware of Auron and Garaz calling him back.

Within an instant, the riders halted, forming a line with lances pointed at him and shouting challenges. Maybe this hadn't been the best idea after all? Carefully, he raised his hands to show he was no threat. Behind the soldiers, the villagers huddled together in fear, a nervous murmuring passing between them. Yes, he didn't look as good as he had when he'd left Hablock—a month ago, was it? It felt like it—but he didn't look like a bandit.

From the front of the group, a single rider approached him, one hand on the sword in the scabbard at his side. This guy was obviously in charge. If the gold armour hadn't given it away, the haughty expression behind his handlebar moustache would've. He looked down on Nicolas with suspicion. He expected this man was used to looking down at a great many people.

'What is the meaning of this?' he demanded in a fine accent.

'We need your help,' he blurted as he looked in turn at each of the lance tips pointed directly at him.

'We?' the man asked as he scanned the bushes, and the riders behind him bristled, ready for action.

If the rustling in the bushes hadn't told him that Garaz had emerged, the soldiers' astonished looks and their leader drawing his sword certainly would've.

'No!' he cried. 'He's with me. He's okay.'

'You have a strange choice of travelling companions, boy,' the man said, not taking his eyes off Garaz nor attempting to hide the distaste in them.

'Um, yeah, but we still need your help,' he pressed.

'Do you know who you're addressing, boy?' one of the soldiers shouted indignantly.

He had no idea, so he shrugged. The man on the horse seemed displeased with this, just like a certain other person who believed that they should be recognised by sight.

'I am Sir Eldric Von Mastien, High Marshall of Yarringsburg,' the man proclaimed.

'Don't you know anything about the kingdom you live in?' Auron jibed as he appeared at Nicolas's side.

Instead of answering, he shot Auron a glare. He was in a delicate situation right now, and talking to people no one else could see might tip it in the wrong direction.

'And you are?' Sir Eldric asked testily.

'Tell him your name is Nick Carnage,' Auron said enthusiastically.

'I'm not saying Nick Carnage,' he snapped back in a harsh whisper.

'Nick Carnage?' Sir Eldric asked.

'No, no,' Nicolas corrected, as Auron chuckled next to him. 'My name is Nicolas Percival Carnegie, from Hablock...my lord,' he finished, remembering to add the title as the soldiers glowered at him.

'Do you always need to introduce yourself so formally?' Garaz whispered. 'I am sure that he does not care for your middle name.'

'Nick Carnage sounds cooler,' Auron muttered to himself, purposely loud enough for Nicolas to hear.

'And why exactly have you stopped the kings' men about their business, Mr Carnegie?' Sir Eldric demanded.

'There's a fort just up the mountain trail,' he began, words coming faster out of his mouth than he intended. 'A necromancer there is kidnapping people. He's doing something big. Some of them are being taken to Stranom Crag, so we were on our way there.'

'For?'

'Well, to try to rescue them,' he replied. 'But then we came across you and...' He didn't really want to say *and now you can do it* aloud.

'I see,' Sir Eldric said as he stroked his moustache thoughtfully. 'Necromancer, you say? And you expect me to take the tale at face value or do you have evidence to back up what you claim?'

'He speaks the truth,' Garaz offered. 'I was taken by them, but this brave young man rescued me.'

'There have been kidnappings, true enough,' the High Marshall remarked. 'That's why we're evacuating local villages to the city. But to commit the kings' men based on the story of a boy on the roadside who travels with...questionable company is a big ask.'

'It's true. I swear,' he protested.

'As long as you swear then.' Sir Eldric's sarcasm was thinly veiled. 'However, it is my duty to keep this kingdom secure, and if your story has even a hint of truth then I am dutybound to look into it. I shall send scouts to the Crag and this fort, I believe I know the one, once we've escorted these good people to safety. If it is true, the king's justice will be swift and decisive, and you will have the gratitude of the whole kingdom, Mr Carnegie.'

'Fancy words do not equal decisive actions,' Garaz muttered under his breath.

Despite his companion's reservations, he felt optimistic, almost elated. This was the best outcome he could've hoped for. This High Marshall obviously didn't take him seriously, but he was going to look into it anyway, and when he did, he would find a fort full of bad guys and a necromancer, just like he'd said. They would be arrested, the hostages would be rescued, and he could go home. It really seemed like an *all's well that ends well* deal. Part of him was a little disappointed that he wouldn't be the one to rescue the girl, but she had a better chance with them.

'Thank you.' He smiled wholeheartedly at the High Marshall before asking, 'What shall we do?'

'Go home and let us do our jobs.'

That was exactly what he wanted to hear.

As the convoy moved away, he breathed in deeply, letting out all the tension and fear as he breathed back out again. On his way home to his family, finally. When he got to hug his mother again, he may ever let go.

'You can't go home yet, so get that right out of your head, kid,' Auron said flatly.

'What? Why not?'

'Because he isn't going to send scouts out until he gets where he's going, wherever that is,' the spirit pointed out as he crossed his arms sternly. 'By the time the scouts get there, look around, report back, and the garrison mobilises, it will be hours. Maybe even tomorrow.'

And there was reality to smash his hopes and dreams. Of course the process would take ages. How had he not thought of that? Well, the answer to that was obvious, but he still cursed himself for allowing hope to creep in thoughtlessly. The hostages still needed immediate help, and they were it.

'Dammit,' he muttered.

'I did not care for that man,' Garaz mused as the convoy disappeared around a corner in the road.

'That's just what his kind are like,' Auron shrugged. 'Noble and way up his own arse. But if you look past his wonderful personality, he is actually very good at his job.'

'He didn't seem to like you much,' he said as he looked at Garaz, not bothering to repeat Auron's words.

'Hardly surprising, given my race,' Garaz replied. 'I am welcome far fewer places than I am unwelcome.'

'But I thought nowadays the Nine Kingdoms were inclusive of all races, since the last wars way back.' He'd definitely read that somewhere. 'There are mixed towns, and towns for other races in each of the kingdoms. I thought that we all...just got along.'

Auron laughed out loud. 'He doesn't know who the High Marshall of his own kingdom is, and he can't recognise one of the greatest heroes of the age, but he can happily bang on about race rights across the Nine Kingdoms,' the spirit mocked.

'Think of it this way,' Garaz said, turning to him, 'is your skin green?'

'No.'

'Then you are included. Good for you.' Garaz turned and walked off in the direction of the Crag.

Auron shook his head admonishingly at Nicolas and followed the orc.

He tried to understand what he'd said wrong. Failing, he jogged after his companions and on to whatever awaited them at this blasted Crag.

CHAPTER 14

'Ah.' Auron nodded sagely. 'The universal symbol for *bugger off or die*. How quaint.'

Totems were dotted around the entrance to Stranom Crag, which—being a simple black hole in the rock—would've been intimidating enough for Nicolas, even had it not been surrounded by sticks in the ground from which hung gaping skulls, each staring at the trio from empty sockets.

'It would appear that visitors are not welcome,' Garaz remarked dryly.

'Brilliant.' Nicolas sighed.

He stared at the skulls, which seemed to be slack jawed at the stupidity of what the group was about to do.

Besides the totems, there was no sign of anyone around the Crag's entrance. No guards and certainly no wagon.

Surely whatever's in there is pretty terrifying if it doesn't feel the need to post guards at the entrance to its lair?

His ember of courage dimmed with every passing second.

Maybe the place would be empty? Maybe the Deities were just playing a big practical joke on him? Who knew what higher beings would find funny? He bet they'd had a good old laugh when he was sick on the floor of the jail. The skulls probably knew what was inside, but he doubted they would talk.

'The answers we seek lie ahead.' There was more than a hint of apprehension in Garaz's voice.

'Yup.' He nodded, ready to turn and run.

'So why are you not moving then?'

'My body is refusing to let me take a single step closer to that place,' he admitted.

'Mine either,' the orc replied ashamedly. 'It is as if this place is giving off some tangible aura that tells every sense I have to turn and walk away.'

'Oh really?' He was glad it wasn't just him being…him. 'I thought I was just being cowardly.'

'You've flirted with it a few times since I've known you, but mostly you're just a bit whiny,' Auron said unhelpfully. 'Though in this case it isn't you. This place stinks of evil. Even I want to turn and walk away.'

The trio studied the opening, as if the rock were going to suddenly change. Or they'd develop the ability to see through it. But no matter the scrutiny, it remained a large, dark hole. Light seemed to have no reach an inch beyond the opening, like it wanted no part of the place either, which did nothing for the courage of people who needed to enter.

'This reminds me of the time I had to face The Goblin King of the Undercity. I—'

'I don't think this is the best time for an anecdote,' he said, unable to take his eyes off the ominous opening.

'There's always time for one of my '*anecdotes*,' as you put it, kid,' Auron huffed, jaw clenched. 'But fine, I tell you what. Daddy will go in first and you kids can stay outside and be all scaredy.' It seemed pride beat apprehension as Auron strode indignantly towards the opening.

At least he didn't have to go first, especially as the light from Auron's aura vanished the minute he entered the Crag, as if it had swallowed him whole.

After a brief but loaded pause, the spirit's head appeared from the opening and gestured for them to follow. Heart pounding and legs feeling like jelly, he forced one foot in front of the other as he approached the Crag. His one comfort was that Garaz seemed to be experiencing similar difficulties. Focusing on the people he needed to rescue, most specifically the girl, he pushed himself onward, overcoming whatever dread the entrance radiated, to enter Stranom Crag.

Inside, the aura pushing against them vanished. Now all he had to contend with was fear of the unknown, the dread of failure, and the prospect of imminent pain and death. He wished he'd waited outside.

In his longing, he made the mistake of looking back towards the entrance. His eyes had almost adjusted to the dark, but the light from the entrance blinded him, and he needed to wait for his vision to clear again. The only positive thing was that there were no immediate signs of life directly inside the cave, just rock and moss and moisture.

Directly ahead of them, a single passage led down. The only light source they had was Auron, but he seemed a bit dimmer inside the cave. The thought of whatever could diminish the aura of a spirit was something he was trying not to dwell on.

Barely being able to see made the initial going slow, as they inched carefully through the passage, intent on not tripping. It was worse for Garaz as he couldn't see their walking lamp, so the orc put a hand on his shoulder as he followed him deeper into the cave on the narrow and uneven path. It was slightly annoying how Auron was able to navigate the passage confidently, tripping being a mortal concern and all.

Other things the spirit didn't have to be concerned by were the closeness of the walls, the humidity that was already soaking his shirt, the drips of water from the stalactites on the ceiling, and the fear of injury. He was trying not to focus on the negative and...failing miserably. The quietness didn't help, leaving him alone with his thoughts as everyone was too afraid to speak for fear of being heard by the wrong ears.

Eventually, reaching a point where it became lighter, the illumination provided by fluorescent fungus clinging lazily to the rock, they took a moment to rest. At least he didn't have to guide Garaz anymore, feeling ill equipped to be responsible for anyone's safety. The irony of that and the reason he was here wasn't lost on him.

'This is worrying,' Garaz whispered. 'We should have come across a guard by now. At least some sign of life. The necromancer's fort was teeming with guards, so why none here? This place must be occupied, or why the totems at the entrance?'

'What do you think, Auron?' Hopefully a professional opinion might ease their anxiety.

'I think that whatever's down here is so bad that it thinks no one would dare intrude on it. Either that, or it's really stupid.'

If Auron's strategy was to double his anxiety, it had worked spectacularly.

'What did he say?' his orc companion enquired.

'He isn't sure.' He tried to spare Garaz the butt-clenching fear coming over him right now. If orcs clenched their buttocks? Or even had buttocks?

Auron made a show of glaring at Nicolas, an indicator that his mistranslation of the spirit's words wasn't appreciated. The hero opened his mouth—probably to rebuke him—when they were interrupted by something that sounded suspiciously like singing.

The sound of singing in this dark place was so strange that it took them a few moments to come to the realisation that there must be someone to do the singing and that it was getting closer. Once both these shoes dropped, and with nowhere to actually hide, he and Garaz pressed themselves to the rock wall as tightly as they could and waited.

Just a few metres ahead, a figure emerged from an opening in the passage they hadn't noticed, due to their angle to it. In the poor light it was difficult to make out any particular features, but Nicolas did catch sight of a face with colourless, almost grey skin, decorated by red sores. Were they just confined to the figures face? He couldn't tell due to the dirty black robe that covered the rest of its squat form. Turning away from them, thankfully, the stooped figure shambled in the direction the group had been heading, carrying a small tray as it sang off-key and merrily to itself. Though he couldn't hear much of the song, the parts he caught seemed to concentrate heavily on virgins and blood, quite graphically. Thankfully the figure took the atrocious song with it as it limped down the corridor and out of sight.

'I know many a bard who would weep to hear music so brutally assaulted,' Garaz whispered, eyeing the direction in which the figure had travelled.

'What was that?' he asked, noticing the concern on Auron's ghostly features.

'A familiar.' Auron look grim. 'That means there are vampires down here.'

'Vampires?' he cried, a little too loudly.

Garaz started, either at the tone of his voice or what he'd said.

'Yup.' Auron nodded, frustratingly matter-of-factly. 'Familiars hang around bootlicking and serving vampires in the ridiculous hope they might get bitten one day and made like their masters. Fat chance. The undead leeches loathe the gross little hangers on, but they are handy for cleaning up after the odd bloody massacre or two. Best the poor creatures can hope for is a lifetime of servitude. Worse, they're around when a vampire gets angry and get the full brunt of it.'

Undead leeches? Bloody massacres? *Vampires?*

'Vampires don't exist,' he protested stubbornly. 'They're make-believe... Like elves.'

'On the contrary,' Garaz corrected, 'elves were very real. They simply left the world as we know a thousand years ago.'

'Yeah, some pretentious crap about it being the time of the younger races, if the stories are to be believed.' Auron scoffed. 'But yeah, they were real, and so are the forces of the undead. Get used to it, kid.'

As easy as that, was it?

'If we are dealing with vampires then our situation is grave indeed,' Garaz noted without a hint of irony.

'Nice pun.' Auron chuckled. 'The orc is funny.'

"*Your* situation is grave indeed,' Nicolas corrected.

His companions turned and looked at him quizzically.

'I'm going home.' And he meant it. 'First mercenaries then a necromancer and now...now, there are vampires. Well, that's it, gentlemen. That right there is my line. I'm done.'

His ember of courage vanished as if a bucket of water had been poured on it. He'd reached his limit, and it was vampires. He had no business down here and was going to rectify that immediately.

'You can't just go home, kid,' Auron argued.

'Watch me.' He began to back down the corridor. 'I'm so out of my depth here it isn't even funny. I wish you both the best of luck, and I'll happily go find that Sir Eldric guy as soon as I leave this cave. I'll make sure he brings a whole army down here.'

'You cannot just—' Garaz began.

'Oh, I bloody well *can* just.' He turned quickly back in the direction the group had come from. If he looked at his companions any longer, he would end up staying. He had to cut the cord here or never. Were those footsteps he could here? Yes, and they were coming from the route to the exit.

'Go,' Auron whispered urgently as he pointed to the tunnel from which the familiar had appeared.

Moving quickly but quietly, the trio slipped into the side tunnel. This one was thinner, forcing them to walk in single file, but they progressed at speed. Soon they emerged into what appeared to be a storeroom. Just like the tunnel, it had been cut from the rock but with no thought towards smooth edges. Jagged rocks poked from the walls and ceiling, and only part of the floor was covered in wooden decking, on which sat shelves holding mining equipment and a group of large barrels. They made for great cover, and the trio secreted themselves behind one in the far corner of the room to take stock of their situation.

'Looks like you're tagging along after all, kid,' Auron noted smugly. 'Nice to have you on board.'

He didn't dignify that with a response. What was there to say? He was trapped, his choice gone. Instead he glared at the spirit, who looked utterly pleased with himself. This was interrupted by Garaz lightly tapping his shoulder.

'Can you ask Auron what he knows about vampires?' he asked in a whisper. 'My own knowledge is limited to myth and legend.'

After clearing his throat—worried his voice would be strangled by the fear of the creatures Auron had said were in these same tunnels—he was about to repeat the question when he saw the look on the spirit's face; he had heard it himself.

'They are gross, blood-drinking creatures who think themselves above the living, in a nutshell,' Auron answered with a look of distaste. 'They see it as a gift to be bestowed only on those truly deserving and have a superiority complex that makes the most inbred noble look modest. Actually, that's just the Elevated, the ones who can pass for human. The others, the Ferals, are pretty much just animals they use as guard dogs. Or attack dogs, depending.'

'Are these *Elevated* here?' Garaz asked after Nicolas relayed Auron's information.

'Yeah.' Auron mimed spitting on the floor. 'Only the Elevated have familiar servants as it makes them fancy, if you see gross subhuman vampire groupies as a marker of social status. They live in small groups, so there isn't much competition for food. There are probably just three or four of them and a handful of Ferals for security.'

'How do you *deal* with vampires?' he asked, shying away from using the word kill as he had no desire to kill anything. Ever.

'In my travels, I've found that lopping the head off is a pretty reliable method of *dealing* with anything,' Auron replied with a wink. 'Though a piece of wood through the heart will do just as well. They are notoriously flammable too. Sunlight kills them, but you'd have to be some kind of genius to lure a vampire outside during the day. They are quite careful about that.'

He didn't want to picture a situation in which he had to try to *lop* the head off anything. Though if it were a choice between that and having his blood drained by some creature with the munchies, he would give it a go. At least he had a sword. His hand tightened on the hilt. Garaz had his stolen club, which seemed more than a little inadequate, a thought which seemed to have occurred to the orc as well, judging by the look on his face.

'I suppose they are working for the necromancer?' Garaz mused.

'Hardly.' Auron snorted as Nicolas repeated the spirit's words. 'They hate necromancers more than anyone else. They see being undead as an exclusive club and take a very dim view of anyone who tries to break into it by running around raising zombies and whatever. Historically, they tend to make a pretty nasty example of any necromancers they come across.'

'So, no one likes necromancers then?' he said to himself after repeating Auron's response to Garaz.

'They don't even like themselves much.' Auron chuckled. 'I'd hate myself if I was a corpse-bothering psychopath.'

He found himself looking back the way they'd come. In his mind, he could see the whole route home. He could even see inside his house—his mother busy organising the baskets for their daily deliveries as his father brought hot, fresh bread from the ovens. It might as well be in another continent now. Would he ever make it back there? The chances seemed less with each passing hour.

The green hand on his shoulder popped Nicolas's little bubble and brought him right back to the present. 'You cannot go back, Nicolas,' Garaz said softly. 'We can only go forwards. I, for one, will not leave innocents to die down here whilst I have breath in my lungs. Whatever dangers, I will face them until the end our journey has in store for us. It is the right thing to do. I know you know this and have the courage to stay with us.'

His companions had a very annoying habit of being right. The orcs words stoked the ember enough that he could continue. Where else would he go anyways?

'I'm staying.' He was unsure whether it was his courage or no discernible exit that kept him here. Either way, he was with them. And if he was stuck here, he should at least try to do some good.

'That orc has a big pair on him, kid,' Auron remarked, impressed.

'That is a strange compliment, but I shall receive it with gratitude,' Garaz replied.

There was a very strange moment when no one was sure exactly what had just happened. Garaz was looking directly at Auron, who was looking back at him in surprise. Nicolas looked between the two, slack-jawed.

'You can hear me?' Auron's tone was excited.

'And see you,' the orc confirmed. 'A pleasure to meet you finally, Dawnblade.'

'You're damn right it is.' Auron smiled before addressing Nicolas. 'It seems your burden as messenger boy is at an end.'

Great. The one thing useful thing he could actually do was now gone. What did he have left to offer? Wracked with self-doubt, he forced a smile. 'Enjoy listening to his stories,' he muttered, slightly petulantly, under his breath.

'How is it you can see me now?' Auron asked, ignoring his remark.

Garaz took a moment to contemplate this. 'Maybe because I am fully dedicated to this quest, and therefore your unfinished business? Though that is only a guess. Who knows how the world of ghosts works?'

'It'll do.' Auron smiled. 'Though maybe the afterlife simply cannot contain my charisma for too long. And I'm a spirit, not a ghost. I don't wear a sheet, big fella.'

'Does he always talk in that way?' Garaz asked Nicolas.

'Way more than he ought to.' He smiled.

Auron ignored the jibe, seemingly too busy being pleased that someone else could see and hear him.

'What's our next step then?' Nicolas asked, not eager to get going but not wishing to stay here chatting either.

'That door,' Auron said confidently, pointing at a small wooden door built into the far side of the chamber.

'You seem very certain.' Garaz did not.

'You have to be in situations like this,' the spirit replied. 'We need to find those people as quickly as we can and preferably without letting anyone know we're here. We know there are people roaming the passage out there, which leaves...that door.'

He did appreciate Auron's dedication to making sure the vampires didn't know there were potential meals strolling around their inner sanctum.

'But what if someone's in there?' he couldn't help but ask.

'Then you deal with them.' Auron shrugged, making a sword-slashing motion with his hand, just to be clear.

'The logic is sound enough, I suppose,' Garaz mused as a stood up carefully, scanning the room first for signs of another presence.

The room remained empty, and the trio emerged from their hiding place and made carefully for the door.

'This cannot be a coincidence,' Garaz whispered as he looked at the mining tools laid out on the racking near them, the picks and shovels with drying mud and dirt on their sharp edges.

He had to agree. The chances of both the vampires and the necromancer randomly deciding to do a spot of digging were very slim.

A groan made them freeze where they stood. It didn't sound like the moan of a beast or monster, more like the sound of someone who'd just woken up and really didn't care for it.

Moving slowly, the trio turned in the direction the moan had come from. Attached to the nearest piece of racking was a black metal chain, which led down to the shackled wrist of a figure lying on the floor.

'It's her,' Nicolas said with a big smile—his first actual smile in days.

CHAPTER 15

She was exactly as Nicolas remembered her, except for being tied to a wooden rack...and unconscious. He was surprised how much detail he'd retained from that brief glimpse through the cage, but it was all there: the beautifully pale skin, the short auburn hair, sculpted cheekbones, and the cute nose. It was strange for his heartbeat to quicken from something other than fear.

'Hey, kid.' Auron clicked his smoky blue fingers in front of his face. 'Standing in the middle of a vampire's lair isn't the best time to get all dreamy eyed.'

'Ah yeah, sorry.' Hopefully, the poor lighting in the room hid his blushing.

'You look a little tall for a familiar.' The girl had one of her green eyes half open and was eyeing them suspiciously.

His mouth opened and closed a few times, but no words came out. He blushed again, and this time Auron and Garaz could definitely tell.

'We are not with them.' Garaz helpful filled the awkward silence. 'My friend here saw you on the wagon, and we came to help you and the other prisoners. My name is Garaz, shaman and spell weaver. This is...'

'Nicolas Percival Carnegie,' he blustered, adding a small bow.

'You really want everyone to know your middle name, don't you, kid?' Auron chuckled in disbelief beside him.

He chose to ignore the amused spirit.

'Nice to meet you,' the girl's tone was curt as she rose and brushed dirt from her dress as best she could with one hand bound.

There was something about the way her hair bobbed as she moved that made his heart skip a beat. From the look of her, she'd been roughed up badly. He had to do whatever he could to help this girl. He took a step towards her.

'Stop,' Auron cried, trying to grab him and pull him back. His hand passed through Nicolas, leaving a chill where a touch should've been.

He stopped. Why was Auron alarmed? Whatever made him jumpy had to be bad.

'Her neck,' Garaz said simply.

The bob of her hair had revealed a thin neck as pale as her face, save for the two bloody circles on it and the small trickle of blood that ran from each.

'Vampire,' he cried, jumping back, landing almost behind Garaz.

The girl looked at Nicolas and Garaz in confusion for a few seconds. 'Oh that,' she said with a cheeky laugh. 'Yeah, they bit me. Turns out they don't like how I taste. The vampire who bit me spat my blood back out like some really spicy food. It was so funny. Earned me a beating, but still funny. So yeah, no vampire here.'

'You understand we cannot take your word for that,' Garaz said levelly.

The girl looked annoyed but seemed to concede the point. 'Well, if it helps, I don't want to drink your blood,' she replied with a sarcastic grin.

'That is exactly the sort of thing a vampire trying to trick you would say,' Auron interjected.

'I'm sorry.' And he really was. 'We need real proof before we release you.' He prayed to all the Deities that she hadn't been made into a vampire.

'I'm chained to a wooden rack.' There was more than a little attitude in her voice now. 'What would you like me to do, exactly?'

'Draw the sword,' Auron told Nicolas.

'Why?'

'The blade is reflective,' the spirit replied. 'Vampires are soulless, blood-drinking lowlifes and therefore cast no reflection. If you can see her in the blade, she's good.'

Drawing the sword from its scabbard, he marvelled at how beautifully reflective the blade was, as if it weren't metal at all. Carefully, he angled it until he could see the girl reflected in it, poking her tongue out at him playfully.

'Happy?' she asked.

She was alive. Not only that, but she hadn't been turned into a vampire. He couldn't believe he'd actually managed to reach her, yet here they were. Emotions surged through him, infatuation and relief being chief among them. Thinking back to one of the adventure stories he had actually read as a child, he knew exactly how to act in this situation. Dropping to a single knee, he held the sword towards her in his open palms, his head bowed slightly.

'Fair maiden,' he declared, completely caught in the moment. 'We have journeyed far and faced many perils to come here, rescue you, and deliver you from this place of evil. I pledge my sword to freeing you from this evil lair and seeing you to safety.'

As soon as he felt the silence around him, reality set in again. What in the Underworld had he just done? Had he just repeated something he'd read in a children's book? Whatever the explanation, he had just made a colossal fool of himself. Rising and sheathing the sword, he did his absolute darndest not to make eye contact with anyone else in the room. But it turned out he didn't need to. He could feel their surprised gazes as if they were hot pokers branding him. With an I, for idiot.

'Where did that come from?' Auron asked, eyeing him suspiciously. 'Been at your mother's romance novels, have you?'

'Doesn't matter,' he muttered quietly, shifting awkwardly on the spot, wishing the ground would swallow him.

'That was quite...an experience,' Garaz said diplomatically.

'Hey, Sir Romancealot.' The girl was staring at him. He couldn't quite look her in her emerald-green, and annoyed, eyes. Though his quick glance did also show him a glint of amusement. 'First, how dare you assume my gender.'

Her face shimmered as if turning to liquid. The features seemed to ebb and flow into and around each other, changing until they hardened again. Into...him. Somehow, his own eyes were staring back at him, his own mouth smirking at him. The strangest part was seeing exactly what he would look like in a dress. He would never forget that.

'And secondly, how dare you assume I need rescuing when I'm quite capable of saving myself.'

Again, the shimmering appeared, but this time, it engulfed her whole body. The shimmering body became liquid and then seemed to shrink, until it hardened again into the body of a small child, who looked up at him with that same smug smirk, despite looking ridiculous in clothes that were now many sizes too big. The metal bonds around her wrist clattered to the floor. With another shimmer, the girl was back to the form in which Nicolas had first seen her.

'Still so keen to whisk me away so I can adore how brave and heroic you are?' She grinned.

He made a few non-committal, nervous sounds.

'You are a shapeshifter?' Garaz asked in awe.

'You're the brains of the operation then,' came the smiling reply. 'You can call me Shift. And for the benefit of your friend here, I will not be referred to as her, she, fair maiden, my lady, or any other such crap. They, their, or them will do nicely.'

'What? How? Who?' he stammered, finally finding some words.

'They...their...them,' Shift replied carefully, as if addressing a buffoon, which was exactly what he felt like.

'It is a pleasure to meet you and see your astounding ability.' Garaz offered Shift a slight bow.

'It comes in handy,' they replied. 'Until today, I didn't realise it made me unappetising to vampires. Every day is a learning day.'

'Ask them how they do that?' Auron was excited. He obviously had never met a shapeshifter before.

'Now isn't the time for backstories.' Nicolas was desperate to leave the room, hoping the memory of him making an utter idiot of himself could be locked away in it forever. Though he knew it would be stuck in his mind, popping up an random moments throughout the rest of his life.

'Who is he talking to?' Shift asked Garaz as they looked at him warily. 'He's done that a couple of times now. Is someone else here or is he a bit mad? And I don't mean madly in love...I already know the answer to that.'

Their teasing infuriated him. Honestly, his own stupidity infuriated him, but he didn't like being reminded of it.

'Now is not the time for backstories,' the orc replied simply.

'Fine.' Shift shrugged. 'But we need to get out of here now. After I made the vampire sick, they beat me and brought me in here. I don't think it'll be long before they decide to come back and finish the job.'

'I thought you didn't need rescuing,' Nicolas muttered petulantly to himself. This wasn't going anything like he'd thought it would. Stupid adventure stories.

Looking up, he found Shift nearly nose to nose with him, and they did not look happy.

'For the record,' they snarled, *you* are not rescuing me. *I* am letting you tag along while I escape. I could turn into a rabbit and hop out of here and leave you to die screaming when a group of angry vampires find you. However, I do not want that on my conscience. Understood?'

He nodded sheepishly.

'Have we met before?' Shift asked, suddenly studying him intently.

'You saw me when you were on the wagon,' he replied. 'You passed me on the bridge.'

'Yeah.' Shift didn't seem convinced. 'I remember that, but I swear I've seen you somewhere else before that.'

'I am sure that it will come back to you,' Garaz interjected. 'Until then, I suggest that we do not dally.'

Shrugging it off instantly, Shift made towards the door, Nicolas and the others following close behind. Before the door, Shift paused for a moment, as if something had just come to mind. They looked back over their shoulder at him and the others.

'I don't want to completely ruin your whole rescue plan.' Nicolas knew that only bad news could follow such a sentence. 'But you ought to know that the rest of the prisoners are already dead. I'm the only one left.' Despite the matter of fact way they delivered the news, he could tell it weighed heavily on them. 'Sorry.'

His heart sank, something that seemed to be reflected in both Garaz and Auron. All those people, dead. Out of all those he had seen in the wagons, he had saved a grand total of two. What could he have done differently? Could he have pushed himself harder? Had his ineptitude made him as responsible for the deaths as those who'd killed them? Battling his doubts head on, he forced them back out of his mind. Whilst they were still in the middle of a vampire lair, he had saved no one, even himself. He could mentally beat himself up when they were all safe, if they made it that far.

* * * *

Beyond the door, a series of nondescript rock passageways led through what was proving to be a large, maze-like complex. It seemed the further into the Crag they ventured, the greater the aura of death the place gave off until you could almost taste it, as if blood and decay were as much a part of the air as oxygen. At some points in the cramped passageways, faint screaming seemed to echo around them, as if even the rock walls were in despair over the terrible acts being committed within their confines.

It wasn't just the hot air and dread that weighed heavily on him. His doubts hadn't left, instead manifesting as an all-consuming guilt which was distracting him from everything going on around him. Even from the outset of following Auron he knew he'd be of no use, that he didn't have what it took. Whether or not he'd even rescued the two individuals with them now was up for debate. Forcing his mind back to the wagon, he tried to picture each of those he had seen, each of those he had allowed to die. Had they suffered? He would never know. The urge to just give up was strong. He prayed for the souls of those he had failed.

'Don't play the numbers game, kid,' Auron whispered as he came up alongside him.

'I'm sorry, what?'

The spirit's white eyes seemed to be staring straight into his mind. 'The numbers game,' he repeated. 'Comparing the number of people you saved to the number you didn't.'

'I wasn't—'

'Yes, you were,' Auron interrupted firmly. 'All heroes do it. Here is a fact, kid: you can't save everyone. It's cold and sad, but it is what it is and cannot be changed. Yeah, mourn the people who died, but their deaths aren't on you. They're on the bad guys who killed them. Usually, by the time I get called in, something's already gone wrong, people have already died. I can't change that. All I can do is make sure as few die after I'm around as possible and that those who do the killing are punished.' The spirit smiled at him warmly, maybe for the first time. 'Be thankful for the lives you did save.'

'I think you could argue that both the people I *'saved'* did most of the work themselves.'

'Doesn't matter,' Auron said with a chuckle. 'You were there to save the orc, and you were here to save Shift. *That's* the important thing. You may think you aren't capable and want to leave, but I can guarantee that ninety-nine percent of people in your shoes wouldn't have made it to the fort, let alone here.'

'Let's tally up how many are saved when we actually get out of here,' he replied in a breezy tone to mask his very real anxiety about them all dying in these caves.

His mind was a confused mix of shame and pride. Auron was right, but he still couldn't quite let go of the fact that he wished he'd done better. He would have to reconcile with that at some point. Maybe when they weren't in a vampire nest. He needed to focus on getting out of here.

Shift swore they remembered the route used to bring them to the storeroom and from there, the route from which all the prisoners had been brought into the Crag. This made it a simple matter of backtracking to the exit. Apparently, there was a lower side entrance around the other side of the Crag that was more concealed and ideal for things like unloading prisoners without being seen.

'Are they sure they're leading us the right way?' Auron asked as they turned to enter another tunnel identical to the last four they'd crept down.

'Are you certain of the route?' Garaz asked their guide. 'You said that the entrance was a lower one, yet we seem to be ascending slightly.'

Shift stopped and turned to them just before a crossing in the tunnel. Even in the dim light, the hint of confusion on their face was clear. Not encouraging.

'Yeah.' They ran a hand awkwardly through their hair. 'Maybe they hit me a little harder than I thought. It may have scrambled a few lefts and rights.'

'Brilliant,' Auron huffed, echoing Nicolas's own thoughts on the matter.

'So, you don't know where we're going?' he asked, still shy of making eye contact with them after he'd gotten swept up in the moment earlier.

'This leads somewhere,' they replied with a shrug.

'That seems to be the best plan we have at the moment,' Garaz said grimly. 'Being on the move is better than staying here, which is much better than going back to where the activity is.'

'Ask them what we can expect,' Auron suggested. 'What did they see before being dragged here?'

He asked the question.

'I only saw three vampires,' they replied thoughtfully. 'We were brought to a big chamber and lined up by those gross servant things. Then the vampires came in. Arrogant scum walked the line like we were some sort of menu, and they were selecting their courses. Once they had decided, they started killing...' Even though they looked away, their sadness was palpable as they trailed off.

'That sounds about right,' Auron muttered.

'Are you certain of that?' Garaz asked.

'Nothing's certain,' the spirit retorted, 'but it aligns with what I've seen.'

'You've hunted vampires before?' Nicolas asked.

'Let's just say we have history, kid,' Auron confirmed, jaw clenched.

'Okay, I have to know,' Shift interrupted, their face illuminated by the neon moss growing on the cave walls. 'You guys are talking to someone, aren't you?'

'Ghost,' he answered simply.

'You have a ghost?' Shift said with raised eyebrows. 'Nice.'

'I am not a ghost, I am a spi—' Auron began in an aggrieved tone.

Sounds of movement nearby caused Auron to stop and listen. Quickly, the group looked for cover. Again, there was none. All they could do was press themselves to the wall and hope luck was with them.

From the intersecting tunnel came a group of familiars doing something that resembled marching. Poorly. The shambling group, none of them really in line, carried old spears marred with rust. Thankfully, they were concentrating so hard on keeping what little formation they had that none glanced towards Nicolas and his companions, and the odd parade soon disappeared.

'They're looking for us,' he moaned quietly.

'No,' Auron said, watching the tunnel entrance. 'I'm not sure what that was, but it was no hunting party.'

'This way.' Shift pointed straight ahead of them, in a different direction to the armed familiars, much to his relief.

Before long, the tunnel opened out on one side, and they found themselves on a walkway overhanging a much larger room. Something about the room made his skin crawl as he crossed the threshold. The chamber was the biggest the group had seen since they'd entered the Crag and by far the most intricately decorated.

Shift tensed as they looked out across the chamber below them. 'It was here,' they said sombrely. 'This is where they killed all those people and nearly killed me.'

A terrified shiver ran up his spine as he finally noticed the faded bloodstains on the floor, obvious even from his elevated perch.

CHAPTER 16

C ut from the rock itself, like every other part of the Crag, the chamber the group overlooked was vast. Unlike the rest of the Crag, however, effort had gone into making this room look like something out of a castle, albeit a dark mockery of one. In stark contrast to the rest of the complex, the floor was even and the walls smoothed and rounded, with images of skulls chiselled into the stone, lit by rows of torches instead of dim cave moss. Four banners adorned the walls, each with different disturbing imagery that made him squirm if he looked at it too closely.

The centre of the room was dominated by a large, ornate banqueting table with heraldry carved into it. Whilst different again from the banners, it was equally as upsetting to the eye. Five throne-like chairs surrounded the table, each placed before a dinner setting. Golden plates, cutlery, and goblets caught the glint of the torchlight.

'Told you I knew the way,' Shift remarked with a glib whisper.

The room stank of blood, and he felt sorry for his new companion, despite their breezy attitude. He couldn't imagine what butchery they must've witnessed here. To the side of Shift, Auron was staring at each banner in turn with disgusted recognition.

'Down,' Shift cried in a low voice.

Obeying instantly with no visible sign of danger, he decided he must be getting used to this. He was having plenty of practice.

Concealing themselves behind some weather-beaten barrels discarded on the walkway, they peered below them. The troop of familiars emerged from an entrance directly beneath them, entered the room in their bastardised formation, and passed the table to approach the large double doors at the far end of the room. The door was covered in skulls, and he didn't believe for a second that they were carved. At least there was no space in the rows. If he did die here he'd hate to have his skull mounted on some vampires door for all eternity.

The familiars split into two lines as they reached the door, flanking it on either side and holding their spears at attention. Were they supposed to be some kind of honour guard? Two without spears moved to the door itself while another, marked by his rusted helmet, stood proudly—if not quite upright—at the head of the group.

'This is the poorest looking honour guard I've ever seen,' Auron remarked as he watched the familiars organise themselves.

From somewhere beyond the double doors, a gong sounded, the deep note resonating through the air around them. At the gong's signal, the two familiars at the door pulled the handles. With a wheezing effort from the creatures, the door opened with a creak that sounded much to Nicolas like an inhuman scream.

The familiar with the helm shouted something, and the familiars in the honour guard held their spears forward in salute.

Emerging from the dark opening was a trio of deathly pale youths, flawlessly groomed in well-styled tunics. Though their hair looked messy, it was obviously the result of calculated effort. Entering the room, the trio looked around them with disinterest, as if perpetually bored. The leader sighed as he walked to a seat.

Behind them were a group who looked like children, but were somehow quite obviously...not. They almost skipped along, their mischievous, malicious eyes darting around their new surroundings. Giggling, the leader—a young girl with long black hair—took her place at the table.

Stomping into the room like a herd of angry beasts came three figures in blood-red armour. Two wore bat-winged helms, but the leader displayed his shaven head, which was tattooed with yes, more skulls. Marching to a seat with his proud chest puffed out, the leader regarded everything around him as if it annoyed him greatly.

Following the warriors were shambling individuals in rags, none of whom looked entirely human. Fierce, blood-red veins covered their white skin, and their noses and teeth were somewhere between animal and human. They stalked the room carefully, as an animal might when it expects to be prey soon.

Once each group had taken its place at the table, the large gong sounded again thrice more, shaking his skull. The familiars stood to even more rigid attention, and a fifth group entered the room. This trio swept in wearing noble finery, the air of dominance preceding them, and long capes trailing behind. The lead figure had slicked, black hair and exuded evil from every pore, his bright red eyes looking at everything as if he owned it. His presence filled the room as he seated himself at the head of the table with a knowing smile. Nicolas found himself hugging more tightly into the rough wood of the barrel he hid behind.

Everyone seated, the double doors were pushed closed, and the honour guard filed away. New familiars entered the room, bringing carafes of a red, thick liquid. As the creatures filled goblets, glares of suspicion and distrust fired between those at the table.

'The Five Families,' Auron whispered through gritted teeth.

'The what?' Nicolas asked quietly.

'Not the time for exposition, kid,' the spirit replied firmly.

Drinks served, the familiars scurried away, leaving their masters to their business. The tension was palpable, and it seemed to him it would only take an errant fart for them to start fighting each other. The exception was the head of the table, who sat back, fingers steepled, with a look of immense satisfaction on his face. Eventually, he rose, picking up his goblet in a fluid motion and raising it high into the air.

'Brothers and sisters,' he greeted in a melodious, accented voice. 'I welcome you all. I hope that proceedings can be cordial now that we all have a drink in hand.'

'What a welcoming invite, considering you are normally much less courteous towards us,' the vampire with the inhuman face said in a phlegmy voice. 'Your *invitation* made it appear as if we were to be your only guests. We did not realise we would be sharing a table with *these*,' he finished, with a contemptuous wave at the others around the table.

'Me too,' boomed the scalp-tattooed warrior, obviously annoyed by the slight but choosing to overlook it. 'I would not have come had I known I had to dine with such—'

'Don't use a bad word,' the girl interrupted in a playful voice, putting a finger to her lips. 'That would make you naughty. And naughty people get punished.'

'Do not threaten me, child,' the warrior replied swiftly, his face darkening.

'How many scars has that child given you?' the vampire with the stylish tunic said in a flat, bored voice. 'Pretty lame.'

'You *dare*, you impudent dog?' the warrior roared as he rose, slamming his fist on the table while his other hand went to the hilt of his sword.

'Trust you to be the first to go for a weapon,' the misshapen vampire tutted disdainfully.

'Do not cross me, Varyn,' the warrior snarled, pointing an accusing finger. 'Don't believe yourself special just because you are slightly smarter than a Feral. I would still be doing you a mercy to cut your grotesque head from your impure shoulders.'

'Enough.'

The voice from the head of the table was almost a whisper, but it echoed around the chamber, and everyone complied instantly. Nicolas winced at the shiver the voice elicited from him as the warrior seated himself, making a show of not really wanting to, before each of the four bowed their heads slightly submissively to the figure.

'As amusing as your squabbling is,' the vampire at the table's head began, 'it is not why you were summoned.' He took his seat, swirling the goblet in his hand lazily in front of him. 'I admit it is unprecedented to have the heads of all Five Families in a single room. We all know the things we have tried to do to each other in the past, sometimes successfully. However, the fact that this gathering is so unusual has your curiosity, does it not?'

Clearly, this vampire had read the room correctly and was basking in that fact as the others grudgingly acknowledged it.

'We're listening,' Varyn said, curiosity as evident in his tone as suspicion.

Seemingly determined to draw out the moment, the figure remained silent. He judged it perfectly too; he spoke just before any of the others became annoyed enough to speak up.

'Ascension.'

It was a single word, but it had a dramatic effect on the rest of the room, who alternated between laughter and shock. Even the vampire in the stylish tunic, as aloof as he'd seemed until now, scoffed openly.

'You brought us here to tell us a bedtime story?' The girl giggled.

'I came all this way for this nonsense,' the warrior snapped, slamming his armoured fist on the table...again.

'You speak of myths, nothing more,' Varyn cried in his slurred speech, outraged.

The black-haired vampire allowed the uproar to wear itself out as he watched, bemused, from behind his goblet. The two vampires who had escorted him looked equally amused. Eventually, the raucousness died down, and the rest of the vampires were silent again.

'Myth, you say?' The vampire grinned coyly. 'Are you sure of that?'

The other vampires seemed wrong-footed by his assured tone. Unsure glances were exchanged.

'What do you know?' the warrior asked bluntly.

'Many things, my dear Barus.' The vampire chuckled. 'For instance, I know that ascension is indeed possible.'

The other vampires waited for the black-haired vampire to elaborate. After a few moments of silence, they finally became impatient with his theatrics.

'Well?' Varyn asked, testily.

'I have an ally,' came the reply. 'One who can facilitate ascension for us.'

'Who is your new friend, Count?' the girl asked.

The count looked off to his side, something catching his attention. 'That I will not say. Not here.'

'We deserve to know,' Barus rumbled. 'Ascension concerns us all.'

'We must meet this ally and find out whether he can actually do what he claims,' Varyn added. 'Or if you have been fed a load of nonsense.'

'No, you must not,' the count replied. 'Because the wheels are already in motion. I haven't invited you here to join in a new endeavour. I have invited you to make you part of something that is nearly complete.'

'You dare begin this without so much as a word?' Barus challenged.

'The word is being given now,' the count replied with a lazy wave of his hand. 'That is why you are here. Though I am no longer sure any of you deserve to be a part of it.'

Again, there was a general uproar.

Again, the warrior rose, hand on the hilt of his sword. 'You disrespect us!' he roared. 'We are leaders of four of the great vampire families, and you disrespect us as if we were pathetic familiars.'

The tension in the room became electric as the count rose from his chair and slammed both his palms onto the table with an echoing boom. 'Am I in a room with four leaders?' he snarled, finally displaying an emotion other than smugness. 'Are any of you deserving of the title? You are, all of you, slipping in your old age.'

'Slipping and sliding.' The girl giggled as her two escorts danced behind her.

'Slipping how?' Varyn asked suspiciously.

The count sighed and rolled his eyes theatrically. 'My honoured brothers and sisters, leaders of vampire families whose names are dreaded by mortals, eternal hunters of the night...surely, I am not the only one here who can smell a human in the room?'

There was another human in here? Twelve vampires raised their noses and sniffed the air around them as Nicolas tried to spot this human. If they were trapped, maybe he could help them escape somehow with a diversion or... Then it clicked. The human in the room was him. At that exact moment of realisation, twelve heads turned in his direction, fangs bared and hissing wildly.

'Welcome, honoured guests,' the count saluted with his goblet, smiling viciously.

'Run,' Shift cried, already doing what they'd suggested.

CHAPTER 17

H e bolted towards the opposite end of the walkway, following his companions in a frantic dash to put as much distance between themselves and the vampires as possible. The opening ahead of him seemed miles away. In his peripheral vision, figures were moving from the banqueting table. Deities, those creatures were fast. As he made the end of the walkway, there was a *thump* behind him. Risking a quick glance, he saw one of the creatures crouched where he'd just been hiding. It must've leapt up from the ground. By the Deities, how were they supposed to escape creatures who could do such feats? With a roar, the creature charged him.

'Come on,' Shift urged from the front of the group.

They ran. With no idea of their direction, and with violent death on their heels. They crashed into walls thoughtlessly in their mad dash. Skin was scraped, but the alternative at slowing down was worse. Footsteps behind him told him how disturbingly close the vampires were getting, but he couldn't look back. If he turned and saw them up close, fear might root him to the spot.

Bursting through an opening in the tunnel, he emerged into another large storeroom full of crates and barrels. The room was well lit with torches, and at the far end, Garaz was waving at him to hurry. How had he gotten so far behind the rest of his group? Was he really so slow? How had the vampires not overtaken him already?

With each step toward Garaz he felt the pain in his legs, but he pushed himself onward.

Looking concerned, the orc raised his arms high. 'Shield your eyes,' Garaz shouted before saying words Nicolas didn't understand.

Even with his eyes covered, the bright flash made him stumble, but he thankfully kept his footing. Removing his hand and blinking away the last few spots of brightness, he turned his head. Behind him, a group of four vampires were scrambling around at the door, cursing and rubbing their eyes, temporarily blinded. He wished the orc could have summoned a fireball to immolate them all, but this would do. Now to make the most of it. Pushing himself ever harder, he charged on.

'Nice.' He smiled as he dashed past his orc companion and out of the room.

Beyond the door were a set of steps leading upwards.

'Bar the door,' Auron shouted as he stood on the steps next to Shift, watching Nicolas and Garaz come through the door with relief.

The orc slammed the wooden door shut and wedged a barrel behind it. Would that be enough to hold them. They were fast, were they strong too? His answer came not far up the stairs when wood splintered behind them. Their makeshift barricade had fallen, barely slowing the vampires.

As they raced up, he could see the top of the stairs beyond Shift and the open door promising another barrier for those chasing them. Then the vampires sprang their trap.

One of the armoured vampires appeared at the top of the stairs, emerging almost at leisure. The creature unclasped the lower half of its helmet, revealing a predatory grin and sharp yellow fangs. His hope turned to dust. They were cornered. The ones behind were on their heels. They were done.

The vampire got here too fast. Then he knew that the vampires could have finished this at any moment, they were toying with them, having sport. There was no hope.

Without breaking stride, Shift charged headfirst at the vampire, whose confident grin slipped as its prey showed no hesitation or fear. As Shift neared the top of the stairs, the vampire drew its sword and stood ready to receive them. Shift had no weapon that he knew of. Were they insane?

But Shift did something unexpected. They threw themselves at the legs of the vampire, crashing into its shins and taking both the vampire's legs from under it as the sword rose to strike. The force of the collision caused the undead creature to fall forwards with a cry and tumble headlong down the stairs.

The rolling vampire passed straight through Auron, who looked vaguely annoyed and violated, before continuing towards him and Garaz. He leapt to the side of the stairway and pressed to the wall, his orc companion doing the same on the opposite wall.

Rolling past them harmlessly, the vampire collided with the pursuers, who were somehow a mere couple metres from him. Had they really been that close? Those chasing them had been so focused on nearly catching their prey that they hadn't paid attention to what was going on ahead of them. Their armoured kin, who'd picked up a bit of speed on his descent, crashed into the four vampires, knocking them into a snarling heap, with several cries of pain as the ridiculously over-spiked armour pierced undead skin.

'Idiots.' Auron laughed.

As Nicolas reached the top of the stairs, he helped Garaz pick up Shift, who seemed in pain.

'Throwing myself into a pair of armoured legs wasn't the most painless idea I've ever had,' they grumbled as they rose, rubbing their shoulders.

'Effective, though.' Garaz smiled warmly.

Wasting no more time, the group ran into the room at the top of the stairs and closed the heavy iron door behind them. The key had been left in the lock, and Garaz turned it with a metallic click. That ought to hold them a bit longer...he hoped.

The room they were now in looked almost like a well. It was circular with brickwork walls that extended high above and far below them, with a single walkway straight across the precipice, leading to a similar iron door, which was closed.

As the others began to cross the walkway, he looked down, and the sheer drop on either side was so overwhelming that he could barely form a coherent thought—except this one: that walkway was definitely not wide enough. The sudden thumping on the iron door got him on it anyway, and he followed his companions and trying to block out the oppressive smell of decay in the room.

Halfway across, he heard something that sounded like the wind, but he couldn't feel it on his skin. Everyone stopped and looked at each other in confusion. The sound grew, and he quickly realised it wasn't a single sound but many overlapping into one large wave of noise bouncing from wall to wall around them.

He edged carefully towards the side of the walkway and tentatively peered over, the others doing the same. Way below them, the ground was dark and strange. He couldn't quite focus on it, and with horror, he knew he wasn't looking at ground, rather a mass of bodies, which were writhing restlessly. He couldn't see the eyes on him, but he felt them.

The overlapping hissing that had made the wind-like noise soon devolved into snarling, which grew in pitch.

'Ferals,' Auron cried in disbelief.

'There must be hundreds of them,' Garaz said, similarly struck.

'So much for *three or four of them and a handful of Ferals.*' He sighed, kicking himself for not having expected this.

Far below, the Ferals were clambering on one another in a futile attempt to reach the walking meals above them. They moved like crazed animals, and he was glad he couldn't make out the details in the dark.

'Good luck with that.' Shift laughed.

'They do not need luck,' Garaz said, pointing.

Several of the Ferals were digging their claws into the brick wall and using it to climb up. Soon, the idea caught on, and the circular wall was writhing with ascending Feral vampires.

'Run,' Shift cried, in one of the most obvious statements he'd ever heard.

He'd thought he'd nearly reached his limit, but the sound of scuttling and growling getting closer was a fantastic motivator.

Luckily, because the well beneath them was so deep, they had plenty of time before the ascending Ferals would reach them. As the last of the party—Nicolas—passed through the door at the far end of the walkway, Garaz slammed it shut and locked it. Nicolas's sigh of relief as the lock clicked was almost euphoric.

He doubled over, panting hard, but at least Shift was doing the same. Even Garaz seemed to be fighting the urge to wheeze. Only Auron stood tall, looking towards the end of the short tunnel ahead of them. His face was grim, but Nicolas was too concerned about his own current state to worry about it.

'We can't stop for long.' Shift stood upright and stretched their back. 'We don't have much time.'

'We don't have any time at all.' Auron's voice was heavy.

Looking up, he saw defeat in Auron's face, and his heart sank. Both he and the orc looked towards the end of the tunnel ahead of them. Shift couldn't see Auron, but they soon picked up the cue from him, searching the darkness ahead.

'You can all come out now,' commanded a familiar voice from beyond the tunnel's end.

Nicolas looked at his companions, and his dread and sense of finality was echoed in their faces. As if to put an exclamation point on their predicament, frantic scratching began on the other side of the iron door, accompanied by hissing and snarling.

'Do not make us have to come in after you.' The voice was almost playful.

'What do we do?' he asked, his panic spreading as he saw nothing reassuring in the faces around him.

'Face our fate,' Auron said before adding in a heartfelt voice, 'I'm sorry, kid.'

He searched the spirit's face for an answer, a spark of hope, but there was only the look of a man sure he was about to have company in the afterlife.

Shift looked towards the tunnel and brushed themselves off, face reluctant yet defiant. 'On our terms then,' they declared firmly, walking towards the opening of the tunnel.

Was that bravery or insanity?

Garaz gave him a solemn pat on the shoulder as he passed.

Taking a deep breath, Nicolas followed.

* * * *

Escape would be impossible now. In front of them, an impenetrable wall of spear wielding familiars, behind which their masters revelled in cornering their prey. At their backs, hundreds of Ferals clawed at the door, hungry for their blood...well, his mainly.

The real gut punch was how close they had come to freedom. In the corner of the large storage area he saw the caged wagon that had brought him here as much as it had Shift, some of the vampires arranged around it as if to purposely draw their attention to it. They must be so close to the exit. That only made the blow of being caught twice as painful.

Safely behind their servants, he saw all the vampires from the banqueting hall as well as a few others, wearing clothes that pointed to their family allegiance. At the head of the group was the black-caped vampire, reeking of self-satisfaction and evil.

The caped vampire paced behind his spear wall, looking at each of the party in turn, though *looking* was too simple a term to describe what he was really doing. His eyes seemed to bore into them, straight into their very souls, doing so with a haughty contempt that made Nicolas feel small. He was being looked at as he may look at a sandwich at dinner time.

'What a curious little group you are,' the count purred, smirking. 'An orc, a foul-tasting creature, a snack...and an old friend.' With a fanged grin he looked towards Auron.

'You can see me then,' Auron replied flatly.

'We, who have transcended mortality and conquered death itself, can see through the veil between the living and the dead.' The vampire smiled self-indulgently.

Nothing like a bit of self-aggrandisement.

'Vampires.' Auron rolled his eyes. 'And we aren't friends.'

The count feigned hurt. 'For shame, Auron of Tellmark,' he chuckled, 'I owe my title and power to you.'

'Only because I killed your predecessor,' he snarled. 'It wasn't a favour. If you'd been there, I would've happily killed you as well.'

'Lucky for me, I do not have the penchant for defiling temples that my predecessor had,' the vampire said thoughtfully before continuing. 'Please, I must know, how was the mighty *Dawnblade* finally laid low?'

From the look Auron was giving the count, Nicolas assumed that were he living, most of the vampires in this room would've already been slain.

'The ghost is the Dawnblade?' Shift whispered to him then gave him wide eyes when he nodded.

'I wouldn't give a disgusting creature like you the satisfaction,' Auron told the vampire.

'You call me a disgusting creature?' the count gasped, once again feigning offence.

'The disrespect!' The cry came from the familiar in the dented helm. He looked outraged to the point of exploding, his whole stumpy body shaking with fury. 'You dare insult a Lord of Death? You will pay for this. I will make you sorry for your words.'

'Calm yourself, Prax,' the count soothed. 'It is simply the last thrashes of an animal run to ground who knows it is done. It seems bitterness has lessened the great hero in the afterlife.'

Auron bristled but said nothing, undoubtedly determined to give him as little satisfaction as possible.

'Who knows that you are here?' the count asked after a pause.

'Ah.' Auron smiled. 'Now we get to the point of the show.'

'Show?' Garaz asked as the count glowered at Auron.

'We…you…should've been dead about five minutes ago. In my experience, there are two reasons a villain keeps you alive when they have you cornered. One, he wants to get off on the sound of his own voice. Two, he wants to know something. Obviously, the count intermingles both reasons beautifully.'

'This vampire cannot be that great,' Garaz mused. 'He is subservient to a necromancer.'

As the other vampires broke into a cacophony of outrage, the count glared murderously at Garaz. He evidently was not fond of spoilers.

'Your *ally* is a filthy necromancer?' Barus shouted, which was apparently the only tone of voice he had.

'Wow,' Shift smiled slyly. 'Vampires taking orders from humans is one thing, but a lowly little necro—'

"*Silence.*' The count's voice was like a fierce gust of wind, echoing from every wall with a tone that commanded obedience.

Nicolas and Shift flinched and covered their ears, and the vampires fell silent quickly. One of the familiars was so shocked by the sudden outburst that he dropped his spear, which clattered to the floor. Before he had a chance to retrieve it, the vampire child stepped forward and snapped the creature's neck with a sickening crack. The familiar fell into a heap atop its lost weapon.

'How dare you assume the Lord of all Vampires takes orders from a human?' the count snarled, fangs bared and haughty exterior melting.

Behind the count, the other vampires—leaders in their own right—blatantly took umbrage with him claiming dominance over them but were smart enough to read the room and keep silent. Though he did have a suspicion those words would come back and bite the count someday, and not in the neck either.

'When the ascension comes, even a certain necromancer will know his place in the order of things,' the vampire snapped.

'He made it sound like you were dancing to his tune.' Auron shrugged, seeming to love having a wound to poke at.

'You...' the count began angrily before finally collecting himself, 'are good, Dawnblade. You try to trick me into saying too much. Sadly, you mistake me for one of those simple bandits you usually spar with. Though, I admit surprise at how much you know.'

'It's really weird watching someone talk to thin air,' Shift muttered to him.

'Being able to see him is weirder,' he replied quietly.

'Part of me thinks I should have you tortured to find out what you know,' the count said as he looked at the group thoughtfully. 'But maybe keeping you alive for longer would be a mistake.'

'Can I eat the skinny human?' the vampire child asked, tugging gently on the count's cape as she bounced on the balls of her feet excitedly.

Was that his fate now, to be eaten by an undead child? The idea of any of these creatures drinking his blood sickened him. The idea he may be turned into a vampire himself was worse. Looking at the rusted spear tips pointed at him, Nicolas decided that if he had to die here, throwing himself upon those would be preferable. Ideally, he'd prefer to escape and live, but it seemed the universe cared little for his preferences. If the best he could do would be to cheat the vampires of a meal, then so be it.

The vampire considered this for a moment. 'No,' he said finally. 'We have no time for such frivolity. There are matters to discuss and events already in motion. No more distractions.'

The girl pouted slightly but said no more as the count clicked his fingers with a smile. As one, the group of familiars marched forwards, deadly spears closing on the party one shuffling step at a time. Despite his earlier decision, he still found himself stepping back from the advancing spears, only to find solid rock behind him. He tried to close his eyes so he wouldn't have to watch his impending death, but they seemed to bulge wider, as if hell-bent on taking in every detail. He wanted to pray, but what good were prayers in a place so evil?

His wide eyes caught a blur of motion at the far end of the chamber, and an arrow imbedded itself through the neck of the vampire Varyn with a wet *thunk*. He gurgled feebly as blood ran from his mouth and staggered to the side, inhuman eyes rolling back into his head.

'By Order of King Tyrus of Yarringsburg, I condemn you foul creatures to death!' Sir Eldric cried as he charged into the room, sword drawn, followed by a troop of armour-clad warriors.

CHAPTER 18

The soldiers filed out of the narrow opening behind Sir Eldric before forming a triangular formation with military efficiency. Shields locked together, they advanced on the vampires, several archers back at the door firing more arrows into the creatures and their servants. The projectiles felled familiars instantly, the vampires only hissing angrily as arrows pierced their skin. They appeared to be much more durable than their servants.

What surprised him most was the vampires' quick reaction once they realised they were under attack. The group reformed, the leaders moving back as their vassals stepped forward, claws and fangs ready and weapons drawn where they had them.

The familiars seemed at a loss, milling uncertainly as the soldiers bore down on them. Two fled, crying pathetically as they limped through an opening and out of sight—something the vampires would surely have issues with later. When the grubby servants did finally take action, it wasn't the kind he'd expected. Instead of reforming their spear rank toward the attackers, the familiars dropped their weapons and flung themselves into the path of the charging soldiers, seemingly elated to die in service of their masters.

Sir Eldric and his men set to dispatching the pathetic creatures. Swords carved through the air, and blood and limbs went flying. The servants died quickly, uttering guttural death cries as they fell, but Nicolas began to understand the goal of their suicidal tactic. Overwhelmed by the sheer weight of numbers, the soldiers' charge slowed until their momentum died altogether. Large bodies piled up around them in a very one-sided melee.

The sacrifice gave the vampires the precious seconds they needed to gather themselves and counter charge. As the soldiers cut down the last of the familiars, they found themselves set upon by fang and claw, many of the vampires using their supernatural agility to leap clean over the bodies of dead familiars and straight into the ranks of their attackers.

Formations quickly broke down into the scrum of battle, a blur of motion from which he could make out little detail.

But what he could see, he didn't want to: a head that flew through the air to strike the rock wall, fangs entering a neck as the man screamed and struggled to break free, claws raking bloody grooves into flesh before the hand was removed at the wrist by a sword. Terrible details that he would never be able to unsee.

All he could do was watch the carnage as if he were somewhere else, somewhere far away. And what he saw was that the vampires seemed to be gaining the upper hand. Though the soldiers were well armoured, the vampires had the superior speed and strength and were using both to great effect. As proven when the count punched straight through one of the soldier's necks with no more effort than plucking a flower. Nonchalantly, the vampire examined his blood covered hand as the soldiers body hit the floor.

Someone grabbed him by the hair, bringing him painfully back to the moment. Why had he just stood there helplessly? Yelping, Nicolas was pulled backwards until a strong arm wrapped around his chest. He flailed and kicked but was held tight in an inhuman grip. In his peripheral vision, he could see part of the head of the vampire that had him—the gleeful yellow eyes and fangs ready to sink into his flesh.

As the vampire moved in for the kill, a large, familiar green hand engulfed its face. From beneath the hand, a white light emerged, illuminating the vampire's face as it screamed, smoke pouring from its burning flesh. The grip on him went slack, and he leaped away from his attacker. When he turned, Garaz was clutching the creature to him as his glowing hand continued its work. The vampire spasmed until finally going limp, its body turning to dust before it even reached the floor.

'What did you do?' he stammered in shock.

'It has been hypothesised that healing magic would have a very detrimental effect on the undead,' Garaz said. 'Glad to see that it was correct.' He glanced briefly at the dust pile by his feet.

'You healed him to death?'

The orc smiled as he grabbed a spear from the floor and swung it ferociously. One of the vampires was making for the iron door, no doubt to let the Ferals in. The shaft of the spear struck the vampire in the side of the head with force enough to snap it in two and propel the vampire headfirst into the wall with a sickening thud. Wooden splinters fell to the floor, and a second later, the vampire joined them.

'Kid, draw your sword!' Auron shouted urgently from beside him.

Finally remembering that he actually had a sword, Nicolas drew the Dawn Blade and held it in front of him. The weapon and its weight felt alien in his hands. Could he even hold it for long, never mind use it? If something comes at you, swing the sword, he told himself, trying to steady his unchecked rapid breathing and the shaking blade he was holding.

'Turn and slice,' Auron shouted as something behind Nicolas seemed to catch his eye.

Doing as bidden, he put all his energy into a horizontal slice of the sword. The blade sailed through the air before him and hit nothing, the momentum of the strike almost turning him full circle as his arms pulled painfully against his shoulder joints.

'I meant slice down,' Auron said in exasperation.

He looked down, belatedly, and the vampire child was in front of him, looking up at him with faux innocent eyes and giggling. The sword must've missed her by a head. Preparing to swing again, the child had already lunged at him, digging her claws into his arm. Pain seared through him, and his arm weakened until it let go of the sword, very much against his wishes.

'Yum, yum.' The child laughed as Nicolas cried out in pain, licking blood from her claws and readying herself to pounce.

Unable to do anything but watch fate play out before him, his eyes became hypnotised by the vampires fangs until a makeshift wooden club sent the vampire child to the floor with a cry. Stepping away from the creature, he saw it scurry away like a scared insect.

'You need to learn to fight,' Shift snapped, grabbing him by the collar and dragging him towards the exit.

At the last second, he remembered to pick up his sword. Auron would be upset if he left it in a vampire nest, though that was the least of his problems right now.

By now, the room had turned fully in the vampires' favour. The soldiers had used their swords to keep the creatures at arm's length as best they could, but their numbers were dwindling as Shift and Nicolas made for the opening from which the soldiers had first emerged. The sound of metal scraping on metal and a roar of triumph signalled that the door to the Ferals chamber had been opened. The amount of the danger they were in seemed to increase by the second.

'Fall back,' Sir Eldric cried as the new threat poured into the room.

The Ferals entered the room like a storm. They had the vampires' speed and strength and the familiars' disregard for their own well-being, a deadly combination. Nicolas watched in horror as they threw themselves directly at swords, shrugging off wounds that would've easily felled a normal man.

This was the first time he'd seen them properly, and they were more frightening than the regular vampires. Their dull, leathery grey skin was a stark contrast to their bright red eyes, which held no semblance of their former humanity. Facially, they were more akin to bats, with large snouts and great, pointed webbed ears. They moved surprisingly fast on such misshapen limbs, and equally well on all fours or upright. There was truly nothing human about them save a vague recollection of how they'd once appeared. Did they understand what they'd become, what they were doomed to live as?

The retreat quickly became a rout as the soldiers fled for their lives, some stupidly abandoning their weapons in the need to get away from the oncoming fanged death. Nicolas and his companions made it into the tunnel as the line collapsed completely. He had made it from the room alive. It was a shame so many had not. How had he survived where seasoned warriors had fallen?

Bloody screams behind them urged them on as they fled the chamber. In front of them were Sir Eldric and several of his men, with several more behind them, though that number continued to dwindle as the vampires dragged down bodies to feast upon, some stopping to feed while others bounded over them to get to their prey. He didn't need to look back to see it happen, he heard the crack of their armour hitting the floor as they fell and the scrapping of metal on stone as they were dragged back by the ravenous horde. The way the men's screams were ominously cut off sent a chill up his spine. There was no going back, no saving them, just the frantic race to escape; a race of darkened corridors, claustrophobic tunnels, and terror. This time, the narrowness of the tunnel worked in their favour, negating the Ferals' superior speed and agility as the creatures bumped into each other and fought to be the first to feed.

'There,' Garaz cried as they turned a corner in the zigzagging tunnel and saw the promise of natural light ahead.

Seeing the sun so close gave Nicolas a determination to live, pouring all of it into his legs and creating one final surge of speed, one final burst towards freedom and safety. There was a blinding light as he burst from the mouth of the Crag. He moved so fast that he lost control of his own body, stumbling into and knocking over one of the skull totems. The wooden pole fell to the floor, the skull spilling from it and rolling along the ground, cracked and broken. He staggered a few steps, then landed on the floor in a heap.

Light turned into images after a few moments, and he could see what was going on around him. All his group had made it out of the Crag, along with Sir Eldric and four of his men. They all lay on the ground, panting with exhaustion in the sun. Auron stood amongst them in a completely neutral state as they all struggled to recover. It was strangely funny, and he was not at all sure why. He let out an involuntary laugh. They were out, they were alive. The sun in the sky was the most beautiful sight he had ever seen.

Hearing massed growling, he turned and looked back towards the entrance of the Crag. The opening of the cave was filled with Ferals, hissing and snarling at the prey they had lost but kept at bay by a line of light inches in front of them. Several took tentative steps forward, only to shriek and fall backwards as their skin sizzled and blistered in the sunlight. None of them made any real attempt to continue their pursuit. As animalistic as they were, they still had a keen survival instinct, it seemed.

'We made it. We're safe.' Shift laughed triumphantly.

'For now.'

The Ferals in the Crag's entrance parted slightly, and the count appeared, glancing at the light of day with pure disgust. Rage emanated from him as he looked at Sir Eldric.

'Your master will pay the price for having you desecrate our home, human,' the count snarled. 'The blood you have spilled here will be returned a thousandfold, and this king of yours shall rue the day he set you pathetic cattle upon us.' Then the vampire turned his head deliberately towards Nicolas and his companions. 'And the suffering you endure will make what we do to them look almost pleasant by comparison.'

'Why don't you come out here and say that, big man?' Auron challenged with a smirk.

'You do not want to still be out here come nightfall,' the count threatened before turning with a dramatic sweep of his cape and disappearing back inside the Crag. The rest of the vampires followed in turn, with a final challenging growl or two in the direction of their lost prey.

* * * *

With the vampire's threat still ringing in their ears, the group made good time away from the Crag. As much as they needed time to rest and recover, the sun wasn't going to stay up forever, and the threat of being brutally killed by vampires once it went down meant that the group didn't have time to dally. Garaz had hastily ministered to the worst of their wounds, including Nicolas's torn arm, but they had time for no more. Sir Eldric knew of a nearby outpost where they could find shelter before making their way back to Yarringsburg for serious reinforcements in the morning. Riding back would've been ideal; however, none of the horses Sir Eldric and his men had ridden to the Crag were where they'd left them.

As they travelled quickly, but cautiously, down the mountain, Nicolas couldn't help keeping half an eye on the sun's position, as if it would vanish should he take his eyes off it for a moment. He didn't know how Auron made a life from this. All the travelling to and fro was one thing, but then there was the constant mortal danger. Half of him wanted to ask the spirit, but the other half didn't want to know the answer.

Nobody spoke as they continued. Were they all trying to come to terms with what had just happened, just as he was? They were probably doing a lot better than him, having the benefit of experience. Though by the haunted looks on some faces he question how right he was about that. Even Garaz and Shift didn't seem complete strangers to a fight, since they didn't freeze like he had. For his part, he kept playing the scene over and over in his head. He should be thankful he'd made it out alive, but he just couldn't stop focusing on the number of times he nearly hadn't.

Reaching some trees, Garaz called the group to a brief halt. Though the soldiers seemed edgy to continue, and Nicolas definitely was, they indulged him. Quickly, the orc pulled up herbs from a nearby tree, setting them on a piece of bark before lighting them with a flint. Rising, he wafted the bark from side to side, spreading the fine-smelling smoke the herbs produced.

'It will mask our scent,' Garaz explained, noticing his quizzical expression.

Nicolas didn't understand why the vampires wouldn't just follow the scent of burning herbs, but if this week had proved anything, it was that he understood little.

Satisfied with his work, Garaz ushered the group to continue.

'I've never run from a villain's lair,' Auron grumbled as the group navigated a short but steep hill. 'And now I have twice in as many days.'

'I'm glad I could be part of it,' he muttered petulantly in response.

'What's the matter with you, kid?' Auron asked, blue features tinged with distaste.

The question was a hammer bursting the dam holding back a reservoir of frustration, anger, fear; of everything that had happened over the last few days that he hadn't time to deal with. 'I'll tell you what's the matter.' The frustration increasing the speed and pitch of his voice with every word. 'I've lost count of the number of times I've nearly died in the past couple of days. I've been thrown off bridges, beaten, locked up, snuck around vampire lairs, and now I have to listen to some dead guy bang on about his glory days and how hard this is on him.' Was he being hysterical, maybe, but he couldn't stop himself now. 'Well, you know what, *I'm* still alive, but I won't be for much longer because a vampire king...yeah, a vampire king has marked me for death. And all so I can help some guy who died answering the call of nature who's decided to do everything in his power to make sure I join him in the afterlife at his earliest convenience.'

For a moment, Auron glared at him, his jaw set indignantly. But it only lasted a moment before his face sagged and there was only sadness in it. 'Okay, kid,' he said, before turning and walking away.

He knew instantly that whatever he'd been through, it was no excuse say what he had just said. He wanted to call Auron back, to apologise, but the shame of his behaviour prevented him from doing it.

'Who is he shouting at?' Sir Eldric asked as he and his men looked nervously toward him, hands on the hilts of their swords.

'Ghost,' Garaz and Shift replied simultaneously.

'Oh.' Sir Eldric seemed unsatisfied by the explanation, but unwilling to press the matter, maybe for fear of the answers. 'Very well then.'

The High Marshall and his men went on their way, with Shift following closely behind.

Only Garaz remained, looking at him with understanding. 'Do I need to tell you that was harsh?'

'No.' He looked in the direction in which Auron had gone and wished he could take it back.

'Give him a moment,' Garaz said, following Nicolas's gaze. 'As brash as he may seem, his death is recent. It must weigh heavily on him, despite appearances.'

'I'm just frustrated with...all of this,' he admitted with a sigh.

The orc laughed aloud, a deep and heartfelt sound.

'What?' he demanded, preparing to take offence.

'You seem under the impression that you have been quiet about this fact until now.' Garaz chuckled. 'Trust me, my friend, I understand how this has affected you, even without you mentioning it at every opportunity. You just need to understand that you are not alone in your frustration. We all feel it and deal with it in our own way.'

'Oh,' he said as he considered this. 'I suppose I may have complained a bit.'

Garaz's expression indicated he was under exaggerating.

'Sorry,' he said, suddenly finding something interesting about his feet so he didn't have to look up and confirm the shame he was feeling.

'As I said, I understand,' Garaz said. 'We have all been thrust into unfamiliar and dangerous territory. The key word is *we*. None of us are alone in this. We are facing this together and will get through it together.'

With that, Garaz made to follow the rest of their party but stopped when Nicolas didn't follow. He gestured for the orc to continue. He just needed a minute to set his head straight.

Leaning against a tree to catch his breath and racing mind, he turned at a rustling in the bushes behind him. For a second, he thought it might be Auron…but he wouldn't rustle anything. Then it had to be one of the party coming back for him. What was coming for him was a figure brandishing a spear, bursting from the bushes with an angry cry.

The figure came at him in a slow, shambling way, suggesting he didn't attack people with spears often. In fact, he came on so slowly, uttering his phlegm-filled curses, that Nicolas had plenty of time to simply step out of the spear's path. Unable to stop himself quickly enough, the figure was forced to continue to the tree itself, the spear impaling the trunk with a deep *thunk*.

With moans and curses and quite a bit of flailing, like a child having a tantrum, the stumpy figure attempted to dislodge the spear, which was stuck fast. So invested in trying to free his weapon, he didn't notice Nicolas walk up behind him and unsheathe his sword. Feeling almost guilty, but knowing it was very necessary, Nicolas hit the figure across the back of the head with the hilt of the sword, sprawling them out instantly on the floor.

'Huh,' he exclaimed, looking at the hilt as if seeing it for the first time.

That played out pretty well. Maybe he was learning something, after all?

'Well done, kid,' Auron exclaimed as he emerged from the bushes to Nicolas's side, without rustling them. 'You caught a bad guy.'

CHAPTER 19

P rogress to the outpost was much slower going with a prisoner in tow. Not only was the familiar naturally slow, but he was belligerent, doing everything he could to impede the group's progress while cursing them as loudly as he could. This situation improved slightly when the soldiers escorting him drew their swords to encourage more cooperation and Shift stuck a sock in his mouth. Though he now wasn't purposely tripping over every stone he came across, the soldiers still had to practically drag him along to make any sort of time against the lowering sun.

As it was about to set, the outpost came into view ahead of them, set just off the main roadway and surrounded by a sturdy wooden fence. Nicolas hoped it would be good defence against whatever the Crag would unleash upon them after dark. The outpost itself was a small place, made up of a single large building with a storage shed at its side and a couple of watchtowers, whose torches were currently being lit as the natural light dimmed. Relief rushed through him at the sight of the building and the safety it promised. The only place he would've been more relieved to be right now was home. Deities, how he missed home.

Yarringsburg guardsmen waited to greet them at the gate, becoming quite flustered when they realised the High Marshall himself was amongst their grubby and beaten number. This flustering became worse when they were informed a vampire attack may be imminent. As commands were shouted and the garrison readying, they were ushered quickly into the outpost. He could've fallen to the ground and sobbed tears of happiness as the heavy wooden beam was put in place across the gate behind them. Torches were lit around the perimeter and defences manned as the group made their way into the barracks. Hopefully, the torches would give any creature with an aversion to fire cause to keep away, but somehow, he doubted it.

The first point of visit for Nicolas, Shift, and Garaz was the barracks' kitchen. He wasn't sure if they were drawn there of their own will, or if the smell of fresh-cooked stew had hypnotised them, taking control of their bodies and minds. Either way, he was famished, and the audible tummy rumbling of his companions suggested they were too. Being part of a battle then fleeing in terror had roused his appetite like a bear woken by a villager poking it. He didn't even care if it tasted as good as it smelled; he was in no mood to be particular in his eating.

Though the benches in the kitchen were little more than hard pieces of wood, they felt almost luxurious when Nicolas took the weight off his aching legs. Without discussion, the group scoffed their hearty meal. For a blissful moment, they were all engrossed in eating, even Garaz, who was doing an impressive job of ignoring the looks he was getting from the soldiers in the outpost. Auron stood in the corner of the room, looking out the window at the ever-increasing darkness in the sky. Whether he was looking for something or just trying to avoid watching them eat, a task he could never perform again, Nicolas didn't know.

When he'd finished his food—though he wished the bowl would magically refill itself—he couldn't put it off any longer. He had something he needed to say. Considering who he was saying it to, he decided to be more careful with his words. 'Thank you for saving my life,' he blurted awkwardly in a way that was completely contrary to how he'd rehearsed it in his head.

Shift looked up from their own food, swallowed the mouthful they were chewing, and smiled brightly. 'You're welcome,' they replied. 'I'm sure in a second or two, you would've kicked that little vampire girl's butt.'

'You reckon?' There was no chance.

'Oh yeah,' Shift replied with a devilish half smile. 'A natural warrior like you, I'm sure you were luring her into a false sense of security before dealing the killing blow.'

The sarcasm was laid on more thickly than he felt necessary, and he flushed first from embarrassment then annoyance, which seemed to please Shift greatly.

'That is incorrect,' Garaz said as he put down his spoon and regarded their new companion. 'He would have dealt the killing blow once he had gotten to his knees, raised his sword, and made a knightly speech to distract his enemy. That is how it is done, is it not, young Nicolas?'

Shift spat out the mouthful they were chewing as they laughed aloud, while the orc smiled genially at him. Even though Auron was facing away from them, Nicolas could see his intangible body shaking with laughter. Despite himself, he laughed too. Maybe a bit of brevity was what everyone needed right now. After more food.

'Am I ever going to live that down?' He chuckled.

'Well, if the vampires have their way, you won't have to live with it long,' Shift said, and the rest of the group laughed again, despite the reality of the statement.

'Do you have to be an ass?'

'I just open my mouth, and out it comes,' Shift replied with a cheeky wink.

'Yeah, well, maybe you should pick a form less pretty so people know what to expect when you start talking,' he joked back, flushing again when he saw the look on Shift's face.

They rested their chin in their hands and looked toward him in a mock dreamy fashion. 'Well, I say, good, sir. Thou doth flatter me.'

He chuckled and poked out his tongue. He retracted it when he noticed Auron had turned and was looking intently at Shift.

'I've never met anyone who could shapeshift like that before.' The spirit was studying them carefully. 'Only wizards, who needed potions or enchantments to do it. I've never come across someone who could do so naturally.'

Nicolas sensed the question Auron wanted to ask and asked it.

'I don't know how I do this,' Shift replied after some thought, studying the back of their hand. 'It's just a natural thing...that I do. I just picture what I want to become and, bam, I'm it. I mean, I can't turn to any old thing. It has to be living, so no inanimate objects. I can't become a chair or anything. I also can't go above or below a certain size.'

'Have you been able to do this since birth?' Garaz asked.

'I assume so,' they shrugged. 'I don't remember any of my early life. It's all blank. One day, I was just there, on a road, with no idea who or where I was. When I realised I could change shape, it was a shock, to say the least, especially to the highwaymen who tied to rob me. I was disorientated and changed gender and race multiple times in front of them. I don't think I've ever seen anyone flee as fast. Except, of course, us when we had vampires on our heels.'

'What did you do?' he asked, enthralled.

'Eventually, the highwaymen regrew their spines, came back, and found me. They saw potential in my gift and introduced me to some people, and I did the only thing I could think of with a skillset like mine—stealing stuff from rich folk. Turns out I was a natural.'

'What a noble use of such a gift,' Garaz said with a raised eyebrow.

'Not at all.' They laughed. 'It has been an adventure, though. Funny story. Just before those mercenaries caught me and took me to the Crag, I was in the forest on my way to a job. I was starving, missed breakfast. So, I see this pretentious kid with a backpack that looked pretty full. I hid behind a tree and shifted into a troll. The look on this kid's face when I emerged was priceless. I reckon he must've soiled his britches. He ran away pretty fast, and I had some good food.'

Feeling his grip on his spoon tighten, he looked at Shift as the realisation their words conjured set it. Half of him couldn't believe it, the other half was mad as a charging ogre.

'I did not *soil my britches,* thank you.' Seething, he sat back, glaring across the table at Shift.

Shift looked at Nicolas oddly for a second then burst out laughing. '*That's* where I know you from,' they cried, actual tears rolling down their cheeks. 'I didn't twig with your face mashed up as it is, and your jacket is ruined. Oh, Deities. Sorry about that, but a person's gotta eat, and your face really was hilarious.'

'You're an ass.' He wanted to say a lot more than that, but he had been made a fool of, again. He thought anything else he may say would only contribute to it. Instead he sat back sullenly.

'Huh,' Auron said to himself more than anyone else. 'Seeing a troll in the forest was just a coincidence, after all.'

'Look, I am sorry.' Shift's voice took a sincere tone. 'I steal stuff, and I was hungry. Nothing personal, okay?'

They held out their hand, and he looked at it distastefully for a second but finally shook it. He supposed that, in hindsight, it was kind of funny. It felt strange thinking back to the forest, like a whole different time, when he'd only just set out from…He stopped himself. He wasn't going home anytime soon and longing for it was only torturing himself. He just wished it was easy as that to stop thinking about it, but it lingered regardless.

'Seems I have something in common with vampires,' he said, after taking his hand back. 'Meeting you left a sour taste in my mouth too.'

Shift offered him faux applause with an impressed smile.

'Though I hate to bring this conversation back to more serious events,' Garaz began, looking at Auron, 'I had a question about the aforementioned creatures. I do not understand this family system of theirs. Admittedly, I know little about them save the popular myths and legends, and I had always taken them for pack creatures, just not to such an extent.'

'Apparently, it used to be a lot simpler hundreds of years ago,' Auron replied. 'They would live in small groups, like you say, with no bearing on each other except when it came to competing for hunting grounds. Over the years, as they began to believe in their superiority to mortals, they evolved their own bastardised version of a society. Now, all vampires are in one of those stupid families. *The Battle Born*, *The Flawless*, *The Regressed*, *The Eternal Young* and *The First*. They all have their own customs, creating new vampires based on their philosophy. The Battle

Born only turn warriors, for example.' The spirit looked away back toward the direction of the Crag in distaste. 'Yet as much as they try to polish it up, they are still the same pack animals they always have been, fighting with each other over territory in some animalistic parody of our own kingdoms. Them all coming together just doesn't happen. Whatever this *ascension* is, it's something big.'

'Then we must discover their intentions,' the orc said thoughtfully as Nicolas related what Auron had said to Shift.

'We do have a source of information,' Shift said as they finished the last mouthful of their stew.

'Indeed, we do,' Sir Eldric interrupted.

Nicolas hadn't heard the High Marshall enter the room, and neither had his companions, given their reactions. Why was every look Eldric gave them from down his nose? The vampires wouldn't care who was noble and not when they came.

'Our prisoner requires questioning,' the High Marshall continued. 'Though it would normally be against my better judgement, I think you should be present. You've been in the low creature's lair and may've seen something that will allow me to wrongfoot the fiend so I can get to the truth of the matter.'

'Oooh, an interrogation.' Shift sounded almost playful about something Nicolas thought was very serious.

'Let us not dally.' Sir Eldric punctuated this by turning haughtily and leaving the room.

Nicolas and his companions quickly followed him.

* * * *

There was a great deal of noise as he approached the door to the jail. The racket appeared to be generated by a single voice, shouting and cursing in a slightly rasping tone. Whatever the owner of the voice was unhappy about, they intended to make it clear to all around.

"*You!*" the familiar shouted, pointing an accusing finger at Nicolas the moment he entered the room. 'You will pay for this. All of you will pay. You will all die. No immortal gifts for you, just bloody death. I tried to kill you for the disrespect you showed my master. I failed, but it doesn't matter, because all your times are coming soon. Verrrrrry soon now that the sun is setting.' The familiar sneered at him, looking infinitely pleased with itself.

'You should have no issue getting him to talk, sir,' one of the soldiers who stood guard in the room offered. 'The foul little bugger has yet to shut up.'

'I will say nothing to betray my masters,' the familiar screeched as he held the bars of his cage, spittle hanging from his dry lips.

The familiar looked almost comical in his defiance, though Nicolas did pity the poor man. His short and stumpy frame showing many signs of uncleanliness and neglect, easy to confirm by his smell. His hair was patchy and straw-like, yet greasy and matted at the same time. No wonder he wore that stupid-looking helmet.

'I disagree,' Sir Eldric said levelly. 'You shall tell us what you know of your own volition, or my men shall beat it from you.'

Nicolas winced. Yes, the pathetic creature had tried to kill him, but he wasn't sure he could stand here and watch him beaten. Even knowing he'd been complicit in who knew how many deaths, he couldn't feel anything but sorry for him.

'Kid, you need to question him,' Auron said from nowhere.

'Me?' He snorted.

'I know a thing or two about getting information from people,' the spirit said, looking at the angry familiar. 'These guys get beaten by their masters regularly. The soldiers will break their knuckles before he talks. We need to play it differently. The familiars take pride in their masters, despite the fact they are disgusting, blood-drinking monsters. Play on that. Because you are the least threatening in the room, he will more likely want to show his status to you. Plus, he is already angry at you and bound to slip if you can get him ranting.'

'Thanks.' He wasn't sure if he'd been complimented or not. 'May I?' he asked the High Marshall, indicating the prisoner.

After a second, Sir Eldric stepped aside and motioned for him to continue. He seemed curious as to what he was going to do, as was the familiar. To be fair, Nicolas was quite curious himself.

'Hello, Prax,' he began in a friendly tone.

The familiar was instantly wrongfooted. Good. He shuffled back in his cell and eyed Nicolas warily. 'You know my name?' Prax asked uncertainly.

'I heard it in the Crag.' He smiled. 'Seems like you're a bit above the rest of your friends.'

'I am First.' Prax puffed his small chest up with pride, yet still looked pathetic. 'Head of those who serve the ones who bridge the gateway between life and death.'

'Nice.' He gave an impressed nod. 'Laying it on a little thick, though.'

Prax looked at him quizzically.

"*The ones who bridge the gateway between life and death*. They're only vampires.'

'They are beyond humanity and above all others,' the familiar snapped petulantly.

'Are they, though?' He scrunched his face. 'They sit in dark, stinking caves drinking blood. They don't seem to be above much, save rats.'

Judging by the look of shock and anger on Prax's face, his gambit was working.

'Oh, we will see who is above whom soon enough when the ascension happens.' Prax snarled.

In response, Nicolas blew a raspberry. Maybe this interrogation stuff was easier than he'd thought.

The familiar looked apoplectic. 'When the necromancer casts his spell, and the thrice-cursed sun is blotted forever from the sky, my masters will ascend to the surface and take what is due them. Humans will become little more than cattle, save for the honoured familiars that serve their masters so faithfully. We shall be elevated and ascend to their side to rule for all eternity,' Prax practically spat at him.

'Preposterous.' Garaz snorted. 'No wizard has the power to perform such a feat, and there is no spell to do so in existence. Utter nonsense.'

'Oh, but this necromancer has a spell and the power to do it.' Prax sneered, evidently loving showing everyone how brilliant his master's plan was. 'The exalted and mighty count, who I have the honour to serve, taught the necromancer the ancient secrets of the blood. He showed him how to draw power from it, the power of others, and make it his own. Soon, he will use that power, and the world will change forever, and it will be glorious.'

'That is what he has been doing with the other wizards...syphoning them?' the orc roared, appalled. 'That is blasphemy and an abomination of the natural order. How could he dare? Why would he?'

He had not seen Garaz angry before and hoped never to again. His yellow eyes tinged red as he ranted at the familiar.

'So that he may be elevated.' Prax was smug in demonstrating his knowledge. 'He will do this service and be raised to immortality as thanks.'

Something about that statement struck Garaz, who calmed down and looked in confused contemplation.

'What of the captives, the ones who came with me?' Shift asked darkly.

'Tribute and fodder.' Prax smiled maliciously through gapped teeth. 'Paid by the necromancer to seal the deal. When the Ascension happens, my masters will still need an army to take what is rightfully theirs, and now we have plenty. When the sun goes out, waves of Ferals will go forth and kill, spreading the spell until the whole world is dark and the food chain is righted again.' The familiar glared at Shift before adding, 'Save for you and your foul-tasting blood.'

Shift picked up a book from the desk just inside the jail door and hurled it angrily at the bars.

Prax jumped back with a whimper as the book struck the bars and fell to the floor with a thud. Then the familiar approached the bars once more, laughing at the reaction he'd elicited. 'Throw your little tantrums whilst you can,' Prax croaked. 'You are running out of time.'

'Insanity,' Sir Eldric scoffed. 'If you seriously believe humanity will stand idly by and allow this, you are as foolish as your masters.'

'Oh, don't worry, good sir.' Prax chuckled. 'You will see the truth when Yarringsburg runs red with blood.'

'You dare...' Sir Eldric threatened, stepping forward, hand on the hilt of his sword.

'Yarringsburg will be where it all begins.' The familiar smiled. 'It will be the capital of the new vampire nation and a holy city for all immortal beings.'

'You will die on our walls long before a single undead creature sets foot in my city,' Sir Eldric shouted.

'Walls will not be a problem—'

The familiar's words were cut short by Sir Eldric's fist.

Prax had pressed his face to the bars, making his nose an excellent target, and Sir Eldric had obliged. Nicolas winced at the sickening crunch accompanied by a spurt of blood. Prax cried feebly before falling to the floor, unconscious.

'Forgive me.' Sir Eldric looked pensive as he rubbed his fist. 'I could not stand idle and hear those threats against my people.'

'You only did what we all wanted to,' Shift said with a sympathetic smile.

'Quite.' The High Marshall looked at the prone familiar. 'When this matter is done I shall take pleasure in arranging this *creatures* execution.'

'It is sad that such a pathetic creature's life should end in such a way,' Garaz said.

'Yes, well, you would say that, would you not, orc?'

Sir Eldric's words caused a palpable tension in the room.

Garaz stiffened and even Shift looked more than a little awkward.

'Meaning?' The orc's tone was defensive already.

The High Marshall turned and looked at Garaz properly in the eye, for the first time, despite the height difference. 'Meaning that, yet again, inhuman creatures are causing mischief,' he said simply. 'And once again, humanity pays the toll.'

'The crimes of these conspirators are against life itself, not just humans,' Garaz retorted.

'And yet it is humans who suffer, humans who are paid as tribute to these creatures, and a human city that is under threat.'

'The familiars are actually human,' Shift said, offence in their voice. 'And the vampires certainly aren't of other species.'

'I would hardly describe these familiars as human any longer.' Sir Eldric rounded on Shift. 'And as for the vampires, they are inhuman creatures, plain and simple. Today, vampires trouble us. Tomorrow, maybe the orcs again. The next day, maybe whatever it is that you are, shape changer. There is always something, and it always comes from outside of us.'

'Now, wait a minute...' Shift said took a step forward, fists balled.

The air in the room went from tense to toxic in the space of a few sentences. Two soldiers in the room had their hands on the hilts of their swords and were ready to draw. He needed to do something, fast.

'We have all had a difficult day,' Nicolas said, stepping between Shift and Sir Eldric. 'I don't think fighting amongst ourselves is the best way to end it.'

After a moment of exchanged glares, Sir Eldric was the first to relent. 'Apologies.' The High Marshall took a breath. 'I have lost men today, and the threat on my home has made me lose my decorum.'

The apology came to him and neither Shift nor Garaz, but he turned and looked at Shift, regardless.

They backed down, grudgingly, after a second or two. 'Accepted,' was all they would say.

Gradually, the tension in the room lessened and everyone seemed, while not at ease, at least not ready to begin throwing fists.

'So, what do we do now?' he asked the room at large.

'I ride to Yarringsburg within the hour to raise defences,' Sir Eldric stated. 'You may stay here tonight to rest, but after that, you are to go home. Your part in this matter is done. And I do mean that this time.'

The High Marshall swept from the room without another word.

CHAPTER 20

His eyes opened to darkness around him. Why had he woken? It was surely the middle of the night. It was surprising he'd slept at all, with the lingering death threat on his head, but a semi-comfortable bed seemed to have negated that. Along, no doubt, with the safety of the wall and armed soldiers around them.

Sir Eldric and an escort of two men had left the outpost quickly after the interrogation. Nicolas had attempted to dissuade him from travelling at night, but the High Marshall's mind was set, insisting that time was of the essence and the safety of Yarringsburg of greater importance than his own life. As much of a pompous idiot the man seemed, you certainly could not cast aspersions on his sense of duty.

Thanks to the faint light coming through the window from the torches outside, he could make out some detail of the room, the illumination showing him that both Garaz and Shift slept soundly—though in the orc's case, it was obvious from the noise he was making. Sitting up, he saw the night sky distorted through the glass window of the room. The idea to step out beneath the stars and get some fresh air suddenly became a very tempting one.

Tentatively, he raised himself from the bed, not wishing an errant creak to wake his companions. He rose and tiptoed from the room, just about avoiding the obstacles between him and the door. He was as surprised as anyone else might be that he made it to the door without waking anyone. Making his way out of the room and down the corridor, he reached the main door of the barracks.

He opened the door slowly, only to be greeted by a familiar blue glow as he stepped outside. 'Can't sleep?' Auron said from beside the door.

He turned to look at his companion and immediately had to turn away as the light cast by Auron's intangible body stung his eyes. Taking a second to recover, he turned back more slowly. 'I just thought I'd get some fresh air,' he answered finally. 'What about you?'

Auron looked up into the sky then back at Nicolas, half-smiling. He was leaning against the wall of the barracks, but at the same time appeared to be floating inches above it. He wasn't sure he would ever get used to the way Auron didn't connect with his surroundings.

'Don't sleep anymore,' the spirit replied. 'Eternal wakefulness is just another joy of being dead.'

Sudden awkwardness overtook him. He had something he needed to say but didn't really want to start the conversation, because admitting to doing something wrong felt awful. But he already felt awful, so he needed to just get on with it and exorcise the demon. He briefly teased his brain with how the conversation would go, before realising that nothing went the way he planned anymore.

'About that,' he began. 'I am sorry about what I said before, the way I spoke to you. It was unfair.'

Auron chuckled. 'Don't worry about it, kid. I've been called worse by worse. Besides, you went from village life to necromancers and vampires in a day. I think the odd freak out is allowed. We're good.' For a second the spirit looked hesitant to continue, but spoke anyways. 'I may seem calm about what happened to me, but there was an *adjustment* period. Just be thankful you didn't get to me any sooner.' There a single hollow chuckle from Auron.

Nicolas still felt guilty but at least there were no hard feelings. He couldn't begin to imagine what Auron had gone through, seeing his body lying there and...

'Talking to your ghost friend?'

The sudden voice beside him made him jump, which evidently pleased Shift greatly, judging by their grin.

'Yeah,' he replied, once he'd regained his composure.

'Neat.' Shift leant against the wall next to Auron. 'Must be nice to have a ghost friend.'

'Great,' Auron muttered. 'Now I'm a fashion accessory. And I'm a spirit, not a ghost. Ghosts are just...well... I'm a spirit.'

'It's weird...but okay,' he told Shift, deciding not to repeat Auron's outrage. 'What was it like to have a gang of thieves as friends?'

'Hardly friends.' Shift snorted. 'You can't get too friendly with people who steal from others and may turn on you at any moment.'

'Sounds like you have a story?' he asked, ignoring the irony of Shift's remark.

'Not one I want to tell,' came the sharp reply.

'Glad to see I am not the only one who cannot sleep,' Garaz said as he appeared at exactly the correct time to diffuse the tension.

'The gang is all here,' Auron smiled. 'Gotten over your spat with High Marshall yet?'

Garaz's face dropped instantly. 'The man is an ass,' the orc replied coldly.

'True enough.' Auron nodded. 'Don't know if he was born like that or evolved into it, but an ass he is. But his heart and duty are all in the right place. He just wants to protect his people. I can relate to that.'

'I can respect that, as well, it is just sad that he is more than a little racist.' Garaz sniffed.

'I'm really hoping it was just the stress talking,' Auron said, though Nicolas wasn't so sure. 'We've all been through it, and sometimes it comes out the wrong way.'

'It's really strange listening to you two talk to someone I can't see or hear,' Shift complained.

'I envy you.' Nicolas chuckled. Turning to Auron, he hoped to see a reaction to a joke he was quite pleased with, but the spirit's expression as he stared off across the courtyard made him tense.

'What is it?' he asked fearfully.

Auron appeared to be looking at nothing. 'The guards on the towers and the walls,' the spirit began, 'I can see their ghosts walking the courtyard.'

That was definitely something, something bad. Now that his attention had been drawn to it, he could actually feel that something was wrong. Garaz relayed what Auron had said to Shift, and they had a very similar reaction to his. All the party stood alert, watching the surrounding area. He reached for his sword and cursed as he realised he'd left the Dawn Blade in his room when he went for his moonlight stroll. He noted for the future: *always carry your weapon everywhere when you have a death threat against you.*

Auron's attention turned to the base of one of the watchtowers. 'Get back inside,' he commanded.

Though he couldn't see anything himself in the shadow of the tower, he most certainly felt the hungry eyes on him.

Carefully, the group edged back through the door. It wasn't the time for making sudden moves. After shutting the door behind them, Garaz pulled the bar across it, jostling it a couple of times to ensure it was firmly in place.

Nicolas stared at the door as if he would suddenly develop the ability to see beyond it to what lay outside. When a single, brutal blow rocked the door, even Auron jumped. The bar and the door held firm. Then the silence came again, until Auron sighed loudly.

'I don't want to alarm anyone,' he said, looking around. 'But I can see the ghosts of the guards from inside the building too.'

Before he had a chance to process this information, they were interrupted by shrill laughter. A figure stepped into the hallway behind them.

'You see! You see! I knew my masters would come for me. I knew your time was nigh. I told you so. And I get to watch you die, and I will enjoy it. Oh yes, I will. Every painful second of it. You will suffer for the pain and insults you wrought,' Prax cried, practically raving as he pointed at the group.

Somehow, the familiar looked even more pathetic in his gloating, his nose at an odd angle to his face, making his speech nasal and grating. His eyes looked crazed, and he shook with righteous fury as he burst into a bout of maniacal, gleeful laughter. The shrill laughter made him wince, but it was abruptly cut off as Prax was hoisted from the floor and his neck snapped with an audible crunch. The stout body went limp instantly and was unceremoniously dropped to the floor, head facing the wrong direction; his presence in the hallway replaced by a figure wearing spiked, blood-red armour.

'He was right about you suffering,' Barus snarled, showing as much fang as possible. 'But wrong about being around to see it.'

'Typical cliché vampire talk.' Auron rolled his eyes, unimpressed.

'Silence, ghost!' the vampire roared at Auron.

Maybe annoying the deadly vampires wasn't the smartest idea?

'Everyone can see him but me.' Shift pouted.

Two more doors in the hallway opened, and four more vampires emerged. All wore the armour of the Battle Born family—face plates open, fangs bared, and curved swords at the ready. He couldn't help but notice that some of the fangs had fresh blood staining their tips. Looking at it made him feel queasy.

'Garaz, I don't suppose you have any spells that can help? Like shooting a fireball or something?' he asked hopefully.

'If I had the ability to shoot fireballs, they would have been unleashed before you asked,' the orc replied, not taking his eyes from the vampires. 'I do, however, have an immediate plan.'

Before he had a chance to ask what that plan was, Garaz turned and threw himself through the nearest window with a sharp smash, followed by the tinkling of broken glass falling to the floor as the orc disappeared into the darkness beyond.

'Huh.' Shift seemed impressed as they jumped through the smashed window after the orc.

He didn't need to look to know that the clomping of boots on wood meant the vampires were charging him. Quickly and unceremoniously, he threw himself through the window as well, leaving Auron alone in the hallway, taunting the oncoming vampires with some choice curses regarding their lineage.

Hitting the floor outside the barracks, he managed to roll with the impact, though he cut himself in several places on broken glass shards. No time to worry about that. The two vampires who'd been waiting on the other side of the door were staring at the people who'd suddenly appeared in confusion. That confusion soon became anger, which manifested itself in the standard fang-bearing and hissing.

'Hey, you!' Auron shouted as his head appeared through the door.

Startled by the sudden sound, both vampires spun towards the door then recoiled at the sight of the bright blue head before them. Garaz used the moment to spring forward, planting his hands around the necks of the vampires and chanting urgently as his hands began to glow again. Within moments, the screaming creatures had crumbled to dust beneath his healing magic, their empty armour spreading across the floor as dust poured from the joints.

As he rose, one of the vampires appeared in the window from which they'd exited the building. Acting purely on instinct, Nicolas grabbed a torch from the mount on the wall beside the window and lunged. The torch struck the vampire squarely in the jaw, the blow sending orange embers dancing into the air as the creature reeled back. The shrieking vampire disappeared from the window as it patted desperately at its now-flaming head.

'They're flammable,' he muttered, looking at the torch in his hand as if it were some sort of holy weapon.

The sound of breaking wood snapped him from his reverie. The door to the barracks blew outwards in a storm of wood shards, throwing Garaz backwards. What was left of the doors themselves were buckled and broken. From the hole they'd once occupied emerged three more vampires and Barus, snarling as they did.

'Shift,' he shouted, pointing.

Shift was nearer the door than Nicolas. Looking at him and the torch in his hand, they seemed to understand his intention instantly. They grabbed the torch from the nearby wall then cried out and charged the vampires.

The lead vampire swung his sword, but Shift was slightly faster, ducking beneath the blade before plunging the torch into the vampire's open mouth mid-roar. The creature made a choking sound then tried to cry out, but the piece of wood jutting from its mouth masked the sound. The vampire dropped its sword, grabbing at the torch and staggering back as the fire took hold of it. Staggering turned to flailing as the burning creature became a walking pyre and fell back into his companions, spreading the fire to them as it clawed at their armour, dragging them down.

The vampires cried in agony as fire consumed them, writhing on the floor to try to put out the flames. Nicolas jumped as a burning shape threw itself through the open doorway. Barus landed in the courtyard beyond the door, his entire right side aflame, screaming in a way no human would've been able to. At inhuman speed, he charged across the courtyard and through the gate of the outpost into the night, the yellow glow of flame showing his path even after he'd vanished.

As effective as Nicolas's idea had been, there was an unfortunate side effect. As the engulfed vampires thrashed and writhed, the fire caught on anything flammable, which was the whole wooden barracks. Soon the entire building was alight, with plumes of thick, black smoke rising into the sky as the group backed away from the choking fumes.

Bright flames engulfed the building like a caressing lover. It was almost hypnotic as the building and fire became one, each individual flame dancing a random, weaving pattern over the wood it consumed. Then something occurred to him.

'The sword.' He bolted toward the ruined door without even thinking.

Garaz and Shift weren't close enough to grab him and stop his foolhardy charge, but they shouted after him. He didn't listen. He was acting on...he didn't know what he was acting on, but it was suddenly very important to him to retrieve the sword.

Coughing almost as soon as he entered the burning barracks, he made his way quickly to where the group had been sleeping. Heat prickled his skin as he dodged licking tongues of flame. Fortunately, so far, the walls had the majority of the fire's attention, so the floor was mostly navigable.

Keeping low to avoid the worst of the smoke, he reached the door of the barrack room, which, thankfully, was open. From there, he could see the bed he had slept in and the sword, the Dawn Blade, next to it in its sheath. Most of the room was still untouched, the fire still making its way steadily down the hallway, but it would not be so for long. He ran into the room and grabbed the sword.

'Kid, wait,' Auron shouted as he appeared at the door.

'It's okay.' Quickly he scooped up the sword. 'I'll be out before the fire cuts me off.'

'No, kid,' Auron said, panic in his voice, 'there were five vampires in here.'

He didn't even really have time to process this information properly before his body dropped, ducking from some imperceptible cue of danger, the curved blade of the sword swinging at his neck missing by a hair's breadth. The vampire, his jaw blacked and burnt, roared with fury and cut down at Nicolas, who was now crouched looking up at his attacker with no way to dodge the incoming blow. The blade bore down on him, and Nicolas closed his eyes, raising his hands out of reflex. Instead of a death strike, however, there was a distinctive *thunk* near his head.

Opening his eyes, he saw he'd raised the sheathed Dawn Blade to block the blow, the leather catching the attacker's sword. The force of the blow still travelled painfully through his arm, but he stood and stepped to the side, lowering the sheath, which caused the attacker to stumble forwards as he refused to let go of his trapped blade. Releasing one hand from the sheath, Nicolas drew the blade and turned into an overhead circular cut, which took the creature's head from its body in one stroke.

'Whoa.' Auron looked at him as if seeing someone new.

Had he just done that? Where had that come from? He...he had killed someone. Nausea clenched in his gut. That creature, though...that creature was already dead. You couldn't kill something that was already dead. He told himself this until he finally calmed, trying not to look at the empty armour and dust pile at his feet.

The sharp, cracking sound of fire consuming wood drew his attention to the door of the room, which the fire had now claimed and was eating away at greedily. Sheathing the sword again, he took a leaf from Garaz's book and threw himself through the nearest window.

CHAPTER 21

The sun bathed the sky a deep red, looking aflame itself as it chased away the darkness, and illuminated the burnt out ruin of the barracks. Pieces of blackened, scorched wood rose from the ground where the building had been, most of it now ash, and trails of smoke still ascended into the bright morning sky. In the courtyard, beneath a watchtower, Nicolas lay exhausted, his companions around him in a similar state, bar one.

'That was a ballsy move, kid,' Auron said as Nicolas stood and stretched wearily. 'You didn't need to go back for the sword.'

'I felt like I did.' He looked at the blade on the ground next to him. 'I don't know why, but I did.'

Even he had to admit that running into a burning building was contrary to all his survival instincts, not to mention his current view of his level of courage.

Auron looked at him with a hint of pride in his smile. 'You certainly used it well enough,' the spirit said with a raised eyebrow, 'for an amateur.'

'Yeah,' he smiled, 'I have no idea where that came from. I had to make do, though, seeing how you said you were going to teach me a thing or two, and it has yet to materialise, despite the near-constant danger we're facing.'

'It's still on my agenda,' Auron replied, with a look verging on embarrassment.

'I guess I got lucky, or I'm just a natural.'

'I may not have called you a natural warrior or an interrogator before, young Nicolas, but you appear to be showing all manner of surprising skills.' Garaz laughed as he sipped some of the water they'd gathered from the nearby well.

Once Nicolas had emerged, coughing, from the burning building, and the immediate threat of vampires had been dealt with, the group had seen to securing what was left of the rapidly dwindling outpost. Fortunately, there had been no further sign of vampire activity during the night as they took it in turns to keep watch; a fruitless gesture as none of them slept anyway. Apparently, the arrogant creatures had assumed seven would be enough to take care of Nicolas and his companions. He'd assumed it would've only taken one.

'So where to next?' he asked, eyeing the wreck of the barracks, its ruins a testament to them cheating death again.

'I thought home?' Garaz replied with confusion. 'Sir Eldric gave you leave to return now that he has the situation in hand.'

He picked up on the slight distaste with which the orc said the High Marshal's name.

'This isn't done.' Something about everything he had heard nagged at him, though he couldn't tell why. 'I don't think defending Yarringsburg will be as easy as Sir Eldric thinks.'

'That is just another thing amongst many that does not make sense in this affair,' the orc noted.

'How so?' Auron asked.

'This necromancer's plan to blot out the sun so the vampires can rise and claim the world in exchange for being made one of them is unachievable,' Garaz began. 'Magic is rooted in life energy, and spells are brought forth and maintained by the life energy of the caster. Vampires cannot do magic simply because they have no life energy. If the necromancer casts this alleged spell of his, which must be ancient magic I have never heard of, then as soon as he becomes a vampire, the spell will break and the sun will return.'

'And all the vampires outside will die.' Nicolas finished Garaz's thought.

'Exactly,' the orc replied. 'And the necromancer would know this. It is a basic principle of magic. No amount of power stolen from other wizards can change the fundamental laws of nature.'

'So, he is doing something that even his *partners* do not know about, some kind of double cross?' Shift asked as they lay back, eyes closed, enjoying the morning sun.

'That doesn't make sense either,' Auron mused. 'Necromancers and vampires hate each other. Necromancers think dominion over the dead is their right, as do vampires. The idea of them teaming up for anything is...ridiculous. Vampires kill necromancers on sight, so how did he approach them in the first place?' The spirit seemed thoughtful for a moment. 'Though I admit the necromancer knows how to keep his partners sweet.'

'The tributes.' Nicolas didn't want to remember those who had died, and what they had become.

'That,' the spirit replied, 'and not having his minions kill us before the vampires could.'

Was he missing something?

'Something didn't sit right about how the vampires got into the compound without raising the alarm,' Auron explained. 'Vampires can be stealthy and subtle but not Battle Born. They live for combat and would love the challenge of fighting professional soldiers. They would've stormed in here so that not even someone under a sleep spell would've missed it. On that premise, I had a nose around. The guard's throats were cut and the gate left open before they arrived. It was Silva, before you ask. The bitch carved a rose into the gate to make sure I knew it was her. I guess we made it personal for the vampires, enough that Silva was told to leave us for them.'

'But how would those mercenaries know we were here?' Garaz asked, frowning at the thought of Silva and her fearsome colleague Grimmark.

'I don't think Sir Eldric made it to Yarringsburg,' Nicolas said quietly. 'They must've intercepted him. It's the only way they could've known.'

The group was silent for a moment as they thought of the High Marshall. Though he was a jackass, none would wish him dead. So much for his earlier idea of finding soldiers to deal with all this. Could they do better where professionals could not? He supposed they were all that was left. First chosen by a stick, now chosen by default.

'Then we have to warn the city.' Shift stood, looking grimly to the mountain. 'I'm missing half this conversation because I can't hear the ghost-hero, wherever he is, but like Nicky here said, this isn't done.'

'You're with us then?' he asked.

Shift paused for a moment. 'I watched those creatures murder innocent people so they could make more of those feral things, which is exactly what they were planning on doing to me,' they replied sombrely. 'I don't think I can just walk away and let others suffer the same fate. I'm with you until this is done. Besides,' Shift said with a cheeky grin, 'the idea of payback is pretty appealing too.'

'We are assembling quite the little group here.' Auron smiled. 'An orc, a shapeshifter, a gh...spirit, and an occasionally whiny kid. I'm sure this will make an excellent story.'

'Glad to be on board,' Shift replied, waving at Auron. 'And hello, by the way.'

It took the spirit a second, but with a smile, he bowed to Shift, who gave a faux curtesy in response.

'I am glad we can all see each other now.' Garaz smiled.

'Does make it a bit easier.' He shrugged. At least he would no longer have to repeat conversations like some kind of parrot. As much as he liked feeling useful, it was starting to wear thin.

'What won't be easy is getting to Yarringsburg in time,' Auron mused. 'All the horses have run off, and it will be a long walk around the mountains, which I don't think we have the time for.'

Why did they have such bad luck when it came to finding horses?

'The familiar did seem to suggest the necromancer was ready,' Garaz offered. 'It could be today when he casts his spell.'

'Not at night then?' he asked.

'No,' the orc replied. 'If he was going to do it, it would have to be during the day.'

'Because how else would you know if it worked unless you do it during the day? Duh,' Shift butted in, rolling their eyes theatrically at Nicolas.

'Which leaves the big question: how are they going to get all those vampires into Yarringsburg during the day?' he asked, ignoring Shift's ribbing. 'They can't just hold large leaves over their heads and hope for the best as they storm the walls.'

'I don't think they're storming the walls at all.' Shift seemed like they knew something. 'This necromancer is in an abandoned fort, right? Well, there are plenty of old thieves' tales of forts that have tunnels that link to castles, should a king ever need a quick escape or discreet exit. I bet there's a tunnel in that fort all the way to Yarringsburg Castle.'

'There's no way they would leave a fort abandoned that had a tunnel straight to the castle sitting under it,' he scoffed.

'They would if the tunnel were old, and they thought they'd blocked it and kept it secret, or if they'd forgotten it was there themselves. Stupider things have happened.'

'But it could be unblocked with the right resources,' Auron said thoughtfully.

'Exactly.' Shift smiled. 'And I bet with enough effort, you could dig an intersecting tunnel from the Crag if you knew exactly where to dig. Even if it is guarded at the castle end of the tunnel, whoever's there will hardly be prepared for a horde of vampires to come spewing out.'

'And then they're already inside the city,' Auron snarled. 'With thousands of victims between them and the city walls as soon as the sun is removed from the equation. By the time news of the attack spreads and the people actually begin to evacuate, the vampires will have chewed their way through half the population. Those who try to flee will jam the gates in panic and will be ready and waiting when the vampires get to them.'

'No one would be prepared even if Sir Eldric had made it back.' Nicolas sighed. 'They would be looking for an attack from the outside.'

'This information, distressing as it is, gives us an opportunity.' Garaz looked almost reluctant to continue.

He looked at the orc quizzically.

Garaz returned his look, intimating that Nicolas should understand what he meant.

'You want to use the tunnel?' he cried as he realised what his companion was alluding to. Was he insane?

'It would be the quickest way to Yarringsburg.' Shift shrugged.

'And they wouldn't expect it,' Auron said with a nod, becoming animated at the idea, which was all well and good when vampires couldn't kill you.

They were all insane.

'Yeah, because they would assume no one's crazy enough to walk down a tunnel behind an army of vampires.' And it'd have to be a special kind of crazy.

'Exactly.' Auron smiled in a really annoying way.

'But if we get there behind them then aren't we still too late?'

'Remember what I said earlier, kid, about ensuring as few people die as possible?' the spirit said heavily. 'We need to get to the city. If we go through the tunnel, we need to accept that some will die, but that we can save many more by actually getting their and stopping this. Or we take a day to walk around this mountain and by the time we get to the city, everyone is dead.'

It was cold and logical, but it made sense. They had but one option.

Looking at his companions one at a time, he saw the resolution in each of their faces.

'Fine.' If it truly was the only way, then so be it. 'I seem destined to spend my days alternately walking up and down this bloody mountain, so I might as well go through it too. Let's go visit the necromancer's fort again.'

'So, we are going for the tunnel in the fort then and not the Crag?' Shift asked.

'I refuse to go back into that vampire nest,' Nicolas said. 'Besides, I'm sure the tunnel will be guarded, and it'll be easier to get into it if those guarding it can't smell us coming.'

Looking back to the burnout remains of the barracks, he looked at the destruction already wrought by these people. He had a question to ask. He already knew the answer, but he needed to say it aloud. 'What do we do when we get to the castle?'

Auron looked at him intently, seeming to know why he was asking.

'Kill the necromancer,' the spirit replied. 'The only way to end this is to break the spell and as much as I know you don't like the idea of killing, there is no way the necromancer goes to all this trouble and just gives up because of some impassioned speech. When he dies, sun comes out, vampires die; or are at least contained until they can be destroyed. It's the only way.'

Auron was right, on both counts. As uncomfortable as he was with the idea, he knew the state of the barracks would be reflected a thousandfold in the city itself if they didn't act. He nodded soberly.

'We have a plan then,' Garaz said in an impressed tone.

'A crazy plan.'

'Those are the best kind, kid.' Auron smiled.

* * * *

Getting ready to depart the outpost hadn't taken long at all. Any supplies they might've collected had burned up with the building. The best they could do was scavenge a few items from the dead soldiers, which wasn't pleasant work. Rifling through the pockets of the dead men he tried not to look at those he stole from. He also tried not to imagine them spontaneously coming back to life to protect their worldly possessions. Part of him wanted some armour for the coming fight, but he couldn't bring himself to strip a dead body. Poor Shift had no choice, as a dress wasn't fitting attire for the task they were about to undertake. He tried to ignore how good they looked in their new outfit as Shift and Garaz picked suitable weapons for themselves. He was content with the Dawn Blade; it had seen him well so far. Well, that one time.

Before they departed the outpost, he'd wanted to give the soldiers a proper burial—it seemed only right—but the others impressed on him that time was of the essence. The best they could do was cover them respectfully in their cold weather capes, while he wished their souls speed to a better place.

Standing over the bodies, he began to wonder what chance their ragtag group had against this evil when men trained to fight had fallen so easily? The odds didn't matter now, though. They were all that was left, and they would do their darndest to stop this necromancer and his allies. Too many lives were at stake to walk away. Maybe even those of the ones he loved. He yearned for home, but knew this was his path now, until it was done. Maybe the Deities were watching them and would think them brave in the face of insurmountable odds, striking the vampires down with bolts of lightning and saving them a job? He laughed at his own fantastical thinking.

As they left the gates, the day felt wrong somehow. It wasn't what had happened that had made him ill at ease, but there was something in the air, like the world itself knew what was coming and was anxious about the outcome. He knew the feeling.

'I suppose this is business as usual for you?' he asked Auron as they travelled the path side by side.

'Usually, I'm alive for it, but yeah, pretty much,' the spirit answered.

'Have you saved the world before?' he asked, the responsibility weighing heavily on him, a fact which Auron seemed to pick up on. Most likely since he couldn't hide it if he tried.

'Usually, the stakes of my fights are not so grave,' he said thoughtfully. 'You meet a lot of warlords and wizards with delusions of grandeur, but no decent follow through. At the moment, I'm not sure if this falls under that category or not.'

'You don't think the necromancer can do it?'

'I think something has changed.' Auron looked to the sky, seeming to feel the same wrongness he'd picked up on. 'I've been noticing it for a while now. There's been more and more trouble in the kingdoms of late, and each time, the stakes get bigger. People are becoming scared. Borders are closing. When I was summoned to Yarringsburg, I'd only just returned from another quest. There was a time I would go a whole year and only quest three, maybe four times at most. This was my sixth, and we're not even at mid-year. Something's brewing and stirring things up, but I can't see what it is.'

'I should like to speak to this necromancer and find where he obtained this spell of his,' Garaz commented, obviously listening to their conversation. 'It is not the sort of thing one finds in a general book of magic. I have heard of nothing like it in all my travels.'

'And information regarding this tunnel of theirs,' Shift added. 'That must be a very closely guarded secret. Not the sort of thing one stumbles on by accident. *Oh look, I've tripped and found a tunnel to the heart of Yarringsburg castle. Time to do some nefarious planning.*'

Nicolas chuckled, but his head was full of notions of heroism and danger, which weren't concepts he was used to dealing with. Looking at Auron, he couldn't imagine what it must be like to live a week of this, let alone a life. These couple of days had nearly wrecked him as it was.

'What's the Hall like?' he asked.

'The Hall of Guardians?' Auron asked.

'Yes.'

'I always pictured it like some grand drinking hall,' Shift said with an almost dreamy look. 'Lots of trophies and art depicting great acts of heroism and statues of champions of old.'

'That's pretty accurate, actually.' The spirit laughed. 'It used to be, at least. At its height, it was a place of merriment and brotherhood. It's much less so now.'

'How so?' Garaz asked.

For a second, it seemed as if Auron was reluctant to talk about it, but he spoke anyway. 'I'm not the first hero to fall recently. I've lost many friends over the past year as we travel all over, fighting new perils. When heroes fall, new potentials are brought in to fill the gaps. It's getting to the point where those called to make up our numbers are…unworthy. More mercenaries than anything, like Silva and Grimmark. The Hall falls on hard times and is becoming a shadow of what it should be. People are losing faith in us as we fail to keep up with the sheer amount of villainy that abounds.'

'So, they are relying more on conventional armies as opposed to champions?' Shift asked.

'Yes,' Auron replied. 'There was a time when kingdoms didn't need outposts like the one we came from, and now they're dotted all over. Local militias are becoming standing armies in their own right. The times are changing.'

'The Deities still have faith in you,' he offered.

Auron looked at him quizzically.

'They sent a message to put you on the right track.' Nicolas hoped it was some comfort to his companion. 'They obviously have faith that you're still up to the task.'

'I wish their faith were as well placed as Silva's arrow.' Auron laughed aloud at Shift and Garaz's sad faces. Nicolas undoubtedly looked similarly forlorn. 'Gallows humour,' the spirit said, shaking his head and smiling. 'At some point, I need to accept that I'm dead.'

'You're still going to succeed, dead or not,' he said with a grin.

'We shall see to it,' Garaz added.

'Yeah,' Shift said. 'Dead or not, this victory will be yours as much as ours.'

Auron smiled and looked towards the trees as if too embarrassed to look his companions in the eye—a feeling Nicolas knew well.

CHAPTER 22

They made decent time to the fort, which put them closer to whatever fate awaited them. At least the proximity of the outpost to the fort made for a straighter run, though the climb upwards was still gruelling. Once he was home again Nicolas promised to never even look at a mountain again.

By late morning, they reached a familiar outcrop—the place he'd hidden when Auron had scouted the fort the first time they were here. Why did that feel so long ago? So much had happened in such a short space of time, most of it either horrible or terrifying or a combination of the two. Thinking to how close the outpost was to the fort, he wondered on how easily all of this would've been avoided if the soldiers had just patrolled the area they protected.

Still, no use focusing of what ifs as the odd companionship, thrown together by circumstance and life-threatening danger, assembled just below the edge of the ridge. The air was warm around them, even in the shade of the rocks, and they were hot from the quick climb, though maybe the sweat on his neck was more from fear than temperature and exertion? Beyond the blind ridge, they could hear nothing save the usual background noise of birds calling to each other.

'You guys wait here while I scout it out,' Auron stated as he looked towards the ridgeline.

'What if the necromancer sees you?' he asked.

'Then we will be blessed with some particularly bad luck.' Auron smiled.

If their luck was running to form, the necromancer should be directly around the corner then.

Auron took several steps from their concealment and stopped dead, an unhappy look on his face. The one Nicolas knew heralded danger.

'You might as well come out,' shouted a familiar voice. 'We know you're there.'

He looked uncertainly at his companions, who returned his look. Auron seemed to be deliberating. Finally, he motioned for them to come out.

'I think we have no choice but to face this one,' he said gravely as Nicolas's heart sank.

He emerged into the open. The fort looked every bit as aged and wrecked as the last time he'd seen it, though the inside was surely a bit worse for wear because of them. Beneath the fort, the makeshift camp had vanished. Those who'd dwelt there, however, had not. Around twenty mercenaries, weapons held in lazy grips, stood on the bridge across the moat, staring at Nicolas and his companions with a doggedness that made him pretty damn uncomfortable. Beyond the troop of thugs were a pair of horses with two very familiar figures upon them.

'That's a shame,' Silva yelled from her horse. 'We were hoping you wouldn't come out. Running you down before killing you would've been much more entertaining.'

Seeing them both again made him shiver. Four times, they'd tried to kill him and failed, and now here he was, stood before them again. From what he could tell, Auron was handling seeing them better than his last encounters. His aura was reddening, but there was no uncontrolled outburst from the spirit. He did look like he wanted to rip their heads clean off their necks, but that was understandable. His eyes were fixed on Silva as if he could kill her from here with a blink.

He thought about what the two mercenaries had nearly done to him, and Shift, and Garaz, and what they'd succeeded in doing to Auron. Inside him Nicolas felt an unaccustomed anger building. How were they sat there so casually after everything they had done? Here before him were kidnappers and murderers and they just...sat there. The mere thought of it made his anger too great to contain.

'Why?' The anger exploded from his mouth. 'Do you think you'll have more luck killing me this time than the last few times you tried? It's getting embarrassing now, guys.'

Where had that come from? Actually, better question: had that been a good idea? Judging by the look on Grimmark's face...no; but the anger in him would not be denied.

'You little goblin turd,' Grimmark roared, making his horse shift uneasily. 'When I'm done with you, I shall wear your jawless skull around my neck as a warning to all others who dare cheek me.'

'Choosing to rile them up first is an interesting strategy.' From the tone in Garaz's voice he could translate *interesting* as *stupid*.

'Trust me,' Auron said through gritted teeth, 'these two bring out the worst in anyone.'

'Is Auron with you?' Silva asked. 'I would so hate for him to miss the deaths of his new friends.'

Auron was clearly fighting to keep his temper, but somehow, he kept control.

'I'll take your silence as a yes,' Silva shouted.

'I am curious,' Garaz shouted back. 'How does kidnapping and murder pay?'

'Very well,' Grimmark answered with a sneering smile. 'Though some I would gladly kill for free. The little runt, for example.'

'Rude.' Nicolas snorted. Skinny, yes. Runt, no.

'How exactly do you plan on spending all that gold?' Shift asked. 'When the vampires take over the world, I doubt it will still be business as usual for the taverns and brothels.'

Both mercenaries burst out laughing.

'I'm torn,' Silva said with a shake of her armoured head. 'Half of me wants to enlighten you, but the other half likes the idea of you dying stupid.'

'They were stupid to come here, so let them die as they lived.' Grimmark roared, 'So what about it, idiots? Are you coming over here or must we come to you?'

'What's the play here?' Shift asked quietly.

He looked at Shift then at the force assembled before them. The anger in his gut became resolution, a resolution which surprised him.

'I'm not about to give them the satisfaction of hunting us down,' he answered, glaring at Grimmark. 'I've been up and down this thrice-damned mountain too many times as is.'

'There are a lot more of them than us,' Shift pointed out unhelpfully.

'I, for one, would rather die here than hunted down as I fled,' Garaz interjected.

Mind made up, he took several steps forward and drew the Dawn Blade from its sheath. He held the sword for everyone to see, its clear blade reflecting the light of the sun beautifully, before using it to draw a line in the dirt directly in front of him. He pointed to Grimmark then to the line then made a rude gesture with his finger.

'Where did that come from?' Garaz looked at him in astonishment.

'If I'm going to die here, might as well make them work for it.' He took satisfaction from the dark look on Grimmark's face, a look way beyond simple anger.

'We'll make a hero out of you yet, kid,' Auron said with a smile. 'Did I mention that 'Nick Carnage' has a real ring to it?'

'That's not my name.' He smiled. 'And even if I was inclined to it, I'm going to die within a minute or two. Maybe next lifetime.'

'Oh, we've got about five whole minutes left, I think.' Shift lazily swung the sword they'd taken from the outpost, most likely getting used to the weight.

Garaz drew his own weapon and readied it as well.

'Go,' Grimmark commanded from his mount.

In front of the mounted warrior, the assembled mercenaries advanced. Axes, clubs, and swords were raised and what began as a fast walk soon became an all-out charge. Nicolas felt strangely at peace as those intent on killing him grew closer, hollering fierce battle cries from faces contorted in anger. He wouldn't give them the satisfaction of flinching or cowering. At least he would go down fighting. Maybe he would even give a decent account of himself. If he swung the sword enough, he was bound to hit something. In the grand scheme of things, dying on his own terms and sending at least one bad guy to the underworld would be a good day's work as far as he was concerned. He'd nearly died so many times in the last few days that the fear didn't overcome him as it previously had. He just hoped his friends didn't suffer.

Briefly he thought of the home he'd never see again. His parents must be worried sick. Part him hoped they never found his body, having to see what the mercenaries would do to it, but another part wanted them to, so that they weren't bound by a hope of his return, one that would never be fulfilled. He offered a silent prayer to them before readying himself.

'Remember how I said I was going to teach you to fight, kid?' Auron said at his side.

'Yeah. Are the lessons going to start soon?' He laughed, hoping he was a quick study.

'Well, I have an idea,' the spirit said in a tone that piqued his curiosity, 'I'm not sure it's a good one, or that it will even work, but if it doesn't, I'm sorry.' Auron seemed awkward for a moment. 'If it does, I'm also sorry.'

'What are you—'

His words were cut off by a flash of blue before his eyes. Instantly, his body froze as if the blood in his veins had been replaced with pure ice. He spasmed, losing feeling in his limbs as he did, the numbness spreading quickly to his core and consuming him completely. His senses dulled, all sound muffled. His mind suddenly felt claustrophobic, as if it were being compressed and invaded. Memories of events he'd never experienced flashed through his head, and thoughts other than his own whispered to him.

When he began to move, it wasn't of his own will. Legs stepped and arms swung in jerky motions with no input from him. His head turned by itself. A hostage in his own body, he'd been violated, utterly and completely.

From his view at the back of his mind, he watched himself advancing on the warriors, his erratic motions gradually becoming more fluid until he was charging at speed, swinging the Dawn Blade before him in a loose figure eight. How was he doing that? He'd barely been able to lift the thing before now.

As the lead warrior closed, a curved blade swung down towards him. Then suddenly his body sidestepped the blow, bringing the Dawn Blade up under the attacker's sword arm as it did. The arm was removed from the attacker's body, circling in the air in slow motion, the blood flying from it in a gross swirling pattern. Before the arm had even struck the floor, the Dawn Blade had been brought around and sent the attacker's head to join his lost limb, the rest of the body following soon after. Perhaps it was better to only see this from a distance. It looked...messy.

An incoming spear was expertly parried with an inside step before the sword's sharp blade was drawn across the stomach of the attacker. The man fell to his knees holding something red and wet in his hands that Nicolas tried not to focus on, face contorted in pain. Without breaking stride, the blade was pulled back and thrust into the stomach of the next attacker before sliding out and being pirouetted through the air to take the head of another. Though he was cut off from his external senses, fulfilment flooded him, as if he were in his element, doing what he was born to do. This sensation being alien to Nicolas, he soon came to understand that it was emanating from the other strange presence in his mind. He thought now he half-understood what was happening.

More warriors closed and things sped up in his mind, events merging into a tornado of violence. The sword would swing, and men would fall, limbs parted from bodies and blood spilling from lethal wounds. Beyond the carnage, the bridge and fort were getting closer with each kill. He felt as if he were strapped to a runaway horse, unable to look away as much as he may want to.

As the battle continued, nausea balled in his belly and his consciousness expanded, rebelling. He could feel his limbs again and some warmth in his body, beginning with his fingers and toes first but working slowly inward. His senses became more attuned, as if he were approaching the end of that tunnel, or maybe it was receding toward him? The sheer volume of sensation now bombarding him threatened to overwhelm him.

Another sword-wielding warrior came at him, and his blade rose to meet it. The swords clashed with the distinctive sound of metal hitting metal. He felt his body step to the side as the Dawn Blade slid away from the warrior's sword, before it was struck diagonally across the man's torso. The warrior contorted inwards as he fell, blood spilling from screaming lips. Then Nicolas fell too.

Falling to his knees and dropping his sword, his body spasmed again. Sensation burst over him, as if everything he could see and hear were turned up to an extreme level for a brief second. Then he vomited. Once he was sure nothing more could come out of him, he rolled to the floor and curled into the foetal position. His body burned from inside out, Whatever he had just experienced, it had shaken him body and soul.

'I'm sorry, kid,' came a weak voice beside him.

Auron lay, kind of, beside him. The spirit seemed to have faded somehow, so much so that he was almost not there at all. His face looked pained.

'What...what did you do?' came the words from his raw throat, the words burning on their way out his mouth.

'I...I possessed you,' Auron replied. 'I wasn't sure it would work, and it wasn't really the time for a lengthy discussion. I didn't realise it would hurt so much. I didn't realise I could feel pain anymore.'

'Did the job, though.' Shift appeared quickly, cradling Nicolas's still shaking body in their arms.

He looked about him slowly, his body feeling strange now he was in control again. Auron's impromptu idea had definitely done the job. Behind him lay around twenty bodies and various discarded weapons, and limbs. It seemed most of the warriors were outright dead, and the few who weren't looked as if they would've preferred to be.

Had he done that? The claws of panic surrounded him, ready to take him in an iron grip, ready to tell him he was a murderer. No. This wasn't him. He hadn't been in control. Those men had died at Auron's hands. He would not have managed more than one, if he got lucky.

Turning back to the bridge, he was gratified by the look of surprise on Grimmark's face. He assumed Silva had a similar look, had he been able to see her expression through that helmet.

'I get why you didn't ask.' He groaned. 'Please don't ever do it again.'

'Be thankful, kid.' Auron laughed weakly. 'I feel like I want to throw up but can't.'

'Whatever they say about the start of your career,' Garaz said as he helped Shift haul Nicolas up, 'none can doubt your skill.'

'Thanks,' Auron said as he rolled onto his back and stared up at the sky.

It took him a few moments to stand by himself as he relearned to control his limbs and fight back the weakness from the possession and all the unfamiliar movements they'd just been made to do. With enough effort and concentration, he was finally standing again, if not completely upright, somehow sword in hand.

He looked toward the bridge. 'Two to go.'

'And three of us.' Shift smiled.

Beyond the group, Silva and Grimmark were looking at each other uncertainly.

'Just one.' He took a stumbling step forwards. 'It's got to be me.'

'Are you sure about that?' Garaz asked as if addressing a complete lunatic.

He was. He didn't know why he was, but he was. 'I promised Auron I would avenge him,' he replied firmly.

'But you've only just learned to stand up again without help,' Shift pointed out.

'Yeah, but I have an advantage.' He smiled.

The others looked at him quizzingly.

'I still have Auron's memories. I know what he knew. It's all fading, but it's there. If I do this now, I can take them. I know it.' It was strange for him to have such certainty, but it came with a price. 'Though I wish the thing about the week on the desert island with the Mer-Princess of the Tidal Kingdom would fade quicker.'

Auron gave a cheeky, but pained, grin. 'She can breathe underwater, and her gills—'

'No,' Shift said, cutting Auron off by holding up a silencing hand.

'Agreed.' Garaz looked at Auron with distaste.

Time was of the essence, so he stepped onto the bridge, sword at the ready.

'Before you do this,' Silva shouted, 'you do remember what happened last time you were on a bridge with us, right?'

Had the edge of bravado gone from her voice? He obviously had the pair uncertain, which he hoped would work to his advantage. In truth, he really hoped they would both just run off, but that seemed unlikely.

'Different bridge, different outcome,' he replied firmly, hoping.

'Yes,' Grimmark rumbled. 'This time, you will die properly.'

The pair of mercenaries didn't run away as Nicolas had hoped. Instead, they dismounted their horses and drew their weapons. Approaching side by side, Grimmark cradled the head of his war hammer while Silva lazily rolled her spear between her hands. They seemed to show caution in the face of the skills he had just demonstrated, whilst he showed caution knowing the skills were no longer there, mostly.

'How many times have you nearly died in the last couple of days?' Silva asked. 'How much longer will your luck hold out, do you think?'

It sounded almost as if they were trying to dissuade him from fighting, though she wasn't wrong about his luck being due to run out. He could only hope he had just enough left for this.

As the gap closed between them, he was surprised to realise that most of Auron's memories had already faded…except for one thing. The hero had purposely left something in Nicolas's mind, a message.

Make them get in each other's way.

Instantly, a plan came to mind, and he did something his opponents wouldn't expect—he charged them, issuing a barely passable battle cry. The sudden charge did catch Silva and Grimmark off guard, but being the experienced warriors they were, the surprise lasted but a second then they too charged, issuing a much more impressive battle cry.

At the very last second before the opponents met, he veered straight towards Grimmark, using the bulk of the big man to keep Silva from thrusting at him with her spear. Roaring, the warrior swung down with his hammer. For a moment he nearly froze at the sight of the bear hammerhead, looking exactly as angry and dangerous as he remembered. Instead he ducked to the outside of the strike, hearing the familiar sound of metal cracking stone.

'Out of the way, oaf,' Silva cried at her partner as she found him a barrier between her and her prey.

Using his momentum, he circumvented Grimmark, rolling around him and striking at Silva from the opposite side. She easily and expertly deflected the blow with the shaft of her spear but was too close to her companion to bring the spear tip to bear, though it didn't stop her trying.

'Careful, wench,' Grimmark snapped as the spear tip missed his nose by millimetres.

The giant warrior swung his hammer again, aiming to take his head right off his shoulders, but he was too fast, ducking the blow and forcing Silva to do the same with a curse. However, where Nicolas could rise quickly, Silva could not, the weight of her armour holding her down. She used her spear to push herself back up, but as she leant forwards on her weapon, trying to right herself, he kicked her in the back of the knee. That was enough to send her falling forwards into Grimmark, though the big man barely moved as she crashed into him. Nicolas wasn't sure he'd even noticed.

Angrily pushing Silva off him, the bear-obsessed warrior swung his hammer in a brutal downward arc, only to find Nicolas already somewhere else again.

'Are you trying to miss me on purpose?' he goaded Grimmark.

That jibe certainly twisted the warrior's tender bits, judging by the reaction it got. With a mighty roar of rage, Grimmark swung the hammer again. Nicolas stepped back from the blow just in time, the hammer missing him by millimetres as he revealed Silva behind him, who'd only now succeeded in righting herself and drawing her sword. Though he couldn't see her face through the featureless helmet, he could easily imagine her current look of surprise.

'Oh,' the warrior said as the hammerhead flew towards her.

Anything else she may've said was drowned out by the loud clang of metal on metal. The head of the hammer struck Silva directly in the chest plate, caving it in and indenting the snarling snout into it as the force of the impact threw her back. Silva was driven to the side of the bridge and thereafter over, scrabbling for purchase on the stone...and failing. The warrior disappeared, a cry and a splash following seconds later.

He ran to the edge of the bridge and looked over. In the water below, ripples worked their way out from where Silva had struck the water, a few tell-tale bubbles showing exactly where she sunk. These became less and less until they disappeared completely, and the water was calm again.

'I told her all that armour would get her in trouble one day,' Grimmark remarked at his side, looking out over the edge of the bridge as well.

Turning in shock, he cursed himself for becoming distracted when the big warrior was still a threat. He began to move, but this time, Grimmark was faster. The big warrior drove the shaft of the war hammer straight into Nicolas's stomach, so hard that he coughed up blood as he doubled over and fell to the floor in agony.

Writhing in pain on the ground, he could only watch as Grimmark's shadow fell over him.

Smiling like someone about to savour a feast, the warrior raised his hammer high. 'Goodbye, pest.' Great, that was the last thing he'd ever hear.

It seemed he wasn't destined to avoid death by hammer on a bridge twice. Above him, Grimmark's arms tensed, but the hammer didn't come down. The warrior seemed to try several times to rectify that, but it wouldn't budge. As the big warrior turned, Nicolas caught a glimpse of the large troll holding the end of the hammer in both hands and snarling with vicious intent.

Grimmark, evidently not fancying a test of strength against a troll, let go of his hammer and drew instead a deadly looking knife from his belt. Before he had a chance to thrust the blade, Garaz appeared and blew some kind of dust into the warrior's face. From his reaction, whatever it was, it was burning. The big man cried in pain, rubbing his eyes furiously. Hands blocking his vision, Grimmark didn't see the hammer coming until it struck him in the jaw.

There was a wet crack, and Grimmark was spun back in towards him, his jaw hung slack and the caved in half of his face was a bloody mess. The big man wavered on the spot before toppling towards Nicolas in seeming slow motion. It was all he could do to shield his vital parts before the warrior fell atop him, his impressive weight pinning Nicolas to the floor. Is this what the guys poor horse had to carry around?

'So, it seems Nick thinks he doesn't need our help,' Shift remarked as he scrambled to free himself from the dead mercenary. 'Apparently, he can do it all by himself.'

'Apparently not.' Garaz stood over him, smiling genially.

'To be fair, he was doing well up until he nearly died and needed saving,' Auron said at Garaz's side, looking like his old self again. Relatively speaking.

'And I suppose he doesn't need any help now?' Shift asked with a raised eyebrow as they came into view.

He didn't know if he was seeing things, but they appeared to be putting their top back on. What he did know was that no amount of squirming would get him out from under the dead mercenary.

'Could you guys help me, please?' he asked sheepishly. Stuck under a large dead warrior was no time for pride.

'We could make a team player out of our fearless solo adventurer yet.' Shift laughed.

'Indeed,' Garaz added with a chuckle.

As the other two went about moving the dead mercenary off him, Auron crouched at his side.

'Nice work, kid.' The spirit's look could only be described as pride.

CHAPTER 23

Though they entered the fort cautiously, it was unnecessary. The only guards were those strewn across the plateau behind them, some in pieces. From the look of it, the place had been abandoned with no intention of return. Unwanted equipment had been thoughtlessly thrown to the floor and left. Nicolas wrinkled his nose at the lingering burnt smell in the air.

From the entrance, the obvious way to go was down, following a path of displaced dirt. The lower they went into the building, the darker and danker it became. Seeing the occasional rat, he tried to hide the shiver of revulsion the vermin triggered. His companions seemed to not care about the creatures, and he didn't want to be singled out as the one who did. Besides, there were likely worse things ahead of them.

In a basement room, they found a large cover stone—or what was left of it. The stone had been broken to pieces, revealing the open tunnel beyond. Judging by its thickness, it must've been a long, arduous task.

'That is a big, dark hole.' He was unable to keep the apprehension from his voice.

'It stinks of evil,' Auron remarked as he looked into it. 'Metaphorically. I can't smell anything.'

From the opening, the tunnel seemed to continue at a decline. Torches were placed at intervals along the earthen walls, but the light did nothing to make it less foreboding.

'This is really the best plan we could come up with?' Shift asked as they turned to the group. It seemed even the happy-go-lucky shapeshifter was nervous now.

'What are the chances that hole is full of vampires?' Not a helpful thing to ask, but Nicolas felt the need to voice his anxiety anyway.

'Hopefully, their attention will be otherwise engaged,' Garaz said as he pulled some herbs from his robe and handed them out.

Following Shift's example, Nicolas stuffed them into his pocket. These were the same herbs Garaz had used when the group fled the Crag to hide their scent, which had proved ineffective when you had mercenaries to tell the pursuing vampires where you were. They couldn't burn them now, but Garaz assured the group they would still have an effect. Which was better than no effect, in his book. Shame there was no herb that actually repelled vampires. If there was, he would've been wearing a coat of it now.

'Relax.' Auron's tone was confident. 'The necromancer left enough guys to guard the fort that he won't be expecting anyone to follow him down the tunnel. Sometimes the element of surprise is better than a hundred trained men.'

'That's good,' Shift smiled, 'because we definitely do not have a hundred trained men.'

'I always feel better when the person who can't be harmed tells me to *relax* just before I enter a long, dark tunnel.' Nicolas laughed, drawing chuckles from all his companions. 'What's the worst that can happen anyway?'

'Vampires can drink our blood dry,' Shift replied.

'They can turn us into vampires, and we spend eternity as mindless beasts killing innocent souls,' Garaz added.

'The necromancer can kill you and resurrect you as zombies to forever do his bidding while the flesh rots on your body, stuck at a never-ending point between life and death,' Auron said thoughtfully.

'Seriously?' he cried. 'That was rhetorical. I didn't want a list!'

There was more general laughter, but it was strained this time with all eyes on the tunnel mouth, as if waiting for something to jump out at them. Gallows humour took the edge off but didn't blunt it completely.

'Well, this isn't going to get any more sensible.' He sighed, walking into the tunnel, with Shift and Garaz behind him.

* * * *

The tunnel had two things in abundance: length and tedium. No matter how far they walked, there was just more tunnel. More earthen walls uncaring about who walked beneath them or why. More wooden beams ensuring that the tunnel didn't collapse, more torches casting dim light and creating dark shadows on the walls around them, and more insects than Nicolas cared to share a confined space with. The only thing ever of passing interest was the odd piece of discarded mining equipment. Though just because they could see nothing ahead, didn't mean the tunnel wasn't occupied, so they moved in silence.

Though the tunnel was quite wide and a few heads taller than Garaz, it managed to be claustrophobic at the same time. The only way to travel was either forwards or backwards, and the view either way was darkness. Or maybe the claustrophobia came from knowing that there was a mountain directly above them. How exactly was the tunnel holding all that weight in check when the ragged walls suggested quick, careless digging? Any second now, the world might fall on them and bury them alive. Or maybe the vampires would jump from the dark and kill them? As Nicolas walked, drenched in sweat, panic walked alongside him, threatening to overtake him at any moment.

He had no idea where they were in relation to the rest of the world, which was disconcerting. He'd never seen the city of Yarringsburg, but the castle was built directly into the mountainside, so at some point they would reach the other side of the mountain and be in the castle. He didn't look forward to seeing the carnage the vampires had wrought. If they were there at all and not still in this tunnel with them.

With no concept of time, the group could've been walking for an hour or half a day when Auron called them to a halt.

'Up ahead,' was all he said as he stared at the tunnel in front of them.

Feverishly, Nicolas looked around for cover, but there was nothing. Even the beams holding up the walls were too narrow to hide behind. All he could do was reassure himself that he had a sword in his hand and had already killed one vampire. Surely, he could replicate that feat a thousand or so times? He pointed the sword ahead of him cautiously.

'What is it?' Garaz asked nervously, looking at Auron.

'There's a break in the tunnel wall ahead of us,' the spirit replied.

Apparently, one of the few benefits of being a spirit was excellent night vision.

Creeping forwards carefully, everyone readied their weapons. Soon he could see the hole in the side of the tunnel wall. There were, thankfully, no signs of life. Or the undead.

'Vampires,' Auron said simply as he looked at the floor.

Up until now, there'd been a steady stream of muddy boot prints on the floor going both ways through the tunnel. From the mouth of the intersecting tunnel and moving ahead of them, the ground had been flattened by a mass of feet hurriedly moving forwards. Where there were any discernible prints in the ground, they were clawed. The walls of the tunnel were also adorned with claw marks, gouged deeply into the mud.

'That would go to the Crag, I take it?' Garaz asked, pointing at the adjoining tunnel.

'Looks like,' Auron replied.

'By the look of it, every feral in that pit passed through here.' Shift looked slightly paler in the torchlight.

'And they were none too grateful for the access either,' the spirit said as he examined area. 'There are bloodstains here. I think it's a fair guess that they belong to the miners who made the opening.'

As bad as that was, there was a positive note here. 'At least we have a few less necromancer minions to fight.'

'Indeed, just a few more Ferals most likely,' Garaz replied, destroying his optimism.

'Either way, judging by the bloodstains here, we're going to be late to the party,' Auron remarked grimly.

'You can tell that just from looking at blood?' he asked, more than a little queasy at the thought.

'Hero work isn't all slaying bad guys and rescuing virgins, kid,' the spirit replied with a wry smile. 'A lot of gross stuff goes with the job as well, like being able to tell the age of a bloodstain at a glance.'

Continuing, their tension increased a hundredfold. There was, apparently, a big difference between *thinking* the tunnel would be full of vampires and *knowing* it. His hands ached from his white-knuckled grip on his sword, and the rest of the group surely felt the same. Even Auron radiated an aura of concern, and he couldn't exactly die again.

That the vampires had done nothing to attempt to conceal their passage through the tunnel didn't help. Indeed, it seemed the creatures were hell-bent on leaving their mark on every surface they could find. They must've been wall to wall as they charged through here.

They'd been following the singular trail for another hour—or maybe two, who knew for sure?—when the nature of the tunnel changed from rough earthen walls to carved stone, more like a castle corridor than a tunnel. Separating the two sections was what was once another cover stone, now a pile of rubble on the floor before them. There were no torches in the section beyond, so they would have to rely on the ghostly light from their heroic companion's aura.

'We must have reached the edge of the city,' Garaz mused as he studied the new terrain.

Wrinkling his nose, Nicolas smelt the musty aroma of air not disturbed for a long time, now tinged with the smell of decay from the creatures who had just passed through here. 'How long since anyone last passed this way?'

'This tunnel is hundreds of years old,' Auron said. 'Back in those days, there was no alliance, easy or not, between the Nine Kingdoms. It was an age of strife, where kingdoms rose and fell weekly, and a king potentially needed a quick getaway. Then peace comes and places like this get forgotten, especially after they are blocked off.'

'I think they're going to pay for their complacency.' Shift ran their finger along a claw mark in the stone beside them.

They were so close to their goal now, just one straight run of quiet darkness before the world around him became crazy again. He could do this. He had to.

Surprisingly, after another half hour, they came to a junction. He'd assumed the tunnel just led to the castle, but here it broke off in two opposite directions. Without any notable markings, how in the underworld would they know which tunnel to take?

'Which way do we go?' Shift asked.

'That way will be the castle,' Auron said, pointing to their left. 'The claw marks go in that direction. But I don't know why the tunnel goes the other way too.'

'Should we see where it goes?' he asked, a little hopefully.

'We do not have the time,' Garaz said, a look of understanding at Nicolas's question on his face. 'The castle is our destination, and that is the way.'

He shrugged; it had been worth a shot.

'We need to go right.' There was something in Auron's tone that made them all turn and look at him. Being the only source of light he was difficult to focus on, but the hero looked grimly to their left and before Nicolas could even ask, he began to hear the sounds himself—scratching against stone. Maybe it was just rats? No. That was a fool's hope. No rat could make a sound so loud. His suspicions were confirmed when the scratching turned into a low growling then several low growls that overlapped each other.

'Run,' he whispered, not needing to see what was coming to know what it was and in what quantities.

None of his companions required elaboration either, turning and running down the right-hand tunnel just as he did. Even Auron ran with them, though maybe it was because he didn't want to lose them. Behind him, he heard a single bark before the sound of massed claws scuttling towards them echoed through the tunnel. Though the stone paving beneath their feet made the claws scratching against it in the distant dark nothing short of terrifying, it did mean there were no obstructions like rocks or roots, allowing the group to flee as fast as they could.

Soon, the tunnel narrowed, forcing them to move in single file, with Nicolas unfortunately somehow ending up at the rear. At least it would force their pursuers to do the same. The only light was the bobbing blue one coming from Auron, which flashed in time with his steps, creating a strobing effect that made it appear they were all moving in slow motion. Beyond Auron, there was blackness, and behind them was blackness—the only difference being that he knew for a fact the blackness behind them wasn't empty.

Then, abruptly, the tunnel ended. It just stopped with no warning, dooming them to be caught. Shift and Garaz scrabbled at the wall, feeling around for a hidden latch or opening and cursing very freely. Nicolas turned and stared back into the darkness, listening to the predatory growling as it grew closer, swearing he caught sight of movement in the black. No, they were not that close. Not yet, but soon.

'On your left,' Auron shouted, pointing.

Turning in that direction, he saw a small side passage, almost invisible in the dark. Stone steps led upwards, and none of them needed an invitation to ascend at speed. Nicolas reached the wood door at the top of the stairs first, desperately yanking the handle. It didn't budge. Why wouldn't it open? The only other thing he could think of was to bang on the door and call for help.

'Move,' Shift shouted behind him.

Pressing himself to the wall, Shift slid past him. Once Shift was at the door, they pulled a small clip from their hair, stuck it into the keyhole, and began to work the lock.

'Hurry, they are at the bottom of the stairs,' Garaz warned as he watched the group's back.

Shift mumbled something about how well Garaz would cast spells with them over his shoulder interrupting.

Behind him, there was definite movement in the dark. What were they waiting for? Why did vampires feel the need to play with their food? Mannerless creatures. He held the Dawn Blade before him, but there wasn't enough room to swing the weapon. If he tried, he would more likely hit Shift and Garaz.

As the movement got closer, Auron jumped between the rest of the party and the oncoming attackers, flailing his arms wildly and shouting. A pair of long claws emerged from the dark, slashing through Auron and making the smoke of his body ebb and flow. The attacking creature, which he thankfully couldn't see clearly, slashed again, more fiercely, and again, roaring with frustration as Auron stood before it, nonchalant, mocking it for failing to kill him. Earning the group valuable seconds.

Shift used them well. There was a click inside the keyhole and when Shift tried the handle again, the door opened, albeit with some effort. Shift disappeared through the opening, and he followed quickly. Once Garaz had followed them, they slammed the door shut. Leaving only Auron in the stairway, continuing to torment his attacker.

They appeared to have entered a cellar of some kind, one not used, judging by the years of dust and cobwebs that covered the old furniture littering the place. At Garaz's urgent suggestion, they made good use of the furniture, barricading the door. Though he helped, his companions were doing the lion's share of the work as he struggled to move the heavy items. His main contribution seemed to be sneezing loudly as the clouds of dust their activity threw up assaulted his nostrils.

'Don't wait on me guys.' Auron declared, almost petulantly, as he entered the room, passing through the door and the makeshift barricade like it wasn't even there.

'You seemed to have the situation under control.' Garaz slumped against the heavy dresser he'd just pressed against the door.

Something banged on the opposite side of the door. Though the barricade looked solid, Nicolas couldn't help but jump at every jolt, which shook the door and the furniture. Shift and Garaz pressed themselves against the barricade to give it what support they could. He joined them, feeling the vibrations through the furniture with each forceful strike. Beyond the door, claws scratched on wood and muted howls of frustration reached them from hunters angry at losing their prey.

'Lucky the stairway is so narrow,' Auron said as he watched the door vibrate. 'If they'd been able to bring their numbers to bear, that door wouldn't last.'

The barricade, as improvised as it was, held firm. Even those on the other side of the door, driven by whatever primitive instincts they had, eventually realised it wouldn't give. The ferocious banging ended as quickly as it had begun, and there was only silence, save for the panting of those holding the barricade in place.

'I suggest we don't dally here long,' Garaz said after a few moments of silence. 'They may begin looking for another way in.'

CHAPTER 24

Aware those hunting them wouldn't simply give up, they wasted no time leaving the cellar. Up the small flight of stairs in the corner of the room was a brightly coloured, vibrant hallway that was a stark contrast to the dingy cellar. Following the hallway, they entered a large reception room, equally colourful and well-appointed with plush sofas and drinks tables laden with half-finished glasses. Paintings adorned the walls, and pillars with small sculptures were dotted around the room. Even the window was well-dressed, with fanciful lace drapes. It was all a bit gaudy for Nicolas's tastes, but maybe this was the norm for city life?

'We're in a brothel,' Auron informed him simply as he took in his surroundings.

'You can tell that at a glance?' he asked with a mix of judgement and surprise.

'Look around properly, kid.'

Doing as bidden, he gave proper attention to the room. His face reddened as he realised the paintings all contained scenes of debauchery and the sculptures on the small pillars were, well...

'Enjoying the view?' Shift asked.

He suddenly realised how long he'd been staring at the...things in the room. He made a few awkward noises, much to his companions amusement.

'Makes sense, I suppose.' Shift smiled as they examined a bust of a bust. 'Those tunnels are for evacuating a king. If the king wasn't in the castle, this would be the second-most likely place for him to be. Kings and prostitutes go together as well as kings and crowns.' They laughed at their own remark.

'Lovely.' Garaz didn't even try to mask the distaste in his voice, wrapping his cloak around him as if it might shut out the environment. He was making a serious effort to touch nothing in the room.

'Well, at least that means we're in the city.' Nicolas said to himself more than the others. 'I didn't think we'd make it this far.'

'I'm happy you were wrong, Lord Pessimism.' Shift examined a small, feathered fan abandoned on the floor.

Nicolas was about to respond when he noticed something off with Auron. The spirit was looking around the room like something was very much amiss.

'What's the matter?' he asked, knowing the spirit well enough now to be worried.

'This place shouldn't be empty,' Auron said seriously.

'Says the authority in the group on the subject of brothels,' Shift smirked.

Now that his attention had been drawn to it and away from the...art, he noticed all the tell-tale signs of a place abandoned in a hurry. There was half-eaten fruit on a table, a spilled drink left soaking on the carpet—all of it told of a hasty exit. And now that he thought about it, should the room be this dim? It was daytime, after all. He didn't know how long their journey through the tunnel had taken, but it couldn't be later than mid-afternoon.

He walked to the window, followed by the others. Initially, he could only see the abandoned street beyond. Why were there no people around? He got the answer when he looked up.

Where there should've been a blue afternoon sky, there was instead a thick, black cloud, an unnatural one. It looked almost like a solid wall, but it swirled and danced, a rolling tempest that completely blocked out the sun, casting everything in twilight grey. The buildings around them were tall, but on the horizon somewhere he could make out a rising column of black smoke that fed the cloud. That must be where the castle was. Once he managed to focus on the cloud properly, it seemed to be moving outwards, though the constant dancing made it difficult to be sure.

'Would that be enough for the vampires?' He already knew the answer.

'Only direct sunlight kills them,' Auron confirmed grimly. 'They could stand in the shade if they wanted to during the day, but that would be the equivalent of standing in the one spot in a burning building that wasn't already on fire.'

'It looks like we're pretty late to the party.' Shift's eyes were on the street below the black sky.

Looking back down, Nicolas now saw that the streets weren't simply empty. Just like the building they were in, there was every sign of people leaving in a hurry, the street littered with the debris of those who'd fled. Even though he was unused to cities, he found the empty streets eerie and desolate. As he scanned the overturned carts and dropped bags, he spotted random blood splatters on the pavement. But they weren't random. They had belonged to people. People going about their day to day when vampires set upon them, biting into their flesh and draining them before using them to bolster their own numbers. He wished he hadn't noticed them, wished the vampires were less messy eaters. His eyes settling instead on a small teddy crumpled in the centre of the road. That sight affected him as much as the rest of the scene combined.

'You sure killing the necromancer will stop this?' It needed to stop, and now.

'I am sure of nothing,' Garaz replied. 'This is magic I have not known or heard of. But if it obeys the base principles of magic, it should be tied to the life essence of its conjuror, so killing the necromancer should break the spell.'

He hated the idea of killing anyone, but the other reality would be much worse. But had he not killed already? For a moment he thought back to all those mercenaries at the fort who had died at his hand. His hand, but not his will. He needed to focus on the here and now and not imagined guilt for things he hadn't done. 'Is the cloud just going to keep expanding until it covers the entire world?'

'Again, I do not know.' The orc's voice gave away his frustration. 'Maybe as the vampires spread so will the cloud, maybe not. This magic is definitely not picked up from a simple spell book.'

'How do you think he got his hands on it?' Shift asked.

'Maybe the vampires had it and gave it to him. Vampires are long-lived and may have access to things long forgotten,' Auron suggested. 'Maybe it was dug up from some ancient ruins. I'd like to know so that wherever it came from can be guarded so something like this never happens again.'

'Maybe the necromancer will just tell us, and we can talk him into stopping the spell somehow?' And maybe he wouldn't have to take a life after all.

The looks he got from his companions told him their opinions on that idea.

'Let us get to the castle first,' Garaz said calmly. 'Then we can get a better understanding of how to proceed.'

Time was now of the essence. The city was in peril. People were dying. The cloud above looked undefeatable to him, but he prayed Garaz's assumptions were correct. If not, who knew if they even could stop it. He tried to imagine a world in which vampires ruled and stopped himself pretty quickly.

Afraid, but determined, he followed the others to the door of the brothel. Garaz opened it, revealing the affluent shopping boulevard in which it was situated. He would've imagined a more backstreet location, but that wasn't the pressing issue right now. What concerned him more was the group of armed men pointing arrows at him and his companions.

'How in the underworld did *you* get here?' Sir Eldric looked at them with a mixture of surprise and fascination. The High Marshall, like the rest of his men, seemed more than a little worse for wear but as pretentious as ever.

'You're alive!' Somehow this seemed like a sign that things were now on an upwards trajectory.

'Not for want of them trying.' The High Marshall sniffed as he approached the group, his men fanning out through the street as they were given the sign that all was well. 'But again I ask, how did you get here? I left you safely at the outpost with strict instructions to go home.'

'The outpost was attacked,' he told Sir Eldric sadly. 'They killed everyone, but we managed to escape. We thought they must've gotten you so we came here to warn people and...help.'

Sir Eldric looked forlorn for a moment, like a man bearing yet another unwanted burden.

'We got here through an old escape tunnel from the necromancer's fort,' Shift added.

'Tunnel?' Sir Eldric spoke to himself more than anyone else. 'How could I not have heard of such a thing?'

'They obviously have better intelligence than you,' Garaz muttered under his breath.

'That explains how the vampires suddenly appeared behind us as we fortified the city walls,' the High Marshall concluded.

'Like I said, we came to help.' The gesture seemed futile when surrounded by armed soldiers.

'Then you are welcome,' Sir Eldric replied surprisingly. 'The situation is grave, and we shall need all the help we can get, whatever form it comes in.' The sideways glance he gave Garaz was not well hid.

'What is the situation?' Garaz asked, apparently noticing the look and deciding to confront the attitude head on.

Sir Eldric seemed hesitant to answer for a moment, as if he didn't want to say it aloud. 'As far as we can tell, the castle has been completely overrun by the creatures. Unfortunately, the entire Royal Family was secured inside the castle at the time...for safety, ironically enough. I made it here early this morning and prepared the city defences, thinking an attack would come from without. The first we knew of our mistake was when that damnable cloud covering the sun began to originate from inside the castle.' The High Marshall sighed heavily before continuing. 'Then the Ferals came. They swept through the inner district, killing in a frenzy and gorging themselves. Afterwards, they fell back to the castle grounds, taking the bodies with them. We have seen nothing since.'

'Why did they stop?' Auron asked, and Nicolas relayed the question.

'That I do not know,' the High Marshall replied. 'Their foul masters must be powerful indeed to rein their Feral brethren in so fully. If I were to guess, they are waiting for the cloud to fully cover the city before they move against us in force.'

'What about the people of the city?' Shift questioned.

'We have evacuated everyone to the far outer district of the city,' the soldier next to Sir Eldric, a captain, chimed in. 'We have advised evacuation of the city, but many are too afraid of vampires attacking them out in the open and refuse to leave. We have established a perimeter and reinforcements are on their way, but...'

The captain trailed off, but he didn't need to finish his sentence. Even Nicolas knew that if the vampires moved en masse, the perimeter would fall long before those reinforcements arrived.

'Ask him what the plan is then,' Auron said. 'You don't simply wander the streets with a small group of men in the midst of a vampire apocalypse.'

Nicolas asked, and Sir Eldric smiled self-appreciatively before replying.

'We will not win this battle by force of arms, but with stealth, strategy, and luck we may yet stay this calamity. And seeing as your little group has a knack for getting into places it should not be in, you are now part of that strategy.' Sir Eldric raised his voice so all his soldiers could hear his words. 'The death that has been visited upon us shall not go unpunished,' he declared. 'I vow that while I have a sword in my hand, these unholy creatures will rue the day they soiled our beloved city and pay for every innocent life they have taken.'

The soldiers beat their fists on their armoured chest plates by way of applause.

Garaz looked less impressed by the posturing; Nicolas was sure the orc had rolled his eyes. 'Let us hope he can live up to his fine words,' he remarked.

'Whatever we can do to help,' Nicolas said, puffing his chest out slightly, eliciting a snigger from Shift.

'The first thing you can do, young Nicolas,' the High Marshal began, 'is step aside and allow us entry.'

Inside the brothel, Sir Eldric and his men, followed by Nicolas and his companions, made for the main staircase that led to the higher levels of the *establishment.*

'He walks with the confidence of someone who's been here before,' Shift remarked as Sir Eldric led them through the building without hesitation.

'Where are we going exactly?' he asked, trying not to look at what was on the walls.

'The master bedroom contains a passage that leads to one of the towers upon the castle wall,' the High Marshall explained. 'It allows members of the Royal Family to visit this place in secret. We will use it to our advantage to make it to the castle unseen.'

"*This* secret tunnel he knows about,' Shift whispered to him. 'Also, exactly how many secret passages does a king need to a brothel?'

'There could be a whole network of tunnels leading from this place to various locations in the city.' Auron smiled. 'The well-to-do of Yarringsburg don't do well when they're seen walking into houses of ill repute. Especially ones on a main road.'

'Perhaps if this place requires so much secrecy, they should not have it at all,' Garaz added.

On the highest floor of the brothel, the party approached a pair of ornate double doors that obviously led to the master bedroom, which turned out to be exactly as lavish as you would expect the master bedroom of such a place to be.

'Touch nothing,' Garaz whispered to Nicolas as he glared in distaste at his surroundings, especially the bed.

'There,' Sir Eldric exclaimed, pointing to a large wardrobe against the back wall of the room. 'Behind that is a—'

His words were cut off by a bump from inside said piece of furniture. Without a moment's hesitation, swords and bows were aimed at the wardrobe. Even Nicolas was ready to fight.

'Reveal yourself,' the High Marshall commanded as he eyed the wardrobe warily.

With a whisper and a whimper, the door of the wardrobe opened slowly. Two maids, fraught and bloody, emerged slowly, shaking. Once they registered who they were sharing a room with, they both fell to their knees and sobbed, the dam of emotion held in for so long breaking into a flood of tears as they held each other tightly.

Sir Eldric laid his sword upon the bed and approached the maids slowly with open hands. 'Hush, dear ladies,' he said softly. 'You are safe now.'

Watery eyed, the sobbing maids looked up into the eyes of their rescuer. 'They killed everyone, my lord,' one of the maids cried amid sobs. 'We were on an errand for our lady. There was screaming and inhuman sounds and so much blood. We found the door to this place open, so we just hid. But those screams...'

Sir Eldric got down on his knee, holding each gently by the shoulder. 'I know,' he said, his voice tender. 'But you are safe now. I, the High Marshall of Yarringsburg, personally guarantee your safety. We are here to drive these creatures away and avenge those they have slain.'

Losing any sense of social etiquette, they grabbed the High Marshall, hugging him tight and sobbing into his tunic. Trauma apparently made one forget one's social rank.

'It's almost like he's putting on a show,' Shift muttered with an unimpressed look.

'There is an element of self-aggrandisement to his manner,' Garaz commented. 'But it seems to have the desired effect.'

Nicolas guessed the orc was referring to the soldiers in the room, all of whom looked in awe at their leader. He had to admit, he was a little inspired too.

'Let him be,' Auron whispered firmly. 'I know he's a snotty ass, but these people need a strong leader right now. That's what he's being. I can respect that.'

'So, he isn't always like this then?' he asked.

'Oh, he's always been like that,' Auron said with a half-smile. 'But today it's okay.'

'If you say so.' Shift sniffed. 'Just seems a little insincere to me.'

'I doubt professional thieves are big on sincerity,' the spirit retorted.

Shift looked at Auron and shrugged as if to say *touché*.

Having calmed the maids sufficiently, Sir Eldric guided them to two of his men with orders to escort them downstairs and then to safety. The maids looked back with appreciation at their saviour and cast wary, distrustful glances at the orc in the room.

Once the maids had been spirited away, Sir Eldric examined the wardrobe in which they'd been hidden. Pressing a small, unassuming circle in amongst a swirling pattern carved into the wood caused a click, and the wardrobe detached itself from the wall on one side. With some effort, a couple of soldiers heaved the heavy piece of furniture aside to reveal a ladder that led down.

'This will get us to the castle wall unseen,' Sir Eldric informed them as his men descended the ladder.

'And what if the vampires have found it already?' he asked.

'We just have to trust to our luck that they haven't,' the High Marshall replied as he began his descent.

'I've only just left a tunnel,' Nicolas muttered as he set foot on the top rung of the ladder. Below him was darkness and the unknown, but at least the soldiers had gone first.

CHAPTER 25

Twenty minutes later, they emerged from the other end of the passage. Sir Eldric was as good as his word, and the tunnel came out inside one of the stone towers that sat at the corners of the wall cutting the castle off from the rest of the city. As Nicolas emerged from the passage, brushing a cobweb from his hair, Sir Eldric's men had already secured the door.

'There is no sign of any vampire activity,' one of the soldiers reported after scouting the stairway ahead of them.

'Doesn't mean they aren't there,' Auron remarked warily to those who could hear him.

'The first thing we have to do is get a better view of what we are facing,' Sir Eldric mused. 'I will go to the top of the tower and see what awaits us.'

'We shall come with you.' Garaz's tone that brooked little argument.

The High Marshall didn't argue, but he cast a glance at the orc that definitely said, *'If you must.'*

What they all saw from the top of the tower made the group gasp and several, Nicolas included, curse aloud.

As he'd emerged from the trap door onto the tower, the first thing that had struck him was Yarringsburg Castle itself. It looked mighty, yet it was dwarfed by the mountain from which it was cut. Extending out from the side of the mountain, the castle boasted a handful of towers. Smoke rose from the tallest one to feed the black cloud above them. That, however, wasn't what made him curse.

From beyond the castle wall extended a large open area, paved and interspersed with trees planted in neat rows and miniature gardens. There were also several statues of notables of old, none of which were unbroken now. The space led to the edge of the city proper, which spread before him from his high vantage point. Hundreds of Ferals occupied the space, snarling, twitching, and hissing, but staying put in a way unnatural to such animalistic creatures.

For a moment this was all too much for him. He found himself fighting his rising nausea as he finally viewed the full scale of the enemy laid before him. Some of the inhuman bodies we only half transformed, wearing shreds of clothes that told him who the person had only recently been. Seeing such terrible creatures wearing fancy suits or laced ladies' day dresses seemed utterly wrong and a testament to the evil gripping this city. Trying to ignore the smell of massed, decaying flesh, he said a silent prayer for all those poor souls, and one for their endeavour. At least if their gambit succeeded, they would be freed from their undead prisons. Was that how Auron felt? Was he looking forward to moving on once they were done? If they succeeded, of course.

And he truly hoped they did. The horde he saw here was a mere fraction of what it could be if these creatures were unchecked, them and their foul masters. Between the Ferals and the wall stood several neater columns of vampires, the so called *Elevated* , arranged in their family units, banners at the front of each column fluttering lazily in the breeze. Similar banners adorned the walls of the castle itself, so there could be no question who it belonged to now. These vampires stood tall and proud, unlike their hunched brethren, seemingly ready to march behind the horde and claim what they believed to be theirs by right.

By the Deities, he would do his best to deny them that.

There was blue sky on the horizon where the cloud hadn't quite covered the city, yet it continued moving slowly outward, as if it had all the time in the world to complete its task. Beneath it, the army waited, most likely until the whole city was in darkness, before they launched their attack. He supposed immortal creatures knew how to be patient when it suited them. What it meant for them, was that there was still time to avert this disaster.

'How do we get in without that lot falling on us?' Shift finally broke the tense silence.

'For that I have a plan,' Sir Eldric said with a knowing smile.

Looking at the mass of vampires, he hoped it was a really good plan.

'We cannot fight that horde head on,' the High Marshall began, 'but we can make them believe we intend to.'

'How?' Garaz asked.

'As we speak, several small groups of soldiers are deploying around the circumference of the castle grounds,' Sir Eldric continued as if he hadn't been asked a question. 'When ready, they will launch arrows into the vampires then retreat. My hope is the vampires believe this a prelude to an attack and launch their own, and that once they do, the way will be clear for us to enter the castle.'

'I wouldn't want to be the one to poke that beast.' Shift cast a sideways glance back at the horde. 'I thought you said your defences wouldn't hold out for long against such an attack.'

'They will not,' Sir Eldric admitted painfully. 'But the attack is coming whether we encourage it or not, so I would rather use it to my advantage and fight on our terms than simply wait to be overrun. Once the horde is away, we will move in and kill this necromancer. With his spell is broken, the sun itself should win the rest of the battle for us.'

'You understand magical theory?' Garaz questioned.

'I know how to ask the correct people for advice,' Sir Eldric replied in a snippy way, seeming to feel challenged by the question.

'Not many of your men will make it back to the line once they launch their attack.' Nicolas hadn't said it for a response, he was merely trying to get his head around the concept.

'No,' the High Marshall replied heavily. 'They know this is most likely a suicide mission. But they also know it is our only hope, and they are prepared to lay down their lives to save this city. Will you do the same, Nicolas?'

He found himself nodding firmly in response without even thinking. Deities, he'd changed in the last few days. The city beyond him needed saving from what seemed to be the purest form of evil he could imagine. Beyond the city lay the rest of the kingdom, including his home and family. This needed to end here and now, and if he could aid that end in coming, then he would.

Sir Eldric smiled and patted him on the back.

'It's a bold strategy.' Auron seemed impressed. 'But sometimes those are the best.'

'And how do we get into the castle once we've cleared the way?' Shift asked. 'There's no way it won't still be guarded.'

'That will be simple enough.' Sir Eldric smiled again.

Nicolas looked out at the horde, the poor souls doomed to be inhuman attack dogs for undead creatures. It didn't seem that any part of this could be simple. 'This is terrible,' he whispered.

'It's tough, kid.' Auron looked equally moved by the scene. 'But like I said before, you can't focus on those who're already dead. You need to focus on those you can keep alive. This hero gig is more about preserving life than avenging death and there are thousands more out there who need our help. There's time to grieve once the battle's won.'

'More hero wisdom?'

'I am full of it,' the spirit replied.

'Yes, you are,' he said with a smile, which was returned with a slight chuckle. 'Like when you told me you were going to teach me to fight. Is that going to be after we face down the army of vampires or any time before when it would actually be useful?'

'It's been a busy few days,' Auron smiled, slightly sheepishly. 'When it comes to it, I'll be by your side, you can count on that.'

'Just try to stay out of me this time.' The memory of the possession caused him to shiver.

'You've killed one vampire. What's a thousand more?' Shift's smile seemed confident, but Nicolas wasn't entirely convinced.

'You will not be short on vampires to practice on,' Garaz added.

He had killed a vampire. Killed. He hated that word. He wasn't a killer, it wasn't in his nature. As much as he kept justifying it to himself that the creature was technically already dead, he still felt a deep guilt in his stomach. Why? It had been a murdering undead monster. Taking some deep breaths he pushed the thoughts away. This was the worst time for his mind to be so conflicted. Those were things to deal with when this was over.

Nicolas found himself almost hopeful when the first part of Sir Eldric's plan worked exactly as the High Marshall had predicted. The black-clouded sky filled with flame-tipped arrows fired from hidden positions in the city. After rising, they curved around to fall back down again, landing in a horde so thick on the ground the archers couldn't have missed had they tried. Where a flaming arrow struck, the vampire instantly combusted, thrashing in pain, sometimes taking a couple of its foul brethren with them. Still, it made barely a dent in the horde. It did give the illusion that a major attack was taking place, though.

After the first volley, the Ferals didn't move. For a moment, it seemed the plan might fail. How could such creatures keep themselves in check so well? They were evidently enraged but made no move to hunt down their attackers.

Then the horn sounded.

Coming from one of the castle's towers, the horn blew a deep bass note that reverberated through space like the roar of a mighty beast. The note was answered by a collective howl of pure bloodlust from the feral vampires, who surged like a great wave of flesh and fang. Running at great speed, like baying hounds, the Ferals funnelled into the streets and soon disappeared.

Once the Ferals had vanished, the ranks of Elevated marched, moving in their neat columns, stepping as one. There were columns of shuffling, half-feral vampires, columns of child-like vampires who were almost skipping, columns of disinterested, well-dressed fanged youths, and columns of red-armoured vampires bearing sword and spear. Behind them all came a column of vampires in ornate battledress and noble attire. The collective rise and fall of feet clapped across the stone paving and could be heard long after they'd disappeared.

And then the way to the castle proper was clear, save for the handful of guards on both the battlements and in front of the gate itself. Apparently, the vampires weren't stupid enough to leave the castle undefended, but arrogant enough to believe it only needed a minimal defence. What were the chances of anyone significant slipping in behind their advancing horde? Hopefully, this arrogance would play in his party's favour.

'They haven't left many,' he noted.

'Enough,' Auron replied simply as he eyed the guards. 'They're still fierce predators individually, don't forget.'

Not likely.

'And there are bound to be more in the castle,' Shift added, 'who'll be called outside long before we cover all that open ground. So how do we enter the castle?'

From his belt, the High Marshall produced a small glass orb, inside which swirled a green cloud. Each of the five soldiers accompanying him had similar orbs on their belts, and removed them at their leader's signal.

'What are those?' Nicolas found the contents of the orbs almost hypnotic.

'Our secret weapon.' Sir Eldric smiled. 'The gas in these orbs come from a special blend of potent herbs, including the ones the orc used. Once the orb is smashed, the gas will expand, confusing the vampires' sense of smell as well as physically blinding them to our approach. We will use this distraction and enter the castle.'

'They will know something is amiss.' Garaz seemed sceptical. Good to know he wasn't the only one.

'Yeah,' Shift added. 'Large green clouds don't just appear without an eyebrow or two being raised.'

'That is true,' Sir Eldric nodded. 'But we have to hope the vampires look beyond the wall for the source instead of within. We will use their confusion to slip by the guards and hopefully, by the time they realise what is actually happening and gather themselves, we will already be inside the castle.'

'It's better than just running and hoping.' Auron shrugged

'It is lucky you have such fascinating devices to hand.' Was there a hint of challenge in Garaz's voice?

'It is preparedness not luck,' Sir Eldric replied testily. 'We live beside a mountain honeycombed with caves such as the Crag. Do you think this the first time we have had issues with vampires? My predecessors found these orbs highly useful in clearing nests in the past, so we always keep a stock on hand for emergencies. Though, admittedly, one this big had never been contemplated. Still, you can never be too careful with all sorts of inhuman creatures abounding nowadays.' Now the challenge was clear in Sir Eldric's voice.

'Meaning what?' The orc was fixing the High Marshall with a steely gaze that was returned in kind.

The High Marshall's men had let their hands slip to the hilts of their sheathed swords. Shift exchanged a look of unease with both Auron and Nicolas.

'Meaning,' Sir Eldric said finally, 'that the kingdom is in danger, and you can never be too careful.'

The stare-down continued for a few more moments, until Garaz gave a huff and disappeared back into the tower. Sir Eldric stared after him for a moment before recomposing himself.

Nicolas went after Garaz and found the large orc leaning against a wall on the other side of the tower, staring menacingly at the floor as if he were ready to stomp on it should it the tile stand out in a way he didn't like.

'What was that?' he asked.

Garaz turned his head toward him, fixing him with the same glare. It made Nicolas tremble slightly, aware of the power of his large green companion. But someone needed to talk him down, and since Shift and Auron were being unforthcoming, it was him by default.

'The man is an ass,' Garaz rumbled with absolute certainty.

'You almost sounded like you were…accusing him of something.' He was on uncertain ground, and it would be disastrous if the group fractured now.

'No, that would make no sense.' Garaz's face softened slightly. 'He means well for his people, I know this. But he exemplifies the kind of racism I have had to face for years. He considers himself the best of humanity but is also everything that can be worst about it. I thought I was used to it by now, but sometimes it still just…riles me.'

'I get it,' Nicolas began. 'I mean, I don't completely get it because it's never happened to me, but I can understand. You know this is the worse time for this, though, right?'

The orc let out a hearty belly laugh. 'It is a sad day indeed when you are lecturing me on keeping my composure in dangerous situations,' Garaz exclaimed, slapping him on the back.

'You're welc— *Hey!*' he cried, as he took in what Garaz had said to him.

'I apologise, young Nicolas, I should not let such a man cause me to lose my composure.'

'You're only human,' he replied then winced when he realised exactly what he'd said. 'Sorry, I didn't mean…'

Garaz smiled at him warmly. 'I know what you meant.'

'It is time,' Sir Eldric said, appearing at the corner. 'Let us dally no more.'

CHAPTER 26

G azing over the edge of the stone towers battlements, Nicolas could now only see a small group of vampires milling about by the castle gate. They seemed at ease and unworried. *He* was worried, though, by what he couldn't see. How many more of the undead creatures lurked inside the castle itself?

Beside him, the soldiers and Sir Eldric were readying their orbs. It was a gambit, to be sure, and he hoped the High Marshall was correct in his assumption that the creatures would believe the distraction originated outside the walls. The man *had* been correct about everything thus far and he strategized extremely well on the fly, but Nicolas couldn't silence his nagging paranoia.

'Are you sure those things will work?' he asked Sir Eldric, indicating the orbs. 'It's quite a distance between the tower and the gate, and they are a little, well...small.'

Sir Eldric looked at Nicolas and smiled, his moustache rising. 'Should I judge things by their size?' he asked. 'You would be considered small, yet you have done much more than someone would have expected of you.'

The point was fair. He'd done so much more than he ever expected of himself. Truly, he didn't know how he had made it to this point. It would be easy just to write it off as luck. Whatever it was, he hoped it kept working, now more so than ever. Looking at his companions, he wanted them all to get through this alive. They were a strange group, people he would never have chosen to face danger with – but he never would have chosen to face danger at all.

Sir Eldric gave the signal, and he and his men threw their orbs with all their might. The small glass balls travelled far onto the outside of the wall but still landed short of the gate. As they smashed on the ground, the vampire guards immediately became alert, moving forward warily to find the source of the disturbance. The green cloud from each orb grew at speed, combining with each other until a thick green mist covered the immediate area both sides of the wall. The distraction was working, but at the same time, he could no longer see the guards he was so worried about.

'It seems luck is on our side,' Auron said as he sidled up to Nicolas.

'It usually is until someone goes and says something stupid like that,' he chided.

'It's not as stupid as going to rescue someone you've never met trapped in a dank cave only to get down on one knee in some kind of romantic knightly gesture,' Shift whispered with a wink.

'Oh, come—' Nicolas started.

'Will you be quiet,' Sir Eldric hissed.

Suitably abashed, he stared at the ground as heat scalded his cheeks. When he glanced up, though, Shift poked their tongue out at the High Marshall the minute he turned his back to them.

The green mist was starting to rise above the tower now, circling his feet. Below, the vampire guards were shouting in confusion. After moving to the bottom of the tower, the group assembled beside the wooden door, awaiting their moment.

'We move in single file,' Sir Eldric commanded. 'Keep eyes on the person in front of you and don't stray. Once we make it to the wall of the castle, we will split into two groups. Mine will circle to the far side of the castle. Nicolas, you and your companions will head for the kitchen access on the east side.'

He would be following Shift, with Garaz following him.

'Remember,' Shift said with mock seriousness, 'you're following me. Don't take this as an ideal opportunity to check out my butt.'

'But...I...I wouldn't,' he stammered.

'Shame.' Shift gave him a cheeky wink. 'It's a cute butt.'

It was, in truth, but not knowing what to say, he turned instead to Garaz.

'Before you ask,' the orc said, holding up a silencing finger, 'I have no intention of attempting to 'check out' your butt as I follow you.'

Shift and Auron sniggered slightly. Again he was the butt of the joke. How could these people make light when faced with such a situation?

Then the time for jokes passed, and they opened the door, slipping out into the green cloud. Instantly Shift became a shadowy outline as the cloud attempted to conceal them form his view. Desperately he tried to keep them in sight, panicking each time he dodged an unforeseen obstacle and had to find them again. What would he do if he lost the group? What if he had lost Shift altogether and was following a vampire now instead? His fears suddenly became allayed as the castle wall appeared abruptly in front of him, causing him to stumble as he tried not to walk directly into it.

'Smooth,' Shift whispered next to him, grinning.

He kept his hand on the wall, in case he suddenly lost it, though how a giant stone wall would suddenly vanish was anyone's guess. Having something solid to touch made him feel more grounded in a world where all he could see was green. The only other member of his party he could see was Shift, barely.

In front of him, a shadow appeared in the mist. He waved to it, assuming Garaz had become as turned around as he nearly had.

'Helig? Is that you?' asked the voice attached to the shadow, between hacking coughs.

The vampire emerged from the smoke, clearly as surprised to see Nicolas as he was to see it. Nicolas immediately went for his sword, but hands sweaty with fear slipped on the hilt. The vampire hissed, displaying its fangs, and walked toward him with evil intent. He could do nothing but watch. With a flash of metal, the creature's head rolled from its shoulders.

'Quickly,' Sir Eldric whispered, taking his arm while the vampire crumbled to dust behind him.

The High Marshall led Nicolas down the wall a little way, slipping around a corner quickly before pressing against the stone. And not a moment too soon, as the partially concealed figures of four vampires passed by in the smoke.

'Lars?' one shouted. 'Lars? Where are you? We need to secure the gate. Lars? Curse this damnable mist.'

Beside him the rest of the party were assembled.

'So far so good.' The hint of surprise in Auron's voice would've unnerved him if he'd had any nerves left.

'So far so good,' Sir Eldric said in a low voice, repeating the words of a spirit he could neither see nor hear. 'Now it is time for us to separate. You are clear on where to go?'

'Yes,' Shift answered. 'We're going in through the kitchen side entrance, and you're going to circle around and enter via a servant door on the far side of the castle.'

'Two groups, twice the chance of success,' the High Marshall said grimly before adding, 'Good luck.' The High Marshall was about to turn to go when Nicolas stopped him.

'Thank you,' he whispered. 'You saved my life just then.'

'Just make sure what you do next makes that effort worth it,' Sir Eldric replied. Not waiting for a response, Sir Eldric and three of his men disappeared into the mist, leaving the other two soldiers to escort Nicolas and his companions.

'Good luck,' he whispered after him, before the group moved off to find the kitchen entrance.

* * * *

That turned out to be an easier task than Nicolas had expected, even with limited visibility. The overturned delivery wagon they stumbled on pointed towards it like a giant wooden arrow. Dodging broken crates of lettuce and carrots, the group tried not to step in the remains of produce crushed in a mad dash to either flee vampire attackers or chase down prey. He couldn't help but wonder what fate had befallen the deliverymen, though he likely already knew. The trail of dying vegetables led to a simple wooden door in the castle's side, which had been smashed open from the inside and was thankfully unguarded.

The kitchen itself looked as if a storm had struck it, a mess of discarded utensils, spilled food, and blood splatter. What had happened in here had been fast and unsubtle.

'I don't think we're going to find any survivors here.' Nicolas tried to not look directly at the drying blood mixed with various cooking ingredients.

'I do not think we will find any survivors in the castle at all,' Garaz said solemnly.

'For creatures who drink blood, they sure do spill a lot of it,' Shift noted in disgust.

'Vampires.' Auron rolled his eyes as he examined the scene. 'They make up for it by being good hunters. I think this was one of the first rooms hit. They would've secured the exits first, made their way into the centre of the castle then up a level at a time.'

There were side pantries to the kitchen, which Sir Eldric's soldiers briefly checked. Nicolas wasn't surprised when he was told there were no vampires in the pantries; he couldn't imagine a vampire hanging around in there snacking on sausages or something.

Double doors led from the kitchen to the corridors of the castle proper. The décor was as extravagant as Nicolas had expected, lavish tapestries on the walls along with coats of arms and armour and paintings of rulers of old. Or had been until the vampires had their way.

'The vampires certainly went out of their way to tear this place up.' Shift looked at a torn painting, and the claw marked walls surrounding it.

'I suppose being forced to live in underground caves gives one a certain anger towards the most privileged,' Garaz suggested, examining a statue missing its head.

'Vampires,' Auron remarked again, as if that explained everything.

One of the eeriest things was the lack of sound in a place that should've been so full of life. It wasn't right. None of this was right at all. It was so silent that every crunch of carpet seemed to echo, calling the vampires to them. None came, but it didn't stop the tension making him feel as if the walls were closing in on them.

At the end of the corridor was another set of double doors, claw marks marring the perfectly carved images of kings of old. Through them was a large dining room that would've been stunning had the vampires not left their mark on it. The bulk of the room was taken up by the massive wooden dining table, surrounded by twelve chairs

'You!' From the king's chair rose a large, red-armoured figure, throwing down the decanter he'd been drinking from. It smashed on the table, throwing shards of glass and liquid across the polished surface.

Barus looked a lot different from the last time the group had encountered him. His pale, hairless face was now a mass of congealed, red scar tissue, his right ear fused to the rest of his face and half his mouth distended. One of his armoured hands was a useless, blackened stump that lay at his side. His formerly pristine blood-red armour was charred and blackened. He looked at the intruders with animalistic rage in the one eye he had left.

'I should be leading an army right now,' he screamed, spittle flying from his mouth. 'But I am *too crippled to be of use*. You have taken my honour and my moment of glory.'

'Funny hearing something that lives in a cave and drinks blood speak of honour,' Garaz replied.

Barus used his good hand to pick up a large war axe, whose dual blades were fashioned as bat wings and which he seemed to have no problem using single-handed. The vampire jumped onto the table and let out a mighty roar. 'Die!'

Manging impressive speed for a creature dragging a useless burnt leg, the vampire ran at them. Cutlery scattered and crockery smashed under his metal boot as his heavy footfalls dented the wood beneath him. Bearing down on his victims, Barus raised the war axe, ready to strike.

'Boo.'

From beneath the table, Auron appeared, jumping up directly into Barus's path, waving his arms. The sight caused the vampire to try to suddenly stop. However, the effect of his momentum and the drink he'd already imbibed made him stumble, and then fall. Dropping his axe, the vampire crashed forwards and slid, coming to a stop just before he flew off the edge of the table, his head dangling over the side as he attempted to get his bearings. Shift sliced down with their sword and took the overhanging head from its neck. It hit the carpet with an almost imperceptible thud before it, and the rest of Barus's body, crumbled to dust, leaving the empty red armour lying on the dining table.

'Even in death, I've still got it,' Auron preened.

'I feel like someone should make a joke about bad table manners.' Shift kicked the pile of dust that had once been Barus's head.

'You make too many jokes for such a dangerous time,' Garaz said, a hint of reproach in his voice.

Shift smiled at the orc and shrugged playfully.

'That worked much better than I thought it was going to.' Auron smiled. 'Lord Barus?'

The door on the far side of the dining hall opened just enough for a head to poke around it. Looking first towards the chair where Barus had been sitting, the vampire quickly noticed the empty, dusty suit of armour at the end of the table. His gaze then went straight to Nicolas and his companions. There was a cry of surprise, and the head disappeared back behind the door.

'After him,' Auron cried.

The gravity of the situation wasn't lost on Nicolas. If the vampire managed to alert the others, this mission would come to a very sudden and bloody conclusion.

Running for the door at full speed, they pursued the fleeing vampire. Emerging into a corridor almost identical to the previous one he saw the creature already at the far end of it. How were they supposed to catch something so fast? He didn't know, but that didn't mean they shouldn't try. Quickly he followed his companions in pursuit of the undead monster

Fortunately, as the corridor ended and turned into the grand entrance hall of the castle, the group found they didn't have to pursue the vampire much further. Unfortunately, there was a reason for that.

The grand entrance hall lived up to its name—or had, until the vampires had gone to work on it, hanging their own profane banners and placing human limbs around as decorative pieces. The row of heads adorning the pedestals lining the room almost certainly belonged to the royal family, regal faces now forever locked in expressions of horror.

The focal point of the room was the grand marble staircase around which a group of eight vampires variously sat or stood. Though he should've been terrified by the group, he found himself more confused. The scene was obviously painstakingly staged to in an attempt to make the vampires look both menacing and nonchalant at the same time. None of the creatures looked like they were sitting or standing naturally. Or even comfortably. A ninth vampire leant against the wall—and this one he recognised. The vampire was gazing pensively into some middle distance with a strange smouldering look on his face, the collar of his tunic turned up and his hair tussled to the tiniest degree.

'It seems we have intruders.' The leader of the Flawless Host sighed.

With another melancholy huff, he pushed himself lazily from the wall and strutted to join his fellows on the stairs, who seemed hung on their leaders every gesture.

'How droll,' the vampire said finally, punctuating his dramatic pause with a flick of his hair.

'Are we boring you?' Shift asked indignantly.

The vampire spared Shift the briefest of unimpressed glances before giving another sigh, a long, drawn-out faux breath as his gaze went back to the middle distance. 'Alas,' he began, leaning against the banister as if the weight of the world were on him. 'The curse of this un-life is that I find nothing truly entertaining anymore.' The vampire pensively rubbed the bridge of his nose. ' Your meek human lives seem to flash by in mere seconds as I walk the path of the immortal. I inhabit the world but find little joy in it.' Again staring back into the middle distance. 'This is my curse. To always be an outcast, desperate to connect but that connection always just out of reach.'

He couldn't help but find the whole show this vampire was putting on a little tiring. His followers seemed to be enjoying it though, lapping up every word.

'Did you practice that in front of a mirror?' Shift asked with a smug smile.

'I, who cannot walk in the sun, cast no reflection.' Change of pose. 'My curse ensures that I may never truly see the creature I have become, that I may never look into...these eyes, again,' the vampire proclaimed, staring back into the middle distance so hard that Nicolas actually turned his head to see if there was something there to look at.

'That is a great shame,' Auron said with a half-smile. 'Because if you *could* see yourself in a mirror, you'd realise that your hair's out of place.'

That got a reaction.

'Silence,' the vampire barked, finally displaying something resembling a personality. 'I am Lord of the Flawless, locked in a cage of eternal perfection. But do not mock, because all who hear the name Val tremble before it from either fear...or envy.'

'Isn't Val a girl's name?' he asked, the words coming before his brain could question the wisdom of upsetting a vampire lord.

There were several chuckles behind him, Shift and Auron's the loudest.

The eyes of all the vampires blazed at him with pure hatred, and Val's face darkened.

'We really need to talk about your gender concepts,' Shift whispered. 'But his reaction was worth it, so I'll let it go this time.'

'Laughter is such a bourgeois concept,' Val snarled. 'Let us see how you laugh when I puncture your neck and dine upon your life essence.'

He was becoming more frustrated than intimidated. Who'd have thought he'd find an undead creature anything other than terrifying? The true mark of how tiresome the vampire was, was the fact that Nicolas would actually rather get to the fighting. 'Even your threats sound lame.'

Val threw himself forwards, claws and fangs bared. There was a moment of shock. He was fast, very fast, faster than Nicolas's brain could process. Instead of *get out the way,* his mind instead sent the command *raise your sword.* So, it fell to Shift to grab him and yank him aside at the last second, the Dawn Blade sweeping wildly through the air as they did. The blur of the vampire's body passed him.

When he turned, the leader of the Flawless was standing still, his back to the room. Around him, his companions and the soldiers had their weapons ready. On the stairs, the other vampires all stood in expectation. Slowly, Val turned. Eyes wide, he brought his hand up to his cheek, to a tiny cut, which seemed to be the sum total of his sword swipe. The vampire touched the cut with two fingers and looked in disbelief at the blood on them.

'You...you have *cut* me,' the vampire whispered, looking at the blood as if it had come from a gaping wound. 'My face...is ruined.'

He didn't know what to say. For some reason, part of him wanted to apologise, but the cut was barely an inch long, and the guy was a murdering vampire.

'Hardly,' Shift replied with a snort.

'The kiss of your blade has forever tarnished my eternal beauty.' Val seemed like he was talking to him, but at the same time talking to no one at all.

'Hardly.' Auron snorted.

'I am...no longer...flawless.'

As if in a trance, Val walked towards the nearest wall and the small table that lay broken on the floor next to it. Reaching down slowly, he picked up one of the table's wrecked legs. With a dramatic, melancholy sigh, Val staked himself through the heart.

'If I cannot have perfection, I will have...oblivion.'

If there were any other words, they disappeared as the vampire's skin turned from flesh to dust and crumbled to the floor with a clattering wooden stake falling atop the pile of dust and empty clothes.

What in the Underworld had just happened? The other vampires, all the Flawless family, began to keen and wail in grief as the group readied themselves for a fight. Instead of a fight, what they got was the strange sight of each of the vampires copying their recently departed master. Each grabbed a broken piece of wood and staked themselves, striking a melancholy pose as their bodies disintegrated around them. They left stunned silence in their wake.

'I am so confused.' He looked at the mounds of dust on the floor. 'I...I...don't know.'

'I...am at a loss to understand what just happened,' Garaz said, confusion on his face.

'Vampires,' Auron shrugged as if that again explained everything.

CHAPTER 27

A fter the...whatever had happened on the stairway, no other vampires impeded their progress. Having Sir Eldric's men to act as guides meant the party made good progress towards the tower and whatever awaited. Ascending through the higher levels of the castle gave them all a greater view of the city. The dark cloud had extended as far as he could see, and columns of smoke from inside the city rose to join it where fires must've broken out. The battle in the streets must be fierce. If they could only hold out for just a little longer.

The view gave him a better perspective of what was at stake. To know it and to see it were two different things. All those buildings before him, home to thousands of innocent people whose lives could hang on what he did. It meant doing something he wasn't comfortable with, but if it was a choice between that and sealing the city's fate then... Well, truthfully, he still didn't know for sure if he could go through with it. Some part of him still hoped to talk his way out of this, talk the necromancer down, convince him to break his own spell so he didn't have to...do what he must. Why was he being so hard on himself? There were four others with him who could kill the necromancer. Why did he keep making it his sole responsibility?

At the top of the stairs at the highest point of the castle, the tower, there was a short corridor to their right and a single door leading to what Nicolas had been told was an observatory. Though the corridor was the same as any other in the castle, it seemed more ominous. Beyond that door was an ending, both for them and the city, whichever way it went.

As much as he tried to steel himself for what awaited, he found it difficult. Mainly because he wasn't sure what awaited. What he wouldn't give to see through the door before they went in. Briefly his eyes caught his reflection in the sword he held. How he had changed in just a few days. There was tiredness and cuts and bruises all over him, but also a determination in his face, a confidence he didn't recognise. If they succeeded, what would he be taking away from all of this?

The group assembled on the landing and looked at the door.

'That's it then?' he asked, trepidation and the weight of their responsibility pressing on him.

'Yes,' one of the soldiers confirmed. 'The castle observatory.'

'So we go in, kill the necromancer, and the cloud goes away?' Shift asked.

Next to Nicolas, Auron seemed ill at ease. 'There's no way it will be that easy,' he said. 'It never is.'

He was right.

Before them, the door opened, and a figure from the room beyond slipped into the corridor. He wore regal robes that would've put even the gaudiest king to shame, and his smile was filled with smugness.

'Here to pay homage to the new king of Yarringsburg and soon to be emperor of Etherius?' the count asked in a smooth voice, seemingly unconcerned about the armed group before him. 'Dawnblade,' the vampire said with an exaggerated bow as he looked at Auron. 'How pleasing to have you here to witness my triumph.'

'Count,' Auron greeted the vampire coldly.

The count looked at the group and something seemed to occur to him. 'If you are here, I take it Barus and Val are dead?' he asked casually.

'Yeah,' Shift answered. 'And not the *walking around in fancy clothes drinking blood* kind of dead either.'

The count shrugged as if it were no matter. 'You killed a useless cripple and a self-important idiot. Well done, you,' he mocked. 'The only irksome issue is that Barus was supposed to lead the Grand Army of the Vampires. But once you ruined him, he was hardly fit for the role. The half-breed's still healing from the arrow wound in the neck, and I would never have let Val lead the horde. They would have stopped every half an hour to preen themselves. I admit myself glad you killed that vain idiot, in all truth.'

'So, you let the child lead your army?' Garaz asked with a raised eyebrow, doing the math of vampire leaders left standing.

'Don't let her look and playfulness fool you.' The count laughed. 'She can be very effective when she has a task to complete. It's a shame I have to unleash an army to put my food in its place at all, but such is life.'

'And that just leaves you to stand here like some sort of gatekeeper?' Shift asked.

'I stand here as the emperor of the Vampire Nation, the very nation about to swallow the world. The spell is cast, and the slaughter my children are reaping will spread it across all kingdoms. Darkness will reign and so will we, despite your continued inconveniences.' The count stopped for a moment and appraised the group. 'If you bow to me now and pay the proper fealty, I may let the familiars keep you as pets.'

'As nice as that sounds, I think we'll pass.' Nicolas tried not to let his sword arm shake in the presence of pure, powerful evil.

'Yeah, the word of an emperor who lives at the whim of a necromancer isn't really worth much.' Shift smiled.

The count's face contorted angrily. 'Avus is a mere means to an end,' he replied. 'Once we have taken this city, he will soon learn his place.'

'Does he know this?' Garaz asked.

'He will soon enough.' The count smiled menacingly.

'Enough talk.'

The words had come from one of the two soldiers, prompting them to charge the count, swords raised and ready. Seconds later, they were both dead in a very sudden and brutal fashion. Nicolas was a little sick in his mouth. Garaz and Shift looked as stunned as he was.

The count took a moment to lick blood delicately from his fingers. 'I think your comrades were right,' the count mused. 'There has been enough talk. It is time for you die. Obviously, I cannot kill the beloved Dawnblade, but fear not, Auron, you will not have to grieve your friends' passings for too long. Once the necromancer has a spare moment, I will get him to banish your soul to the Underworld, old friend. Wouldn't do to have you floating around...haunting stuff.'

'I am not your friend, you pointy-fanged, preening, full of yourself, puddle of insect piss,' Auron snapped.

The count evidently took umbrage but didn't dignify Auron with a response. Instead, he closed on the group, doing so as if he had all the time in the world, savouring his moment.

'Ideas?' Garaz asked as he took a fighting stance.

'Die quickly but valiantly?' Nicolas had nothing better to offer.

'There are three of you,' Auron counselled. 'Use your numbers to keep him on the back foot and don't underestimate his speed or strength. Keep moving and wait for an opening.'

'I have a better idea.' Before Nicolas could ask what it was, Shift threw something towards the count.

The small glass orb smashed directly in the count's face, instantly encasing his head in a cloud of green smoke as the vampire roared in anger. As the smoke spread throughout the corridor and the vampire coughed and cursed,

'Thief,' Shift shrugged as they saw the question in his eyes.

'Nicolas,' Garaz said urgently, 'go and take care of the necromancer. We shall hold the vampire here.'

'Are you—'

'Go!' Auron shouted.

He didn't need telling a third time. Though visibility in the corridor had quickly become zero, it was a straightforward task to keep to the wall and advance. Fortunately, knowing where the vampire was in the cloud was simple due to the curses he was spitting out.

Reaching the door with a bump, Nicolas was about to open it when there was a sound behind him.

'Die, insect!' the count roared as he emerged from the smoke, running at Nicolas.

Preparing himself for a death equally brutal to the soldiers who had accompanied them, he was surprised when the count stopped short. With his own look of surprise and a choking sound, the count flew back into the smoke, yanked by his own elaborate cape.

'Thanks, guys,' he whispered.

With the sounds of fighting behind him, Nicolas slipped into the observatory, wishing his friends well and hoping he was up to whatever lay beyond. Despite his hopes otherwise, it seemed it would all be down to him now.

* * * *

As soon as he had entered the observatory the hairs on his arms stood on end, his skin prickling at the energy in the air. There was a metallic taste to the air and his senses dulled in the power around him. A single figure sat cross legged on the central platform where a telescope had once resided before being torn from its perch and discarded, head bowed as if in prayer. His topless back was covered in strange writing that made him queasy to look at. Around the figure swirled black smoke, which seemed to emanate from inside him before being channelled towards a large black crystal that hovered in the air in front of him. From the crystal, the smoke shot through the hole in the roof to feed the cloud that consumed the sky.

They were the only two occupants, though the multitude of bloodstains covering the star charts on the walls and the equipment laden tables suggested it had been heavily occupied only recently. He had no time to dwell on whatever bloody last stand may have occurred here. The necromancer was here. He had the advantage. The man hadn't seemed to notice he was no longer alone.

Part of him, a naïve part, still wanted to try and talk this out. But he couldn't give up his one advantage. The idea of taking a life, no matter how deserving, made him sick to his stomach, a fact that the idea of stabbing him in the back doubled. But this was not an honourable combat type of situation like heroes in the stories. So many had died already because of this man and so many more could. He couldn't risk it, he had to go in for the kill.

Creeping toward the necromancer, he could hear the man was chanting under his breath. The energy that came from him pushed against Nicolas like a wind. Despite that, he pressed on and raised the sword.

'Don't.' The necromancer spoke as if Nicolas were a child with a crayon poised to write on the wall.

He was so surprised by the sudden word that he stepped back.

The necromancer stood. Nicolas had forgotten how tall the man was. Without his robe on, he was also very slender, looking almost malnourished. The necromancer turned and despite the sweat glistening on his body and the look of sheer effort and exertion in his eyes, he smiled warmly. The nimbus of power shimmering around him made it difficult to look directly at him, but he persevered. This wasn't the time to stare at his shoes.

'Mr Nicolas Percival Carnegie,' the necromancer smiled warmly. 'How nice to have someone to talk to who isn't a vampire.'

'Talk to?' he asked. What exactly was going on? Whatever he'd expected from the necromancer, a nice chat was last on the list.

'Of course,' the necromancer said with an open-armed gesture. 'This is a historic day, and it's nice to be able to share it with someone other than those loathsome creatures.'

Now Nicolas was completely lost. 'The vampires, you mean?'

'Yes.' The necromancer curled his lip in distaste. 'Disgusting, pompous monsters, the lot of them. But needs must.'

'I'm sorry.' He was completely lost now. 'You don't like vampires?'

'Who does?' the necromancer laughed, a harsh, grating cackle. 'They don't even like each other.'

'Then why are you helping them take over the world?' Auron asked as he appeared at Nicolas's side, his face calm in a way that Nicolas's was definitely not.

'And the Dawnblade himself. Who better to share today with?' He gave them another genuine-looking smile.

'You can see me then,' Auron stated flatly.

'I am a necromancer. Of course I can see the dead. I see them all around me.'

Auron looked around the room but seemed to be looking specifically at things Nicolas couldn't see. 'You can see them all?'

'He means the screaming wizards,' the necromancer winked at Nicolas before turning back to Auron. 'Yes, I can.'

'Why don't you banish them?' he asked. 'Surely having ghosts screaming at you all day drives you mad?'

The necromancer laughed again. 'Why would I do that?' he asked. 'The sound is glorious to me. All those wizards who thought that they were so much better than me and now their spirits are trapped here at my whim, bound to me because I took their feeble lives. Their discontentment is like birds chirping in the morning.'

The necromancer paced the room, pointing into random areas of empty space which presumably contained a ghost.

"You are a disgrace to magic. Necromancy is an affront to nature. You are a filthy degenerate, and so on and so forth,' he almost sang as he circled the room with satisfaction. 'At least I'm alive, you pompous old fools.'

Great, the guy was full-on crazy. Suddenly the idea of talking him round seemed very remote. But still...

'Not for long,' he said, trying logic anyway. 'When the vampires make you one of them, you'll hardly be alive anymore.'

The necromancer stopped pacing and looked at him with confusion. Then his face changed, and he began to laugh. With every laugh, the cloud around him jumped and danced. 'Those creatures won't give me what they think I want, even if I did want it, which I don't.' He tapped his nose in a conspiratorial way.

'Oh, you're just dying to tell us, aren't you?' Auron sighed. Obviously, this was familiar territory to him.

'You want to know why I'm helping them take over the world?' the necromancer said theatrically. 'Here's the big twist, my friends. I'm not.'

Nicolas pointed towards one of the windows in the room. From it, you could see the city covered in black cloud and still aflame, the city the necromancer was helping to destroy. He gave an expression he hoped accurately conveyed that he begged to differ.

'Oh that,' the necromancer replied as if only just noticing it. 'The thing is, the vampires think I'm going to help them take over the world in exchange for being turned into one of their filthy kind. What they really intend to do is kill me the minute they take over the city. The idiots don't even realise that killing me would break the spell, which is something I'm going to do in about ten minutes anyway.'

'But the sun will come back out and the vampires will all die.' This was starting to give him a headache.

'And he'll be the hero who saved the city. Maybe even the world,' Auron interjected, shaking his head with a look of utter contempt on his face.

'Precisely,' came the very gleeful reply.

'But you loosed an army of vampires on the city.' Nicolas needed to try to understand why someone would even contemplate doing this. Could he even make sense of the ideas of a madman? 'The people will hardly love you for that.'

'Only if they know the truth.' The necromancer looked out of the window onto the burning city. 'But that won't be the narrative people hear. Once the *dust* settles, so to speak, people will want to know how the spell was broken. Who brought the sun back out and defeated an entire army of vampires singlehanded? Who saved the city and the world? And so, I shall emerge, this humble necromancer, shunned by society, but ready to step up and save it when its need was most dire. Breaking the grip of the vampires as it tightened around their necks. They will love me.'

'That's what this is all about?' He didn't think he'd ever been so disgusted in his life. 'All this death and carnage...to make people like you?'

The necromancer grew more serious for a moment. 'I've been looked down on my whole life for the gifts I possess. I've been hounded from town to town, spat upon, had children curse my name. I have gifts to share that nobody wants, secrets no one will listen to. Now people will see how useful necromancy can be. Me and the rest of my kind will be welcomed back to civilisation with open arms, to take our place amongst the scholars and wizards of the world where we belong. All thanks to me...and if I'm gifted an estate and title for my trouble, well, who am I to argue?'

'No one's going to believe you just happened along,' Auron scoffed.

'I do have some friends,' the necromancer replied with a half-smile. 'Sponsors who see the real value of my work, who gave me the resources to ensure my vision becomes reality. They will ensure the story's told the right way.'

'Brilliant.' Auron snorted. 'Hundreds dead just so a necromancer can get over his inferiority complex.'

'Careful, ghost,' the necromancer warned. 'Yesterday, I was just a humble necromancer. Today, I will be reborn Avus Arex, Hero of Yarringsburg and Scourge of Vampires.'

'You're no hero,' Nicolas snarled. 'You're a murderer and a villain.'

'Pfft, sheath your self-righteousness, pup, it has no place here.' Avus scoffed.

'Everyone will know exactly what you are, because I'll tell them. Every single person I meet,' he shouted, anger boiling up from inside him.

Avus Arex laughed again. 'It's very bold of you to assume that you're leaving here alive, Nicolas,' he said. 'As nice as it's been to have someone to brag to, you know I'm about to kill you, right?'

'I was going to say the same to you,' he declared, pointing the sword towards the necromancer.

Any previous hesitancy about taking a life was shed. The moral rights and wrongs faded away in a certainty that this man, this murderer, had to die. The weight lifted, he knew he was ready. What may come of it, he would deal with that later.

Avus Arex raised his hand and flicked his wrist almost lazily. There was no visible contact, but it was as if a charging troll had hit him. His body was thrown clear across the room to slam painfully into the stone wall, driving the air from his lungs completely. He heard the metallic clang of his sword hitting the floor, but the room was spinning too fast to see where it had gone.

'Do you have any idea how much magical energy is coursing through my veins right now?' Avus asked, looking at his hand as if it were brand new. 'Of course you don't, or you wouldn't have made that feeble attempt to threaten me.'

'Don't worry, kid, I'm here.'

Auron was running towards him. Instantly, he knew what the spirit was planning to do. He didn't look forward to it, but if it was the only way to get the job done then so be it. Then, Auron stopped dead in his tracks. His white eyes looked around wildly and though he appeared to be trying, he couldn't move.

'No,' The necromancer approached Auron and appraised his ethereal form. 'Some might call trying to possess the boy so he can actually fight cheating.' He said with a wagging finger. 'And some might call trying to do that in front of someone who can command the dead...stupid.'

Still Auron couldn't move, but the contempt for the necromancer burned from his essence as clearly as the black cloud danced around Avus's.

Finding Avus distracted with his gloating, he had a moment to recover. Shakily, he pushed himself up from the floor. Taking a moment to ensure he would stay standing, he brushed himself off and raised his fists in front of him. There he stood, glaring defiantly at the topless man with clouds of magical energy dancing around him. The necromancer slowly raised an eyebrow.

'Seriously?' Avus gave a harsh laugh. 'I've shown you but a fraction of what I can do, and you want to challenge me to a fist fight?'

'No, I want to kick your ass.' Oh Deities did he want to.

Another harsh laugh came from Avus, and with a flick of his hand, he drew Nicolas through the air towards him, to be left hovering just off the ground, eye level with the tall necromancer. He couldn't move the top half of his body, his arms restrained to his sides and his head held in an unseen grip to keep him eye to eye with Avus.

The necromancer looked Nicolas in the eye with a smile before punching him in the stomach. He heaved and gasped as his diaphragm spasmed, pain rippling through him. Hacking violently, he saw blood flying from his mouth. His breaths were wheezy and uneven. He wanted to cradle his stomach, to crumple to the ground, but the magic held him firmly in place. No wait, that wasn't quite true. It seemed as if he could still move his legs.

'I'm not one for the rough stuff,' Avus gloated as he blew on his knuckles, clearly proud of his punch. 'But I think I acquitted myself quite well there. Still fancy duking it out with me, Nicolas Percival Carnegie, or would you rather I just kill you now?'

'Today, it's Nick Carnage, you walking dragon anus.' He smiled, relishing the confused look on the necromancer's face.

With all his might, Nicolas swung his leg upwards. It wasn't much, but the area he targeted was pretty sensitive, so it wouldn't take much. Avus's mouth became an exaggerated 'O' as the kick connected with his balls. Wheezing hard, the necromancer held his groin as he fell to his knees.

The magical grip on Nicolas slackened, and he made the short drop to the floor. He may not have been a natural fighter, but he knew not to waste an advantage when he had one. Driving himself forward, he brought his fist crashing across the necromancer's cheek. The smacking sound satisfying, he followed up with his other fist. This time he felt something crack beneath the blow, the necromancer's cheek bone most likely. Knuckles burning with pain, he used the most obvious tool he had left and drove his forehead straight into the necromancer's nose. There was an audible crunch and warm blood spurted across his face. Avus let out a muted cry of pain as he fell back to the floor.

The price Nicolas paid for that broken nose was the spinning room, the headbutt disorientating him. Using a nearby table to steady himself, he saw Avus lying the floor, howling as he held his nose, blood escaping from between his fingertips. The necromancer's legs open, he was almost begging for another shot to the groin, and Nicolas was happy to oblige. He took a run up and was about to swing when a hand shot out and he found himself propelled into the air.

The walls of the room passed by him at speed, for a moment he wondered if he was headed toward the hole in the ceiling, destined to shoot through the sky until he left Etherius entirely. His back struck hard wood, answering his question and jarring his spine painfully. Arching his back involuntarily, he cried out when whatever force had lifted him from the ground simply let him go.

Falling, he winced rather than watch himself speed towards the ground, shielding his head with his forearms in an attempt to protect at least part of himself. If he survived the fall at all. His body struck a table with force, the legs of the table giving out beneath the impact, the table crashing to the floor with him, items on it either dispersed to the ground of digging into him painfully. His entire body felt numb, that wasn't good. His eyes struggling to focus, he saw his arm at his side, a thick splinter of wood embedded in the skin, his forearm torn and bleeding freely. Moving slowly, as if underwater, he reached to the splinter and pulled it out with a wince, casting it aside as blood flowed freely from the wound and he felt an echo of the pain to come.

Knowing he was still in a very dangerous situation he tried to rise, pushing up with his arms and legs. It felt as if a mountain were atop him. Shaking limbs soon gave out under the strain and he collapsed back to the table. He needed to move. He couldn't just lay here and wait for...

Forcibly, his body was turned over, a hand gripping his throat tightly. He let out a choked cry, the edges of his vision blurring as he was lifted from the ground, his airways compressed. Sharp fingernails dug into his neck, drawing blood. Desperately, he clawed at the hand holding his neck, but the grip gave nothing. Spots appeared before his eyes, along with the necromancer's face, bloody nose sideways and eyes burning with rage.

'You...dare,' Avus snarled, struggling to talk properly with his ruined nose and spitting blood with every syllable.

Desperately he tried to push the necromancer off of him, striking the arm holding him up. The grip tightened even more, and his limbs went limp. There was simply no way he could fight any more. He was done. He'd come so close to ending this madness but ultimately, he'd failed. At least he had the small satisfaction of the injuries he'd given the necromancer being the last thing he saw.

'Die,' Avus screeched with a maniacal smile.

The necromancer raised his free hand, which was coursing with black energy. Something terrible was about to happen to him, but he accepted it. The failure was harder to accept, but at least he'd made a stand, for all the good it had done. Hopefully, someone else would save all the families he'd let down. And his family...would they ever know what had happened to him?

Gravity suddenly caught him, and he fell to the floor, grip broken and air fighting its way back into his lungs. On his knees, he coughed and attempted to regain himself. When he looked up through watering eyes, Avus still stood tall over him, but now the blade of a sword protruded from a bloody wound in his stomach. Avus was looking down at the blade in disbelief.

'Evil never triumphs whilst the righteous stand against it,' Sir Eldric snarled from the other end of the sword, worse for wear but impressive, nonetheless.

Avus turned his head to the side to see who'd impaled him and raised his hand, still coursing with energy, towards his attacker. But before he could utilise it, Sir Eldric withdrew his blade with a disgusting sucking sound and took the necromancer's head off with a single clean swing. The head bounced on the floor in front of Nicolas. In a moment of forgivable pettiness, he spat on it.

As the necromancer's headless torso fell first to its knees and then to the floor, the aura in the room changed, the black cloud of energy around the necromancer vibrating fiercely. The vibration made its way as a pulse towards the crystal, causing it to crack and shatter almost to dust. The thread of black energy feeding from the crystal into the sky evaporated instantly, and Nicolas was sure he could already see the first rays of sunlight in the sky.

By the Deities, had they actually won? Was this what victory felt like? He wanted to be elated, but he was in so much pain. Slowly propping himself up on the edge of the nearest window, he watched the light come back to Yarringsburg.

CHAPTER 28

W hen a hand touched Nicolas's shoulder, he jumped with more energy than he'd thought he had left, turning and raising his fists to fight. Sir Eldric looked impressed. The High Marshall was cut and bruised, his clothes torn. It looked as if he'd just as much of an adventure getting here as Nicolas had.

'Thank you for saving me...again.' He glanced at the still closed door to the room. Curiosity got the better of him. 'How did you get up here?'

'It was not easy,' Sir Eldric replied, gesturing to the state he was in, 'but one doesn't get to be High Marshall without knowing all the secrets ways of the castle.' He pointed behind him.

Nicolas followed Sir Eldric's direction to a bookcase of old texts that was slightly ajar, revealing a passageway behind it. Suddenly, he realised his role in all this.

'Were we just a distraction?' he asked. 'We were to keep the vampires busy so you could slip up here and do the deed?' He forced his eyes away from the necromancer's headless corpse.

'Partly,' Sir Eldric admitted with a shrug. 'But splitting our group still doubled our chances for success, though I did hope you might keep the bulk of the vampires busy.' The High Marshall looked him over, he doubted he was a good sight right now. 'I am glad you survived.'

Being used as bait was...annoying, but he understood the gambit. In the end, he was still alive, and they had succeeded. 'Fair enough.' He shrugged.

From the corner of the room came a hearty laugh. He turned, and Auron was staring at something in particular with a large smile on his blue face.

'What's so funny?' he asked.

'The necromancer's ghost is here.' Auron didn't take his eyes off the scene that captivated him so. 'A pit to the Underworld has opened, and he's trying to claw the sides of it to keep himself here. But there are a lot of angry ghosts around him stamping on his fingers and...oh, there he goes. So long, jackass, have fun in the Underworld.' He waved.

Nicolas burst out laughing as sunlight filled the room.

'You did great, Nicolas.' Auron smiled at him with pride.

'You used my name...my proper name?'

'When you help save the world, I can't very well keep calling you *kid,* can I?' He smiled.

Pride swept over him. He had helped. Maybe he hadn't done the lion's share of the work, but he'd been here, and he had tried, and they had won. That was something. Their group had—

'Shift and Garaz!' he shouted as he bolted for the door, scooping up the Dawn Blade on his way.

He swung it open, and the figure of the count filled the corridor beyond. The vampire held Garaz off the ground with a single hand, hissing at the orc's bloodied face. The counts other hand moved slowly to the back of Garaz's head, appearing ready to snap the orc's neck. To the side of them, Shift lay face down on the carpet, unmoving. The last threads of green smoke still lingered in the air.

Hearing the door, the count turned his head, eyes widening as he saw Nicolas, before his face contorted in rage.

'You,' the vampire snarled.

'Me.' What was left of him anyways.

Dropping Garaz, who landed in a heap on the carpet, the count turned to him, the shadows in the hallway seeming to lengthen and gather around the vampire lord. Gulping, he realised the primal fury that was about to be unleashed upon him. How could he stand against that? He could barely stand. As bloody and beaten as he was, seeing his friends lying prone on the floor, not knowing if they were alive or dead, he knew that if standing was all he could do, then he would make his last stand here, for them.

'You have undone my great work, child,' the counts voice trembled with rage. 'But you shall not savour your victory. Your story ends here.'

Story? That word triggered a memory and he suddenly looked at the sword in his hand, the reflective blade.

With a roar of frustration that stabbed his eardrums, the vampire began to stalk toward him. Backing away under the full force of the approaching storm that was the count's wrath he retreated back into the observatory. The count smiled, licking one of his fangs in anticipation.

'You reek of fear, boy,' the advancing vampire purred. 'It smells delicious.'

Stopping beneath the hole in the observatories roof, Nicolas smiled back at the creature. 'All you're about to smell, is burning.'

As the vampire looked at him quizzically, he angled the Dawn Blade into the shaft of light coming through the observatory roof. Turning the sword, soon the area around the counts eyes was illuminated by a reflected beam of pure sun light. The vampire roared in pain. As much as he wanted to look away, watching the vampires face burn was strangely fascinating. Quickly the count brought his cloak over his face, but the damage was done. Stumbling back into the door frame, the count's cloak dropped, revealing cauterised scar tissue where his eyes had one been.

'I can't see...I can't see...' the vampire moaned.

Cradling his ruined eyes and cursing, the count didn't see the shadow that loomed over him, but Nicolas did. With a slowness that told of weariness and great pain, Garaz rose until he stood tall over the vampire, enraged, his eyes red pinpricks of light beneath his brow. With a mighty cry the orc brought his sword swinging into the neck of the vampire. The blade cut deep into the creatures flesh and the count began to make a choking sound, blood running from between his lips. But the sword hadn't cut straight through, and the vampires head was still attached to the neck, albeit barely. Unable to tear himself away from the sight, he watched Garaz take a scruff of the count's hair and pull the vampires head from his neck with a wet tearing sound that made him wince. Discarding the head disdainfully as the count's body crumbled to dust, the orc slumped to his knees, breathing heavily.

As much as he wanted to check on Garaz, Nicolas knew that Shift had yet to move, whereas the orc was obviously alive. Moving as quickly as his body let him, he ran to Shift then took them in his arms and turned them over carefully. Their arm was at an incorrect angle and looked bruised and swollen. He couldn't tell if they were breathing as he tenderly cradled their head in his lap, searching for signs of life.

'Do not try to kiss me,' Shift murmured weakly.

'What?' he asked, slightly affronted.

'You heard.'

'I wasn't.'

Shift opened a single eye and regarded Nicolas. 'Me lying on the floor with a broken arm is no time for you to get romantic.'

'I wasn't!' he protested.

'Are they okay?' Auron asked as he leant over Shift.

'Fine,' he answered dryly.

'Nice move with the sword, kid,' the spirit said. 'Whoever you learned that from knows his stuff.'

The idea that they were all badly beaten and Auron was still self-aggrandising made him laugh aloud.

'I take it from the sunlight outside that we won?' Garaz asked as he limped up to the trio.

'Yes.' He smiled. 'We won.'

＊ ＊ ＊ ＊

Nicolas would be the first to admit he'd never been interested in tales of heroism, but in the few he *had* heard, this was the point where everything was supposed to go back to normal and everyone lived happily ever after. For the city of Yarringsburg, it wasn't quite as simple as that.

Victory had been swift once Avus Arex was slain, which had happened in the nick of time. The vampires had been seconds from completely overrunning the defenders of the city. By all accounts, it had been one hell of a fight, with many stories of bravery, self-sacrifice, and fighting against the odds, coupled with stories of brutality and terrible carnage. But in the end, the horde of vampires had nearly proven too much to hold back. Fortunately, the simple idea that their plan had been based on—kill the necromancer and the sun returns—had proven correct. With his death, the sun had retaken the sky, with the vampires out in the open.

The unfortunate side effect of several hundred vampires combusting as one was a raging inferno in the centre of the city, absorbing the blazes already underway to create a virtual storm of flame and smoke. The defenders found themselves going from defending the city from a horde of the undead to defending it from a primal element of nature itself. In this, they were reinforced by the citizens of Yarringsburg, who rallied with buckets of water and earth to fight the blaze before it burned their homes completely to ash. It was a dogged fight, but eventually a successful one, though the damage to the city would take years to repair.

There was also the dust cloud. The deaths of thousands of vampires caused a mass dust cloud to descend on the city, almost like a fog that refused to settle. People took to covering their faces so they didn't breathe in flakes of dead vampire. Though apparently some despicable profiteers took to gathering the dust and selling it as some kind of miracle cure-all.

Reinforcements from the outer towns and garrisons arrived just before nightfall, providing fresh troops to tend the wounded, help fight the last of the fires, and hunt down and exterminate the few vampires who'd managed to get inside before they were burnt to ash. The cornered creatures didn't last long against vengeful hunters.

As the sun rose anew on Yarringsburg, large columns of smoke still rose into the sky, defiant to the fact that the fires which had created them were extinguished. People were blackened with soot and smoke and flecked in dust. Coupled with the exhaustion they all felt, the people of Yarringsburg looked like ghosts of themselves, even though, all told, they had endured. The cost had been high, though. Much of the city's central district was in ruins and though there was no official tally of the dead yet, it was easily in the hundreds. People mourned their lost loved ones and grieved for the royal family, whose line had indeed been extinguished by the vampires.

In the absence of any direct descendants to the throne or leadership from the Royal Council, who'd also been in the castle at the time of the attack, Sir Eldric had taken charge and done an admirable job. He appeared to be everywhere at once, delivering food, bolstering morale, and getting involved tackling fires and hunting straggling vampires. Emergency hospitals were set up for the injured and a shanty town was hurriedly constructed outside the city in order to give shelter to the massed homeless. By the middle of the next day, work crews had already been organised to clear rubble and begin the rebuilding process. The city and kingdom would heal but would bear the scars of what was popularly referred to as the *The Sunless Day* for years to come.

But Yarringsburg would not need to do this alone. Aid soon began to arrive from many of the other Nine Kingdoms of Man once news spread of the attack. Old rivalries were ignored in the new spirit of cooperation, allowing the people of Yarringsburg to stand tall even in their privation.

Sir Eldric became a legend overnight. Killing a necromancer and by proxy several hundred vampires in a single blow tended to inflate one's reputation even before factoring in all the good work he did afterward. By the end of the next day, there was a popular movement to have him named the new king.

* * * *

Nicolas leant against the wall of the city gate, enjoying the cool stone on his back in contrast to the warm morning sun. A new group of workers had just arrived at the city to the tune of the continued sawing and hammering of those already engaged in rebuilding. From the look of them and the tools they'd brought, they were stone masons and carpenters. Their arrival was marked by a wave of cheering that extended from the edge of the shanty town surrounding the city to the bustling crowd around the gate itself. After dismounting their wagons, the leaders of the group were guided to marshalling stations just inside the city gates, where work details were organised and dispatched.

Though it had been several days since the battle, the city still smelled of burning. He was almost used to it now—the lingering smell of death from the massed funeral pyres outside the city less so. But soon that would no longer be his problem.

To his right, nestled against the city wall, was a large mound of dust—all that was left of the vampires—which it had become custom to spit on as you walked past, to avert bad luck. It was surprising how much saliva these people could produce with the dry air around them.

Outside the city gates, the shanty town, a sea of tents, stretched as far as he could see. Random columns of smoke from cookfires rose between the tents and children ran around, noisily at play. Though all these people had been displaced, there was a good spirit in the camp. Presumably if the alternative was being killed and made into a vampire, a few weeks in a tent seemed glorious in comparison. The people of Yarringsburg had been brought together by the tragedy as never before.

'Boo,' Auron said matter-of-factly as he appeared at Nicolas's side.

Looking at his companion, he couldn't suppress a small smile. For all that they'd been through over the past days, Auron was still flawless, if blue, while Nicolas was bruised and battered. Garaz had treated the worst of his wounds but had wanted to help the city healers as soon as he was able, despite their protests. It was a shame not all help was happily accepted in Yarringsburg.

'Still here then?' he asked.

'Apparently so,' Auron replied. 'I thought my spirit would've passed on as soon as Silva died, and then when the necromancer did, but no, still here. I think I can feel it coming, but I just want to linger here a little longer and see the city well. Then it will be time to go. Which is sad, but I'm definitely curious what the afterlife is like.' The spirit chuckled thoughtfully. 'I've had a long and bloody life. It's time to put my feet up.' Auron looked at him for a moment. One of those piercing gazes he did every so often. 'Have you thought about continuing?'

'Adventuring?'

'Yeah,' Auron said, choosing his words carefully. 'You may not have the most natural gift for it, but you're better than you give yourself credit for and your heart is in the right place. Sometimes, that counts a lot more than experience or ability.'

Strangely enough, he *had* thought about it a lot over the last few days as he'd helped to clear rubble and search for survivors. He would've been lying if he said he wasn't tempted. The idea of helping people appealed to him. But in the end, he'd seen too many terrible things—things he never wanted to think about again, much less repeat, so there was only one real answer for him, one place he wanted to be.

'My heart's place is at home.' He ignored the disappointment that nagged at him upon speaking those words.

'Fair enough.' Auron sounded disappointed but understanding. 'I would shake your hand if I could.'

'Me too.' He looked at his friend.

'So, Nicky's plan all along was to kiss his way through all of us?' Shift asked as they approached with Garaz in tow. 'Now I don't feel special anymore.'

'I wasn't going to kiss him.' He made a face at his companion.

'Judging by the look you two were giving each other, I disagree.' Shift smiled.

'Nicolas has made no attempt to kiss me,' Garaz stated simply. 'I feel strangely left out.'

'You can shut up too,' Nicolas snapped playfully.

Both his companions still looked worse for wear, but then they'd had no real chance to rest as they helped get Yarringsburg back on its feet. Shift's arm hung limply in a sling across their chest. Garaz insisted he'd healed the bone while Shift protested that it still hurt. Nicolas had an idea Shift was pulling a fast one to get out of the heavy work with the relief effort. The orc looked tired and pale, having expended a great deal of energy treating the injured, only resting when forced to.

'So, we are doing our goodbyes then?' Shift asked as they looked at the full pack at Nicolas's feet.

'Appears so.' he smiled. 'There are enough people here now that I feel I can make my way. Besides, I am way overdue at home. My parents were going to kill me.' Thank the Deities he'd thought to send a courier to let them know he was still alive. 'What about you two?'

'I'll hang here a few more days until my arm heals, then I was thinking of heading south,' Shift said with a wink. 'I tend not to stay in one place too long.'

'Because you rub people up the wrong way so quickly?' he teased.

Shift punched him playfully on the arm with their free hand.

'How about you Garaz?' Auron asked. 'You sticking around?'

The orc shaman thought for a moment before he replied. 'No, my friend,' he said. 'Since *non-human* elements did such damage to the city there is more than a little...distaste for anyone who does not have the correct look.'

Nicolas hadn't wanted to acknowledge it openly, but he'd seen evidence of this over the last few days. There was a general undercurrent of dislike towards the non-human residents of Yarrinsgburg, many of whom had been savvy enough to get out of town while the getting was good. There were already some men on street corners speaking of humans banding together against threats from *'out there.'* Hopefully, the general anger and resentment would naturally fade as the city pulled itself back together.

'That's probably a good idea.' He peripherally noted the glares directed towards the orc.

'It shouldn't be,' Shift protested. 'We were instrumental in saving the city, after all.'

'We were,' he soothed. 'But it was actually Sir Eldric who did the deed.'

'On the back of our hard work. Where's our credit? A knighthood maybe? Some gold, at least?' Shift pouted.

'The city needs someone strong to rally around,' Auron counselled. 'Let him have his moment. So what if we're a footnote in the official history? We know what we did.'

'Says the man with a thousand glorious deeds to his name.' Garaz chuckled.

'Correction,' Auron said with mock seriousness, 'I just stopped counting at a thousand.'

They all laughed, and Nicolas hoped this moment stuck in his head for the rest of his life. It would be a good memory during a time when he'd had plenty of bad.

'It's been a blast,' Shift smiled, noting his expression.

'That it has,' he admitted.

Nicolas yelped as a pair of thick green arms wrapped around him.

'It has been an honour, Nicolas Percival Carnegie.' Garaz's words were from the heart.

'Still say that Nick Carnage sounds better, a real hero name.' Auron laughed.

'I tried it once and I don't think it fit,' he murmured, still locked in the orc's iron grip. 'Maybe next time.'

Garaz let go, and Nicolas, once his lungs could function properly again, gave him a firm handshake. Then he turned to Shift, opening his arms.

'Nope,' they said with a smile.

'Maybe next time.' He smiled back.

Not that he ever planned on there being a next time. Though thinking of it reminded him of something he'd nearly forgotten.

'Uh, Auron,' he said quietly. 'About that...' He indicated the sheathed sword by his pack. By rights, it was Auron's, though he could no longer wield it.

'Keep it.' The spirit looked at the weapon lovingly. 'Call it a reminder. Of us. And of what you can do when you aren't overthinking it or panicking.'

'Like I'd ever forget any of that.' He laughed.

With that, he hefted his pack onto his shoulders, took up the sword, and found he had no words. There was nothing he could say that would accurately express how he felt in this moment. Over the last few days, he'd become so close to such a ragtag group of people. He'd laughed with them, despaired with them. Run with them, and fought with them. Nearly died with them...and he now felt closer to them than to anyone else.

Instead of words, he offered a genuine smile and an exaggerated bow before he turned and walked from the city gates. He couldn't help turning back to wave before the group was out of sight. It was returned.

* * * *

Thankfully, the worst thing about the return journey to Hablock was the anticipation of being home, which seemed to make it last an age. But with every step he knew he was that little bit closer to home and family, and he had some beautiful scenery to distract him from time to time. He also had the satisfaction of knowing his time away had been in the service of doing something good, not that he planned on ever sharing that with anyone. Some of the trip he spent trying to think of a plausible way to explain his bruises.

As happy as he knew he would be to be home, he really felt it when the village square of Hablock came into sight on the horizon, finding himself breaking into a run down the countryside tracks. His body may be banged up from the events he had been thrust into, but finally seeing what he had longed for through all of it gave him new energy.

On the final stretch to the village he was unsurprised to see a crowd waiting for him. He thought he'd been spotted by some field hands a while back, they must've spread the word. That, or the crowd had been here since he'd left. Indistinct figures became expectant faces as he grew closer and he couldn't stop the beaming smile on his face, despite how much it irritated his bruises. As he saw his parents break from the crowd and run to him he couldn't help but cry aloud. 'Mum, Dad.'

Dropping his pack, he sped toward them. Gripping them both as tightly as they gripped him when they met.

'We were so worried,' his mother sobbed into his shoulder.

'You were only supposed to be gone a day,' his father shouted with mock outrage, a tear in his eye too.

As the embrace broke, his mother took his head in her hands. 'Deities, Nicolas are you okay?' She appeared to search him for visible wounds. 'We thought...all sorts.' Her voice was full of emotion.

He was okay, he really was. Despite his haggard state, he was elated to finally be home, pushing the lingering thoughts of the three people he found himself missing to the back of his mind.

'I'm okay,' he confirmed. 'And I'm so glad to be home.'

'We've both prayed for you night and day,' his mother said.

He'd done a fair bit of that himself. 'They worked.' He smiled.

'What happened?' his father asked in earnest.

'I delivered the message...it just took a little longer than I thought.'

His parents looked sceptical, but they respected the fact that he clearly didn't want to talk about it. Which he most certainly did not.

'Proud of you, son,' his father said, moving to grab his discarded pack as his mother took his shoulder and led him back toward the cheering crowd in the square.

The welcome home party lasted well into the night. When Nicolas did finally make it to his bed, he slept for an entire day, the Dawn Blade at the side of his bed with only its sun-carved hilt showing.

Epilogue

Yarringsburg Castle smelled of a strong mixture of fine aromas as servants continued to scrub clean every surface they could find. There were scents in the air he could identify and many he could not, all mixing together to make the air sickly sweet. But still, underneath it all, was the smell of blood. It would take a long time for the smell to go completely, which was unsurprising as the stuff had been all over most of the walls and carpets not a week before.

Eldric, now king of Yarringsburg, turned down the corridor leading to his chamber, and the servants stopped their work instantly to turn and bow to him. This had happened in every corridor since he had entered the castle, and crowds had cheered and chanted his name in every street between the castle and the temple where he had been proclaimed king.

As he walked down the corridor, his feet squelched slightly upon the still-wet carpet. He could not blame the servants for that. The place had been a slaughterhouse, after all, and they were all new, their predecessors being the ones whose slaughter had soiled everything so. Eldric stopped several times to speak to various servants who looked up at him with awe and shock that he would deign to notice them. Every time, his personal guard would stop and then follow him again in perfect step. Again, these men were new to the role but had taken it on admirably, though it helped that he had handpicked them all.

Eldric proceeded to the end of the corridor and the large pair of ornate wooden doors that marked the entrance to the king's chambers. As he approached the door, he could make out the heraldry carved into them—the heraldry of his predecessor. Eldric wanted no trace of his predecessor left in the castle, but these things took time. He made a mental note to bring it up with his new chancellor in the morning.

When he reached the door, the two golden-armoured guards before it stood smartly to attention. Eldric nodded to them, and one moved to open the door. Beyond the opening door, he could see his new home, taking a moment to soak it all in. Before the coronation, he had been staying in his old chambers. He could have insisted on staying here immediately, but it had seemed crass to do so until everything was official and may have ruffled some feathers amongst the traditionalists. For now, he needed to keep up appearances. That would change, but again, all in good time.

'That will be all, captain,' Eldric said, half-turning to view the leader of the five-man troop behind him.

'Very good, my king,' the captain replied smartly, striking his gauntlet to his chest before dispersing his men along the corridor to stand watch.

My king. Eldric had heard that term a lot today but still got a satisfied tingle whenever he did. He nodded to the captain and proceeded into what were now his chambers.

The doors closed behind him, and he was finally alone for the first time since sunup. The first part of his chamber was a study filled with old books, an antique desk, and an ornate fireplace that kept the room at a perfect temperature. Circling the room, his hands outstretched, he touched everything that was now his: books and papers and furniture and ornaments.

The room beyond was his sleeping chamber, with a huge four post bed. This was the first area in the castle where he could not smell the lingering taint of blood. He would commend the servants for that later, as the efforts to get it out of this room in particular must have been immense.

Next to the requisite dressers and wardrobes was a standing mirror, and Eldric took a moment to admire himself. He looked resplendent in his velvet tunic with cape and furs—as much a king as any of a royal bloodline ever had. He touched the pommel of his gold-hilted sword then removed the crown on his head and studied it.

It was a simple design elevated by the gems and carvings that adorned it, giving the right message of humbleness yet greatness. Turning, he placed the crown upon the stand by his bed and removed his sword of office, hanging it in place upon the wall.

Then he stopped dead. The hair of the back of his neck rose and goosepimples ran across his flesh. The air around him had a metallic tinge to it. He turned back to the mirror. Where there had once been a reflective surface, there was now a moving pool of rippling green energy that swirled and dipped and bubbled before him silently.

'*Enjoying your moment of glory, good king?*' A soft yet penetrating voice seemed to come from nowhere, and everywhere.

'I think I deserve to bask in my accomplishment,' Eldric replied, not taking his eyes from the mirror.

'*Of course you do,*' the voice replied. '*It is not every day that a man becomes king. You have earned it, Eldric.*'

'I would not be here without your help, your guidance,' he replied, knowing that acknowledgement was expected.

There was a moment of silence in which he somehow felt the pleasure of the voice addressing him.

'*I trust everything is in order?*' the voice asked.

'Yes,' Eldric replied with a smug half smile. 'Everyone who may have known anything is dead. I believe that should tie up any loose ends nicely.'

'*Surely you know better than most that some things that die do not stay dead?*'

'The necromancer never met me directly, dealing with the same third party who hired the mercenaries. The vampires had no clue what they were really involved in, stupid, arrogant creatures. Maybe one or two survived the burn and the purge afterwards, but the Five Families are gone and so is all their strength.'

'*Silly man thought he was going to be a hero.*' The voice chuckled, a dark edge to it now.

'He actually believed people would think him the saviour of Yarringsburg. You should have seen the look on his face when I killed him,' Eldric said with a predatory grin.

'*And the king?*'

'He suspected something was going on, but he had no clue what. That was why he summoned that idiot. *The Dawnblade*. Fortunately, Silva and Grimmark saw to that complication,' Eldric answered. 'Losing those two was a blow. Not having them here to let me into the castle made a certain amount of *improvising* necessary, but it worked out well enough. Shame to lose good help, though. They could have been useful with what's to come.'

'*Are there any to challenge your claim to the throne?*'

'No.' Eldric smiled. 'Charging into the vampire's nest shouting the king's name prompted the filthy creatures to be very thorough when it came to eliminating the royal bloodline.'

'*Those who stand tall with power cannot always see the drawn knives of those beneath them,*' the voice mused.

Was that directed at him? Was his loyalty being questioned? 'I know who I serve, and I believe in what we are doing.'

'Of course you do, King Eldric,' the voice soothed. 'I know you are loyal. That is why you were chosen.' The voice enquired after a second, 'What of this 'Nick Carnage' and his companions?'

'Nicolas is nothing.' Eldric sneered. 'As far as anyone worth anything is concerned, he was only peripherally involved. If they knew about him at all. I am the saviour of Yarringsburg. The fact that Nicolas and his friends believed they had any effect on the outcome of these events *at all* is laughable. I would have killed the necromancer regardless of their involvement.'

'Do they need silencing?'

He gave that a moment's thought. 'They know nothing. Everyone believes the necromancer worked alone and it is done. Nicolas has disappeared back to the nothing village he came from, and the others have dispersed in different directions. Killing him and his companions would be a waste of time, at best, and at worse, lead to questions being asked. Leave them where they are and let them rot in their mediocre lives.'

'Very well,' the voice replied. 'Take the time to settle into your new role, King, and cement your position. Then the real work can begin in earnest.'

'Soon?' Eldric questioned.

'Wheels are turning in the other kingdoms as we speak. Pieces move and events unfold in our favour,' the voice said with a hint of smugness. 'We have great things to accomplish, King Eldric, but all in due course. We did not get this far by being impatient.'

'Of course, Maestro.' He bowed to the mirror, to his master.

The mirror solidified again, leaving Eldric's reflection staring back at him. But the voice still lingered in the air briefly before fading away itself.

'We shall change the world,' it whispered before vanishing.

King Eldric smiled.

ACKNOWLEDGEMENTS

The fact that you're reading this is amazing to me. When I first had an idea for a story and started typing away during the first year of lockdown, I had many fanciful ideas about one day holding a book that I had published in my hands. I say fanciful, because I always tried to temper myself. Sometimes it sounded more like negativity, *'Well, nothing will come of it, but at least you're having fun writing it'*. But I never let it stop me writing.

Letting someone read my first draft, that was scary. That's why I chose my Mum. I may never have chosen to let anyone read it, but she asked and I said yes. When she came back and told me how great it was I was surprised. If I can get someone who doesn't read fantasy to enjoy a fantasy novel then maybe I had something here? (I said that whilst privately hoping it wasn't just my Mum being nice because...well, she's my mum).

So what did I do? I kept working. I kept learning and kept taking that next step. And now you are holding in your hand the outcome of not only countless hours of work, but also a labour of love.

My wife asked me the other day when I first started writing this book, and the sequels that I'm currently working on. I couldn't say for sure, because right now it seems like I've always been writing, and I love it. I love the world I've created and the characters in it, even when I'm doing unpleasant things to them (I just don't love myself so much then).

But it wasn't all me who made this happen, and I have to acknowledge those who helped along the road to getting this work published. The first of those was my Mum, Christine, who gave me the push to get the publication ball rolling. I also need to thank wife, Shona, for providing a sounding board when I was trying to get my head around publishing and marketing concepts. My editor Dani gets a big thank you, not simply for her amazing work, but for always being patient with my newbie questions (I'm sure I asked some daft ones). I am also thankful to everyone who contributed to my Kickstart toward the novels publication costs. They were all a big part of making this a reality.

Lastly I'm thankful to you, the reader, for looking on a shelf or scrolling on an online shopping platform and thinking, *'Hmm, this seems alright'*. It means so much to me to share my story and world with you. Thank you for supporting this independent author on his own adventure.

Enjoy.

About the Author

Andrew Claydon is a UK author from Somerset. His debut novel, the first of many in the *Chronicles of the Dawnblade* series, is called *The Simple Delivery*. Currently, he writes from a desk in the corner of his kids bedroom, trying to ignore the glares of the cat who likes to sleep in there during the day whilst he types away.

When he isn't writing, he loves to read sci/fi and fantasy novels. It's one of the things that inspires him to write himself. He also enjoys playing Warhammer 40,000 and is a keen wrestling fan.

He has degrees in both history and psychology, as well as black belts in several martial arts.

When he isn't creating vast fantasy worlds and populating them with good guys and bad guys to run around fighting each other, he works as a supermarket baker.

Connect with me –
Subscribe to my newsletter for the latest publishing news at:

www.andrewclaydonauthor.co.uk

Or follow me on social media:
Facebook: Andrewclaydonauthor
Instagram: @authorandyc
Tiktok: @authorandyc

Strange Companions
Chronicles of the Dawnblade
Book 2
By Andrew Claydon
Coming 2022/23

Printed in Great Britain
by Amazon

81395393R00144